C.J. CHERRYH

CYTEEN

"CYTEEN could easily make Cherryh into SF's next household name."

—*Newsday*

"Churning with political intrigue and heavyweight powerbrokering, thick with knotty conspiracies and plot. Cherryh's backdrop is a complex and thoughtful one . . . aficionados of futuristic imaginary power-politics and those intrigued by the possibilities of human-biological manipulation, will find much to ponder here."

—*Kirkus Reviews*

"Unmistakable weight and ambition . . . readers will find much to enjoy."

—*Publishers Weekly*

"A massive, multi-faceted novel that tackles a variety of ethical, social, and political issues . . . Cherryh's world building is ambitious and her main characterizations are well individualized . . . ultimately fascinating in concept and detail. Decidedly a major work."

—*Booklist*

"A multi-dimensional epic . . . a thought-provoking study of society."

—*Other Realms*

"A psychological novel, a murder mystery, and an examination of power on the grand scale, encompassing light-years and outsize lifetimes."

—*Locus*

Also by C.J. Cherryh

Cyteen: The Betrayal
Cyteen: The Rebirth

Published by
POPULAR LIBRARY

C.J. CHERRYH
CYTEEN
THE VINDICATION

POPULAR LIBRARY

An Imprint of Warner Books, Inc.

A Warner Communications Company

POPULAR LIBRARY EDITION

Popular Library®, the fanciful P design, and Questar® are
registered trademarks of Warner Books, Inc.

This work is published in paperback in three volumes and was
originally published in hardcover as one volume entitled *CYTEEN*.

Book design by H. Roberts
Cover illustration by Don Maitz

Popular Library books are published by
Warner Books, Inc.
666 Fifth Avenue
New York, N.Y. 10103

W A Warner Communications Company

Printed in the United States of America

Originally published in hardcover by Warner Books.
First Printed in Paperback: April, 1989

10 9 8 7 6 5 4 3 2 1

CYTEEN:
THE VINDICATION

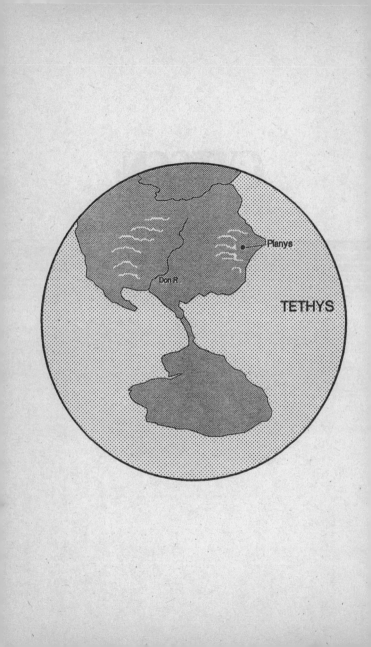

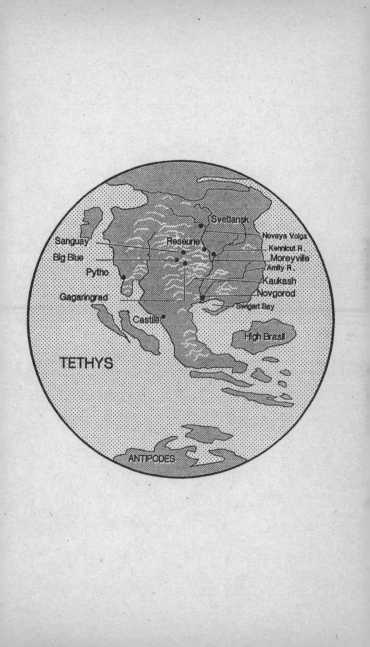

Svetlansk

Novaya Volga

Reseune

Kennicut R.

Sanguay

Moreyville

Big Blue

Amity R.

Pytho

Kaukash

Gagaringrad

Novgorod

Swigert Bay

Castile

High Brasil

TETHYS

ANTIPODES

2420: 10/3: 2348

AE2: Minder, this is Ari Emory. I'm alone. Give me references on psychogenesis.

B/1: Stand by. Retrieving.

Ari, this is Ari senior. Stand by.

The program finds you are 14 chronological years, with accesses for 16 years. This program finds you an average of 10 points below my scores overall.

Your psych scores are 5 points off my scores.

Your Rezner score has not been updated since age 10.

You are 5 points off qualification for access.

AE2: Base One: can my accesses reach data on Bok: keyword, clone?

B/1: Stand by. Retrieving.

Accesses inadequate.

AE2: Try endocrinology: keyword, psychogenesis. Gehenna: keyword, project. Worm: keyword, psych.

B/1: Accesses inadequate.

2420: 11/1: 1876:02

AE2: Minder, this is Ari Emory. I'm alone. Reference: psychogenesis.

B/1: Stand by. Retrieving.

Ari, this is Ari senior. Stand by.

The program finds you are 14 chronological years, with accesses for 16 years. This program finds you an average of 7 points below my scores overall.

Your psych scores are 1 point above my scores.

Your Rezner score has not been updated since age 10.

You are qualified to access files. Stand by.

Ari, this is Ari senior. These files can be read only from Base One Main Terminal. All relevant and resultant files are being stored in your personal archive under voice-lock.

You have used a keyword. You now have access to my working notes. I apologize in advance for their sketchy quality. They're quite fine when I was younger, but disregard a lot of the things dated pre-2312: they're useful if you want to see the evolution of thought: psychogenesis was something I was working on as early as 2304, but I didn't have the key studies in endocrinology until I had studied a good deal more; you can benefit from my study notes in those years, but I wasn't on the right track until 2312, and I didn't get the funds I needed until 2331. I benefited a great deal by Poley's work in that same decade: we disagreed, but it was an academic, not a personal difference. We exchanged considerable correspondence, also in the archives. By the year 2354, at the close of the Company Wars, my notes are much less coherent and a great deal more meaningful.

That you have accessed these notes means something has worked.

You have matched my ability. I hope to hell you have a sense of morality.

Your Base can now access all working notes. Good luck.

AE2: Base One: can my accesses reach data on Bok: keyword, cloning?

B/1: Stand by. Retrieving.

AE2: Try endocrinology: keyword, psychogenesis. Gehenna: keyword, project. Worm: keyword, psych.

B/1: Stand by. Retrieving.

B/1: The Bok clone failed because it was assumed genetics and training would create a genius. It was more than a scientific failure; it was a human tragedy. The project files are now available to your Base . . .

B/1: Endocrinology is a multitude of files. They are now available to your Base.

B/1: Gehenna is the name of a G5 star. Newport colony at Gehenna was a project I handled for Defense. This program is searching House Archives for outcome.

There is presently human life on the planet.

They have survived there for 65 years.

This indicates *some* chance it is a viable colony.

This was a Defense Bureau operation which I elected to undertake for reasons my notes will make clear to you. It was also, unknown to Defense, but within the parameters of their mission requirements, an experiment.

I designed a very simple program. The operational sentence was: You were sent from space to build a new world: discover its rules, live as long as you can, and teach your children all the things that seem important.

No further tape was sent. This was by design.

Integrating any individual of this population into mainstream cultures poses extreme risks. Examine the environment as well as the program. That was the aspect I could not adequately examine. Consult all files and understand what I have done before attempting any intervention.

Quarantine should be extended until results can be projected through 30 generations.

All relevant files are now available to your Base.

B/1: A worm is a deep-set-linked program which has the capacity to manifest itself in subsequent generations of a population without changing its character.

CHAPTER

I

_____ i _____

The lenses crowded close on each other, a solid phalanx of cameras bristling with directional mikes like ancient spears. Behind that, the army of reporters with their Scribers and their individual and zealously securitied com-links.

Behind her, Florian and Catlin, and a miscellaneous assortment of what might be uncle Giraud's aides and staff; but eight of them were Reseune Security, and armed, under the expensive tailoring.

She had chosen a blue suit, recollecting the public image of the little girl with the cast, the little girl who had lost her mother and caught the sympathy of people the length and breadth of Union. She had thought about sweeping her hair up into Ari senior's trademark chignon; but she only parted it in the middle, the way it wanted to fall anyway, and swept it up on the sides and let it fall behind, with combs sprigged with tiny white quartz flowers to hold it. A minimum of makeup . . . just enough for the cameras: her face had lengthened, acquired cheekbones; acquired a maturity that she had consciously to lighten with a little smile at favorite reporters, a

4

little deliberate flicker of recognition as her eyes found them—an intimation of special fondness.

So they might hold back some of the worst questions. People liked to have special importance, and those she favored were the ones who favored her; and old Yevi Hart, who had a hard-nosed reputation and who, in the year after she lost her mother, had turned halfway nice. She had been Working on him for years, a little special look, a little disappointment when he would ask the rough questions. This time she looked at him with a secret between-them glance, knowing he had the first question. *All right, Yevi, go, we both know you're just doing a job: you're still an old dear.*

He looked at her and seemed to lose the thread of his question a split second. His dour face looked worried. He took another breath, wadded up his question-slip and shoved his hand in his coat pocket. "Young sera, —"

"I'm still Ari, Yevi." A tilt of her head, a little sad smile. "I'm sorry. Go on."

Third breath. "Ari, you're applying for majority. The Centrists are suing the Science Bureau to prevent the grant. How do you answer their charge that you've been deep-taught and primed to perform by Reseune staff, that you were created specifically as a legal device to give Reseune and your relatives control of Emory's property?"

She outright laughed. She *was* amused. "One: I've never had deep-tape at all; I learn like any CIT. Two: if—"

"Follow-up."

"Let me get just through these things, Yevi, and then the follow-up. Can I?"

A grim nod.

"Two," she said, holding up fingers, and smiled. "I think they must have meant I was primed for the specific answers to reporters' questions, because if we had tape that could teach me my courses just like that, it would be wonderful—we could sell it all over Union and that would give my relatives a *lot* of money; but the Centrists have to know that's not so, so they must mean primed for the questions, and that means you're letting Reseune see the questions at least a day in advance. That's not the case, is it?"

"Absolutely not." Yevi looked a little cornered. "But if—"

"Three." Another finger. A chorus of blurted questions. "Just a second, I don't want to skip a question. Ser Corain says my relatives created me as a puppet to let them control my predecessor's estate; they say I shouldn't have my majority because it's just a trick to maintain a cover-up about Emory's involvement in Gehenna. That's really two questions. A, if I get my majority I own the rights, my relatives don't, and that means they actually *lose* their control of them, legally; they will go on advising me, but any businessperson gets advice in technical things like investments and research, and that doesn't mean the advisers own him. There's more than my relatives at Reseune—there are thousands and thousands of people I need to listen to—the way my predecessor did even when she was sitting in Council. B, —"

"Ari, —"

"Just let me get the other part of the question. Then the follow-up. I want to do all of them. B, that getting me my majority is a trick to cover Emory's involvement in Gehenna. *I* have access to the Gehenna notes, and I'm perfectly willing to testify to the Council as soon as I *have* my majority. Until then I'm a minor and I can't. So it seems to me that the Centrists' suit is covering up things, because if they really want to know what I know, why are they trying to keep me from being able to go under oath? Those files are under my voice-lock, and not even computer techs could get them out without messing things up and maybe losing real important pieces of it, just gone, for good. Not even my relatives have read the Gehenna files. I'm the only one who has them, and ser Corain is filing suit to keep me from being able to testify."

The reporters all started yelling. She pointed at Yevi. "Yevi still has his follow-up."

Yevi said: "What would be the reason?" Which was not his original follow-up, and some of the other reporters objected.

"I wish I could ask ser Corain," she said. "Maybe there's something in there."

"Follow-up."

"Yevi, I *have* to get to this m'sera, she's been waiting."

"What keeps your uncles from reading the files?"

Ouch. Good question. "Me. I have a special program my predecessor left for me. My voice is a lot like hers, and my geneset *is* hers, so when I was old enough to identify myself to the computer, it opened up these areas; but it's got a lot of security arrangements, and it won't let me access if there's anybody else going to hear; and it can tell."

"Follow-up!" the woman yelled over the shouting. "Can't *you* record it with a tape or something?"

Another good question. Remember this woman and be careful. "I could if I was going to allow it, but I'm not going to. My predecessor went to a lot of trouble about security and she warned me right in the program that I had to take that very seriously, even about people I might trust. I did, even if I didn't understand, and nobody at Reseune tried to get me to tell what was there either. Now I think it was a good idea, because it seems to be something real important, and I think the Council ought to be the ones to decide who gets to hear it, not any fifteen-year-old kid and not just any one part of the government either, because there's too much fighting going on about it and I don't know how to decide who to tell. The Council is supposed to decide things like that. That's the way I understand it. —Ser Ibanez."

"Can you tell us if there's anything in the files that you think would damage the reputation of your predecessor?"

"I can tell you this, because if anything happened to me it's terribly important people should know it: Gehenna has to stay quarantined. My predecessor was under Defense Bureau orders, but it scared her; and that was why she left things sealed for me. —Ser Hannah."

Chaos broke out. Everyone was shouting.

"Wasn't that irresponsible of your predecessor—if it was that important? Why did she keep it secret?"

"It was a Defense secret and it *was* quarantined. She *did* tell some people. But a lot of them are dead, and some of them probably don't understand what she did. *I* don't know it all yet. That's the bad thing: you have to be as smart as she was before you can work with the problem. She's dead and nobody else understands what she understood. That's why they made me. I'm *not* a Bok-clone situation. I *am* a Special, and someday I'm going to be able to understand what happened there. Right now nobody does. But she did leave instructions, and I'm not giving them to anybody until Council asks me under oath, because I'm not going to muddy up the waters by talking until I *can* swear to what I'm saying and the whole universe knows I'm an adult and I'm not lying. If I did it any other way, people could question whether I was telling the truth or whether I knew what I was doing."

They shouted and pushed and shoved each other. She felt Florian and Catlin move up on either side, anxious.

But she Had them. She was sure of it. She had gotten out exactly what she wanted to say.

—————————————— ii ——————————————

"Release the damn broadcast!" Corain yelled into the securitied phone, at Khalid's chief of staff, who swore Khalid was not available. "God! I don't care if he's in *hell*, get hold of him and get that release, you damn fool, it's gotten to my office, and thirty-five top reporters sent it downline—what do you mean security hold?"

"This is Khalid," the Councillor cut in, displacing the aide. "Councillor Corain, in light of the content of the interview we've requested a security delay of thirty minutes for the child's own protection. We seem to have a major problem."

"We *have* a major problem. The longer that hold stays on, the more that *hold* is going to become news, Councillor, and the longer it stays, the more they're going to ask why. We *can't* stop that broadcast."

"Assuredly we can't. There were too many news-feeds. I told you not to allow the interview. A minor child is making irresponsible charges on extremely sensitive matters, with international implications. I suggest we answer this with a categorical denial."

"It would have been foolhardy *not* to allow it. You can't keep the news-services away from the kid, and you saw what she can do with innuendo."

"She's obviously well-instructed."

"Instructed, *hell*, Khalid. *Take that damned hold off!*"

There was long silence on the other end. "The hold will go

off in fifteen minutes. I strongly suggest you use the time to prepare an official statement.''

"On *what*? We have nothing to do with these charges.''

Again a silence. ''Neither have we, Councillor. I think this will require investigation.''

It was a securitied line. *Any* communication could be penetrated if one could get access to the installers; or to the other end of the transmission.

''I think it will, Admiral. There will be a Centrist caucus in one hour. I hope you will be prepared to explain your position.''

''It's completely without substantiation,'' Khalid said to the cameras, on the office vid, while Corain rested his chin on his hand, glancing between the image on the screen and the newsfeed that an aide slipped under his view: *NP: DEFENSE BUREAU SPOKESMAN DECLINES COMMENT ON ACTION* and *CP: KHALID CALLS CHARGES FABRICATION*.

''. . . nothing in those files to substantiate any continued quarantine order. It's exactly what I say: Giraud Nye has come up with a piece of fiction, an absolute piece of fiction, and tape-fed it to a minor child who is in no wise fit or competent to understand the potential international repercussions. This is a reprehensible tactic which seeks to use the free press to its own advantage—utterly, utterly fabricated. I ask you, consider whether we will *ever* see documentation of the child's representations—files which a fifteen-year-old girl *maintains* she alone has seen, which she cannot—I say *cannot* produce— unless others produce these putative files *for* her—files which an impressionable fifteen-year-old child maintains were left for her by her predecessor. I will tell you, seri, I have grave suspicions that no such secret files *ever* were made by Ariane Emory, that no such *program* was ever created by Ariane Emory to give ghostly guidance to her successor. I suspect that any such *program* was written much closer to hand, that the child has been *programmed*, indeed, programmed—a process in which Reseune is absolutely expert, and in which Councillor Nye himself is an acknowledged authority—in fact a Special who gained his status as a result of his expertise in that very field. The child is a pawn created by Reseune to place legal and emotional obstacles in the way of matters of paramount national interest, and callously used and manipulated to maintain the privilege of a moneyed few whose machiavellian tactics now bid fair to jeopardize the peace. . . ."

Reporters were waiting at the hotel. "Are you aware," someone shouted, "of Khalid's accusations, Councillor Nye?"

"We heard them on the way over," uncle Giraud said, while Security maintained them a little clear space in the foyer, while cameramen jostled each other.

"*I* have an answer," Ari said, ignoring Florian's arm as he tried, with other Security, to get her and uncle Giraud on through the doors. "I *want* to answer him, can we set up in a conference room?"

". . . Thank you," the girl said, made a very young-girl move with both hands getting her hair back behind her shoulders, and then grimaced and shaded her eyes as a light hit her face. "Ow. Could you shine that down? Please?" Then she leaned forward with her arms on the conference table, suddenly businesslike and so like Emory senior that Corain's gut tightened. "What's your question?"

"What do you think about Khalid's allegations?" some reporter yelled out over the others.

Chaos. Absolute chaos. The light swung back into the girl's face and she winced. "Cut it off," someone yelled, "we don't need it."

"Thanks." As the light went off. "You want me to tell what I think about what the admiral says? I think he knows better. He used to be head of Intelligence. He sure *ought* to. It's not real smart either, to say I'm programmed. I can write psych designs. *He's* trying to run a psych on everybody, and I can tell you where, do you want me to count it off for you?"

"Go ahead," voices yelled out.

The girl held up one finger. "One: he says there's nothing in the files about a quarantine. He says he doesn't *know* what's in the files in Reseune: that's what he's complaining about. Whichever way it is, he's either trying to trick you or he's lying about what's in the files.

"Two: he says my uncle tape-fed me the stuff. He doesn't know any such thing. And in fact it's not true.

"Three: he says I don't understand what it could mean in international politics. Unless he knows what's in those files, he doesn't know as much as I do what it could mean.

"Four: he makes fun of the idea my predecessor left a program for me. That's a psych. Funny stuff breaks your concentration and makes you not think real hard about what he's really saying, which is that it's impossible. It's *certainly* possible. It's a simple branching program with a voice-recognition and a few other security things I don't want to talk about on vid, and I could write it, except for the scrambling, and that's something my own security understands—he's fifteen too. I'm sure Councillor Khalid does, if he was in Intelligence, so it's a pure psych.

"Five: he says my uncles write all the stuff. That's a psych like the first one, because he can just say that and then everybody wonders. I can give you one just exactly like it if I said Khalid won the election because he made up the rumor Gorodin was against the military retirement bill, and because of the way news goes out to the ships in space, and it being right before the vote, the vote was already coming back and being registered by the time Gorodin's saying it wasn't true even got to a lot of places. I heard that on the news. But I guess people forget who it is that makes up lies."

"Oh, my God. . . ." Corain murmured, and rested his head against his hands.

"I think that's done it," Dellarosa said. "I'd advise, ser, we hold a caucus *without* Defense. I think we need to draw up a position on this."

Corain raked his hand through his hair.

"Dammit, he can't even sue her for libel. She's a minor. And that went out live."

"I think the facts are, ser, the military may have had real practical reasons for preferring Khalid in spite of the rumor. But I think he's taken major damage. *Major* damage. I wouldn't be surprised if we don't see a challenge from Gorodin. We need to distance ourselves from this. We need a position statement on these supposed secret files. We need it while this broadside barrage is still going on."

"We need—" Corain said, "we *need* to call for a Science Bureau select committee to look into this, *past* Giraud Nye, to rule on the girl's competency. But, dammit, you *saw* that performance. The girl *got* Khalid, extemp. He played a dirty little in-Bureau game he'd have gotten away with because no one could pin it on him *or* his staff—but no one's going to forget it in *that* context."

"Nye told her."

"Don't make that mistake. Khalid just did. And he's dead. Politically, he's dead. He can't counter this one."

"She could charge anyone with being in those damn files!"

"She could have charged Khalid. But she didn't. Which probably means they exist and she's going to produce them. Or she's keeping her story clean . . . that she's waiting on Council. I'll tell you the other problem, friend. Khalid's going to be a liability in that office."

"Khalid's got to resign."

"He won't! Not that one. He'll fight to the bloody end."

"Then I suggest, ser, before we even consider Gorodin, who's stuck with the two-year rule, we explore who else might be viable for us inside that Bureau. How long do you think this is going to go? One bit of garbage floats to the surface—and other people start talking to the press. One more—and it becomes a race to the cameras."

"Dammit."

He had insisted Khalid take the hold off the news releases.

And there was no practical way to answer the charges, except to stall with the Bureau hearings. Which Nye could rush through at lightning speed. More exposure of the girl to the news-services.

No way. Withdraw opposition.

Then the girl got herself a full Council hearing.

And the repercussions of revelations on Gehenna went to the ambassadors from Alliance and from Earth.

The girl was *not* bluffing.

"One thing," he said as Dellarosa was leaving, "one thing she absolutely beat him on. *Find* somebody in Defense who makes speeches people can *understand*, for God's sake."

Justin watched and watched, every nuance, every shift in the replay. He had missed the whole afternoon, buried in the sociology lab; and he watched it now, once and twice, because the keyword response in the vid recorder had gotten all the references to the hearings, to Ari, to all the principals.

He shook his head, hands under chin, elbows on knees.

"Remarkably accurate retention," Grant said, beside him on the couch. "For a CIT. She hit every point she wanted to make, certainly. And confused them about the rest."

The tape reached Khalid's second refutation, the cold, passionless statement that Ari had been prompted with that accusation by Giraud Nye, that Giraud used her as his voice because it was otherwise actionable.

Justin shook his head again. "He may have given it to her. But the kid's sense of timing is impeccable."

"Khalid mistook his opponent," Grant said. "He thought that it was Giraud all along."

"Vid off," Justin said, and there was silence in the room.

Grant reached across and shook at his knee. "Do you think Khalid—is capable of harming her?"

"I think that man is *capable* of anything. I don't know. He won't move on—won't move on *her*. She's too hard a target. I'm going to call Denys."

"Why?"

"CIT craziness. Politics. She's too hard a target. *Jordan* works for Defense."

Grant's face went expressionless. Then showed shock.

"I don't think we should put that through the Minder. We should *go* to him."

"How in hell do we get an interview with Denys at this hour? There's no way he'll open the door to us."

"Security," Grant said after a moment. "We ask him to meet us in Security."

"I appreciate your concern," Denys said, the other side of the desk from them, themselves in two hard chairs, Seely standing by the wall, in the interview room.

Justin remembered the place—too well. "Ser, I—don't call

it an irrational fear. Order him not to answer any calls from the base.''

"We don't need any moves against Defense on record," Denys said. "That in itself—could call unwelcome attention to your father. Possibly you're being alarmist . . .''

"Khalid has reason to want an incident, ser. And my father is sitting there without protection. They can *tell* him damned well anything. Can't they?''

Denys frowned, thick fingers steepled, then interlocking. "Seely. Move on it. Now.''

"Yes," Seely said, and left.

Grant rose from his chair, following Seely with his eyes. *Then* the thought came; and Justin stood up, suddenly facing two armed guards in the doorway.

"What is he going to do?" Justin asked, looking at Denys. "That wasn't an instruction. *What is he going to do?*''

"Relax," Denys said. "Relax, son. Sit down. Both of you. There are contingency plans. You're not the first one to think of these eventualities. Seely understands my meanings perfectly well.''

"What contingencies?''

"Dear God, we certainly don't intend any harm to your father. Sit down. Please. You have a very active imagination tonight.''

"What is he going to do?''

"He's simply going to go to the front desk and they'll transmit a code, which you don't need to know, which simply advises Planys lab to go on extreme alert. That means Reseune Security trusts no one who is not Reseune Security. And no one comes in or goes out who's *not* Reseune Security. We simply claim a laboratory incident. Very simple. Since Jordan has the highest-level Security flag at Planys—rest assured, he's not available to any calls, except from us. Sit down.''

Justin sat, and Grant did.

"There," Denys sighed. "Thank you. I appreciate your level of paranoia, Justin. It's finely honed, God knows. I never undervalue a good set of nerves. Storm-sense. Seely—never needs the weather warnings. Isn't that an odd thing—in a mind so rational? —What did you think of her?''

Off the flank and unforeseen. Justin blinked, instantly

wary—and that in itself was a reaction he did not want. "Of Ari? Ari was brilliant. What else could she be?"

"I have a little pride invested in her," Denys said. "You know she brought up her psych scores six points in less than a month, when the rascal got the notion she had to. I told the committee exactly that. And they wouldn't believe she was laying back. Forgive me. I'm also extremely nervous until we get her back here safe, inside *our* perimeters."

"So am I. Honestly."

"I believe that. I truly do. I must tell you—our concern with your father has been in an entirely different context during this trip. I told you I would tell you—when Ari became aware of her predecessor's—death."

"You've told her, then."

Denys bit his lip and studied his hands. "Not all of it. Not yet." He looked up. "On the other hand—I sweated through that first interview. At one point I was sure Ari was going to say—in response to *why* the first Ari didn't make better provision for passing on the information—that Ari was murdered. And then the reporter would have keyed right onto the relationship of the murder to that information—no valid connection, of course. But I felt for a split second that was exactly where it was going—and then Ari changed course. Thank God. I really don't want her to hear the words 'the Warrick case' for the first time—in front of the cameras. Or in the hearings. She's flying home tonight. Totally unscheduled departure, Science Bureau chase planes with full radar coverage. You see we're likewise very paranoid. Giraud is, I think, going to break the news to her on the way. So I've warned you."

iv

"Ari," Giraud said, settling into the seat Florian had vacated for him, across from her, while *RESEUNE ONE* flew through the dark and there was nothing but stars out the windows— stars and the running lights of the planes Giraud said were flying with them.

Because they had to worry about electronic interference and all sorts of things that even Florian and Catlin frowned over.

Because they had challenged a very dangerous, very desperate man who had all kinds of contacts, and because the world had crazy people in it who might try something and try to blame it on Defense.

She would be very glad, she thought, when she felt them touch down at Reseune. Enemies didn't much bother her, except the kind who might aim another plane at you or take out your navigation or who might be Defense trying to blame it on extremists or extremists trying to blame it on Defense.

"We're doing fine," uncle Giraud said. "Radar's perfectly clear. Our escort is enough to keep them honest. I imagine you're anxious for your own bed tonight."

Oh, damn, we've got the Minder checkout to go through when we get back to the apartment, and Florian and Catlin are tired as I am. I just want to go to bed. And I can't sleep.

"I did worry today," Giraud said, "about one thing I was afraid they were going to throw at you. That—we really haven't wanted to go into. But I think—and Denys thinks— I've talked with him on the Bureau system—that you need to know."

God, get to it!

"You know your predecessor was murdered. And that it was somebody in Reseune."

"Who?"

"A man named Jordan Warrick."

She blinked and felt the sting of exhaustion in her eyes. There was only one Warrick at Reseune *she* had ever met. "Who's Jordan Warrick?"

"A Special. The absolute authority in educational design. Justin Warrick's father."

She rubbed her eyes and slid up a little in her seat, looking at Giraud.

"I didn't want you to find that out in front of the cameras. I certainly don't want you to find it out from Council next week. Jordan and Ari had personal and professional difficulties; and political ones. He accused Ari of tampering with his work and taking credit from him—as he saw it. They quarreled— Do you want to hear this in detail?"

She nodded.

"Most likely, and he claims this was the case, it wasn't premeditated. They fought—a physical fight—and she hit her head—at which point he panicked and tried to cover up what had happened. It happened in the cold lab down in Wing One basement. The section is very old, the cryogenics conduits are completely uncovered; he created a break, blew the line, shut the door—it *still* swings, it has to do with the way the building settled, and the door is unfixable; but we've disabled the lock. In short, Ari froze to death in a release of liquid nitrogen from a pipe rupture. It was relatively painless; she was unconscious from the blow. Jordan Warrick—being a Special—had a Council hearing. It was an absolutely unprecedented case—Specials don't commit murder. And his mind—whatever his faults—is protected by law. He did agree to accept a transfer out of Reseune. He lives at Planys. Justin does visit him now and again.''

"Did he know about it?''

"Justin didn't have any idea what was going to happen. He was only seventeen. He'd attempted—using resources of his father's—to smuggle Grant out of Reseune and into Novgorod—Jordan wanted to get the directorate at RESEUNESPACE, and Grant's status as an X-number meant it might have been hard to get him to go with them. But it went wrong, the contacts Justin used—friends of his father—happened to have ties to the Abolitionists, who attempted a very misguided intervention with Grant. I've always entertained a private suspicion that Grant figured in the argument Jordan had with Ari. Grant had to be rescued; he was in hospital that night, in very precarious shape—and Justin was visiting him about the time the murder happened, so there's no question about Justin's whereabouts. He had no idea his father was going to see Ari. He certainly had no notion what his father would do.''

She felt a little sick at her stomach. "He's my *friend*.''

"He was seventeen when all this happened. Just two years older than you are. None of it was his fault. He lives at Reseune—his father lives at Planys under a kind of perpetual arrest. You understand, I think, why we've been very anxious about your contacts with him. But he's never initiated them; he's been very careful to follow the rules that let him live at Reseune. He was able to finish his education; he's made a home at Reseune, he causes no one any trouble, and it didn't seem fair to punish him for something which absolutely was none of his doing, or to send him where he wouldn't have the facilities to pursue his work. He's very bright. He's a very troubled man, a very confused one, sometimes, but I hope he'll work out his own answers. Most of all we've worried about the chance he would do something or say something to hurt you—but he never has. Has he?''

"No." *Remember the source*, Ari senior would say, *had* said, advising her how to deal with deceptions. *Remember the source*. "Why didn't he go to Fargone? Valery did. Valery was only four years old and he never hurt anybody."

"Frankly we wanted Justin where we could see him," Giraud said, going right past the matter of Valery. Of course. "And we didn't want him in prolonged contact with any ship crew or within reach of outside communications. His father's friends—are Rocher and that crowd, the Abolitionists—who are one of the reasons we have that escort flying off our wings."

"I understand." She needed to think about it for a while. She had no desire to talk about it with uncle Giraud; not right now.

"We knew it would upset you," Giraud said, trying for a reaction out of her.

She looked at him and let the situation flow right through her, bland as could be, the night, the planes outside, the news about Justin, Giraud's evading the Valery question. So they could get blown up. So the whole world was crazy. But she had figured it was dangerous when she made up her mind she was going to mention the Gehenna things—when she had warned uncle Denys and uncle Giraud what she was going to do, and they had been nervous about it. But one thing about Giraud—once things went inertial he had a cool head and he came across with the right things at the right time: if she had to pick somebody to be with her in Novgorod she figured Giraud was one of the best. And what he was saying had to be true: it was too easy to check out.

She sighed. "It does upset me," she said, "but I'm glad I know. I need to think about it, uncle Giraud."

He looked at her a moment, then fished in his pocket, and

pulled out a little packet, reached and laid it on her side of the table.

"What's that?"

Giraud shrugged. "No shopping this trip," he said. "But I did remember this little thing in a certain shop. I had Security pick it up. They hadn't sold it."

She was bewildered. She picked it up, unwrapped the paper and opened the box. There was a pin with topazes of every shade, set in gold. "Oh," she said. "Oh!"

"So much jewelry came with Ari's estate," Giraud said, and got up to go back to his own seat at the back. "I thought you should have something that was only yours."

"*Thank* you, uncle Giraud." She was entirely off her balance.

And more so when she looked up at him. The way the light came down on him from the overhead in that second made his skin look papery and old; he walked by and put his hand on her arm and his hand showed deep creases. Old. Of course he was.

Something that was only yours. That rattled around in her head and found such a central place to light that she turned the thought over as often as she did the pin, turning all the facets to the light—whether Giraud had just Worked her or whether it was just that her uncle had this thing about young girls or maybe—maybe a single soft spot that had started back when she was little had just grown along with her, until he finally really had thoughts like that. After all the rotten things he had done.

He had Got her good, that was sure.

One thing that was truly hers. So very few things were.

"What is it, sera?" Florian asked, and: "It's pretty," he said.

"Nice," Catlin said, coming to take the seat beside her, and reached out a hand to touch it.

Of course they were hers. Ari and Ari blurred together and came separate and blurred together again, with very little discomfort nowadays. Ari senior had collected real trouble in her lifetime, but that was all right, she didn't like Ari's Enemies either. They had murdered Ari and now she had Security with her everywhere and planes flying beside just to be sure she got home, to Ari's bed and Ari's comforts and Ari's Reseune, in all—

She didn't mind being Ari, she decided. It was not a bad thing to be. It was a little strange. It was a little lonely a lot of the time, but that was all right, there were enough people to keep it from being *too* lonely. There was a lot to keep up with, but it was never boring. She would not be Maddy or 'Stasi, or even Amy—Amy, closest, maybe, but she had rather be Ari, all the same, and travel to Novgorod and have Catlin and Florian with her—not forgetting that: Amy had no company. Just her maman and her maman's staff, who were no fun.

Being Jane would have been all right. She thought about Ollie, suddenly, hurt because he never wrote; but Ollie wouldn't, Ollie was so correct when he had to be.

He might not even be alive anymore. People could die at Fargone and it took so long to find it out.

She put the pin back in the box. "Put that in my carry, will you?" she said to Florian. "I don't want anything to happen to it." When there was a chance she would wear it where Giraud could see it. He would like that.

"Are you tired, sera?" Catlin asked. "Do you want us to put out the lights?"

"No. I'm fine." But she felt after the lap robe, and tucked it up around her, listening to the drone of the engines.

She could write to Fargone. But it was not wise right now. Anything she did would make her Enemies nervous and maybe put other people in danger, like hanging a sign out over them saying: This is a friend of mine.

Her friends didn't have Security to protect them, if they came outside Reseune and Reseune's other holdings. She had to think about things like that now.

From now on.

——————————— **V** ———————————

Ari, this is Ari senior.

You've gained your majority. You are 15 chronological years. This program deals with you as 17. Your accesses have widened.

You may now access all working notes to the year of my death and all history up to 2362, which is the year I resigned as Reseune Administrator to take up the Council Seat for Science.

When I was 17, in 2300, Union declared itself a nation and the Company Wars began.

When I was 35, in 2318, I sat as Proxy Councillor for Science during the illness of Lila Goldstein, of Cyteen Station, who subsequently died.

When I was 37, in 2320, I yielded the seat to Jurgen Fielding, of Cyteen. The Special Status bill passed and I was one of 5 persons accorded that privilege.

When I was 48, in 2331, I became Director of Wing One at Reseune, on the death of Amelie Strassen; I went on rejuv in that year.

When I was 62, in 2345, I became Administrator of Reseune, on the death of my uncle Geoffrey Carnath. The Company Fleet in those years had succeeded in interdicting Union warships from all stations Earthward of Mariner, and attempted to blockade merchanters from dealing with Cyteen and Fargone and to destroy any merchanter registered to Cyteen. Heavy losses of ships and the need for workers and trained military personnel had brought Reseune into the war effort: from the years 2340 to 2354, Reseune increased in size over 400%.

Actions which I took during those years: franchising of production centers; automation of many processes; building of mills to relieve dependency on scarce transport; expansion of agriculture; establishment of Moreyville as a shipping center; establishment of RESEUNEAIR as a commercial carrier for the Volga area; establishment of Reseune's legal rights over franchised production centers; establishment of Reseune as legal guardian of all azi, no matter where produced; establishment of Reseune as sole producer of all tape above skill-level.

I consider the latter measures, which make it possible for Reseune to guide and oversee all azi throughout Union, to be among the most important things I have ever done—for the obvious reasons of the power it conveys, for moral reasons of the azi's welfare, and for two reasons less apparent . . . . 1. that it gives us the leverage to terminate the production of azi at some

future date, to prevent the establishment of a permanent insti-
tution of servitude in Union or elsewhere; 2. See file under
keyword: Sociogenesis.

When I was 69, in 2352, Union launched its last major of-
fensive of the war; and came to me with the outline of the Ge-
henna project.

See file under keyword: Gehenna, keyword: private file.

When I was 71, in 2354, the Company Wars ended with the
Treaty of Pell.

When I was 72, in 2355, the Gehenna Colony was dis-
patched, as a contingency measure. My advice to the contrary
was overruled by Adm. Azov, Councillor of Defense.

When I was 77, in 2360, I challenged Jurgen Fielding for
the Science seat.

When I was 79, in 2362, final vote tabulations gave me the
seat, which I hold at the time I am writing these notes.

It's one thing, young Ari, to study older people as a fact in
psychology; it's quite another thing to be aware of the psychol-
ogy of old age in yourself—because you do get old inside, even
if rejuv holds your physical age more or less constant.

The difference rejuv has made in human psychology is a
very profound difference: consider . . . without rejuv, the body
begins to change by age 50 and specific deteriorations begin
and grow acute enough within the next 20 to 30 years to cause
disability. That is the natural aging process, which would lead
to natural death between the ages of 60 and 110 at the outside,
varying according to genetics and environment.

In individuals without rejuv, the 20-to-30-year period of de-
cline in functions, followed by a period of diminished function
and degenerative disease, works a considerable psychological
change. In eras when no rejuv was possible, or in places such
as Gehenna, where no rejuv is available, there are sociolog-
ical accommodations to having a large portion of the popula-
tion undergoing this slow diminution of physical and in a few
cases mental capacity. There may be institutions and customs
which provide support to this segment of the population, al-
though, historically, such provisions were not always optimum
or satisfactory to the individual faced with the psychological
certainty that the process had begun. With rejuv, we contem-
plate natural death at, considering mere percentages, a little

*greater lifespan, ranging in my time between 100 and 140 . . .
bearing in mind that rejuv is still a tolerably new phenomenon,
and the figure may increase. But rejuv was a discovery on
Cyteen, was available for the first time during my mother's
generation, and the sociological adjustments were still extremely rapid during my early years: keyword: Aging,
keyword: Olga Emory: keyword: thesis.*

*At the time I write these notes, the major change has not
been so much length of life, although that has had profound
effect on family structures and law, due to the fact most people
now live near their parents for a century or more, and frequently enter into financial partnership in their estates, so that
inheritance, as you have done with my estate, is quite rare:
estates usually progress rather than leap from one individual
to the other nowadays.*

*The major change has been the combination of advanced ex-
perience with good health and vitality. The period of decline is
usually brief, often under 2 years, and frequently there is no
apparent decline. Death has become much more of a sudden
event; and one enters one's 140's with the expectation one will
die, but faces it, not in the depressive effects of degenerative
illness, but as an approaching time limit, a fearful catastrophe, or, quite commonly, with the I'm-immune attitude which
used to characterize much younger individuals.*

*I digress with a purpose. I cannot predict for your time and
your age what old age may be. I do know this, that the sense of
limitations sets in early at Reseune, because of the very nature
of our work, which is so slow, and involves human lifespans.
By my 70's, I saw an experiment launched which I knew I
might not see the end of. And you may not. But that knowledge
is something foreign to you, at your age.*

Remember this, when you read beyond 2345.

*Changes happen. Therefore I have made access to certain
keyword areas of my diary slower to access beyond the year
2362, based on a series of examinations this program will administer. I have fears for your psychological health if you attempt to deceive this program in this regard: expert as you may
become at analyzing tests and guessing which answers are key
to obtaining more information, I ask you to trust my mature
judgment in this, remembering that I write this with the per-*

*spective of a woman who knows you in ways no one else does—
even if you know how to trick the program, answer it with absolute honesty. If an emergency arises and you must get that
information, your skill should enable you to lie to the test and
get what you need; but bear in mind two things: first, as I once
told you, this program is capable of protecting Reseune from
abuse, and certain attitudes, even if they are pretended, may
cause it to take defensive actions; of course this means if you
are a scoundrel, you can perhaps lie in the other direction, but
your psych profile does not presently indicate you are one, or
you would not be getting this information right now. Second, I
will withhold no part of my working notes, and there will be
nothing in those hidden portions that you will need for anything but personal reasons.*

*Last of all I remind you of this: I am safely dead and incapa-
ble of shock. The program will draw a firm line between your
fantasies and your real actions as observed through House
records. Treat the program with absolute honesty. You will occasionally see a new question surface, as your actions within
the House or your chronological age activates a new aspect of
the test. Never lie, even if you suspect the truth may cause the
program to react. It is designed to detect lies, deceptions, eva-
sions, and various other contingencies, but then, I knew I
would be dealing with a very clever individual—with my im-
pulses, if I am correct.*

*I will tell you that I have caused deaths and hurt others in
my life. I will tell you something terrible: I have a certain sa-
distic bent I try to control. Self-analysis is a trap and I have
had to do more of it to write this program than I have liked to
do. I will tell you that my sexual encounters with CITs have
been unsatisfactory from my adolescence onward; that they
have inevitably ended in professional antagonism and ended a
few valuable friendships; that the events of my childhood, lurid
as some of them were, contributed more to my sense of independence and my sense of responsibility toward others. That
my uncle was cruel to me and my household taught me compassion.*

*But that my compassion made me vulnerable to others, all
CITs, whose egos did not take well to my independence and my
intellect, caused me great pain; in plain language, I fell in love*

about as often as any normal human being. I gave everything I had to give. And I got back resentment. Genuine hatred. I tried, God knows, not to trample on egos. But my mere existence challenges people, and I challenged everyone past their endurance. Nothing I could do was right. Everything I did fractured their pride. My azi could deal with me, as yours can with you. But I felt an essential isolation from my own kind, a sense that there was an area of humanity I would never adequately reach or understand—on a personal level, no matter my brilliance or my abilities. That is a painful understanding to reach—at nineteen.

That pain created anger; and that anger of mine helped me survive and create. It drove me into that other aspect of myself, my studies of human thought and emotion—challenging all my ability, in short, which in turn fed back into the other situation and exacerbated it with lovers yet to come. I think that that cycle of sexual energy and anger are interlocked in me to such an extent that I cannot control it except by abstinence, and as you are no doubt aware, abstinence is not an easy course for me.

I hesitate even to warn you, because that frustration had an important, even a beneficial effect on my work. I reached a point in my 70's when I had surpassed every mind around me. Jane Strassen, Yanni Schwartz, Denys and Giraud Nye, and of course Florian and Catlin, were among the friends who still challenged me. But I passed even them. I went more and more inward, and found myself more and more solitary in the personal sense. Then I confess to you that I was extremely happy in my professional work, and I was able to confine my sexual energies to a mere physical release, on a very frequent basis, which, with the satisfactions of my work and the company of a few reliable friends, kept me busy. In some ways I was very lonely, but in the main I was happy. It was a very productive period for me.

But now, above a century, I know that I am launched on projects none of which I will finish, that I am doing things that may save humankind or damn it, and I will never know the outcome.

Most of all that anger drives me now, impatience with the oncoming wall, impatience with time and the limits of those around me; there is no chance to stop and breathe, or rest. I can no longer travel freely, no longer fly, the dream I had of seeing space is something I have no right to indulge in, because security is so difficult and finishing this work is so important. Sex used to relieve the tensions; now it interlocks with them, because the anger is linked with it and with everything I do.

The most terrible thing—I have hurt Florian. I have never done that in my life. Worse than that—I enjoyed it. Can a child understand how much that hurt? Worst of all—Florian understands me; and forgives me. Whatever you do, young Ari, use the anger, don't let it use you.

Because the anger will come, the pain will come, because you are not like everyone else, no more than I could be.

You are not *my life's work. I hope that does not touch you in your vanity, and that you will understand why I reactivated my psychogenesis study and devoted so much of my time to creating you. My life's work is not psychogenesis, but sociogenesis, and no one but you has ever heard that word in any serious context.*

I have shifted the entire course of humanity by the things I have done. Your own unique perspective as a psychogenetic replicate can tell you something of the damage that might be done to Union if people became aware *of what I have done. It had to be done, by everything that I saw.*

But I worked increasingly alone, without checks, and without consultation with anyone, because there was *no one who understood what I understand.*

I can tell you in capsule form, young Ari, as I have told the press and told the Council repeatedly: but few seem to understand the basics of what I am saying, because it runs counter to short-term goals and perceptions of well-being. I have not been able to model simply enough the complex of equations that we deal with; and I fear demagogues. Most of all I fear short-term thinkers.

The human diaspora, the human scattering, is the problem, but Centrism is not the answer. The rate of growth that sustains the technological capacity that makes civilization possible is now exceeding the rate of cultural adaptation, and distance is exceeding our communications. The end will be-

come more and more like the beginning, scattered tribes of humans across an endless plain, in pointless conflict—or isolate stagnation—unless we can condense experience, encapsulate it, replicate it deliberately in CIT deep-sets—unless psychogenesis can work on a massive scale, unless it can become sociogenesis and exceed itself as I hope you will exceed me. Human technology as an adaptive response of our species has passed beyond manipulation of the environment; beyond the manipulation of our material selves; beyond the manipulation of mind and thought; now, having brought us out of the cradle it must modify our responses to the universe at large. Human experience is generating dataflow at a rate greater than individuals can comprehend or handle; and the rate is still increasing. We must begin compression: we must compress experience in the same way human history compresses itself into briefer and briefer instruction—and events on which all history depended rate only a line in passing mention.

Ultimately only the wisdom is important, not the event which produced it. But one must know accurately what those things are.

One must pass the right things on. Experience is a brutal and an imprecise teacher at best.

And the time at which all humanity will be within reach, accessible to us—is so very brief.

You will see more than I could, young Ari. You may well be the only mind of your day able to grapple with the problem: I hope that events have handed you my power undiminished; but no matter, if I have fitted you to hold on to it I have also fitted you to acquire it. Most of all, govern your own self. If you survive to reach the power I have had, you will walk a narrow boundary between megalomania and divinity. Or you will let that anger reach humankind; or you will abdicate in cowardice.

If I have failed with you, I have failed in everything, and I may have created nothing worse than presently exists; or I may have doomed at least half of humanity to wars or to stifling tyranny.

If I have succeeded, there is still work to be done, to keep the hand on the helm. Situations change.

If I had done nothing at all, I foresaw a war that the human species might not survive: too much of it resides only on two planets and depends on too few production centers. We are too young in space; our support systems are still too fragile, and our value systems still contain elements of the stone ax and the spear.

That conviction is the only moral assurance I will ever have.

Study the Company Wars. Study the history of Earth. Learn what we are capable of.

Study Gehenna. This program has ascertained re-contact has been made. People have survived there. Its generations are shorter than ours. Gehenna is the alarm system.

Your Security clearance is now active in the Science Bureau with rank of: Department head, Reseune Administrative Territory.

Further explanation is filed in Reseune Security: access via Security 10, keyword: clearance.

---

vi

"No, ser," Ari said, hands folded on the table. The microphones picked up her voice and carried it, making it huge, a caricature of a young girl's voice. She sat by herself at a table facing the Nine. Uncle Giraud sat in the Science seat; there were Nasir Harad, and Nguyen Tien; Ludmilla deFranco; Jenner Harogo; Mikhail Corain; Mahmud Chavez; and Vladislaw Khalid—whose looks toward her were absolute hostility. Corain had asked the question.

"No, ser, I won't give you a transcript. I've said why. It wouldn't be all of it. And that's worse than nothing. I'm *telling* you the important things. Adm. Azov sent the colony even when Ari told him not; she didn't want it because it was too dangerous. And he went ahead.

"This is the important thing—let me say this—" she said, when Corain interrupted her. "Please."

"I doubt you would forget," Corain said dryly.

Harad's gavel came down. "Go on, young sera."

"This is important," Ari said. "This is the most important part. Adm. Azov came to my predecessor wanting a colony planted on that world because it was an Earthlike planet and it was right next to Pell. Defense wanted to make sure if Alliance got there in fifty years or a hundred they were going to find a planet full of Union people, or an ecological disaster that could contaminate the planet with human-compatible diseases . . .''

It disturbed the Council. Heads leaned together and the gavel banged down again.

"Let the girl finish."

"That was in the notes. They wanted Reseune to build those too. They wanted Ari to design tape so the azi they sent would always be Union, no matter what, and they would cause trouble and work from inside Alliance once Alliance picked them up off the world. Ari tried to tell them they were crazy. But they wouldn't listen.

"So Ari listened to everything they wanted, and she ordered some immunological stuff, I don't know what, but my uncle is going to talk about those. What they essentially did was use viruses to transfer material, and that was all done pretty much like we use for genetic treatment—and they picked some things they hoped would just help the colonists' immune systems; but there was another contractor Ari didn't trust and she didn't know what they might dump onto Gehenna that Reseune didn't know about."

"Do you know the name of that contractor?" Corain asked.

"It was Fletcher Labs. It was May of 2352. That's all she knew."

That made the Councillors nervous. An aide came up and talked to Khalid. Several others took the chance.

"But she was in charge of actually organizing the colony," Corain said then, when things settled down. "Describe what she did."

"She was in charge of picking the azi and training them; and she did the main instructional tape. They wanted her to do all this stuff you *can't* do. Like all these buried instructions. What she did, she made the primary instruction deep-tape; and she axed the azi's contracts in a way that meant if there weren't any CITs they were contracted to the world itself."

"She disregarded the Defense Bureau's instructions. That's what you're saying."

"If she'd done what the military wanted the whole colony would likely have died out; or if they lived past the diseases the third or fourth generation would be really dangerous—psychsets interact with environment. They didn't want to hear that.''

"Time," Chairman Harad said. "Councillor Chavez of Finance.''

"You consider you're qualified to pronounce on that," Chavez said, following up.

"Ser, that's a real basic.''

"I don't care if it's a basic," Chavez said, "you're consistently reading in motives or you're attributing them to people only one of whom you know anything about, and you're not making it clear where you're quoting and where you're interpreting. I'm talking about your predecessor, young sera, who is the one whose notes you're supposed to be testifying to. Not your own interpretations of those notes.''

"Yes, ser." Ari drew a long breath, and restrained her temper behind a very bland look. "I won't explain, then.''

"I suggest you respect this body, young sera. You attained your majority last week; it means, young sera, that you are obliged to act as an adult.''

She looked at Councillor Chavez, folded her hands again and sat there.

"Go on, young sera," Harad said.

"Thank you, ser Chairman. I'm sorry; I'll explain only if you ask. Ari wasn't technical about it: she said: quote: Defense insisted. I explained the hazards of environmental interactions in considerable detail. Their own psychologists tried to make them understand what I was saying; unfortunately the admirals had already made up their minds: the system of advancements in the military makes it damn near impossible for a Defense Bureau bureaucrat to back off a position. Even if—''

"Young sera," Chavez said. "The Council has limited time. Could we omit the late Councillor's profane observations?''

"Yes, ser.''

"Go on.''

"That was the answer.''

"You didn't answer. Let me pose the question again. What, specifically, was Emory's argument to Defense?''

"I can't answer without explaining.''

"What did Emory say?"

"She said they shouldn't do it because the environment would affect the psychsets and the tape couldn't be re-adjusted for the situation. And Defense couldn't tell her enough about the environment. That was the first reason she said they were crazy."

"She knew that when she made the original design. Why did she do it in the first place?"

"Because she did it during the War. If humanity had wiped itself out of space and gotten the planets too, it was one more place humanity might survive. It was real dangerous, but it wouldn't matter if they were the only ones."

"What was the danger?" ·

"You're going to get upset if I tell you again."

"Tell me."

"Letting a psychset run in an environment you don't know anything about. Do you want me to explain technically why that's dangerous?"

The Expansionists all laughed behind their hands. Even Tien, who was Centrist.

"Explain," Chavez said with a surprising lot of patience. She decided she liked him after all. He was not stupid. And he could back up when he got caught.

"Deep-tape is real simple and real general: it has to be. If you make aggression part of the set, and they're in an environment that threatens them, they'll expand the aggression all over everything, and it'll proliferate through the rest of the sets all the way to the surface; or if you put in a block *against* aggression, it could proliferate the same way, and they couldn't take care of themselves. Deep-tape gets all the way down to which way you jump when something scares you. It hits the foundation of the logic sets. And it almost has to be slightly illogical, because on pure logic, you don't move till you understand it. The deep-sets are a bias toward fight or flight. Things like that. And the Defense Bureau didn't give Ari senior any chance to design real deep-sets that might be a whole lot better for Gehenna. They came in and wanted her to program adult military-setted azi to colonize, and they wanted it in one year. She said that was garbage. She argued them into taking a mix of soldiers and farmers. So she composed a genepool of types that might have all the skills *and* the deep-sets she figured might hold *some* right answers to the environment, whatever it was.''

"In other words she lied to the Bureau."

"She had to. They were going to go throw their own azi onto the world without her help, and they were telling their own psychology branch to break the law and try to run a deep-set intervention on them. Their own psych people said that was stupid, and some of them were threatening to talk to the Council, but Adm. Azov told one of them he could end up on Gehenna himself if he kept objecting. That's what that man told Ari. Then she thought about bringing it to Council, but she thought about the chance of the whole human race getting wiped out, and that was when she made up her mind to go along with it, but to do it safer than Defense was going to do it.

"She couldn't just go back and mindwipe all those azi and start over. That was another crazy suggestion the military had. Reseune didn't have enough facilities. And you don't recover from mindwipe that well that they could just dump them off on another planet and leave them there with no psych help. So she couldn't work with the deep-sets. She just studied all the deep-sets and worked up something real simple: she told the azi it was their planet and they had to take care of it and survive and teach their children what was important, that was all. As positive as she could. Because she didn't know how long Gehenna would be lost, and how much that would change.

"And that's the danger in it. Their generations are real short. There's already been a lot of change. Alliance is scared of them because they're afraid there's something on the planet like a secret base, that's the way I understand it; but if there's anything like that, it's not in the notes. Mostly I hear it's the azi that did survive, and there's not much left of CIT culture. That means the program did take.

"There's too many people to mindwipe—thousands and thousands. They'd have to mindwipe them all the way down, and that's a lot of psych work, and they haven't got a Reseune. Councillor Nye can tell you what it would take—"

"It would take a facility the size of Reseune," Giraud said, "doing nothing else, for at least ten years; and the re-integration of that many mindwiped individuals into ordinary society would tax anything *any* of us have. We're talking about thirty thousand individuals. Or more. They're still trying to estimate. No one has a place to disperse those people—they'd still cluster. Cluster means community; community means cultural identity. Alliance hasn't got the population base to absorb them. *We* don't. Don't even mention turning them loose on Earth.''

"They probably can't find all of them," Ari said. "Anyway. So they can't get them off. They'll always be different; and they'll always be a problem. They're an azi population. They're *not* like CITs. They're just going to be crazy according to CIT thinking. Teaching their kids is part of their mindset; and if you bring them into the 25th century that's *another* environment that's going to hit that program and proliferate changes. That's Emory's word on it. If it's second generation, you could integrate them back, but there's even fourths now. Once it hits fourth, she said, you're into something real different. And they don't have rejuv. The Olders die off before they're a hundred. I've heard it's more like forty or fifty. That doesn't give them time to live with their kids or teach them much about being grown up. They're already more different from us than we are from Earth. That's Emory talking.''

"I'm out of questions," Chavez said.

"We're going to recess for lunch," Harad said. "And take ser Tien's questions after—are you holding up to this, young sera?"

"I'm doing all right," she said. "After lunch is fine. Thank you, ser.''

"It vastly disturbs me, sera," Tien said, from the dais where the Nine sat. He spoke very quietly, very politely, which was the way the man talked. "I have to tell you I'm concerned with the security clearance the Science Bureau has given you—not, understand, that I think you're not an exceedingly mature young woman. But we're dealing with things that could mean war or peace, and things that have been thrust on you very prematurely. Do you ever talk to your friends about these things?''

"No, ser, absolutely not." It was a fair question. All along, Tien had been fair.

"Do you understand the importance of not talking to reporters about this?"

"Yes, ser. I do. The only people I've discussed this with are Denys Nye, Giraud Nye, and the Council, exactly; and my azi, but they're not in the room when I work with the System on this either, and they don't know everything. Certainly they don't talk: they're Reseune Security, and their psychset is against discussing anything about me, even little things."

"We understand that. Can you estimate how much of the data you're not telling us?"

Oh. Very good question. "My predecessor had some theories about what would happen on Gehenna." Try to answer without answering. "But they're complicated, and I can't report on those because they're all in design-structure, and they're something that's going to take me a long while to sort through. Science Bureau is going to provide us the Gehenna data as it comes in—"

"To you?"

"Ser, to whoever's working on this project, but likely to me, yes, since I'm the one with my predecessor's notes."

"Time," Harad said. "Adm. Khalid."

"Let's keep to the question of the notes," Khalid said. "And why those notes, if they exist, haven't been turned over to a competent researcher."

"She *is* technically rated as a Wing supervisor," Giraud said. "And she is competent."

"She has no business with the notes," Khalid said. "Or do we believe that Reseune is being steered by a fifteen-year-old and a dead woman? That raises more questions about the competency of Reseune's administration than it does about hers. I have no quarrel with the child. I do have with Reseune. I find evidence of gross mismanagement. *Gross* mismanagement. I think we have more than enough evidence to extend this investigation into Reseune's actions in creating this situation."

"You can do that," Giraud said, "but it won't get you those notes."

The gavel came down. Repeatedly.

"Young sera," Khalid said. "You *can* be held in contempt

of a Council order. So can your Administrator and the other people who are prompting you.''

Ari took a drink of water. When it was quiet she said: ''You can arrest people, but what you want to know is science and you have to ask scientists, and we're it. Bucherlabs hasn't got anybody who can read it. Neither does Defense. I'm already telling you what's in the notes and what you'll find if you go to all that trouble. If you don't think I'm telling the truth now, are you going to believe me then?''

The gavel banged again. ''Councillor. Sera. If you please. Councillor Khalid.''

''We're dealing with an immature child,'' Khalid said, ''who's being pushed into this position by Reseune Administration. I repeat, we need to widen this probe until we get at individuals who *are* responsible. This is a question of national security. The Military Secrets Act—''

''The Councillor is out of order,'' Giraud said.

''—requires an investigation of any mishandling of classified information. The mishandling that allowed a fifteen-year-old child to go in front of news cameras to leak information that *never* should have become public—''

Again the gavel. ''Councillor, we operate under rules, let me remind you. This is not a debate.''

''A diplomatic crisis is at issue. Our enemies have a pretext to break treaties, *including* the arms treaty, which is not to our advantage. They're talking about *plots*, seri, completely ignorant of what azi are and what they're capable of. This is the result of practicing diplomacy in the press.''

''The Councillor is out of order,'' Giraud said.

''Admiral,'' Harad said, ''your time is running. Have you a question for the witness?''

''I have. Under oath, young sera, and bearing in mind you *can* be prosecuted for perjury, how long have you known about these files?''

''About the Gehenna files? They surfaced when I used the keywords.''

''When?''

''The day after you won the election.''

''Where did you get the keywords?''

"Denys Nye suggested them." That was a bad thing to have to admit. "But—"

"Meaning they didn't exist until then. Thank you, young sera. That explains a great deal."

"That's a psych, ser. It doesn't prove anything. I had to know. My clearance—"

"Thank you, we've *had* your answer."

"No, you've made up one."

"The Council will not take disrespect, sera."

"Yes, ser. But I don't have to take being called a liar. You threatened us; I applied for my majority; that triggered—"

"It's not you who's lying, sweet. You've been deceived right along with the Council. Your uncle made those files. He's made them from the beginning. There's no secret, protected system. There are simply records Reseune doesn't want to release, for very clear reasons, and Reseune created *you* to stand between the Council and Reseune's mismanagement."

"No, ser, I'm under oath. I am and you're not. My getting my majority triggered the notes. So when you withdrew your suit, that did it. That's the truth. And *I'm* under oath."

There was a little shifting in seats. A snort from Catherine Lao.

"Your uncle made the files and prepped you for this whole business."

The gavel banged. "That's enough, Councillor. Next question."

"I don't think we're listening to anything in this diplomatic fiasco," Khalid said, "but Denys Nye's constructions. Reseune is playing politics as usual, and it's held too much power too long."

"Do we mention the power in the Defense Bureau?" Giraud said.

"We have a clear case of conflict of interest on the Council. And we have embassies from Pell and Earth asking questions we had rather not answer."

"We have a clear conflict of interest as regards Defense," Giraud said. "Since your Bureau ordered this Gehenna mess over the protests of Science. *As* the witness has testified."

"Time," Harad said, and brought the gavel down.

"I'm due time to respond to that," Khalid said.

"Your time is up."

"I'd hate to accuse the Chairman of partisan politics."

Bang! "You are out of order, Councillor!"

Ari took another sip of water and waited while the Chair wrangled it out. Corain was making notes. So were Lao and a lot of the aides. Corain might have put Khalid up to it, making him the villain, since Khalid already had trouble. There was a challenge to Khalid's seat shaping up—already, a man named Simon Jacques. Much less flamboyant. Reseune had preferred Lu, but Lu's age was against him; and there was under-the-table stuff going on: Corain had talked very secretly with Giraud and Jacques was a compromise they both could swallow, to get rid of Khalid. But that didn't mean Corain wouldn't let Khalid go after Reseune. It just meant that, under that table, Corain didn't want Reseune swallowed up by Defense any more than he wanted it to exist at all.

Meanwhile Khalid had broken off negotiations on a big Defense contract with Reseune. It was a fair-sized threat, but Khalid certainly wasn't doing any more than stalling, because there wasn't anywhere else to get tape from.

And the law that protected azi wound a civil rights issue right into Reseune's right of exclusivity on tape-production, because Reseune *was* the legal guardian of all azi, everywhere—Reseune *could* terminate all azi contracts with Defense—which they wouldn't do, of course, but, Giraud said, Defense had been fighting for years to get access to the birth-to-eighteen tapes for its soldiers, and Reseune would never give them up. That was why Khalid wanted to nationalize Reseune. Khalid said there had been mismanagement at RESEUNESPACE—meaning Jenna Schwartz; but he made it sound like it was present management, meaning Ollie, and that made her damned mad; Defense also said it was worried about something being buried in the training tapes; and Khalid was threatening to bring a bill to break Reseune's monopoly on tape and licensing—

Fine, Giraud said: Khalid didn't have the votes; Khalid's position was already unpopular with his own party—who didn't want *more* azi labs, they wanted fewer; so the whole Gehenna thing was a lever all sorts of interests were using. Corain would have liked to have used it much more, except Corain was worried about Khalid.

It was all very crazy. The stock markets were going up and down on rumors. Chavez, of Finance, was furious and sent a shut-down order on the wave of the rumors, so no ship could leave port for a few days, because they didn't want *that* market-dive information packet going off at trans-light across Union and clear to Pell and Earth, they wanted to get the market stable again before they let any ship leave; and that had the Trade Bureau upset and Information howling about trade censorship. It was a real mess. In fact everybody was getting anxious.

Council won't take this kind of stuff, Giraud had said. And grimly: this is getting very serious, Ari. Very serious.

There was, Giraud had said, a hard-line faction in the military that had been building up for years—a lot of them the old guard who blamed Gorodin and Lu for spending too much on the Fargone project and not getting the programs they wanted; *they* backed Khalid in the election, and they wanted more shipbuilding and more defense systems Sunward; but that was also along the Alliance corridors, and that made the Centrists nervous.

While everybody thought Jacques was a front for Gorodin and might resign and appoint Gorodin proxy if he got elected; and Lu's friends were mad about the double cross.

Crazy.

"We have this entire crisis," Khalid was saying, arguing with Harad, "because Reseune can sit in perfect immunity and level charges contained in documents only the Science Bureau can vouch for. Of *course* the Science Bureau is pure of Reseune influences!"

Giraud was right. Khalid was a disaster with the press, but he was fast on his feet and he was smart. You couldn't discount him.

But Harad brought down the gavel again. "Councillor Lao."

"The question is . . ." Thank God it was Lao's turn next. Uncle Giraud was out, because of conflict of interest. Harad of State was out because he was presiding. ". . . very simply, why a quarantine?"

"They're unpredictable, Councillor. That's the whole thing. We have huge computers that run sociology projections, when we work with psych-sets: we try to balance populations so they end up with wide enough genepools and we check out the psychsets we use to make sure that we haven't put something together that's going to turn up social problems when everybody becomes CIT. This thing—this whole planet—is completely wild and it's all artificial, it's got no relation at all to Terran history—it's just Gehennan. We don't know what it is. That's what made Ari nervous. These azi-sets could have been under God-knows-what interventions while they still had kat and they knew they were in trouble; God knows what their Supervisors decided to tell them; or even if there were Supervisors at the last—" Tell them *that*, get them off the question about predictive sociology. "Take these people into the Alliance or into Union and they're *there* from now on, and they're *different*. Ari didn't say you should never do it. She said there's a period after which it's a lot better to let Gehenna alone and let it grow up, so you can see what it's going to do when it comes into the mainstream culture. Maybe it never will get along with us. Maybe it'll be something very good. We just don't know at this point."

"How *will* you know? Didn't she run those checks?"

"It changes with every generation. It relates to all those psychsets. It relates to the whole mix. Our sociology programs are always improving. Ari ran it every ten years or so until she died. But her data was all just the initial stuff; she was just testing it against the new Sociology programs. We've got to set up to run with the new data. We have to do all the sets with the master-program and then we have to integrate them—that's Sociology does that. Reseune is transferring data over right now to run it. But it's huge; it takes a lot of computer time. And we need up-to-date stats. We can tell Council a lot. But we can't do it overnight and there's nothing, sera, absolutely nothing that laymen can do with that kind of stuff, either, the only computers that can run it are ours. So the best thing, the thing Reseune wants, is to keep that planet exactly the way Alliance wants to—just as little contact as possible while we do the data-collecting. It's like trying to get a good level measure with somebody bouncing the instruments, if people keep meddling there. We have to input all the influences—because just the discovery team landing there had to have done something.''

"This is not," Khalid said, "a playground for the Science Bureau.''

"Nor for Defense, ser," Lao said sharply.

The gavel came down.

She lay flat on the bed in the hotel, limp, while Florian and Catlin rubbed the kinks out, and she went to sleep that way, unexpectedly, just out, pop, gone.

She woke up under the covers and Florian and Catlin had the light down very low, Catlin was stretched out on the other bed, and Florian was sitting in the chair in the corner.

"God," she said, which woke Catlin instantly. "Get to *sleep*. There's battalions of Security in the hall, aren't there?"

"Yes, sera," Florian said. Catlin said: "There are twenty-seven on duty."

"Well, *go to sleep*."

Which was short, for people who loved her enough to stay awake after a day like this one, but she was still falling-over tired, and she did, just grabbed the pillow with her arm, tucked her head down and burrowed until she had a dark place.

Florian turned out the lights anyway; and she heard him cross the room and sit down on the other bed and start undressing.

She headed out again, then, a slow drift. Tomorrow morning was uncle Giraud's turn to testify. Then Secretary Lynch of Science; Secretary Vinelli of Defense; Adm. Khalid—O God, Khalid, then her again, as soon as they got through. She hoped Giraud and Lynch did all right. But when Vinelli got up there, and Khalid, Giraud could cross-examine like everybody else.

Not saying, of course, that Khalid wouldn't go over uncle Giraud and Secretary Lynch the way he had headed at her.

It was going to be a long week.

Or two.

We're going to win about the quarantine, Giraud had predicted at the outset. There's no way Union can do anything like move in on Gehenna without bringing in warships, and there's no way we're going to go to war with the Alliance to get access to Gehenna. What we can lose is what position Union takes about those people on Gehenna—whether they regard them as Union citizens and use that as a lever with the Alliance; or whether they negotiate a joint protectorate with the Alliance; and the hawks have a real stake in that: it's Khalid's political clout that's at issue here—

The Centrist and the Expansionist coalitions were exactly that: coalitions. The hawks were trying to pull something different together by breaking off bits of both, *that* was what had surfaced in Khalid's rise. They were too high-up in the government to call them eetee-fringes. They were *real*: the whole thing that Ari senior had been worried about had come true, the old Earth territorial craziness had found itself an issue and a time to surface—

And here she was holding Ari senior's argument in both hands behind her back— *You know what it would do to Union if they found out what I've done*, Ari senior had said. So she couldn't tell them: she couldn't get the things about Sociology even Sociology didn't know they had done—for Ari senior. She couldn't tell Council about the deep-set work Ari had done, or the fact that Ari had been planning—and installing— imperatives in the azi work crews, in the military, in a whole lot of places—including the deep-sets of the Gehenna azi.

The thing was already going on. By design, thirty percent of the azi Ari senior had designed and turned out of Reseune, and thirty percent of all the azi everywhere who used Reseune tape, would have kids and teach them, all across Union. A certain number of those azi had gotten their CIT papers as early as 2384, on Fargone, then in other places. A lot of them were in Science, a whole lot were in Defense: the Defense azi couldn't get CIT papers till they retired—but they were mostly male and they could still have kids or bring tank-kids up. A lot would do that, because *that* was in the deep-sets. The rest of those azi were scattered out through the electorates, heavy in Industry and Citizens, just exactly where the Centrists were strongest—a mindset that was biased right in its deep-sets, toward Ari senior's way of things.

And even other psych people wouldn't likely see what she had done—unless they were onto it—or unless they were as good as Ari senior, simply because what she did was a very accepted kind of program, a very basic kind of azi mindset. She had *showed* Council, she had even told them the program—and they couldn't see what it did with all those military psychsets, because the connections were so wide and so abstract—except when a living azi mind integrated them and ran with them in the social matrix.

That was what had scared Ari senior so bad.

There were thousands and thousands by now: not a whole lot yet proportionate to all of Union, but the program was running, and those tapes were still turning out azi. Even out of Bucherlabs and Lifefarms, in the simpler, gentle types they trained—there were attitudes designed to mesh with the psychsets of Reseune azi in very special ways.

Look up the word pogrom, *Ari had said, in her notes to her. And see why I am afraid for the azi if people find out too soon what I have done.*

Or too late.

I don't know what I have done. But the Sociology computers in my time can't see beyond twenty of our generations. I do. I've tried to devise logarithmic systems—but I don't trust them. The holes in my thinking could be the holes in the paradigms. Field Too Large is what the damned thing spits back on my wide runs.

I'm becoming emotional about those words.

I'll tell you: if anyone threatens to access these files but you—there is a program that will move them and re-key them in such ways that they will look like a whole lot of different kinds of records and *continually lie about file sizes and other data so that searchers will play hob finding them.*

But for God's sake don't use it until they're breaking the door down: it's terribly dangerous. It has defensive aspects.

I will give you the keywords now to disorganize the System. It has three parts.

First keyword: the year of your birth.

Second keyword: the year of mine.

Third keyword: annihilate.

Then it will ask you for a keyword to re-integrate Base One. Have one in mind and don't panic.

It was a little comfort, knowing that was in there. Knowing she could hide what was going on.

But *she* wouldn't have had just one answer in the computer, to protect something that important.

She didn't think Ari had.

She tossed over on her other side and burrowed again.

And finally she said: "Florian. . . ."

vii

Ari stepped off the plane and into the safeway, and walked the long weary way to the terminal, to get her baggage. Just the briefcase and her carry-bag, that Florian and Catlin had.

Night-flight again, with the escort. Which was a news story unto itself, but all Giraud would say was 'precautions.'

And all the public got was: 'quarantine justified.'

There were people going to be filming here, too—Reseune Information gave a live feed to Cyteen Station, and the station distributed it everywhere. Ships were on their way, the whole of Cyteen commerce was moving again, and the world took a collective breath.

Not knowing all of it, but feeling things were steadier. They were. The markets were up on bargain-hunting and in some ways healthier, because there had been a lot of built-up war-scare that just burst like a bubble, Defense stocks were taking a beating, but diversifieds were doing fine, shipping stocks were soaring again, the futures market was shifting: the Cyteen market believed in peace again after a bad scare, and there was a lot of anti-hawk feeling coming to the surface in the Information polls, which encouraged the shyer voices to speak up and dragged the undecideds back to the peace camp.

After three bad weeks, you could say you wanted peace with the Alliance and sound like a responsible moderate—not a Universalist-eetee, who wanted all the human governments to build a capital in the Hinder Stars—never mind that Earth had over five thousand governments at last count; or a Pax agitator, the sort that had bombed a rush-hour subway car and killed thirty-two people last week in Novgorod.

The police were afraid there was some kind of a pipeline

from the Rocher Abolitionists to the Paxers. They might have gotten the explosives from mine-camp pilferage or maybe just making the stuff: there were possible crime connections, everything from the illicit tape-trade to illegal drugs to the body trade, and a lot of the ones the police could get at were z-cases, just wipe-outs the real criminals used to do the work and take the hits.

The familiar walk from the plane to the safeway doors, the quiet, beige cord-carpet, the sight of Reseune Security guards *talking* with each other in more than coded monosyllables and moving easily, like there was more than a synapse-jump between a sudden noise and hosing-down the room—made her want to melt down on the spot and just sleep for a week, right there, right then, knowing she was safe.

But cameras met her at the exit into the terminal, Security reacted, the few reporters who had gotten passes shoved mikes at her and asked why Giraud had stayed—"He's still got some clean-up," she said. "Office things."

Some secret meetings, staff with staff, Secretary Lynch's staff with Chavez's staff, which was a pipeline from Corain, but that was, God knew, not for the reporters.

"Do you feel confidence in the decision?"

"I think people are going to do the right things now. I think I made them understand—everything's fine if they just treat those people all right—"

"The Gehennans, you mean."

"Yes, the Gehennans. The Science Bureau is going to advise the Alliance ambassador we need some real close communication—that's what's going on right now. But that's the Bureau and the Secretary; and Councillor Harad's office. I think everything's going to work out fine."

Time, well time, to calm the situation down: that was her job; and Giraud's; and Harad's.

"There's no truth to the rumor about a secret base on Gehenna."

She made a deliberate surprise-reaction. "Absolutely not. No. It's not about that at all. I *can* let something out: they're going to make an official statement tomorrow morning: there was some real illegal bacteriological stuff done there. It was our fault. It shouldn't have happened. And we don't need that stuff coming back.''

The reporters got excited. They were supposed to. And it was absolutely true, it *was* one of the cautions, the one they could give out right away, and one of the most urgent ones. ''What *sort* of bacteriological stuff?'' they asked.

''Designed stuff. Viruses. It's not fatal to humans; the Gehennans tolerate it fine. But there are a lot of questions. They did some stuff back in the War that shouldn't have been done. I can't talk about more than that. Councillor Harad said I could say that; he's going to hold a news conference tomorrow morning. I'm sorry—I'm *awfully* tired, and they're signaling me come on—''

''One more question! Is the rumor accurate the Councillor is going to propose talks with Alliance?''

''I can't talk about that.'' Thank God Catlin just grabbed her by the arm and Florian body-blocked and adult Security and uncle Denys' staff got there, Seely in plain-clothes, like always, and Amy and Maddy and Sam closing in—doing the Family-homecoming number—getting her *out* of there—

Getting her all the way to the bus, where she could hug Amy and Maddy and Sam for a whole different reason, for real, because Giraud had let her in on the secret, that a Family reception at the airport was the best way in the universe to get a wedge in on the reporters, get her out, and still give the cameramen the kind of human-interest endshot that left the right kind of feeling with everybody—*who* showed up to do the airport-rescue depended on the kind of impression they wanted to give out.

So uncle Denys sent her the youngers, no official stuff, no indication to the outside world what Reseune's *official* reaction was, no high administrators who could get caught for follow-up by the reporters—just a real happy group of kids slipping in with the Security people, real Family stuff.

Damn, they carried it off smooth as Olders could have.

And left the reporters to guess who they were and to focus on something just human, about Reseune, about the fact Reseune wasn't long-faced and worried and just ordinary kids showed up to welcome her home, after they had seen so much of Reseune Security and asked questions about the chase planes.

Fade-out on happy kids.

People grabbed on to things like that real fast.

"I want to sleep," she said.

"Bad news," Amy said. "They're waiting for you in the front hall." Amy patted her shoulder. "Everybody wants to see you. Just to say welcome back. You were great, Ari. You were really *great*."

"Oh, God," she mumbled. And shut her eyes. She was so tired she was shivering all over. Her knees ached.

"What happened in the hearings?" Maddy asked.

"I can't say. Can't. But it was all right." Even her mouth had trouble working. The bus made the turn and started up the hill. She opened her eyes and remembered she had her hair against the seat back. She sat up and felt to see if it was mussed, and straightened it with her fingers. "Where's my comb?"

Because she was not going into the hall with her hair messed if people had come to see her.

Even if she was falling on her face.

Uncle Denys himself was at the door; she hugged him and kissed him on the cheek and said into his ear: "I'm so awful tired. Get me home."

But Florian had to go ahead to check the Minder before she could even have her bed. *Especially* now.

And she walked the hall through all the Family and the staff; and got hugs and flowers and kissed Dr. Edwards on the cheek and hugged Dr. Dietrich and even Dr. Peterson and Dr. Ivanov—him a long, long moment, because whatever else he had done, he had put her together right; and she had gotten mad at him, but she knew what he had done for her— "You and your damn shots," she said into his ear. "I held together fine in Novgorod."

He hugged her till her bones cracked and he patted her shoulder and said he was glad.

She got a little further. Then: "I've got to rest," she said finally to sera Carnath, Amy's mother, and sera Carnath scolded everybody and told them to let her through.

So they did; and she walked to the lift, went up and over to her hall, and her apartment, and her bed, clothes and all.

She woke up with somebody taking them off her, but that was Florian and Catlin, and that was all right. "Sleep with me," she said, and they got in, both of them, one warm lump, like little kids, right in the middle of the bed.

viii

The Filly loved the open air—there was a pasture bare of everything, where the horses could get a long run—good solid ground, and safe enough if you kept the Filly's head up and never let her eat anything that grew in the fields. Sometimes the azi that worked the horses when Florian was busy used her and the Mare's daughter to exercise the Mare instead of using the walker; but when the Filly was out with her or Florian on her back she really put on her manners, ears up, everything in her just waiting for the chance to run, which was what the Filly loved best.

It made uncle Denys nervous as hell when he got reports about her riding all-out.

Today she had Florian by her on Filly Two, both horses fretting at the bits and wanting to go. "Race you," she said, and aimed the Filly at the end of the field, to the kind of stop that had once sent her most of the way off, hanging on the Filly's neck—she had sworn she would *kill* Andy and Florian if they told; and she was very glad no one had had a camera around.

All the way there with both horses running nearly neck and neck; and it would have taken somebody on the ground to see who was first. Florian could try to be diplomatic. But the fillies had different ideas.

"Easier back," Florian said. The horses were breathing hard, and dancing around and feeling good. But *he* worried when they ran like that.

"Hell," she said. For a moment she was free as the wind and nothing could touch her.

But racing was not why they were out here, or down in AG, or why Catlin had special orders up in the House.

Not why Catlin was walking out of the barn now—a distant bit of black; with company.

"Come on," she said to Florian, and she let the Filly pick her pace, which was still a good clip, and with ears up and then back again as the Filly saw people down there too, and tried to figure it out in her own worried way.

<hr>

ix

Justin stood still beside Catlin's black, slim impassivity, waiting while the horses brought Ari and Florian back—big animals, coming fast—but he figured if there were danger of being run down Catlin would not be standing there with her arms folded, and he thought—he was sure . . . that it was Ari's choice to scare him if she could.

So he stood his ground while the horses ran up on them. They stopped in time. And Ari slid down and Florian did.

She gave Florian her horse to lead away. She had on a white blouse, her hair was pinned up in Emory's way; but coming loose all around her face. The smell of the barn, the animals, leather and earth—brought back childhood. Brought back the days that he and Grant had been free to come down here—

A long time ago.

"Justin," Ari said. "I wanted to talk to you."

"I thought you would," he said.

She was breathing hard. But anyone would, who had come in like that.

Catlin had called his office, said come to the doors; he had left Grant at work, over Grant's objections. No, he had said; just—no. And gotten his jacket and walked down, expecting—God knew—Ari, there.

Catlin had brought him down here, instead, and no one interfered with that. But no one likely interfered much with anything Ari did these days.

"Let's go sit down," Ari said now. "Do you mind?"

"All right," he said; and followed her over to the corner where the fence met the barn. Azi handlers took the horses inside; and Ari sat down on the bottom rail of the metal fence, leaving him the plastic shipping cans that were clustered there, while Catlin and Florian stood a little behind him and out of his line of sight. Intentionally, he thought, a quiet, present threat.

"I don't blame you for anything," she said, hands between her knees, looking at him with no coldness, no resentment. "I feel a little funny—like I should have put *something* together, that there was something in the past—but I thought—I thought maybe you'd gotten crosswise of Administration. The family black sheep. Or something. But that's all history. I know nothing is your fault. I asked you to come here—to ask you what you think about *me*."

It was a civilized, sensible question. It was the nightmare finally happening, turning out to be just a quiet question from a pretty young girl under a sunny sky. But his hands would shake if he was not sitting as he was, arms folded. "What I think about you. I think about the little girl at the New Year's party. About the damn guppies. I think about a sweet kid, Ari. That's all. I've had nightmares about your finding out. *I* didn't want what happened. I didn't want fifteen years of walking around the truth. But they couldn't tell you. And they were afraid I would. That I would—feel some resentment toward you. I don't. None."

Her face was so much Ari's. The lines and planes were beginning to be there. But the eyes were a young woman's eyes, worried—that rare little expression he had seen first that day in his office—over a jar of suffocated baby guppies. *I guess they were just in there too long.*

"Your father's at Planys," she said. "They say you visit him."

He nodded. A lump got into his throat. God. He was not going to break down and go maudlin in front of a fifteen-year-old.

"You miss him."

Second nod. She could feel her way to all the buttons. She *was* Emory. She had proved it in Novgorod, and the whole damn government had rocked on its pinnings.

"Are you mad at me about it?" she asked.

He shook his head.

"Aren't you going to talk to me?"

Damn. *Pull it together, fool!*

"Are you mad at my uncles?"

He shook his head again. There was *nothing* safe to say. Nothing safe to do. She was the one who needed to know. He knew everything. And if there was a way out for Jordan it was going to be in her administration—someday. If there was any hope at all.

She was silent a long time. Just waiting for him. Knowing, surely, that he was fracturing. Himself, who was thirty-four years old; and not doing well at all.

He leaned forward, elbows on knees, studied the dust between his feet, then looked up at her.

No knowledge at all of what the first Ari had done to him. Denys swore to that. And swore what he would do if he opened his mouth about it.

I won't, he had said to Denys. *God, do you think I want her into that tape?*

She hasn't got it, Denys had assured him. *And won't get it.*

Yet—had been his thought.

There was nothing but worry in the look Ari gave him.

"It's not easy," he said, "to be under suspicion—all the time. That's the way I live, Ari. And I never did anything. I was seventeen when it happened."

"I know that," she said. "I'll talk to Denys. I'll make it so you can go visit when you like."

It was everything he had hoped for. "Right now—" he said, "there's too much going on in the world. The mess in Novgorod. The same reason they have you flying with an escort. There's a military base right next to Planys. The airport is in between the two. Your uncle Denys is worried they might try to grab my father; or me. I'm grounded until things settle down. I can't even talk to him on the phone. —And Grant's never even gotten to go. Grant—was like his second son."

"Damn," she said, "I'm sorry. But you *will* get to see him. Grant, too. I'll do everything I can."

"I'd be grateful."

"Justin, —does your father hate me?"

"No. Absolutely not."

"What does he say about me?"

"We stay off that subject," he said. "You understand— every call I make to him, every second I spend with him—

there's always somebody listening. Talking about you—could land me back in Detention.''

She looked at him a long time. Shock, no. But they had not told her that, maybe. There was a mix of expressions on her face he could not sort out.

''Your father's a Special,'' she said. ''Yanni says you ought to be.''

''Yanni says. I doubt it. And they're not even going to allow the question—because they can't touch my father—legally—so they don't want *me* unreachable. You understand.''

That was another answer that bothered her. Another moment of silence.

''Someday,'' he said, ''when things are quieter, someday when you're running Reseune—I hope you'll take another look at my father's case. You could do something to help him. I don't think anyone else ever will. Just—ask him—the things you've asked me.'' *But, O God, the truth . . . about that tape; about Ari; the shock of that—no knowing what that will do to her.*

She's not *like her predecessor. She's a decent kid.*

That tape's as much a rape of her—as me.

God, God, when's she *going to get the thing? Two more years?*

When she's seventeen?

''Maybe I will,'' she said. ''—Justin, *why* did he do it?''

He shook his head, violently. ''Nobody knows. Nobody really knows. Temper. God knows they didn't get along.''

''You're his replicate.''

He lost his breath a moment. And got caught looking her straight in the eyes.

''You don't have a temper like that,'' she said. ''Do you?''

''I'm not like you,'' he said. ''I'm just his twin. Physical resemblance, that's all.''

''Did he fight with a lot of people?''

He tried to think what to say; and came up with: ''No. But he and Ari had a lot of professional disagreements. Things that mattered to them. Personalities, mostly.''

''Yanni says you're awfully good.''

He wobbled badly on that shift of ground and knew she had seen the relief. "Yanni's very kind."

"Yanni's a bitch," she laughed. "But I like him. —He says you work deep-set stuff."

He nodded. "Experimental." He was glad to talk about his work. Anything but the subject they had been on.

"He says your designs are really good. But the computers keep spitting out Field Too Large."

"They've done some other tests."

"I'd like you to teach me," she said.

"Ari, that's kind of you, but I don't think your uncle Denys would like that. I *don't* think they want me around you. I don't think that's ever going to change."

"I want you to teach me," she said, "what you're doing."

He found no quick answer then. And she waited without saying a thing.

"Ari, that's *my* work. You know there *is* a little personal vanity involved here—" Truth, he was disturbed; cornered; and the child was innocent in it, he thought, completely. "Ari, I've had little enough I've really done in my life; I'd at least like to do the first write-up on it, before it gets sucked up into someone else's work. If it's worth anything. You know there *is* such a thing as professional jealousy. And you'll do so much in your life. Leave me my little corner."

She looked put off by that. A line appeared between her brows. "I wouldn't steal from you."

He made it light, a little laugh, grim as it was. "You know what we're doing. Arguing like the first Ari and my father. Over the same damn thing. You're trying to be nice. I know that—"

"I'm not trying to be nice. I'm asking you."

"Look, Ari, —"

"I won't steal your stuff. I don't *care* who writes it up. I just want you to show me what you do and how you do it."

He sat back. It was a corner she backed him into, a damned, petulant child used to having her way in the world. "Ari, —"

"I *need* it, dammit!"

"You don't *get* everything you need in this world."

"You're saying I'd steal from you!"

"I'm not saying you'd steal. I'm saying I've got a few

rights, Ari, few as they are in this place—maybe I want my name on it. *And* my father's. If just because it's the same last name.''

That stopped her. She thought about it, staring at him.

"I can figure that,'' she said. "I can *fix* that. I promise you. I won't take anything you don't want me to. *I don't lie*, Justin. I don't tell lies. Not to my friends. Not in important things. I want to learn. I want you to teach me. Nobody in the House is going to keep me from having any teacher I want. And it's you.''

"You know—if you get me in trouble, Ari, you know what it can do.''

"You're not going to get in any trouble. I'm a wing supervisor. Even if I haven't got a wing to work in. So I can make my own, can't I? You. And Grant.''

His heart went to long, painful beats. "I'd rather not be transferred.''

She shook her head. "Not really *move*. I've got a Wing One office. It's just paper stuff. It just means my staff does your paperwork. —I'm sorry.'' When he said nothing in her pause: "I *did* it.''

"*Damn* it, Ari—''

"It's just paperwork. *And* I don't like having stuff I'm working on lying around your office. —I can change it back, if you like.''

"I'd rather.'' He leaned his arms on his knees, looking her in the eye. "Ari, —I told you. I've got little enough in my life. I'd like to hang on to my independence. If you don't mind.''

"They're bugging your apartment. You know that.''

"I figured they might be.''

"If you're in my wing, I can re-route the Security stuff so I get it, same as uncle Denys.''

"I don't *want* it, Ari.''

She gave him a worried, slightly hurt look. "Will you teach me?''

"All right,'' he said. Because there was no way out of it.

"You don't sound happy.''

"I don't know, Ari.''

She reached out and squeezed his hand. "Friends. All right? Friends?''

He squeezed hers. And tried to believe it.

"They'll probably arrest me when I get back to the House."

"No, they won't." She drew her hand back. "Come on. We'll all walk up together. *I've* got to get a shower before I go anywhere. But you can tell me what you're working on."

X

They parted company at the quadrangle. He walked on, heart racing as he walked toward the Wing One doors, where the guard always stood, where—quite likely, the guard was getting an advisement over the pocket-com; or sending one and getting orders back.

He had seen enough of Security's inner rooms.

He walked through the door, looked at the guard eye to eye—offering no threat, trying without saying a thing to communicate that he was not going to be a problem: he had had enough in his life of being slammed face-about against walls.

"Good day, ser," the guard said, and his heart did a skip-beat. "Good day," he said, and walked on through the small foyer into the hall, all the way to the lift, all the time he was standing there expecting to get a sharp order from behind him, still expecting it all the way down the hall upstairs. But he got as far as his office, and Grant was there, unarrested, looking worried and frayed at the edges.

"It's all right," he said, to relieve the worst of Grant's fears. "Went pretty well. A lot better than it could have." He sat down, drew a breath or two. "She's asked me to teach her."

Grant did not react overmuch. He shrugged finally. "Denys will put the quietus on that."

"No. I don't know *what* in hell it is. She got us transferred. I," he said as Grant showed alarm, "got us transferred *back* to Yanni's wing. But right now—and until she gets it straight with Security—we're not Wing One. That's how serious it is—if she's telling the truth; and I haven't a reason in the world to doubt it. She *wants* me to work with her. She's been talking with Yanni about my work, Yanni told her—damn him—he thinks I'm on some kind of important track, and young sera *wants* what I know, wants me to show her everything I'm working on.''

Grant exhaled a long, slow breath.

''So, well—'' Justin swung the chair around, reached for his coffee cup and got up to fill it from the pot. ''That's the story. If Security doesn't come storming in here— You want a cup?''

''Thanks. —Sit down, let me get it.''

''I've got it.'' He retrieved Grant's cup and gave him the rest of the pot and a little of his own. ''Here.'' He handed Grant the cup. ''Anyway, she was reasonable. She was—''

Not quite the little kid anymore.

But he didn't say that. He said: ''—quite reasonable. Concerned.'' And then remembered with a flood of panic: We're in her administration at the moment; if there's monitoring going on, it's not routed just to Denys, it's going straight to her. My God, what have we said?

''We'll be under her security for a little while,'' he said with that little Remember the eavesdroppers sign, and Grant's eyes followed that move.

Trying to remember what he had said, too, he imagined, and to figure out how a young and very dangerous CIT could interpret it.

ARCHIVES: RUBIN PROJECT: CLASSIFIED CLASS AA

DO NOT COPY
CONTENT: Computer Transcript File #19031 Seq. #9
Personal Archive
Emory II

2421: 3/4: 1945

AE2: Base One, enter: Archive. Personal.

I think I ought to keep these notes. I feel a little strange doing it. My predecessor's never told me to. But they archived everything I did up to a few years ago. I imagine everything on Base One gets archived. Maybe I should put my own notes in. Maybe someday that'll be important. Because I think I *am* important.

That sounds egotistical. But that's all right. They wanted me to be.

I'm Ari Emory. I'm not the first but I'm not quite only the second either. We've got so much in common. Sometimes I hate my uncles for doing what they did to me—especially about maman. But if they hadn't—I don't know, I wouldn't want to be different than I am. I wouldn't want to not be me. I sure wouldn't want to be other people I could name. Maybe the first Ari could say that too.

I know she would. I know it even if she never told me.

I'd say: That's spooky.

She'd say: That's damned dangerous.

And I know what she'd mean. I know exactly what she'd mean by that and why she'd worry about me—but I know some things she didn't, like how I feel and whether the way I think about her is dangerous, or whether being a little different from her is dangerous. I'm pretty sure I'm all right, but I don't know if I'm close enough to her to be as smart as she was or to take care of the things she left me, and I won't know the things that made me smart enough until I'm good enough to look back on how they made me and say—they needed that. Or, they didn't.

I'm riding about fifteen to twenty points above her scores in psych—at the same chronological age. And I'm two points ahead of her score two years from now. Same in most of my subjects. But that's deceptive because I've had the benefits of the things she did and the way she worked, that everybody does now. That's spooky too. But that's the way it'd have to be, isn't it? Tapes have gotten better, and they've tailored so much of this for me, specifically, off her strong points and weaknesses, it's no wonder I'm going faster. But I can't get smug about it, because there's no guarantee on anything, and no guarantee I'll stay ahead at any given point.

It's spooky to know you're an experiment, and to watch yourself work. There's this boy out on Fargone, who's like me. Someday I'm going to write to him and just say hello, Ben, this is Ari. I hope you're all right.

Justin says they're easier on him than on me. He says maybe they didn't have to be so rough, but they couldn't take chances with me, and when I'm grown maybe I can figure out what they really could have left out.

I said I thought that was damned dangerous, wasn't it? Doing psych on yourself—is real dangerous, especially if you're psych-trained. I'm always scared when I start thinking about how I work, because that's an intervention, when you really know psych, but you don't know enough yet. It's like—my mind is so hard to keep aimed, it wants to go sideways and inside and everywhere—

I told Justin that too. He said he understood. He said

sometimes when you're young you have to think about things, because you're forming your value-sets and you keep coming up with Data Insufficient and finding holes in your programs. So you keep trying to do a fix on your sets. And the more powerful your mind is and the more intense your concentration is, the worse damage you can do to yourself, which is why, Justin says, Alphas always have trouble and some of them go way off and out-there, and why almost all Alphas are eccentric. But he says the best thing you can do if you're too bright for your own good is what the Testers do, be aware where you got which idea, keep a tab on everything and know how your ideas link up with each other and with your deep-sets and value-sets, so when you're forty or fifty or a hundred forty and you find something that doesn't work, you can still find all the threads and pull them.

But that's not real easy unless you know what your value-sets are, and most CITs don't. CITs have a trouble with not *wanting* to know that kind of thing. Because some of them are real eetee once you get to thinking about how they link. Especially about sex and ego-nets.

Justin says inflexibility is a trap and most Alpha types are inward-turned because they process so fast they're gone and thinking before a Gamma gets a sentence out. Then they get in the habit of thinking they thought of everything, but they don't remember everything stems from input. You may have a new idea, but it *stems* from input somebody gave you, and that could be wrong or your senses could have been lying to you. He says it can be an equipment-quality problem or a program-quality problem, but once an Alpha takes a falsehood for true, it's a personal problem.

I like that. I wish I'd said it.

And once an Alpha stops re-analyzing his input and starts outputting only, he's gone completely eetee. Which is why, Justin says, Alpha azi can't be tape-trained past a certain point, because they don't learn to analyze and question the flux-level input they get later, and when they socialize too late, they go more and more internal because things actually seem too fast and too random for them, exactly the opposite of the problem the socialized Alphas have—too fast, though, only because they're processing like crazy trying to make more out of the input than's really there, because they don't understand there *is* no system, at least there's no micro-system, and they keep trying to make one out of the flux they don't understand.

Which is why some Alphas go dangerous and why you have trouble getting them to take help-tapes: some start flux-thinking on everything, and some just go schiz, destructure their deep-sets and reconstruct their own, based on whatever comes intact out of the flux they're getting. And after that you don't know what they are. They become like CITs, only with some real strange logic areas.

Which is why they're so hard to help.

I think Yanni is right about Justin. I think he's awfully smart. I've asked my uncle Denys about him, about whether they don't make him a Special because of politics; and Denys said he didn't know whether Justin qualified, but the politics part was definitely true.

Ari, Denys said, I know you're fond of him. If you are, do him and yourself a favor and don't talk about him with anybody on staff—especially don't mention him in Novgorod.

I said I thought that was rotten, it was just because of what his father did, and it wasn't his fault any more than it was mine what my predecessor and his father were fighting about.

And then uncle Denys said something scary. He said: No. I'm telling you this for his sake. You think about it, Ari. He's very bright. He's possibly everything you say. Give him immunity and you give him power, Ari, and power is something he'd have to use. Think about it. You know Novgorod. You know the situation. And you know that Justin's honest. Think about what power would do to him.

I did think then, just like a flash, like lightning going off at night, and you can see everything, all the buildings you know are there, but you forget—you forget about the details of things until the flash comes—and it's gray and clearer than day in some ways. Like there could be color, but there's not quite enough light. So you can see everything the way you can't see it in daylight.

That's what it is when somebody throws light on what you've got all the pieces of.

His father is at Planys.

That's first.

Then there are all these other things—like him being my teacher. Like—we're best friends. But it's like Amy. Amy's my best friend but Florian and Catlin. And we couldn't get along till Amy knew I could beat her. Like she was going to *have* to do something about me until she knew she couldn't. Then we're all right.

Power stuff. Ari was right about that too—about us being territorial as hell, only territory is the wrong word. Territory is only something you can attach that idea to because we got used to the root concept when we were working with animals.

That's what Ari called science making itself a semantic problem. Because if you think territoriality you don't realize what you're really anxious about. We're not bettas.

The old Greeks talked about moira. Moira means *lot* in Greek. Like your share of things. And you can't grab somebody else's—that's stealing; you can't not do your own; that's being a coward. But figuring out what yours is would be a bitch, except other people and other animals help you define what your edges are when they react back: if they don't react back or they don't react so you can understand them you get anxiety reactions and you react with the fight or flight bias your psychset gives you, whether you're a human being or a betta. I got that from Sophocles. And Aristotle. And Amy Carnath and her bettas, because she's the first CIT friend I ever had I worked that out with, and she breeds fighting fish.

It's not territory. It's equilibrium. An equilibrated system has tensions in balance, like girders and trusses in a building.

Rigid systems are vulnerable. Ari said that. Equilibrated systems can flex under stress.

The old Greeks used to put flex in their buildings, moving joints, because they had earthquakes.

I'm leading up to something.

I think it has to do with me and Justin.

I don't trust too much flex any more than too little. Too much and your wall goes down; too little and it breaks.

I'm saying this for the record. If I was talking to Justin or Yanni or uncle Denys I'd say:

Non-looping paths don't necessarily have to be macro-setted on an individual level.

Except then—

—then you have to macro-set the social matrix, which you can do—

—but the variables are real killers to work out—Justin's proved that.

God, talking with yourself has some benefits.

That's what Ari meant by macro-values. That's what she was talking about. That's how she could be so damned careless about the random inputs with her designs. They all feed into a single value: the flux always has to reset off the central sets. That's what Justin was trying to explain to me: flux re-set functions.

Gehennans identify with their world. That's the whole center of what Ari did with that design. And no flux-thinking can get at that.

But where does that go?

Damn! I wish I could tell it to Justin. . . .

Define: world. There's the worm. God! It could be one, if you could guide that semantic mutation.

Pity we have to input words instead of numbers. Into a hormone-fluxed system.

Justin says.

Justin says semantics is always the problem; the more concrete a value you link the sets to, the better off your design is with the computers—but that's not all of it. The link-point has to be a non-fluxing thing—Justin says—

No! Not non-flux. Slow-flux. Flux relative or proportional to the rest of the flux in the sets—like a scissors-joint: everything can move without changing the structure, just the distance down the one axis—

No. Not even that. If the flux on the macro-set has a time-lag of any kind you're going to increase the adaptive flux in the micro-sets in any system. But if you could work out that relevancy in any kind of symbological matrix—then you can get a numerical value back.

Can't you?

Doesn't that do something with the Field Size problem? Isn't that something like a log, if the internal change rates in the sets could be setted; and then—

No, damn, then your world is fine until it gets immigrants; and the first random inputs come in and give you someone who doesn't share the same values—

Immigration—on Gehenna—

Could change the definition of *world* . . . couldn't it?

Damn, I wish I could ask Justin about these things. Maybe I know something. Even if I am sixteen. I know things I can't tell anybody. Especially Justin. And they could be terribly dangerous.

But Gehenna's quarantined. It's safe—so far. I've got time. Don't I?

Justin resents what I did, when I made him be my teacher. I know he does. He frowns a lot. Sometimes Grant looks worried about the situation. Grant's mad at me too. He would be. Even if both of them try to be nice. And not just nice. They *are* kind. Both. They're just upset. Justin's been arrested every time I got in trouble. A lot of things that weren't fair at all. I know why they did it. Like what my uncles did to me. But they were never fair to him.

So it's not like I blame him for his mad. And he keeps it real well: I can respect that. I have one of my own that I'll never forgive. Not really. He knows it's not my fault about his father and all. He knows I'm not lying when I say he and Grant can both go see his father when all this political mess clears up, and I'll help him every way I can.

But he's still hurting about his father. Maman was clear away on Fargone and I never even heard from her again, but she was far away, out of reach, and after a while it didn't hurt so awful much. *His* father is on Cyteen, and they can talk, but that's bad too, because you'd always have to be thinking about how close that is. And now they can't even talk by phone and he's worried about his father, I know he is.

Then I go and tell him he's going to give me his research,

that he's been working on with his father and he hopes could help his father—that's something I did, me. People have been terrible to him all his life and everything he's got he's fought to have, and some kid comes in and wants everything he's done—and *I'm* the one who gets him in trouble— That's my fault, I know it is, but I've got to have his stuff. It's important. But I can't tell him why and I can't tell him what I want. So he just goes azi on me. That's the only way I can describe it—just very cool and very proper.

We work in his office mostly. He says he wants witnesses when he's around me. The Warricks have had enough trouble, he says.

He gives me some real work, because he says I'm not bad, and I can do the frameworks. And then I catch him sometimes, because when I'm really, really doing my best, and especially when I come up with something all the way right, he forgets his mad for a second or two and he loosens up and something shines out of him, that's a hell of a precise description, isn't it? But he gets interested in what we're doing and the ice thaws a bit, and he's just—all right with me. For about two or three minutes, until he remembers that everything he teaches me is going away from him and into me. And I think he thinks I'm going to rob him of everything. And I wish I could make him understand I'd like to help him.

Because I do. I hurt when he's cold with me. It feels so good when he's happy.

Hell if I can give him what's mine, but I don't need to take what's his. And he's a lot like me, everybody's messed with his life.

If I could figure out something, if I could figure out something of Ari senior's that I *could* give him, maybe that would make it fair. Because I know so much, but I don't know enough to make it worth anything. And maybe I'm sitting still with something I think is a real little piece, but that would be worth a lot to him.

Because, oh, he's smart. I know, because when he tells me his reasons for what he does, he has a lot of trouble, because he just *knows* some of these things. He said once

I'm making him structure his concepts. He said that's good. Because we *can* talk, sometimes Grant gets into it, and once, it was the best day we ever worked together, we all went to lunch and talked and talked about CIT and azi logic until I couldn't sleep that night, I was still going on it. It was one of the best days I ever remember. And they were happy, and I was. But it sort of died away, then, and everything got back to normal, things just sort of got in the way and Justin came in kind of down, the way he does sometimes, and it was over. Like that.

I'm going to Get him one of these days, though. I'm going to Get both of them. And maybe this is it.

Maybe if I just run through everything I've got on this model thing, maybe it won't work, I guess if it did someone would have thought of it—

No, dammit, Ari, Justin said—I should never tell myself that.

Don't cut ideas off, he says, till you know where they go.

If I could do something *real*, —

What would he do, —get mad, because then I'd be getting closer to what he's working on, and he'd resent that?

Or get mad, because he'd want it all to be his idea?

Maybe he would.

But maybe he'd warm up to me and it could be the way it is sometimes—all the time. That's what I wish. Because so much bad has happened. And I want to change that.

CHAPTER
2

There were new tapes. Maddy brought them. Maddy did the ordering of things like that, because her mother didn't mind, and uncle Denys said that it would be a scandal if it were on *her* account: which Maddy might have figured out, Maddy was not really stupid, but it pleased Maddy to be involved in intrigue and something she truly did best.

So that was a point Maddy got on her side. That kind of favor was something Maddy could use for blackmail, Ari thought, except there was no percentage in it. If Maddy ever wanted to use it in Novgorod, that was all right, she would be grown then and people would not see the sixteen-year-old—just a grown woman, who was, then, only like her predecessor—whose taste for such things was quietly known. Strange, Ari thought, how people were so little capable of being shocked in retrospect: old news, the proverb ran.

And Maddy could be free as she liked with sex, because Maddy was just Maddy Strassen, and the Strassens had no power to frighten anyone—outside Reseune.

It was a quiet gathering. The Kids. Period. Mostly she just

wanted to relax, and they sat around watching the tape quite, quite tranked, except Florian and Catlin, and drinking a little—except Florian and Catlin. Sam spilled a drink—he was terribly embarrassed about it. But Catlin helped him mop up and took him to the back bedroom and helped him in another way, which was Catlin's own idea, because Sam and Amy were having trouble.

God, life got complicated. *Amy* had a fix on Stef Dietrich; and that was hopeless. Sam had one—well, on herself, Ari reckoned; and that was the trouble, that Amy got seconds on a lot of things in life. And Amy was interested in a lot of things Sam wasn't. And vice versa. She wished to hell Sam would find somebody. Anybody.

But he didn't. And Sam was the main reason why she didn't go off to the bedroom with Tommy or Stef or anyone who came to the apartment; but he wasn't the only reason. The main one was what it had always been, the same reason that she was best friends with Amy and Sam and Maddy and kept everyone else at arm's length—because Sam was always in the way to get hurt, there was no way to shut him out, nor was it fair, and yet—

And yet—

Of all the boys he was the only one who really liked just *her*, herself, from before he ever knew she was anybody.

And that made her sad sometimes, because all the others would be thinking about themselves and what it meant to them, and how she was a Special and she was rich and she was going to be Administrator someday, and making her happy was very, very important—

Which was a lot different than Sam, who loved her, she thought, who really truly loved her. And she loved him—what time she was not frustrated that he existed, frustrated that he had to love her *that* way, frustrated that he was the focus of all her other frustrations and never, ever, deserved them—

Because she would not sleep with Stef Dietrich if there never had been a Sam. That was still true.

For one thing it would kill Amy. Amy could stand to be beaten by Yvgenia, but not by her—in this. No matter that Amy was still gawky and awkward, and never *worked* at her appearance . . . until she took after Stef, and then it was almost pathetic. Amy, with eyeshadow. Amy, fussing with her hair, which was loose now, not in braids. After Stef, who was so damned handsome and so sure of it.

While Sam was a little at loose ends, not quite betrayed, but a lot at a loss. And if Stef had antennae for anything, he knew damned well he had better walk a narrow line between Yvgenia and Amy.

And it left her, herself, to watch the tapes and afterward, after Florian and Catlin had showed everyone out, to lie on the couch and stare at the ceiling in a melancholy not even they could relieve.

"Come to bed, sera," Florian said.

Worried about her.

Worried and absolutely devoted.

The ceiling hazed in her sight. If she blinked the tears would run and they would see them.

But the tears spilled anyway, just ran from the outside edge of her eye, so she blinked, it made no difference.

"Sera?" There was profound upset in Florian's voice. He wiped her cheek, the merest feather-touch. And was certainly in pain.

Dammit. Damn him. Damn him for that reaction.

I'm smarter than Ari senior. At least I haven't fouled up things with Sam and Amy. They've fouled it up with each other.

I don't understand CITs. I really truly don't understand CITs.

Azi are so much kinder.

And they can't help it.

"Sera." Florian patted her cheek, laid a hand on her shoulder. "Who hurt you?"

Shall we kill him? she imagined the next question. For some reason that struck her hysterically funny. She started laughing, laughing till she had to pull her legs up to save her stomach from aching, and the tears ran; and Florian held her hands and Catlin slid over the back of the couch to kneel by her and hold on to her.

Which only struck her funnier.

"I'm—I'm sorry," she gasped finally, when she could get a breath. Her stomach hurt. And they were so terribly confused.

"Oh. I'm sorry." She reached and patted Florian's shoulder, Catlin's leg. "I'm sorry. I'm just tired, that's all. That damn report—"

"The *report*, sera?" Florian asked.

She caught her breath, flattened out with a little shift around Catlin and let go a long sigh. "I've been working so hard. You have to forgive me. CITs do this kind of thing. Oh, God, the Minder. I hope to God you didn't re-arm the system—"

"No, sera, not yet."

"That's good. Damn. Oh, damn, my sides hurt. That thing—calling the Bureau—would just about cap the whole week, wouldn't it? Blow an assignment, miss the whole damn point. Amy's making a fool of herself and Sam's walking wounded—CIT's are a bitch, you know it? They're a real pain."

"Sam seemed happy," Catlin said.

"I'm glad." For some reason the pain came back behind her heart. And she sighed again and wiped her eyes. "God, I bet that got my makeup. I bet I look a sight."

"You're always beautiful, sera." Florian wiped beneath her left eye with a fingertip, and wiped his hand on his sleeve and wiped the other one. "There."

She smiled then, and laughed silently, without the pain, seeing two worried faces, two human beings who would, in fact, take on anyone she named—never mind their own safety.

"We should get to bed," she said. "I've got to do that paper tomorrow. I've got to do it. I really shouldn't have done this. And I don't even want to get up from here."

"We can carry you."

"God," she said, feeling Florian slip his hands under. "You'll drop me—Florian!"

He stopped.

"I'll walk," she said. And got up, and did, with her arms around both of them, not that she needed the balance.

Just that she needed someone, about then.

Ari bit her lip, perfectly quiet while Justin was reading her report. She sat with her arms on her knees and her hands clenched while he flipped through the printout.

"What is this?" he asked finally, looking up, very serious. "Ari, where did you get this?"

"It's a world I made up. Like Gehenna. You start with those sets. And you tell them, you have to defend this base and you teach your children to defend it. And you give them these tapes. And you get this kind of parameter between A and Y in the matrix; and you get this set between B and Y, and so on; and there's a direct relationship between the change in A and the rest of the shifts—so I did a strict mechanics model, like it was a fluxing structure, but with all these levels—"

"I can see that." Justin's brow furrowed, and he asked apprehensively: "This *isn't* Gehenna, is it?"

She shook her head. "No. That's classified. That's my problem. I built this thing with a problem in it, but that's all right, that's to keep it inside a few generations. It's whether all the sets change at the same rate, that's what I'm asking."

"You mean you're inputting the whole colony at once. *No* outsiders."

"They can get there in the fourth generation. Gehenna's did. Page 330."

He flipped through and looked.

"I just want to talk about it," she said. "I just got to thinking about whether some of the problems in the sociology models, you know, aren't because you're trying to do ones that work. So I'm setting up a system with deliberate problems, to see how the problems work. I changed everything. You don't need to worry I'm telling you anything you don't want to know. I just got to thinking about Gehenna and closed systems, and so I made you a model. It's in the appendix. There's a sort of a worm in it. I won't tell you what, but I think you can see it—or I'm not right about it." She bit her lip. "Page 330. One of those paragraphs is Ari's. About values and flux. You tell me a lot of things. I looked through Ari's notes for things that could help you. That's hers. So's the bit on the group sets. It's real stuff. It's stuff out of Archive. I thought you could use it. Fair trade."

It was terribly dangerous. It was terribly close to things that people weren't supposed to know about, that could bring panic down on the Gehennans; and worse.

But everybody in Reseune speculated on the Gehenna tapes,

and people from inside Reseune didn't talk to people outside, and people outside wouldn't understand them anyway. She sat there with her hands clenched together and her stomach in a knot, with gnawing second thoughts, whether he would see too much—being as smart as he was. But he worked on micro-systems. Ari's were macros—in the widest possible sense.

He said nothing for a long while.

"You know you're not supposed to be telling me this," he said in a whisper. Like they were being bugged; or the habit was there, like it was with her. "Dammit, Ari, you *know* it— What are you trying to do to me?"

"How else am I going to learn?" she hissed back, whispering because he whispered. "Who else is there?"

He fingered the edges of the pages and stared at it. And looked up. "You've put in a lot of work on this."

She nodded. It was why she had blown the last assignment. But that was sniveling. She didn't say that. She just waited for what he would say.

And he *did* see too much. She saw it in his face. He was not trying to hide his upset. He only stared at her a long, long time.

"Are we being monitored?" he asked.

"My uncles," she said, "probably." Not saying that *she* could. "It might go into Archive. I imagine they take every chance to tape *me* they can get, since I threw them out of my bedroom a long time ago. Don't worry about it. It doesn't matter what they listen to. There's no way they'll tell *me* no, when it comes to what I need to learn. Or give you any trouble."

"For somebody who held off the Council in Novgorod," Justin said, "you can still be naive."

"They won't do it, I'm telling you."

"Why? Because you say so? You don't run Reseune, your uncles do. And will, for some years. Ari, —my *God*, Ari—"

He shoved his chair back and got up and walked out.

Which left her sitting there, with Grant on the other side of the cluttered little office, staring at her, not quite azi-like, but very cold and very wary, like something was her fault.

"Nothing's going to happen!" she said to Grant.

Grant got up and came and took the report from Justin's desk.

"That's his," she said, putting a hand on it.

"It's yours. You can take it back or I can put it in the safe. I don't think Justin wants to teach you any more today, young sera. I imagine he'll read it very carefully if you leave it here. But you've grounded him. I don't doubt you've grounded me as well. Security would never believe I wasn't involved."

"You mean about his father?" She looked up at Grant, caught in the position of disadvantage, with Grant looming over her chair. "It doesn't make any difference. Khalid's not going to hold on to that seat. Another six months and there won't be any problem. Defense is going to be sensible again and there won't be any problem."

Grant only stared at her a moment. Then: "Free Jordan, why don't you, young sera? Possibly because you *can't*? —Please go. I'll put this up for him."

She sat there a moment more while Grant took the report and took it to the wall-safe and put it inside. Then Grant left.

Just—left her there.

So she left, and walked down the hall with a lump in her throat.

He was better, at home, with a drink in him. With the report in his lap—he had gotten it from the safe, and when Grant said that it was dangerous to carry about, he had said: So let them arrest me. I'm used to it. What the hell?

So he sat sipping a well-watered Scotch and reading the paragraph on 330 over and over again. "God," he said, when he had gone through it the second time, sifting through the limitation of words for the precious content. It was valuable—was like a light going on—in a small area, but there was nothing small or inconsequential where ideas had to link together. "She's talking about values here. The interlock of the ego-net and the value sets in azi psych and the styles of integration— why some are better than others. I needed this—back at the start. I had to work it out. Damn, Grant, how much else I've done—is already in Archives, just waiting there? That's a hell of a thought, isn't it?"

"It isn't true," Grant said. "If it was, *Ari* would have been doing the papers."

"I think I know why I interested her," he said. "At least— part of it." He took another drink and thumbed through the report. "I wonder how much of this is *our* Ari's. Whether it's something Ari senior suggested to her to do—and gave her the framework on—or whether Ari just—put this together. It's a graduation project. That's what it is. A thesis. And I can see how Ari must have looked at mine—when I was seventeen and naive as hell about design. But there's a lot more in this. The model work is first rate."

"She's got a major base in the House computers to help her," Grant said. "She can pull time on nets you couldn't even consult when *you* were her age—"

"On facilities I didn't know existed when I was her age. Yes. And I hadn't had her world-experience, and a lot of other things— I was younger—in a lot of ways—than she is right now. Damn, she's done a lot of work on this. And typically, she never said a thing about what she was working on. I think it *is* hers. This whole model is naive as hell, she's planted *two* major timebombs in the center-set, which is overkill if she's trying to get a failure—but she's likely going to run it with increasing degrees of clean-up. Maybe compare one drift against the other." Another drink and a slow shake of his head. "You know what this is, it's a bribe. It's a damn bribe. Two small windows into those Archived notes, and both of them completely unpublished material— And I'm sitting here weighing what else could be there—that could make everything I'm doing obsolete before it's published—or be the key to what I *could* do—what I could have done—if Ari hadn't been murdered—And I'm weighing it against losing years of contact with Jordan. Against the chance neither one of us might ever—"

He lost his voice again. Took a drink and gazed at the wall.

"Because there's no choice," he concluded, when he had had several more swallows of whiskey and he was halfway numb again. "I don't even know why, or what part of this report is real, or how much of Gehenna is in here." He looked at Grant; and hated himself for the whole situation he was in, because it was Grant's chances of Planys that had been shot to hell, equally as well as his. Grant had sat at home waiting on all his other visits—because the whole weight of law and custom and the practical facts of Grant's azi vulnerabilities to manipulation and his abilities to remember and focus on instruction—had barred him from Planys thus far.

Now their jailers had the ultimate excuse, if they had ever needed one.

"I had no idea," he said to Grant, "I had *no* idea what she was working on, or where this was going."

"Ari is not entirely naive in this," Grant said. "If Gehenna is what she's working on—and she wants to work on it with you—she knows that won't sit well in some circles; *and* that you'll understand right through to the heart of the designs and beyond. Ari is accustomed to having her way. More than that, Ari is convinced her way is all-important. Be careful of her. Be extremely careful."

"She knows something, something that's got to do with Gehenna, that hasn't gotten into public."

Grant looked at him long and hard. "Be careful," Grant said. "Justin, for God's sake, be careful."

"Dammit, I—" The frustration in Grant's voice got to him, reached raw nerves, even past the whiskey. He set the glass down and rested his elbows on his knees, his hands on the back of his neck. "Oh, God." The tears came the way they had not in years. He squeezed his eyes shut, tried to dam them back, aware of painful silence in the room.

After a while he got up and added more whiskey to the ice-melt, and stood staring at the corner until he heard Grant get up and come over to the bar, and he looked and took Grant's glass and added ice and whiskey.

"Someday the situation will change," Grant said, took his glass and touched it to his, a light, fragile clink of glass on glass. "Keep your balance. There's no profit in anything else. The election count will be over by fall. The whole situation may change, not overnight, but change, all the same."

"Khalid could win."

"A meteor could strike us. Do we worry about such things? Finish that. Come to bed. All right?"

He shuddered, drank the rest off and shuddered again. He could not *get* drunk enough.

He slammed the glass down on the counter-top and pushed away from the bar, to do what Grant had said.

──────────────── **ii** ────────────────

Ari, Justin's voice had said on the Minder, *be in my office in the morning.*

So she came, was waiting for him when he got there, and he said, opening the door—he had come alone this time, almost the only time: "Ari, I owe you an apology. A profound apology for yesterday." He had her report with him and he laid it down on his desk and riffled the pages. "You did this. Yourself. It was your idea."

"Yes," she said, anxious.

"It's remarkable. It's a really remarkable job. —I don't say it's right, understand, but it's going to take me a little to get through it, not just because of the size. Have you shown this to your uncle?"

She shook her head. It was too hard to talk about coherently. She had not slept much. "No. I did it for you."

"I wasn't very gracious about it. Forgive me. I've been that route myself, with Yanni. I didn't mean to do that to you."

"I understand why you're upset," she said. "I do." Grant was likely to come in at any time and she wanted to get this out beforehand. "Justin, Grant took into me. He was right. But I am too. If Reseune is safe again you can travel. If it isn't, nothing will help, and this won't hurt—in fact it makes you safer, because there's no way they can come at you *or* your father without coming at me, because your father's worked on your stuff, and that means he's working with you and you're working with me, and all he has to do, Justin, all he has to do, if he wants my help—is not do anything against me. I don't even care if he likes me. I just want to work things out so they're better. I *thought* about the danger in working with you, I did think, over and over again—but you're the one I need, because you work long-term and you work with the value-sets and that's what I'm interested in. I'm not a stupid little girl, Justin. I know what I want to work on and Yanni can't help me anymore. Nobody can. So I have to come to you. Uncle Denys knows it. He says—he says—be careful. But he also says you're honest. So am I—no!" —As he opened his mouth. "Let me say this. I *will not* steal from you. You think about this. What if we put out a paper with your name and mine *and* your father's? Don't you think that would shake them up in the Bureau?''

He sat down. ''That would have to get by Denys, Ari, and I don't think he'd approve it. I'm sure Giraud wouldn't.''

''You know what I'd say to my uncles? I'd say—someday I'll have to run Reseune. I'm trying to fix things. I don't want things to go the way they did. Let me try while I have your advice. Or let me try after I don't.''

He scared her for a moment. His face got very still and very pale. Then Grant showed up, coming through the door, so he drew a large breath and paid attention to Grant instead. ''Good morning. Coffee's not on. Yet.''

''Hint,'' Grant said, and made a face and took the pot out for water.

''Ari,'' Justin said then, ''I wish you luck with your uncles. More than I've had. That's all I'll say. Someday you'll find me missing if you're not careful. I'll be down in Detention. Just so you know where. I'm rather well expecting it today. And I'm not sure you can prevent that, no matter how much power you think you have in the House. I hope I'm wrong. But I'll work with you. I'll do everything I can. I've got a few questions for you to start off with. Why did you install two variables?''

She opened her mouth. She wanted to talk about the other thing. But he didn't. He closed that off like a door going shut and threw her an important question. And Grant came back with the water. They were Working her, timing everything. And he had said what he wanted to say.

''It's because one is an action and one is a substantive. *Defend* will drift and so will *base*. And there's going to be no enemy from offworld, just the possibility of one, if that gets passed down. And they're not going to have tape after the first few years: Gehenna didn't.''

Justin nodded slowly. ''You know that my father specializes in educational sets. That Gehenna has political consequences. You talk about my working with him. You know what you're doing, throwing this my way. You know what it could cost me. And him. If anything goes wrong, if anything blows up—it comes down on us. Do you understand that?''

''It won't.''

''*It won't.* Young sera, do you know how thin that sounds to

me? For God's sake be wiser than that. Not smarter. *Wiser.*
Hear me?''

God. Complications. Complications with Defense. With politics. With him. With everything.

''So,'' he said. ''Now you do know. I just want you to be
aware. —Your idea about semantic drift and flux is quite
good—but a little simple, because there's going to be occupational diversity, which affects semantics, and so on—''

Another shift of direction. Firm and definitive. ''They stay
agricultural.''

He nodded. ''Let's work through this, step by step. I'll give
you my objections and you note them and give me your answers. . . .''

She focused down tight, the way Florian and Catlin had
taught her, mind on business, and tried to hold it, but it was not
easy, she was not azi, and there was so much *to* him, there was
so much complication with him, he was always so soft-spoken,
Yanni's complete opposite. He could come off the flank and
surprise her, and so few people could do that.

He could go from being mad to being kind—so fast; and
both things felt solid, both of them felt real.

She felt Grant's disapproval from across the room. There
was nothing she could gain there: win Justin and eventually she
won Grant, it was that simple. And she had made headway
with Justin: she added it up in its various columns and thought
that, overall, complicated as he was, he had given her a great
deal.

---

iii

''He was nice about it,'' she said to Florian and Catlin at dinner. ''He truly was. I think it was real.''

''We'll keep an eye on him,'' Florian said.

They did much less of their work at the Barracks nowadays.
Just occasionally they went down to take a course, only for the
day. They had taken one this day. Catlin was sporting a scrape
on her hand and a bruise on her chin, but she was pleased with
herself, which meant pleased with the way things had gone.

Mostly they did their study by tape. Mostly things were real, nowadays. And they watched the reports they got on the Defense Bureau, and all the comings and goings of things in the installations that bordered on Reseune properties.

There had been a lot of dirty maneuvers—attempts to create scandal around Reseune. Attempts to snare Reseune personnel into public statements. Khalid was *much* better behind the scenes than in front of the cameras, and he had gained ground, while Giraud told her no, no, there's no percentage in debating him. He can make charges. The minute you deny them you're news and the thing is loose again.

But she had rather have *been* news so she could throw trouble into Khalid's lap.

There had been a scare last week when a boat had lost its engines and come ashore down by precip 10: some CITs had taken offense at the level of security they ran into, and said so, which a Centrist senator from Svetlansk had used to some advantage, and proposed an investigation of brutality on the part of Reseune Security.

Never mind that the CIT in question had tried to repossess from Security a carry-bag that had turned out to contain a questionable number of prescription drugs. The CIT claimed they were all legitimate and that he had a respiratory ailment which was aggravated by stress. He was suing for damages.

There was a directive out to Security reaffirming that Reseune stood by the guard. But Florian worried about it; and Catlin did, when Florian pointed out that it could be a deliberate thing, and if someone hadn't thought of creating an incident with Reseune Security in front of cameras, someone surely would now, likely Khalid, and likely something in Novgorod.

Let me tell you, she had said, when they brought it up with her, *don't* worry about it. If that was engineered, *that's* a fallout that could benefit our enemies. *Don't* doubt your tape; react, and react on any level your tape tells you. If I'm alive I can handle whatever falls out—politically. Do you doubt that?

No, they had said solemnly.

So she slammed her hand down on the table and they jumped like a bomb had gone off, scared white.

"Got you," she said. "You're still fast enough. That was *go* and *stop*, wasn't it? Damn fast."

Two or three breaths later Florian had said: "Sera, that was good. But you shouldn't scare us like that."

She had laughed. And patted Florian's hand and Catlin's, Catlin all sober and attentive, the way Catlin got when she was On. "You're *my* staff. Do what *I* say. Not Denys. Not your instructors. Not anyone."

So when Florian said, *We'll keep an eye on him*, there was a certain ominous tone to it.

"He's my friend," she said, reminding them of that.

"Yes, sera," Catlin said. "But we don't take things for granted."

"Enemies are much easier to plan for," Florian said. "Enemies can't get in here."

It was sense they gave her. They were things she had known once, when they were children, in uncle Denys' apartment.

"Hormones," she said, "are a bitch. They do terrible things to your thinking. Of course you're right. Do what you have to."

"Hormones, sera?" Florian asked.

She shrugged, feeling uncomfortable. But there was no jealousy about it. Just worry. "He's good-looking," she said. "That gets in the way, doesn't it? But I'm not crazy, either."

She felt strange about that, after. Scared. And she thought of times when she had had a lot less flux going on.

So she thought of Nelly; and thought that it had been much too long since she had seen her; and found her the next morning, a Nelly a little on the plump side, and very, very busy with her charges in the nursery.

Nelly had a little trouble focusing on her, as if the changes were too sudden or the time had been too long. "Young sera?" Nelly said, blinking several times. "Young sera?"

"I got to thinking about you," she said to Nelly. "How are you doing? Are you happy?"

"Oh, yes. Yes, young sera." A baby began crying. Nelly gave it a distracted look, over her shoulder. Someone else saw to it. "You've grown so much."

"I have. I'm sixteen, Nelly."

"Is it that long?" Nelly blinked again, and shook her head. "You were my first baby."

"I'm your oldest. Can I buy you lunch, Nelly? Put on your coat and come to lunch with me?"

"Well, I—" Nelly looked back at the rows of cribs.

"I've cleared it with your Super. Everything's fine. Come on."

It was very strange. In some ways Nelly was still only Nelly, fussy with her own appearance—fussy with hers. Nelly reached out and straightened her collar, and Ari smiled in spite of the twitch it made about self-defense, because there was no one else in the universe who would do that now.

But she knew before lunch was half over that the small wistful thought she had had, of bringing Nelly back to the apartment, was not the thing to do.

Poor Nelly would never understand the pressures she stood—or, God knew, the tape library.

Nelly was only glad to have found one of her babies again. And Ari made a note to tell the nursery Super that Nelly should have reward tape: that was the best thing she could do for Nelly—besides let her know that her eldest baby was doing well.

That her eldest baby was—what she was . . . Nelly was hardly able to understand.

Only that Nelly straightened her collar again before they parted company, Ari treasured. It made a little lump in her throat and made her feel warm all the way down the hall.

She went out to the cemetery, where there was a little marker that said Jane Strassen, 2272-2414. And she sat there a long time.

"I know why you didn't write," she said to no one, because maman had gone to the sun, the way Ariane Emory had. "I know you loved me. I wish Ollie would write. But I can guess why he doesn't—and I'm afraid to write to him because Khalid knows too much about people I'm fond of as it is.

"I saw Nelly today. Nelly's happy. She has so many babies to take care of—but she never cares what they'll be, just that they're babies, that's all. She's really nice—in a way so few people are.

"I know why you tried to keep me away from Justin. But we've become friends, maman. I remember the first time I saw him. That's the first thing I remember—us going down the hall, and Ollie carrying me. And the punch bowl and Justin and Grant across the room; and me. I remember that. I remember the party at Valery's after.

"I'm doing all right, maman. I'm everything all of you wanted me to be. I wish there was something you'd left me, the way Ari senior did. Because I wish I knew so many things.

"Mostly I'm doing all right. I thought you'd like to know."

Which was stupid. Of course maman knew nothing. She only made herself cry, and sat there a long time on the bench, and remembered herself with her arm in the cast, and aunt Victoria, and Novgorod and Giraud, and everything that had happened.

She was lonely. That was the problem. Florian and Catlin could not understand flux the way she felt it, and she wished when it grew as bad as it was, that there had been maman to say: Dammit, Ari, what in hell's the matter with you?

"Mostly I'm lonely, maman. Florian's fine. But he's not like Ollie. He's mostly Catlin's. And I can't interfere in that.

"I wish they'd made an Ollie too. Somebody who was just mine. And if there was, Florian would be jealous—but of him being another azi and close to me, not—not about what a CIT would be jealous of.

"I'm not altogether like Ari senior. I've been a lot smarter about sex. I haven't fouled up my friends. They've fouled each other up. 'Stasi's not speaking to Amy. Over Stef Dietrich. And Sam's hurt. And Maddy's just disgusted. I hate it.

"And I'm fluxing so badly I could die. I want Florian and I know it's smart to stay to him. But I feel like there's something in me that's just—alone all the time.

"And I feel bad about thinking it, but Florian doesn't touch the lonely feeling. He just feels good for a while. And even while we're doing it, you know, sometimes everything's all right and sometimes I feel like I'm all alone. He doesn't know all my problems, but he tries, and he'll never tell me no, I have to tell myself no for him. Like I always have to be careful. *That's* the trouble.

"I think it's like floating in space, maman. There's nothing around me for lightyears all around. There's times that I'd rather Florian than anybody, because there's no one understands me like he does when I'm down or when I'm scared. But there's a side of me he just can't help, that's the problem. And I think he knows it.

"That's the awful thing. He's starting to worry about me. Like it was his fault. And *I* don't know why I'm doing this to him. I'm so mad at myself. Ari talked about hurting Florian— her Florian. And that scares hell out of me, maman. I don't ever want to do that. But I am, when I make him feel like my problems are his fault.

"Did you ever have this with Ollie?

"Maybe I should just go down to the Town and try it with some of the azi down there, that do that kind of thing. Maybe somebody like a Mu-class, who knows? A grown-up one. Somebody I can't mess up.

"But that kind of embarrasses me. Uncle Denys would have a fit. He'd say—O God, I couldn't discuss that with him. Besides, it would hurt Florian's feelings. Florian would be a little disgusted if I did it with Stef, but he wouldn't be *hurt*.

"Some azi from the Town, though—I couldn't do that to him. I don't think Ari senior ever did anything like that. I can't find it in any records. And I looked.

"I think I'm being silly. I love Florian, truly I do. If there's trouble it's *my* trouble, not his. I should go back and be twice as nice to him and quit being selfish, that's what I ought to do. Lonely is all in my head, isn't it?

"Mostly. Mostly, I guess it is.

"Damn, maman, I wish you'd written. I wish Ollie would.

"He's CIT now. He's Oliver AOX Strassen. Maybe he thinks it would be presumptuous, to write now, like I was his daughter.

"Maybe he's just turned that off. He'll never stop being azi, down in his deep-sets, will he?

"I thought about having the labs make another of him.

"But you taught him the important things. And I'm not you, and I can't make him into Ollie. Besides, Florian and Catlin would be jealous as hell, like Nelly was, of them. And I'd never do that to them.

"Wish you were here. Damn, you must have wanted to strangle me sometimes. But you did a good job, maman. I'm all right.

"Overall, I'm all right."

_____ iv _____

"It won't work," Justin said. "Look. There's going to be an increase in flux in the micro-sets. I can tell you what will happen."

"But it could be proportional. That's what I'm asking. If it's proportional, that's what I'm saying, isn't that right?"

He nodded. "I know what you're saying. I'm saying it's more complicated. Look here. You've set up for matrilineal education. That means you've got the AJ group, there, that's going to go with PA—there's your trouble, you've got a fair number of Alphas, maybe more than you ought to have. God knows what they're going to make out of your instructions."

"I asked Florian and Catlin how they'd interpret that instruction to defend the base. Florian said you just build defenses around the perimeter and wait if you're sure you're the only intelligence there. Catlin said that was fine, but you train your people for the next generation. Florian agreed with that, but he said they couldn't all be specialists, somebody had to see to the other jobs. But their psychsets aren't in the group. Ask Grant."

"Grant?"

Grant turned his chair around and leaned back. "I'd tend to agree with them, except everybody will have to be trained to some extent or you can't follow your central directive and you'll have some who aren't following it except by abstraction. Once you get that abstraction, that growing potatoes is defense, then you've got a considerable drift started. *Everything* becomes interrelated. Your definition of *base* may or may not drift at this point, and if I were in charge, I'd worry about that."

That was a good answer. She drew a long breath and thought about it.

And thought: *Damn, he's smart. And social. And in his thirties. Maybe* that's *the trouble, with me and Florian. Florian and Catlin are still learning their own jobs. And so am I. But Grant—*

Grant's a designer. That's one difference.

"I've handled that abstraction," she said, "so that there is a change like that. Because they're not stressed and there isn't an Enemy early on. But I think you're right, two variables is going to blow everything full of holes."

"*Maintain* would have been a more variable word than *defend*," Justin said, "but *defend* brings all sorts of baggage with it, *if* any of your group are socialized. And you say three are. The AJ, the BY and one of the IUs. Which means, you're quite right, that you've got three who are likely going to do the interpretation and the initial flux-thinking; which means your value-sets are going to come very strongly off these three points. Which is going to hold them together tolerably well to start with, because they're all three military sets. And they're likely going to see that 'defend the base' is a multi-generational problem. But your Alpha is likely to be less skilled at communication than the Beta. So I'll reckon that's your leader. The Beta."

"Huh. But the Alpha can get around her."

"As an adviser. That's my suggestion. But the smarter the Alpha is, the less likely his instructions are going to make any immediate sense. He'll dominate as long as it's a matter of azi psychsets. But he'll lose his power as the next generation grows up. Won't he? Unless he's more socialized than the Beta."

"They don't have rejuv. It's a hard life. They're going to die around fifty and sixty. So the kids won't be much more than twenty or so before they're going on just what they could learn."

"Your Beta's instructions are likely to be more near-term, less abstract, more comprehensible to the young ones."

"My Alpha founds a religion."

"God. He'd have to be awfully well socialized. And machiavellian. Besides, it's not an azi kind of thing to do."

"Just practical."

"But, given that he does, would the kids *understand* the value of the instruction? Or wouldn't it just go to memorizing the forms and ritual? Ritual is a damned inefficient transmission device, and it generates its own problems. —I think we'd better start working this out in numbers and sets, and get some solid data, before we get too far into speculations. I'm not sure your Alpha can win out over the Beta in any sense. You're likely to lose virtually all his input. And you're likely to end up with a matrilinear culture in that instance—and a very small directorate if it's by kinships. The question is whether kinships are instinctive or cultural . . . I'm cheating on that, because I've read the Bureau reports on Gehenna. But they're not going to resolve it, because there were CITs in the Gehenna colony.''

She had lunch with Maddy; and heard the latest in the Amy-'Stasi feud. Which made her mad. ''I could kill Stef Dietrich,'' Maddy said.

''Don't bother,'' Ari said. ''I'll bet Yvgenia's already thought of that.''

Mostly she thought about the colony-problem, around the edges of the Amy-'Stasi thing. And thought: *Damn, the minute anything goes CIT, everybody's crazy, aren't they?*

The office was shut when she got back. She waited at the door and waited, and finally Justin showed up, out of breath.

''Sorry,'' he said, and unlocked. (Although she could have had Base One do it, through Security 10, but that was overkill, and made Security records, and meant papers. So she didn't.)

''Grant's got some stuff over at Sociology,'' he said. ''He's running a paper for me. I *do* get work done outside of this—''

He was in a good mood. It cheered her up. She took the cup of coffee he made for her and sat down and they started at it again. ''Let's assume,'' he said, ''that whether or not kinships are instinctual, your socialized azi are likely to replicate the parent culture.''

''Makes sense,'' she said.

''Likely quite thoroughly. Because they'll place abstract value on it, as the source of the orders.''

She had never noticed the way he bit at his lip when he was thinking. It was a boyish kind of thing, when mostly he looked so mature. And he smelled good. A lot like Ollie. A *lot* like Ollie.

And she couldn't help thinking about it.

He and Grant were lovers. She knew that from gossip in the House. She couldn't imagine it.

Except at night, when she was lying in the dark looking at

the ceiling and wondering what made them that way and whether—

—whether he *had* any feelings about her, and whether it was all just worry about Security that made him want Grant there all the time. Like he needed protection.

She liked being close to him. She always had.

She knew what was the matter finally. She felt the flux strong enough to turn everything upside down, and felt a lump in her throat and outright missed his next question.

"I—I'm sorry."

"The second-generation run. You're assuming matrilineal."

She nodded. He made a note. Tapped the paper. She got up to see, leaning by the arm of his chair. "You should have had an instructional tape in the lot to cover family units. Do you want to input one?"

"I—".

He looked over his shoulder at her. "Ari?"

"I'm sorry. I just lost things a minute."

He frowned. "Something wrong?"

"I—a couple of friends of mine are having a fight. That's all. I guess I'm a little gone-out." She looked at the printout. And felt sweat on her temples. "Justin, —did you ever—did you ever have trouble with being smart?"

"I guess I did." A frown came between his brows and he turned the chair and leaned his arm on the desk, looking up at her. "I didn't think of it like that, but I guess that was one of the reasons."

"Did you—" O God, this was scary. It could go wrong. But she was in it now. She leaned up against the chair, against him. "Did you ever have trouble with being older than everybody?" She took a breath and slid her hand onto his shoulder and sat down on the chair arm.

But he got up, fast, so fast she had to stand up to save herself from falling.

"I think you'd better talk this over with your uncle," he said.

Nervous. Real nervous. Probably, she thought, uncle Denys *had* said something to him. That made her mad. "Denys doesn't have a thing to say about what I do," she said, and came up against him and held on to his arm. "Justin, —there's nobody my own age I'm interested in. There *isn't* anybody. It doesn't hurt, I mean, I sleep-over with anybody I want. All the time."

"That's fine." He disengaged his arm and turned and picked up some papers off his desk. His hands were shaking. "Go back to them. I engaged to teach you, not—whatever."

She had trouble getting her breath. That was a *hell* of a reaction. It was scary, that a man reacted that way to her. He just gathered up his stuff, went to the door.

As the door opened and Grant stood there taking in what he saw, with small moves of his eyes.

"I'm going home," Justin said. "Closing up early today. How did the run go?"

"Fine," Grant said, and came in and laid it down, ignoring her presence, ignoring everything that had gone on.

"The *hell*," Ari said, and to Justin: "I want to talk to you."

"Not today."

"What are you doing? Throwing me out?"

"I'm not throwing you out. I'm going home. Let's give us both a little chance to cool off, all right? I'll see you in the morning."

Her face was burning. *She* was shaking. "I don't know what my uncle told you, but *I* can find something to tell him, you just *walk* out on me. Get out of here, Grant! Justin and I are talking!"

Grant went to the door, grabbed Justin's arm and shoved him out. "Get out of here," Grant said to him. And when Justin protested: *"Out!"* Grant said to him. "Go home. Now."

They had the door blocked. She was scared of a sudden— more scared when Grant argued Justin out the door and closed her in the office.

In a moment Grant came back. Alone. And closed the door again.

"I can call Security," she said. "You lay a hand on me and I'll swear Justin did it. You watch me!"

"No," Grant said, and held up a hand. "No, young sera. I'm not threatening you. Certainly I won't. I ask you, please, tell me what happened."

"I thought he told *you* everything."

"What did happen?"

She drew a shaken breath and leaned back against the chair. "I said I was bored with boys. I said I wanted to see if a man was any different. Maybe he hit me. Maybe he grabbed me. Who knows? Tell him go to hell."

"Did he do those things?"

"He's screwed everything up. I need him to teach me, and all I did was ask him to go to bed with me, I don't think that was an insult!" Damn, she hurt inside. Her eyes blurred. "You tell him he'd *better* teach me. You tell him he'd *better*. I need him, damn him."

Grant went azi then, and she remembered he *was* azi, which it was easy to forget with him; and she was in the wrong, yelling at him and not at Justin; she had a license that said responsibility, and she wanted to hit him.

"Young sera," he said, "I'll tell him. Please don't take offense. I'm sure there won't be any problem."

"'There won't be any problem.' Hell!" She thought of working with him, day after day, and shook her head and lost her composure. "Dammit!" As the tears flooded her eyes. She pushed away from the chair and went for the door, but Grant stopped her, blocking her path. "Get out of my way!"

"Young sera," Grant said. "Please. *Don't* go to Security."

"I never asked for this. All I asked was a polite question!"

"*I'll* do whatever you want, young sera. Any time you want. I have no objection. Here, if you want. Or at your apartment. All you have to do is ask me."

Grant was tall, very tall. Very quiet and very gentle, as he reached out and took her hand. And there was very little space between her and the desk. She backed into it, her heart going like a hammer.

"Is that what you want, young sera?"

"No," she said, finding a breath.

And did, dammit, but he was too adult, too strange, too cold.

"Sera is not a child. Sera has power enough to have whatever she wants, by whatever means. Sera had better learn to control *what* she wants before she gets more than she bargained for. Dammit, you've cost him his father, his freedom, and his work. What else will you take?"

"Let me go!"

He did then. And bowed his head once politely, and went and opened the door.

She found herself shaking.

"Any time, young sera. I'm always available."

"Don't you take that tone with me."

"Whatever sera wishes. Please come tomorrow. I promise you—no one will bring the matter up if you don't. Ever."

"The hell!"

She got out the door, down the hall. Her chest hurt. Everything did.

Like the part of her that was herself and not Ari senior—had just fallen apart.

I fell in love about as often as any normal human being. I gave everything I had to give. And I got back resentment. Genuine hatred.

. . . isolation from my own kind. . . .

She caught her breath, reached the lift, got in and pushed the button.

Not crying. No. She wiped the underside of her lashes with a careful finger, trying not to smear her makeup, and was composed when she walked out in the hall downstairs.

She knew what the first Ari would tell her. She had read it over and over. *So, well, elder Ari, you were right. I'm a fool once. Not twice. What now?*

--------- V ---------

Grant walked into the cubbyhole of the second floor restroom and found Justin at the sink washing his face. Water beaded on white skin in the flickering light second floor had been complaining about for a week. "She's gone home," Grant said, and Justin pulled a towel from the stack and blotted his face with it.

"What did she say?" Justin asked. "What did *you* say?"

"I propositioned her," Grant said. "I believe that's the word."

"My *God*, Grant—"

Grant turned on the calm, quiet as he could manage, given the state of his stomach. "Young sera needed something else to think about," he said. "She declined. I wasn't sure that she would. I was, needless to say, relieved. Very fast work for young sera. I was so sure you were safe for an hour."

Justin threw the towel into the laundry-bin and folded his arms tight about his ribs. "Don't joke. It's not funny."

"Are you all right?"

"I'm having flashes. Oh, God, Grant, I— *Dammit!*"

He spun about and hit the wall with his hand and leaned there, stiff, hard-breathing, in that don't-touch-me attitude that absolutely meant it.

But Grant had ignored that before. He came and pried him away and folded him in his arms, just held on to him until Justin got a breath and a second one.

"I—lost—my sense of where I was," Justin said finally, between small efforts after air. "God, I just—went away. I couldn't navigate. She's—God knows. God knows what I said. It just blew up—she—"

"—she *needed* a firm no. It's doubtless a new thing for her. Calm down. Now is now."

"A damn *kid*! I—had—no finesse about it, absolutely none, I just—"

"You were expressing a polite and civilized no when I walked in. That young sera doesn't recognize the word isn't your fault. Young sera may call Security and young sera may lodge charges, I have absolutely no idea. But if she does, you have a witness, and I have no trouble about going under probe. Young sera needs favors from *you*. I politely suggested she consider the trouble she's caused and show up tomorrow with a civilized attitude—at which time *I'm* going to be there; at all times hereafter, I assure you." He pushed Justin back at arm's length. "She's sixteen. Personalities aside, she's quite the other end of the proposition—a year younger than you were. A great deal more experienced, by all accounts, but not—not in adult behavior. Am I right? She has no idea what she's dealing with. No more than you did."

Justin blinked. Rapid thought: Grant knew the look. "Go back to the office."

"Where are *you* going?"

"To make a phone call."

"Denys?"

Justin shook his head.

"Good God," Grant said. And felt as if the floor had sunk. "You're not serious."

"I'm going alone, if she'll see me. Which is far from likely at this point."

"No. Listen. Don't do this. If you're having flashback, for God's *sake* don't do this."

"I'm going to straighten it out. Once for all. I'm going to tell her what happened—"

"No!" Grant seized his arm and held on, hard. "Administration will have your head on a plate—*listen to me*. Even if she took your side she hasn't got the authority to protect you. She hasn't got anything, not really. *Not* inside *these* walls."

"What in hell do we do? What do we do when they take us in and they trump up a rape charge—what happens when we end up in a ward over in hospital under Reseune law? All they need is a statement from her. . . ."

"And you're going to go over to her apartment and talk to her. No."

"Not her apartment. I don't think I can handle that. But somewhere."

---

vi

Justin took a sip of Scotch as the waiter at *Changes* brought the three to their table—Ari in an ice-green blouse with metallic gray beading, Florian and Catlin in evening black.

Evening at *Changes* was a dress occasion. He and Grant had taken pains, both of them in their best. Dress shirts and jackets.

"Thank you," Ari said, when the waiter pulled the chair back. "Vodka-and-orange for the three of us, please."

"Yes, sera," the waiter murmured. "Will you want menus?"

"Give us a while," Justin said. "If you will, Ari."

"That's fine." She settled in her chair and folded her hands on the table.

"Thank you for coming," Justin said as soon as the waiter

left. "I apologize for this afternoon. For Grant and myself. It was me. Not you. Absolutely not you."

Ari shifted back in her seat, her lips pressed to a thin line. And said not a thing.

"Has your uncle Denys called you?"

"Have you called him?"

"No. I don't think he wants to hear what happened. I don't know to what extent he can come back on you—"

"Only because he's the Administrator," Ari said. "There's nothing he'll do to me."

"I wasn't sure." He saw the waiter coming back with the drinks, and waited during the serving.

Ari sipped hers and sighed. "Whose credit is this on?"

"Mine," Justin said. "Don't hesitate." As the waiter discreetly took himself off. It was a private corner, quite private: a sizable addition to the bill assured it. "I want to assure you first of all—I'm perfectly willing to go on working with you. I want to tell you—what you're doing—is full of problems. But it's not empty exercise. You've got some ideas that are—fairly undeveloped right now. I still don't know to what extent you've modeled this on reality—or borrowed from your predecessor. If it's considerable borrowing—it would be remarkable enough that someone so young is working integrations at all. If any portion of it is original—I have to be impressed; because there is a center of this that, if I were going faster, and not taking the time to demonstrate your problems—I would simply throw into research, because I think it's a helpful model."

"You can do that, if you like." Not spitefully. Reasonably. Quietly.

"Perhaps I'll do both. With your permission. Because I'm very afraid it's classified."

"Grant can do it."

"Grant could do it. With your permission. And Yanni's. We work for him."

"Because you refused to be transferred. I can still do that."

He had not expected that. He took a drink of Scotch. And was aware of Grant beside him, subject to whatever mistakes he made. "I wouldn't think," he said, "that you'd be thinking about that after the scene this afternoon."

Redirect. Shift directions.

She sipped at the vodka-and-orange. Sixteen, and fragile—in physiology. In emotions that the alcohol could flatten or exacerbate. Flux-thinking at its finest, Grant was wont to say. Puberty, hormones run wild, and ethyl alcohol.

Oh, God, kid, back off it: it did me no favors.

Power. Political power that was still running in shockwaves across Union; threats of assassination. And all the stress that went with it.

"I'm glad you want to talk about it," Ari said, on a slight sigh following the vodka. "Because I need you. I study my predecessor's notes—on kat. I *know* things. I've talked to Denys about putting the stuff into print. Organizing everything. I said I wanted you to do it and he didn't want that. I said the hell with that."

"Ari, *don't* swear."

"Sorry. But that was what I said. I could have sat down and said I wouldn't budge. But it's real good, politically, if the Bureau gets it about now. Sort of proof that I'm real. So you'll know pretty soon what's mine and what's Ari's. I'll tell you something else you can guess: not *all* the notes are going out. Some aren't finished. And some are classified." She took another sip. The glass hardly diminished. "I've thought about this. I've thought real hard. And I've got a problem, because you're the one who's working on deep-sets, you're the one who could teach me the actual things I need— Giraud's very bright; but Giraud's not down the same track. Not at all. I don't *want* to do the things he does. Denys is bright. He's very near-term and real-time. Do you want to know the truth? Giraud isn't really a Special. *Somebody* had to have it, to get some of the protections Reseune needed right then. The one who is, is Denys; but Denys wouldn't have it: it would make him too public. So he arranged it to get Giraud the Status."

He stared at her, wondering if it *was* true, if it *could* be true.

"It's in Ari's notes," Ari said. "Now you know something on Denys. But I wouldn't tell him you know. He'd be upset with me for telling you. But it's why you should be careful. I've learned from uncle Denys for years. I still do. But the work I really want is macro-sets and value-sets. You're the only one who's working on the things Ari *wanted* me to do. I listen to her."

"Listen to her—"

"Her notes. She had a lot to tell me. A lot of advice. Sometimes I don't listen and I'm generally sorry for it. Like this afternoon."

"Am I—in the notes?"

"Some things about you are. That she talked Jordan into doing a PR. That she and Jordan did a lot of talking about the Bok clone problem and they talked about the psych of a PR with the parent at hand—and one like the Bok clone, without. It's interesting stuff. I'll let you read it if you want."

"I'd be interested."

"Stuff on Grant, too. I can give you that. They're going to hold that out of the Bureau notes, because they don't want it in there, about you. Because your father doesn't want it, uncle Denys says."

He took a mouthful of Scotch, off his balance, knowing she had put him there, every step of the way.

Not a child. *Wake up, fool. Remember who you're dealing with. Eighteen years asleep. Wake up.*

"You didn't walk in here unarmed," he said. "In either sense, I'll imagine."

She ignored that remark, except for a little eye contact, deep and direct. She said: "Why don't you like me, Justin? You have trouble with women?"

A second time off his balance. Badly. And then a little use out of the anger, a little steadiness, even before he felt Grant's touch on his knee. "Ari, I'm at a disadvantage in this discussion, because you *are* sixteen."

"Chronologically."

"Emotionally. And you shouldn't have the damn vodka."

That got a little flicker. "Keeps me quiet. Keeps me from being bored with fools. Drunk, I'm about as eetee as the rest of the world."

"You're wrong about that."

"You're not my mother."

"You want to talk about that?" *Off* the other topic. "I don't think you do. Shows what the stuff's doing to you."

She shook her head. "No. Hit me on that if you like. I threw that at you. So you're being nice. Let's go back to the other thing. I want just one straight answer—since you're being nice. Is it women, is it because I'm smarter than you, or is it because you can't stand my company?''

"You want a fight, don't you? I didn't come here for this."

Another shake of the head. "I'm sixteen, remember. Ari said adolescence was hell. She *said* relations with CITs always lose you a friend. Because people don't like you up that close. Ever. She said I'd never understand CITs. Myself—for my own education—once—I'd like to have somebody explain it to me—why you don't like me."

The smell of orange juice. Of a musky perfume.

This is all there is, sweet. This is as good as it gets.

Oh, God, Ari.

He caught his breath. Felt his own panic, felt the numbing grip on his wrist.

"Sera," Grant said.

"No," he said quietly. "No." Knowing more about the woman eighteen years ago than he had learned in that night or all the years that followed.

And reacting, the way she had primed him to react, the way she had fixed him on her from that time on—

"Your predecessor," he said, carefully, civilized, "had a fondness for adolescent boys. Which I was, then. She blackmailed me. And my father. She threatened Grant, to start running test programs on him—on an Alpha brought up as a CIT. Mostly, I think—to get her hands on me, though I didn't understand that then. Nothing—absolutely nothing—of your fault. *I* know that. Say that I made one mistake, when I thought I could handle a situation when I was about your age. Say that *I* have a reluctance when I'm approached by a girl younger than I was, never mind you have her face, her voice, and you wear her perfume. It's nothing to do with you. It's everything to do with what she did. I'd rather not give you the details, but I don't have to. She made a tape. It may be in your apartment for all I know. Or your uncle can give it to you. When you see it, you'll have every key you need to take me apart. But that's all right. Other people have. *Nothing* to do with you."

Ari sat there for a long, long time, elbows on the table. "Why did she do that?" she asked finally.

"You'd know that. Much more than I would. Maybe because she was dying. She was in rejuv failure, Ari. She had cancer; and she was a hundred twenty years old. Which was no favorable prognosis.''

She had not known that. For a PR it was a dangerous kind of knowledge—the time limits in the geneset.

''There were exterior factors,'' he said. ''Cyteen was more native when she was young. She'd gotten a breath of native air at some time in her life. That was what would have killed her.''

She caught her lip between her teeth. No hostility now. No defense. ''Thank you,'' she said, ''for telling me.''

''Finish your drink,'' he said. ''I'll buy you another one.''

''I knew—when she died. Not about the cancer.''

''Then your notes don't tell you everything. I will. Ask me again if I'm willing to take a transfer.''

''Are you?''

''Ask Grant.''

''Whatever Justin says,'' Grant said.

vii

''We've got a contact,'' Wagner said, on the walk over to State from the Library, ''in Planys maintenance. Money, not conscience.''

''I don't want to hear that,'' Corain said. ''I don't want you to have heard it. Let's keep this clean.''

''I didn't hear it and you didn't,'' Wagner agreed. A stocky woman with almond eyes and black ringleted hair, Assistant Chief of Legal Affairs in the Bureau of Citizens, complete with briefcase and conservative suit. A little walk over from Library, where both of them happened to meet—by arrangement. ''Say our man's working the labs area. Say he talks with Warrick. Shows him pictures of the kids—you know. So Warrick opens up.''

''We're saying what happened.''

''We're saying what happened. I don't think you want to know the whole string of contacts. . . .''

''I don't. I want to know, dammit, is Warrick approachable?''

"He's been under stringent security for over a year. He has a son still back in Reseune. This is the pressure point."

"I remember the son. What's he like?"

"Nothing on him. A non-person as far as anything we've got, just an active PR CIT-number. Defense has a lot more on him. Doppelganger for papa, that's a given. But apparently either Warrick senior or junior has pressured Reseune enough to get a travel pass for the son. He's thirty-five years old. Reseune national. Reseune had so much security around him when he'd come into Planys you'd have thought he was the Chairman. There's an azi, too. An Alpha—you remember the Abolitionist massacre over by Big Blue?"

"The Winfield case. I remember. Tied into Emory's murder. That was one of the points of contention—between Warrick and Emory."

"He's a foster son as far as Warrick is concerned. They don't let him out of Reseune. We can't get any data at all on him, except he is alive, he is living with the son, Warrick still regards him as part of the family. I can give you the whole dossier."

"Not to me! That stays at lower levels."

"Understood then."

"But you can get to Warrick."

"I think he's reached a state of maximum frustration with his situation. It's been, what, eighteen years? His projects are Defense; but Reseune keeps a very tight wall between him and them, absolutely no leak-through. The air-systems worker— we've had him for—eighteen months, something like. What you have to understand, ser, Reseune's security is very, very tight. But also, it's no ordinary detainee they're dealing with. A psych operator. A clinician. Difficult matter, I should imagine, to find any guard immune to him. The question is whether we go now or wait-see. That's what Gruen wants me to ask you."

Corain gnawed at his lip. Two months from the end of the Defense election, with a bomb about to blow in that one—

With Jacques likely to win the Defense seat away from Khalid and very likely to appoint Gorodin as Secretary.

But Jacques was weakening. Jacques was feeling heat from the hawks within Defense—and there were persistent rumors about Gorodin's health—and countercharges that Khalid, who had been linked to previous such rumors—was once more the source of them.

But Khalid *could* win: the Centrist party had as lief be shut of Khalid's brand of conservatism—but it could not discount the possibility in any planning. The Jacques as Councillor/ Gorodin as Secretary compromise Corain had hammered out with Nye, Lynch, and the Expansionists—was the situation Corain had rather have, most of all, if rumors were true and Gorodin's health was failing, because Gorodin was the *Expansionists'* part of the bargain.

Wait—and hope that a new hand at the helm of the military would enable them to work *with* Defense to get to Warrick in Planys; or go in on their own and trust to their own resources. And risk major scandal. That was the problem.

If Khalid won again—Khalid would remember that his own party had collaborated in the challenge to his seat. Then he would owe no favors.

Then he could become a very dangerous man indeed.

"I think we'd better pursue the contact now," Corain said. "Just for God's sake be careful. I don't want any trails to the Bureau, hear?"

viii

"I didn't know I was going to do that," Justin said, and tossed a bit of bread to the koi. The gold one flashed to the surface and got it this time, while the white lurked under a lotus pad. "I had no idea. It just—she was going to find out about the tape, wasn't she? Someday. Better now—while she's naive enough to be shocked. God help us—if it goes the other way."

"I feel much safer," Grant said, "when you decide these things."

"*I* don't, dammit, I had no right to do that without warning—but I was in a corner, it was the moment—it was the only moment to make the other situation right. . . ."

"Because of the tape?"

"You do understand it, then."

"I understand this is the most aggressive personality I've ever met. Not even Winfield and his people—impressed me to that extent. I'll tell you the truth: I've been afraid before. Winfield, for instance. Or the Security force that pulled me out of there—I thought that they might kill me, because those might be their orders. I've tried to analyze the flavor of this, and the flux was so extreme in me at that moment in the office doorway—I can't pin it down. I only know there was something so—violent in this girl—that it was very hard for me to respond without flux.'' Grant's voice was clinical, cool, soft and precise as it was when he was reasoning. ''But then—that perception may have to do with my own adrenaline level—and the fact the girl *is* a Supervisor. Perhaps I misread the level of what I was receiving.''

''No. You're quite right. I've tried to build a profile on her . . . quietly. Same thing her predecessor did to me. The choices she makes in her model, the things she'd do if she were in the Gehenna scenario—she's aggressive as hell, and self-protective. I've charted the behavior phases—menstrual cycles, hormone shifts—best I can guess, she's hormone-fluxed as hell right now; I *always* watch the charts with her. But that's never all of it.'' He broke off another bit of bread and tossed it, right where the spotted koi could get it. *''Never* all of it with her predecessor. That mind is brilliant. When it fluxes, the analog functions go wildly speculative—and the down-side of the flux integrates like hell. I've watched it. More, she *originated* the whole flux-matrix theory; you think she doesn't understand her own cycles? *And* use them? But *young* Ari made me understand something I should have seen—we deal with other people with such precision, and ourselves with such damnable lack of it—Ari is having difficulties with ego-definitions. A PR does, I should know; and it can only get worse for her. That's why I asked for the transfer.''

''Fix her on us?''

He drew several long breaths. Blinked rapidly to clear away the elder Ari's face, the remembrance of her hands on him.

''She's vulnerable now,'' he said on a ragged breath. ''She's looking for some sign of the human race—on whatever plane she lives on. That's the sense I got—that maybe she was as open then as I was—then. So I grabbed the moment's window. That's what I thought. That she's so damn self-protective—there might only be that chance—then—in that two seconds.'' He shuddered, a little, involuntary twitch at the nape of the neck. ''God, I hate real-time work.''

''Just because you hated it,'' Grant said, ''doesn't mean you weren't good at it. I'll tell you what this azi suspects—that she would *regret* harm to one of us. I don't think that's true with a CIT. If she ever does take me up on my proposition— No,'' Grant said as he took a breath to object; Grant held up a finger. ''One: I don't think she will. Two: if she does—trust me to handle it. Trust me. All right?''

''It's not all right.''

''No, but you'll stay back: do the puzzling thing, and trust me to do the same. I think you're quite right. The puzzling thing engages the intellect—and I had far rather deal with her on a rational basis, I assure you. If you can commit us to your judgment in the one thing—trust me for mine and don't make me worry. I wouldn't have been in half the flux I was in, except I wasn't sure you weren't going to come back into the office and blow everything to hell, right there. I can't think and watch my flank when it's you involved. All right? Promise me that.''

''Dammit, I can't let a spoiled kid—''

''Yes. You can. Because I'm capable of taking care of myself. And in some things I'm better than you. Not many. But in this, I am. Allow me my little superiority. You can have all the rest.''

He gazed a long time at Grant, at a face which had—with the years—acquired tensions azi generally lacked. He had done that to him. Life among CITs had.

''Deal?'' Grant asked him. ''Turn about: trust *my* judgment. I trust yours about the transfer. So we can both be perturbed about something. How much do you trust me?''

''It's not trusting *you* that's at issue.''

''Yes, it is. Yes. It is. Azi to Supervisor . . . are you hearing me?''

He nodded finally. Because whatever Ari could do—*he* could hurt Grant.

He lied, of course. Maybe Grant knew he did.

"There's a tape," Ari had said to Denys, in his office, and told him *which* tape.

"How did you find out about it?" he had asked.

"My Base."

"Nothing to do with dinner at *Changes* last night."

"No," she said without a flicker, "we discussed cultural librations."

Denys hated humor when he was serious. He always had. "All right," he said, frowning. "I certainly won't withhold it."

So he sent Seely for it. And said: *"Don't* use kat when you see this, don't expose Florian and Catlin to it, for God's sake *don't* put it where anyone can find it."

She had thought of asking him what was in it. But things were tense enough. So she talked about other things—about her work, about the project, about Justin—without mentioning the disagreement.

She drank a cup and a half of coffee and exchanged pleasant gossip; and unpleasant: about the elections; about the situation in Novgorod; about Giraud's office—and Corain—until Seely brought the tape back.

So she walked home with it, with Catlin, because she was anxious all the time she had it in her carry-bag; she was anxious when she arrived home and contemplated putting it in the player.

Her insecurity with the situation wanted Florian and Catlin to be beside her when she played it—

But that, she thought, was irresponsible. Emotional situations were *her* department, not theirs, no matter that sera was anxious about it, no matter that sera wanted, like a baby, to have someone with her.

I wouldn't have advised this, Denys had said—distressed, she picked that up. But not entirely surprised. *But I know you well enough to know there's no stopping you once you start asking a question. I won't comment on it. But if you have questions after you've seen it—you can send them to my Base if you find them too personal. And I'll respond the same way. If you want it.*

Meaning Denys wasn't putting any color on the situation.

So she closed the door on the library and locked it; and put the tape into the player—*not* taking a pill. She was no fool, to deep-study any tape blind and unpreviewed, and without running a check for subliminals.

She sat down and clenched her hands as it started—fascinated first-off by the sight of a familiar place, familiar faces—Florian and Catlin when they would have been a hundred twenty at least; and Justin—the boy was clearly Justin, even at the disadvantage of angle—he would be seventeen; and Ari herself—elegant, self-assured: she had seen newsclips of Ari this old, but none when Ari was not simply answering questions.

She listened—caught the nervousness in Justin's voice, the finesse of control in Ari's. Strange to *know* that voice so well, and to feel inside what it was doing—and to understand what kat would do to that experience, for someone skilled at tape-learning: she felt a little prickle down her back, a sense of hazard and involvement—*conditioned response*, a dim, analytical part of her thoughts said: the habits of this room, the physiological response of the endocrine system to the habit of taking kat here, and the lifelong habit of responding to tape— Azi must do this, she thought. And: The emotional context is kicking it off. Thank *God* I didn't trank down for this.

As muscles felt the sympathetic stimulus of nerves that *knew* what it felt like to walk and sit, and speak, and a brain that understood in all that context that Ari was On, and that her pulse was up, and that the target of her intentions was a Justin very young, very vulnerable, picking up the signals Ari was sending and reacting with extreme nervousness—

Back off, she told herself, trying to distance herself from the aggression Ari was radiating. *Disinvolve.*

The switch was beside her. She only had to reach to it and push it to cut it off. But the sexual feeling was too strong, toward an object otherwise out of reach—toward a Justin not quite real, not the man she knew, but Justin all the same.

She saw the glass fall—realized then what Ari had done to him, and that he was in terrible danger. She was *afraid* for him; but the muscles she felt move in response to that falling glass were Ari's, the impulse she felt through the heat of sex

was concern for the orange juice spill on the damned uphol-
stery— *Her* couch—

Oh, God, she should shut this off. Now.

But she kept watching.

———————————— X ————————————

It was a simple computer-delivered *See me: my office, 0900.*
—Denys Nye. ——that brought him to the administrative wing,
and to the door that he dreaded.

So she had the tape, Justin thought; so Denys knew about
the dinner at *Changes.*

He had *not* expected Giraud with Denys. He froze in the
doorway, with Seely at his back, then walked in and sat down.

"Let's dispense with what we both know," Denys said,
"and not bicker about details. What in hell do you think you're
doing?"

"I thought about coming to you," he said, "but she was
embarrassed as well as mad. I figured—if I did—come to
you—she might blow. I thought you wanted to avoid that."

"So you took a wide action. On your own judgment."

"Yes, ser." Denys was being reasonable—too reasonable,
with Giraud sitting there staring at him with hostility in every
line of his face. "And knowing you'd call me."

"She has the tape," Denys said. "That surprised me,
Justin, that truly surprised me."

Giraud's not the Special. Denys is. . . .

"I'm flattered, ser. I don't expect to surprise you. But that
wasn't why I did it. I wish you'd *let* me explain. Ari—"

"I don't need your explanation. Neither of us does."

"It's a simple adolescent infatuation—"

"She's been sexually active since she was thirteen. At least.
And this fascination is thoroughly in program. We're not
worried about that. Her predecessor had a pattern of such
things. That you're young, male, and working at close quarters
with her— No question."

"I haven't encouraged it!"

"Of course not. But you've tried to manipulate her by that
means."

"That's not so. No."

"Sins of the heart, if not the intellect. You took her on, you've taught her, you've tried to steer her—admit it."

"*Away* from that kind of thing—"

Denys leaned forward on folded arms.

"That," Giraud said, "is intervention, in itself."

"Not to harm her," Justin said, "or me." Giraud had only to speak and reactions started running through him, kat-dream, deep as bone. He could not help that flutter of nerves, could not forget the whip-crack that voice could become . . . in his nightmares. He looked at Denys, feeling a tremor in his muscles. "I tried to keep it all low-key, non-flux."

"Until yesterday," Denys said, "when you decided to handle a situation yourself. When you exacerbated a situation—and decided to handle it . . . by handing her a major key. That is an intervention, you're an operator, you knew exactly what you were doing, and I want you to lay that out for me in plain words—consciously and subconsciously."

"Why should I?" His heart was slamming against his ribs. "Duplication of effort, isn't it? Why don't we just go over to Security and save us all time and trouble?"

"You're asking for a probe."

"No. I'm not. But that's never stopped you."

"Let's have a little calm, son."

Jordan. Oh, God.

He means me to think about that.

"Answer the question," Giraud said.

"I did it to save my neck. Because she's a damned dangerous enemy. Because she could as well blow up in your direction. What in hell *else* was charged enough to knock her back and make her reassess?"

"That's a tolerably acceptable answer," Denys said. Confusing him. He waited for the redirect and the flank attack. "The question is—what do you think you've induced? Where is your intervention going? What's her state of mind right now?"

"I hope to God," he said, his voice out of control, "I hope to God—it's going to make her careful."

"And sympathetic?"

"*Careful* would do."

"You're courting her, aren't you?"

"God, no!"

"Yes, you are. Not sexually, though I imagine you'll pay that if you have to—if you can gain enough stability to handle the encounter. But you'd much rather avoid it. 'Hell hath no fury'? Something like that in your considerations? Politics may make strange bedfellows, but bedfellows make deadly politics."

"I just want to survive here."

"In her administration. Yes. Of course you do. Protect yourself—protect Grant. The consequences of enmity with us—have only a few years to run, is that what you're thinking? A couple of old men—weighed against the lifespan of a sixteen-year-old whose power is—possibly adequate to work for you if you could maneuver your way into her considerations. A very dangerous course. A *very* dangerous course, even for a man willing to sell—what you were willing to sell her predecessor—"

Temper. Temper is . . . only what he wants here.

"—but then, your choices *are* limited."

"It doesn't take a probe," Giraud said, his deep voice quite gentle, "to know what your interests are. —And the latest business on my desk—I think you'll find quite—amusing in one sense. Alarming, in the other. The Paxers—you know, the people who blow up Novgorod subways, have decided to invoke your father's name—"

"He hasn't a thing to do with it!"

"Of course not. Of course not. But the Novgorod police did find some interesting documents—naming your father as a political martyr in their cause, stating that *the new monstrosity in Reseune* is a creation of the military—that assassinating Ari and creating maximum chaos would lead to a Paxer government—"

"That's crazy!"

"Of course it is. Of course your father knows nothing about it."

"He doesn't! My God, —"

"I said—of course. Don't let it upset you. This has been going on for years. Oh, not the Paxers. They're comparatively new. All these organizations are interlocked. That's what makes them so difficult to track. That and the fact that the people that do the bombing are z-cases. Druggers and just general fools whose devotion to the cause involves letting themselves be partial-wiped by amateur operators. *That* kind of fools. I thought I should tell you—there are people in this world who don't care anything for their own lives, let alone a sixteen-year-old focus of their hostilities. And they're using your father's name in their literature. I'm sorry. I suppose it *doesn't* amuse you."

"No, ser." He was close to shivering. Giraud did that to him. Without drugs. Because in not very long, there would be, he knew that; and not all the skill in the world could prevent it. "I'm not amused. I know Jordan wouldn't be, if he heard about it, which he hasn't, unless you've told him."

"We've mentioned it to him. He asked us to say he's well. Looking forward, I imagine, to a change of regime in Defense. —As we all are. Certainly. I just wanted to let you know the current state of things, since there are ramifications to the case that you might want to be aware of. That your father murdered Ari—is not quite old news. It's entered into threats against her successor's life. And Ari will be aware of these things. We have to make her aware—for her own protection. Perhaps you and she can work it out in a civilized way. I hope so."

What is he doing? What is he trying to do?

What does he want from me?

Is he threatening Jordan?

"How does your father feel about Ari? Do you have any idea?"

"No, ser. I don't know. Not hostility. I don't think he would feel that."

"Perhaps you can *find* out. If this election goes right."

"If it does, ser. Maybe I can make a difference—in *how* he feels."

"That's what we hope," Giraud said.

"I wouldn't, however," Denys said, "bring the matter up with Ari."

"No, ser."

"You're a valuable piece in this," Giraud said. "I'm

sorry—you probably have very strong feelings about me. I'm used to them, of course, but I regret them all the same. I'm not your enemy; and you probably won't believe that. I don't even ask for comment—not taxing your politeness. This time I'm on your side, to the extent I wish you a very long life. And the committee is agreed: thirty-five is a little young for rejuv—but then, it seems to have no adverse effects—"

"Thank you, no."

"It's not up for discussion. You have an appointment in hospital. You and Grant both."

"No!"

"The usual offer. Report on schedule or Security will see you do."

"There's no damn sense in my going on rejuv—it's my decision, dammit!"

"That's the committee's decision. It's final. Certainly nothing you ought to be anxious about. Medical studies don't show any diminution of lifespan for early users—"

"In the study they've got. There's no damn sense in this. Ari's on the shots, damn well sure she is—"

"Absolutely."

"Then why in hell are you doing this?"

"Because you have value. And we care about you. You can go on over there. Or you can go the hard way and distress Grant—which I'd rather not."

He drew a careful breath. "Do you mind—if I go tell Grant myself? Half an hour. That's all."

"Perfectly reasonable. Go right ahead. Half an hour, forty-five minutes. They'll be expecting you."

―――――――――― **xi** ――――――――――

Another damned wait. Justin lay full-length on the table and stared at the ceiling, trying to put his mind in null, observing the pattern in the ceiling tiles, working out the repetitions.

Full body scan and hematology work-up, tracer doses shot into his bloodstream, more blood drawn. Dental checks. Respiration. Cardiac stress . . . *you have a little hypertension*, Wojkowski had said, and he had retorted: *God, I wonder why.*

Which Wojkowski did not think was amusing.

More things shot into his veins, more scans, more probings at private places and more sitting about—lying down for long periods, while they tried to get him calm enough to get accurate readings.

I'm trying, he had said, the last time they had checked on him. *I'm honestly trying. Do you think I like waiting around freezing to death?*

Complaining got him a robe. That was all. They finally put him on biofeedback until he could get the heart rate down, and got the tests they wanted.

Why? had been Grant's first and only question—a worried frown, a shrug, and a: *Well, at least we do get it, don't we?*

Which, for an azi, could be a question. He had never thought that it was, never thought that Reseune could go so far as to deny him and Grant rejuv when it was time for them to have it or vengefully postpone it beyond the point when they should have it, to avoid diminished function.

Thinking of that, he could be calmer about it. But he had sent a call through to Base One: *Ari, this is Justin.*

Grant and I have been told to report to hospital. We've been told we're to go on rejuv, over our protests. I want you to know where we are and what's happened. . . .

Which got them nothing. Base One took the message. No one was reading it. They could try for admission to Ari's floor, but open confrontation with Administration was more than Ari could handle. *No one answering,* he had said to Grant.

It's only one treatment, Grant had said.

Meaning that one could still change one's mind. It took about three to eight weeks of treatments for the body to adjust—and become dependent.

Nothing permanent, yet.

"You're going to be coming here for your treatments," Wojkowski had said.

"For *what*?" he had said. "To have you watch me take a damned pill? Or what are you giving me?"

"Because this was not elective. You understand—going off the drug has severe consequences. Immune system collapse."

"I'm a certified paramedic," he had snapped back. "Clinical psych. I assure you I know the cautions. What I want to know, doctor, is what else they're putting into the doses.''

"Nothing," Wojkowski had said, unflappable. "You can read the order, if you like. And see the prescriptions . . . whatever you like. Neantol. It's a new combination drug: Novachem is the manufacturer, I'll give you all the literature on it. Hottest thing going, just out on the market. Avoids a lot of the side-effects.''

"Fine, I'm a test subject."

"It's safe. It's safer, in fact. Avoids the thin-skin problem, the excessive bleeding and bruising; the calcium depletion and the graying effect. You'll keep your hair color, you won't lose any major amount of muscle mass, or have brittle bones or premature fatigue. Sterility—unfortunately—is still a problem.''

"I can live with that.'' He felt calmer. Damn, he wanted to believe what Wojkowski was saying. "What are *its* side-effects?''

"Dry mouth and a solitary complaint of hyperactivity. Possibly some deleterious effect on the kidneys. Mostly remember to drink plenty of water. Especially if you've been drinking. You'll tend to dehydrate and you'll get a hell of a hangover. We *don't* know what the effects would be of switching off the regular drug and onto this. Or vice versa. We suspect there could be some serious problems about that. It's also expensive, over ten thou a dose and it's not going to get cheaper anytime soon. But especially in the case of a younger patient— definitely worth it.''

"Does Grant—get the same?''

"Yes. Absolutely.''

He felt better, overall, with that reassurance. He trusted Wojkowski's ethics most of the way. But it did not help get his pulse rate down.

Ten thousand a dose. Reseune was spending a lot on them, on a drug Reseune could afford—and he could not.

Not something you could find on the black market.

Substitutions contraindicated.

A dependency Reseune provided, that Reseune could withhold—with devastating effect; that nothing like—say, the Paxers or the Abolitionists—could possibly provide.

An invisible chain. Damn their insecurities. As if they

needed it. But it took something away, all the same: left him with a claustrophobic sense that hereafter—options were fewer; and a nagging dread that the drug might turn up with side-effects, no matter that lab rats thrived on it.

Damn, in one day, from a young man's self-concept and a trim, fit body he had taken pains to keep that way—to the surety of sterility, of some bodily changes; not as many as he had feared, if they were right; but still—a diminishing of functions. Preservation for—as long as the drug held. A list of cautions to live with.

A favor, in some regards, if it did what they claimed.

But a psychological jolt all the same—to take it at someone else's decision, because a damned committee decided—

What? To keep a string on him and Grant? In the case they tried to escape and join the Paxers and bomb subways and kill children?

God. They were all lunatics.

The door opened. The tech came in and asked him to undress again.

Tissue sample. Sperm sample. "What in hell for?" he snapped at the tech. "I'm a *PR*, for God's sake!"

The tech looked at his list. "It's here," the tech said. Azi. And doggedly following his instructions.

So the tech got both. And left him with a sore spot on his leg and one inside his mouth, where the tech had taken his tissue samples.

Likely his pulse rate was through the ceiling again. He tried to calm it down, figuring they would take it again before they let him out, and if they disliked the result they got, they could put him into hospital where he was subject to any damn thing *anyone* wanted to run, without Grant to witness it, where neither of them could look out for the other or lodge protests.

Damn it, get the pulse rate down.

Get out of here tonight. Get home. That's the important thing now.

The door opened. Wojkowski again.

"How are we doing?" she asked.

"We're madder than hell," he said with exaggerated pleasantness, and sat up on the table, smiled at Wojkowski, trying not to let the pulse run wild, doggedly thinking of flowers. Of river water. "I'm missing patches of skin and my dignity is, I'm sure, not a prime concern here. But that's all right."

"Mmmn," Wojkowski said, and set a hypogun down on the counter, looking at the record. "I'm going to give you a prescription I want you to take, and we'll check you over again when you come in for your second treatment. See if we can do something about that blood pressure."

"You want to know what you can do about the blood pressure?"

"Do yourself a favor. Take the prescription. Don't take kat more than twice a week—are you taking aspirin?"

"Occasionally."

"How regularly?"

"It's in the—"

"Please."

"Two, maybe four a week."

"That's all right. No more than that. If you get headaches, see me. If you have any light-headedness, see me immediately. If you get a racing pulse, same."

"Of course. —*Do you know what goes on in the House, doctor? —Or on this planet, for that matter?*"

"I'm aware of your situation. All the same, avoid stress."

"Thanks. Thanks so much, doctor."

Wojkowski walked over with the hypo. He shed the robe off one shoulder and she wiped the area down. The shot popped against his arm and hurt like hell.

He looked and saw a bloody mark.

"Damn, that's—"

"It's a gel implant. Lasts four weeks. Go home. Go straight to bed. Drink plenty of liquids. The first few implants may give you a little nausea, a little dizziness. If you break out in a rash or feel any tightening in the chest, call the hospital immediately. You can take aspirin for the arm. See you in August."

There was a message in the House system, waiting for him when he got to the pharmacy. *My office. Ari Emory.*

She did not use her Wing One office. She had said so. She had a minimal clerical staff there to handle her House system clerical work, and that was all.

But she was waiting there now. Her office. Ari senior's

office. He walked through the doors with Grant, faced a black desk he remembered, where Florian sat—with a young face, a grave concern as he got up and said: "Grant should wait here, ser. Sera wants to see you alone."

The coffee helped his nerves. He was grateful that Ari had made it for him, grateful for the chance to collect himself, in these surroundings, with Ari behind Ari senior's desk—not a particularly grandiose office, not even so much as Yanni's. The walls were all bookcases and most of the books in them were manuals. Neat. That was the jarring, surreal difference. Ari's office had always had a little clutter about it and the desk was far too clean.

The face behind it—disturbing in its similarities and disturbing in its touch of worry.

Past and future.

"I got your message," Ari said. "I went to Denys. That didn't do any good. We had a fight. The next thing I did was call Ivanov. He didn't do any good. The next thing I could do, I could call Family council. And past that I can file an appeal with the Science Bureau and the Council in Novgorod. Which is real dangerous—with all the stuff going on."

He weighed the danger that would be, and knew the answer, the same as he had known it when he was lying on the table.

"There could be worse," he said. His arm had begun to ache miserably, all the way to the bone, and he felt sick at his stomach, so that he felt his hands likely to shake. It was hard to think at all.

But the Family council would stand with Denys and Giraud, even yet, he thought; and that might be dangerous, psychologically, to Ari's ability to wield authority in future, if she lost the first round.

An appeal to the Bureau opened up the whole Warrick case history. That was what Ari was saying. Opened the case up while people were bombing subways and using Jordan's name, while the Defense election was in doubt, and Ari was too young to handle some of the things that could fall out of that kind of struggle—involving her predecessor's murderer.

They might win if it got to Bureau levels—but they might not. The risk was very large, while the gain was—minimal.

"No," he said. "It's not a matter of pills. It's one of the damn slow-dissolving gels, and they'd have the devil's own time getting the stuff cleared out."

"Damn! I should have come there. I *should* have called Council and stopped it—"

"Done is done, that's all. They say what they're giving us is something new; no color fade, no brittle bones. That kind of thing. I *would* like to get the literature on it before I say a final yes or no about a protest over what they've done. If it's everything Dr. Wojkowski claims—it's not worth the trouble even that would cause. If it costs what they say it does—it's not a detriment; because *I* couldn't afford it. I only suspect it has other motives—because I *can't* afford it, and that means they can always withhold it."

Her face showed no shock. None. "They're not going to do that."

"I hope not."

"I got the tape," she said.

And sent his pulse jolting so hard he thought he was going to throw up. It was the pain, he thought. Coffee mingled with the taste of blood in his mouth, where they had taken their sample from the inside of his cheek. He was not doing well at all. He wanted to be home, in bed, with all his small sore spots; the arm was hurting so much now he was not sure he could hold the cup with that hand.

"She—" Ari said, "she went through phases—before she died—that she had a lot of problems. I know a lot of things now, a lot of things nobody wanted to tell me. I don't want that ever to happen. I've done the move—you and Grant into my wing. Yanni says thank God. He says he's going to kill you for the bill at *Changes*."

He found it in him to laugh a little, even if it hurt.

"I told uncle Denys you were going on my budget and he was damn well going to increase it. And I had him about what he did to you, so he didn't argue; and I put your monthly up to ten *with* a full medical, *and* your apartment paid, for you and Grant both."

"My God, Ari."

"It's enough you can pay a staffer to do the little stuff, so you don't have to and Grant doesn't have to. It's a waste of your time. It's a lot better for Reseune to have you on research—and teaching *me*. Denys didn't say a thing. He just signed it. As far as I'm concerned, my whole wing is research. Grant doesn't have to do clinical stuff unless he wants to."

"He'll be—delighted with that."

Ari held up a forefinger. "I'm not through. I asked uncle Denys why you weren't *doctor* when you'd gotten where Yanni couldn't teach you anymore, and he said because they didn't want you listed with the Bureau, because of politics. I said that was lousy. Uncle Denys—when he pushes you about as far as he thinks he can get away with, and you push back, you can get stuff out of him as long as you don't startle him. Anyway, he said if we got through the election in Defense, then they'd file the papers."

He stared at her, numb, just numb with the flux.

"Is that all right, what I did?" she asked, suddenly looking concerned. Like a little kid asking may-I.

"It's—quite fine. —Thank you, Ari."

"You don't look like you feel good."

"I'm fine." He took a deep breath and set the cup down. "Just a lot of changes, Ari. And they took some pieces out of me."

She got up from behind the desk and came and carefully, gently hugged his shoulders—the sore one sent a jolt through to the bone. She kissed him very gently, very tenderly on the forehead. "Go home," she said. Her perfume was all around him.

But through the pain, he thought it quite remarkable her touch made not a twitch—no flashback, nothing for the moment, though he knew he was not past them. Maybe he escaped it for the moment because it hurt so much, maybe because for a moment he was emotionally incapable of reacting to anything.

She left, and he heard her tell Florian he should walk with them and make sure they got home all right, and get them both to bed and take care of them till they felt better.

Which sounded, at the moment, like a good idea.

—————————— xii ——————————

B/1: Ari, this is Ari senior.

You've asked about Reseune administration.

My father set it up: James Carnath. He had, I'm told, a talent for organization. Certainly my mother Olga Emory had no interest in the day to day management of details.

Even the day to day management of her daughter, but that's a different file.

I mention that because I fit somewhere in between: I've always believed in a laissez-faire management, meaning that as long as I was running Reseune, I believed in knowing what was going on in the kitchens, occasionally, in the birth-labs, occasionally, in finance, always.

An administrator of a facility like Reseune has special moral obligations which come at the top of the list: a moral obligation to humankind, the azi, the public both local and general, the specific clients, and the staff, in approximately that order.

Policies regarding genetic or biological materials; or psychological techniques and therapies are the responsibility of the chief administrator, and decisions in those areas must never be delegated.

Emphatically, the administrator should seek advice from wing supervisors and department heads. All other decisions and day to day operations can be trusted to competent staff.

I devised a routine within the House system coded MANAGEINDEX which may or may not be in use. Go to Executive 1 and ask for it, and it will tell you the expenses, output, number of reprimands logged, number of fines, number of requests for transfer, number of absences, medical leaves, work-related accidents, anti-management complaints, and security incidents for any individual, group of individuals, office, department, or wing in Reseune, and use that data to evaluate the quality of management and employees on any level. It can do comparisons of various wings and departments or select the most efficient managers and employees in the system.

It will also run a confidential security check on any individual, including a covert comparison of lifestyle data with income and output.

It operates without leaving a flag in the system.

Remember that it is a tool to be used in further inquiry and interview, and it is not absolutely reliable. Personal interviews are always indicated.

I was a working scientist as well as chief Administrator, which I found to be generally a fifteen-hour-a-day combination. A pocket com and an excellent staff kept me apprised of situations which absolutely required my intervention, and this extended to my research as well as my administrative duties. Typically I was in the office as early as 0700, arranged the day's schedule, reviewed the emergencies and ongoing situations via Base One, and put the office in motion as the staff arrived, left on my own work by 0900, and generally made the office again briefly after lunch, whereupon I left again after solving whatever had to be done.

I had a few rules which served me quite well:

I did my own office work while no one was there, which let me work efficiently; I had Florian and Catlin sworn to retrieve me from idle conversations—or from being accosted and handed business. Florian, I would say, handle this. Which usually meant it went to the appropriate department head; but sometimes Florian would check it out, and advise me personally. As he still does. Now that I'm Councillor for Science, it's much the same kind of thing. I absolutely refuse to be bogged down by lobbyists. That's what my staff is for. And they're to hand me investigative reports with facts and figures; which I then have cross-checked by Reseune security, and finally, finally, if there seems to be substance that interests me, I'll have my full staff meet with the interest group; and I will, if the reports are reasonable—but not in other than a businesslike setting and with a firm time limit for them. It's quite amazing how much time you can waste.

Delegate paperwork. Insist the preparers of reports include a brief summary of content, conclusion and/or recommended action; and that they follow strict models of style: this will appear petty, but I refuse to search a report for information which should have been prominently noted.

Give directions and reprimands early and clearly: an administrator who fails to make his expectations and his rules clear is inefficient; an administrator who expects a subordinate to pick up unspoken displeasure is wasting his time.

Learn a little bit about every operation. On one notorious occasion I showed up in the hospital and spent two hours walking rounds with the nurses. It not only identified problems up and down the line, but the whole MANAGEINDEX of Reseune shifted four points upward in the next two weeks.

Most of all, know your limits and identify those areas in which you are less adept. Do not abdicate authority in those areas: learn them, and be extremely careful of the quality of your department heads.

This program finds you have the rank of: wing supervisor.

You are seventeen years old; you have held your majority for: 1 year, 4 months.

You have a staff of: 6.

You have one department head: Justin Warrick, over Research.

He has a staff of: 2.

This program is running MANAGEINDEX.

There have been 0 complaints and 0 reprimands.

There have been 0 absences on personal leave.

There have been 2 medicals in Research.

Your Research department staff has a total of 187 Security incidents, 185 of which have been resolved. Do you wish breakdown?

AE2: No. I've read the file. None of these occurred in my administration.

B/1: Projects behind schedule: 0.

Projects over budget: 0.

Project demand: 12.

Project output: 18.

Projects ongoing: 3.

Wing expenses, 3 mo. period: C 688,575.31.

Wing earnings, 3 mo. period: C 6,658,889.89.

This wing has the following problems:

1. security flag on: 2 staff in: Research: Justin Warrick, Grant ALX.

2. security watch on: 1 staff in Administration, Ariane Emory.

3. security alert: flag/watch contacts.

Status: Reseune Administration has signed waiver.

Your wing has an overall MANAGEINDEX rating of 4368 out of 5000. MANAGEINDEX congratulates you and your staff and calls your high achievement to the attention of Reseune Administration.

Your staff will receive notification of excellent performance and will receive commendations in permanent file.

xiii

The vote totals ticked by on the top of the screen and Giraud took another drink. "We're going to make it," he said to Abban.

After-dinner drinks in his Novgorod apartment. Private election-watch, with his companion Abban, who very rarely indulged. But Abban's glass had diminished by half since the Pan-paris figures had started coming in. Pan-paris had gone for Khalid in the last election. This time it went for Jacques by a two percent margin.

"It's not over," Abban said, dour as usual. "There's still Wyatt's."

The stars farther off the paths of possible expansion were very chancy electorates for any seat. The garrisons tended to be local, resisting amalgamation into other units, and voted consistently Centrist.

But Pan-paris augured very well . . . coming out of the blind storage on Cyteen Station: the computers spat up the stored results of other stations as Cyteen polls closed simultaneously, on-world and up at Station, and the tallies began to flood in.

"I told you," Giraud finally felt safe to say. "Not even with Gorodin's health at issue. Khalid's far from forming a third party. He certainly can't do it with support eroding inside his own electorate. Then we only have Jacques to worry about."

"Only Jacques," Abban echoed. "Do you think he'll keep a bargain? I don't."

"He'll appoint Gorodin. He knows damn well what reneging on that deal would do for him. All we have to hope is that Gorodin stays alive." He took a drink of his own. "And that he hurries and makes an appearance. *Hope* he's not going to wait overlong on proprieties."

The moderate do-nothing Simon Jacques for Councillor; Jacques to appoint Gorodin as Secretary of Defense, then

Jacques to resign and appoint Gorodin proxy Councillor, back to his old seat—after which there was bound to be another round with Khalid.

But by then they had to have a viable Expansionist candidate ready to contend with Khalid. The two-year rule applied: meaning Khalid, having lost the election, could not turn around and re-file against the winner until two years had passed; which meant Jacques could hold the seat for two years without much chance of challenge—but if Jacques resigned directly after election, it would be a race to file: whoever filed first, Gorodin or Khalid, could preclude the other from filing because they were each a month short of the end of the prohibition from the election that had put *Khalid* in: which was sure to mean a Supreme Court ruling on the situation—the rule technically only applying to losers, but creating a window for an appeal on the grounds of legal equity.

That meant it was wiser to leave Jacques in office for as long as the two-year rule made him unassailable—while Gorodin— the health rumors were *not* fabricated this time—used what time he had to groom a successor of his own . . . because the one thing no one believed was that Gorodin would last the full two years.

A successor whom of *course* Jacques was going to support. Like hell. Jacques knew himself a figurehead, knew his own financial fortunes were solidly linked with Centrist-linked firms, and the next two years were going to be fierce infighting inside Defense, while Khalid, stripped of his Intelligence post, still had pull enough in the military system to be worrisome. The estimate was that Lu, tainted with the administrative decisions Gorodin's war record to some extent let him survive, had a reputation for side-shifting that did not serve him well in an elected post; and he was old, very old, as it was.

"We're running out of war heroes," Abban said. "Doubtful if Gorodin can find any of that generation *fit* to serve. This new electorate—I'm not sure they respond to the old issues. That's the trouble."

Seventy years since the war—and the obits of famous names were getting depressingly frequent.

"These young hawks," Giraud said, "they're not an issue, they're a mindset. They're pessimistic, they believe in worst-cases, they feel safe only on the side of perceived strength. Khalid worries me more as an agitator than as a single-electorate hero. He appeals to that type—to the worriers of all electorates, not just the ones who happen to be in Defense. It's always after wars—in times of confusion—or economic low spots, exactly the kind of thing a clever operator like Khalid *can* find a base in. There are alarming precedents. Lu would be the best for the seat, still the best for the seat and the best for the times—but this damned electorate won't vote for a man who tells them there are four and five sides to a question. There's too much uncertainty. The electorate doesn't want the truth, it wants answers in line with their thinking.''

"One could,'' Abban said, ''simply take a direct solution. I don't understand civs, I especially don't understand civ CITs. In this case the law isn't working. It's insanity to go on following it. Eliminate the problem quietly. Then restore the law.'' Abban *was* a little buzzed. "Take this man Khalid out. I could do it. And no one would find me out.''

"A dangerous precedent.''

"So is losing—dangerous to your cause.'' ·

"No. Politics works. When the Expansionists look strong, these pessimist types vote Expansionist. And they'll turn. We had them once. We can have them again.''

"When?'' Abban asked.

"We will. I'll tell you: Denys is right. Young Ari's image has been altogether too sweet.'' Abban's glass was empty. He filled Abban's and topped off his, finishing the bottle. ''When our girl took into Khalid in front of the cameras—that threw a lot of Khalid's believers completely off their balance, but you mark me, they blamed the media. Remember they always believe in conspiracies. They weren't willing to accept Ari as anything solid—as *anything* that can guarantee their future. And *won't*, until she makes them believe it.''

"Which alienates the doves.''

"Oh, yes. When she went in front of those cameras head to head with Khalid—it was damned dangerous. She pulled it off—but there was a downside. I argued with Denys. Her insistence on bringing Gehenna out public again—I'm sure inflamed the hawks and scared the hell out of a few doves—enough to bring the Paxers out in force. She may have attracted the few peace-pushers who aren't more scared of her than him, and may have lost him a few of his, but she didn't gain any of *his* people. It's Gorodin they're re-electing. Gorodin's an old name, a safe name. They're not about to go with a young girl's opinion. Not the worry-addicts.''

More figures ticked by. Widening margin, Jacques' favor.

"I'll tell you what worries me,'' Giraud said, finally. "Young Warrick. He's going to be very hard to hold. How's our man doing—the one with the Planys contact?''

"Proceeding.''

"We document it, we find some convenient link to the Rocher gang or the Paxers and that's all we need. Or we create one. I want you to look into that.''

"Good.''

"We need to leave the Centrists with very embarrassing ties— There have to be ties. That will keep Corain busy. *And* keep young Warrick quiet, if he has any sense at all.''

"Direct solutions there are just as possible,'' Abban said.

"Oh, no. Jordie Warrick himself can be quite a help. We keep putting off the travel passes. Start a security scandal at Planys airport. That should do. Leak the business about young Warrick going on rejuv. Our Jordie's damned clever. Just keep the pressure on, and he'll get reckless—he'll throw something to the Centrists; and our man just funnels it straight to the Paxers. Then we just turn the lights on—and watch them run for cover.''

"And *young* Warrick?''

"Denys wants to salvage him. I think it's lunacy. At least he took my advice—in the case we *have* a problem. The Paxers have handed us a beautiful issue. The doves hate them because they're violent—the hawks hate them for the lunacy they stand for. Let our Ari discover the Paxers are plotting to kill her, and that Jordan Warrick is involved with them; and watch those instincts turn on in a hurry. Watch her image shift then—on an issue of civil violence and plots. Absolutely the thing we need. Attract the peace-party *and* the hawks—and cultivate enemies that can only do her political good.''

"Mark *me*, young Warrick is a danger in that scenario.''

"Ah. But we've been very concerned with his welfare. Planning for his long life. Giving him rejuv puts that all on record, doesn't it? And if Ari's threatened—she'll react. If Jordan's threatened—so will young Warrick jump. You give me the incident I need, and watch the pieces fall. And watch our young woman learn a valuable lesson.'' A moment he stared at the screen and sipped at the wine. ''I'll tell you, Abban: you know this: she matters to me. *She's* my concern. Reseune is. Damned if Jordie Warrick's son is going to have a voice in either. Damned if he is.''

Cyteen Station results flashed up, lopsided.

''That's it,'' Abban said. ''He's got it now.''

''Absolutely. I told you. Jacques is in.''

xiv

Catlin brought sera coffee in the home office, while sera was feeding the guppies in the little tank she had moved in from the garden-room—sera was quite, quite calm, doing that: it seemed to *make* her calm, sometimes, a sort of focus-down. Catlin could figure that. She also knew that it was a bad time, sera was waiting for answers from a protest she had filed with Administration; sera—outward evidence to the contrary—was in a terrible temper, not the time that Catlin wanted at all to deal with her. But she tried.

''Thank you,'' sera said, taking the mug and setting it on the edge of the desk, and fussing with the net and a bit of floating weed.

Sera never even looked her way. After a while Catlin decided sera was deliberately ignoring her, or was just thinking hard, and turned and walked out again.

Or started to walk out. Catlin got as far as the hall, and found herself facing her partner's distressed, exasperated look.

So Catlin stopped, drew a large breath, and went back to stand beside sera's desk, doggedly determined that sera should notice.

She had, she thought, rather have run a field under fire.

''What is it?'' sera said suddenly, breaking her concentration.

''Sera, —I need to talk to you. About the Planys thing. Florian said—I was the one who heard. So it's mine to say.''

It took a moment, sometimes, for sera to come back when she was really thinking, and especially when she was mad, and she brought some of that temper back with her. Because she was so smart, Catlin thought, because she was thinking so hard she was almost deep-studying, except she was doing it from the inside.

But that was a keyword—Planys. That was precisely what sera was mad about; and sera came right back, instantly, and fixed on her.

"What *about* Planys?"

Catlin clenched her hands. *You're* best at explaining things, she had objected to Florian. But Florian had said: You're the one heard it, *you* should tell it.

Because Florian came to pieces when it came to a fight with sera.

And it could.

"This Paxer group in Novgorod," she began.

There had been another subway bombing in Novgorod. Twenty people killed, forty-eight injured.

"What's *that* to do with Planys airport?"

"In security. They're—" She never could go through things without detail. She never knew what to leave out with a CIT, even sera, so she decided to dive straight to the heart of it. "Sera, they're pretty sure there is some kind of contact. The Pax group—they're the violent part. But there's a group called the Committee for Justice—"

"I've heard about them."

"There's overlap. Security is saying that's definite. One is the other, in a major way. They're doing stickers in Novgorod, you understand—someone just walks through a subway car and puts one up. Most of them say Committee for Justice. Or Free Jordan Warrick. But a few of them say No Eugenics and Warrick Was Right."

Sera frowned.

"It's very serious," Catlin said. "Security is terribly worried."

"I understand how serious it is, dammit. —What does this have to do with Planys airport security?"

"It's complicated."

"Explain it. I'm listening. Give me all the details. *What* does Security know?"

"The Novgorod police know the Paxer explosives are

homemade. That's first. There's probably just a handful of people—real Paxers—in Novgorod. The police are pretty sure they're a front for Rocher. But they can't find Rocher. So they're sure he's living on somebody else's card. That's not hard to do. Nothing's hard to do, when there are that many people all crowded up in one place. There's probably a lot of connection between the Committee and the Paxers and Rocher—everybody. So the Novgorod police got the Cyteen Bureau to get Union Internal Affairs on it, on the grounds it's a problem that crosses the boundaries between Reseune and—''

"I know Reseune Security is on the case. But tell it your way.''

"—and Cyteen. Which lets the Justice Bureau call on us to help the Novgorod police. They can't do the kind of stuff we'd like to—Novgorod is just too big. The police are *talking* about card-accesses on every subway gate, but that just means they'll always have somebody else's keycard, and they'll kill people to get them. A lot of things they could do to stop the bombings are real expensive, and they'd slow everybody down and make them take hours getting to and from work. They say Cyteen Station is getting real nervous and they *are* doing keycard checks and print-locks and all of that. So they've decided the only real way to get the Paxers is to infiltrate them. So they have. You just send somebody inside and you get good IDs and you start searching the keycard systems on *those* markers and you start taking a few of them out, you aggravate whatever feuds you find—make them fight each other and keep increasing your penetrations until you can figure their net out. *That's* the way they're working it.''

"You mean you know they're already doing it.''

Catlin nodded. "I'm not supposed to know. But yes, sera, they are. And they know the airports are one of the places where some of the illegal stuff they get is getting through security, and that's how it's going to spread *outside* Novgorod, which is what the rumor is. That there's going to be a hit somewhere else. *That's* what's going on out there.''

"They're not grounding traffic, are they?''

"No, sera. People don't know it's going on. They don't need to know. But they're most worried about Planys and Novgorod. Novgorod because it's biggest and there's the shuttleport. And Planys because they think there's a problem there.''

Sera closed the lid on the tank and laid the net down. "Go on. Take your time."

"They're terribly worried," Catlin said. "Sera, they're not talking about Jordan Warrick in the posters. It's against *you*. People are scared about the subways. That's the Paxers' job. People aren't being very smart. They have all these signs to tell them to watch about people leaving packages, and there's a rumor out that the police have installed this kind of electronics at the subway gates that'll blow any explosives up when it passes through that point, but that's not so. People are calling the city offices and asking about more ped-ways, but that's stupid— you can leave a package in a ped-tunnel that can kill just as many people. So all they can do is put up with it, but people are getting really upset, that's what they're saying, and when they're upset enough, the Committee comes out more and agitates with some lie they'll make up about you when they need it. They're not sure even this isn't something Khalid's behind, but that's just something Security wishes they could prove. But *that's* why they're doing all this stuff with the airports, and that's why Justin can't get a pass. And that's not the worst, sera. There *is* somebody who's getting stuff in and out of Planys. It's connected to Jordan Warrick. That's what's going on. That's why they're stopping Justin and Grant from going there.''

Sera stayed very still a moment. Mad. Terribly mad and upset.

It was not hard to figure why sera partnered with Justin Warrick: Catlin knew the reasons in that the way she had known, after she had seen Florian attack a problem, that Florian was everything she needed in the world.

And when somebody was your partner, you felt connected to them, and you had rather anything than think they could fail you.

A long time sera stood there, and finally she sat down at her desk. "I don't think they know," sera said.

"Not unless there's somebody working inside Reseune, sera. And that's not likely. But not everybody at Planys is Reseune staff. That's where the hole is. And they're not going

to plug it. They're going to see what's going on first. Jordan
Warrick is linked to the Abolitionists. And maybe to respectable people. Nobody knows yet. They're trying to find out if
those groups are doing this.''

Sera's face had gone terribly white, terribly upset.

"Sera?" Catlin said, and sat down in the interview chair and
put her hand on her sera's knee. ''Florian and I will go on trying to find things out, if you don't tell Denys about us knowing. That's the best thing. That's what we need to do.''

Sera's eyes seemed to focus. And looked at her. ''There's
not a damn thing Justin knows about it.''

"They're going to let him talk to his father, sera. They're
going to monitor that—very closely. They're going to give his
father a lot of room, actually let up the security—''

"To trap him, you mean. God, Catlin, to *push* him into it,
what do they think people are made of?''

"Maybe they will,'' Catlin said. "I'm not worried about
that. I'm worried about Justin being *here*. I'm worried because
he's going to be upset when he can't go to his father. Sera, —''
This was terribly hard to say. She had it in her hands of a sudden, the whole picture that had been worrying her and she
made a violent gesture, cutting sera off, before she lost the way
to say it. "The trouble is in Novgorod. With people who hate
you. And Jordan Warrick was with these people a long time
ago. It doesn't matter whether it's his fault or their fault—what
matters is they're making him a Cause. And that's power. And
when he's got that—''

"He's got to do something with it,'' sera said.

Catlin nodded. "And Justin's real close to you, sera.
Justin's inside. And his father's a Special in psych—and he's
your Enemy. That's real dangerous. That's terribly dangerous,
sera.''

"Yes,'' she said, very quiet. "Yes, it is.'' And after a moment more: "Dammit, why didn't Denys *tell* me?''

"Maybe he thought you might talk to Justin, sera.''

"I could *fix* this,'' sera said. "I could fix this— Damn,
I'd—''

"What would you do, sera?'' That sera might have an idea
did not surprise her at all. But it disconcerted her to see sera's
shoulders fall, and watch sera shake her head.

"Politics," sera said. "Pol-i-tics, Catlin. Dirty politics. Like our friends who aren't speaking to each other. Like *fools*, Catlin, who won't tell anyone the truth about what they want—like people want Reseune destroyed for a whole lot of reasons, and some of them are sane and some of them are crooked as hell. Like crazy people who blow up subways for peace. What does reason matter?"

Catlin shook her head, confused.

"I want to know who these people are," sera said in a hard voice. "I want to know, Catlin, whether any of them are of azi ancestry. Whether any of them are azi or whether this is a CIT craziness Reseune didn't have anything to do with." And a moment later: "I've got to think about the other. I've got to think about it, Catlin."

"Sera, *please* don't go to Justin with this. Don't tell him."

A long silence. "No," she said. "No. That's not the thing to do."

2423: 11/5: 2045

AE2: Base One, what data do you have on: keyword: assassination: keyword: Ariane Emory: keyword: death?

B/1: Ari senior has a message.

Stand by.

Ari, this is Ari senior.

You've asked about assassination.

This program will assess your current security problems while this message plays.

Most of all, beware the people you know. The others you would in no wise allow to approach you.

You've asked about death. First, don't mistake my limits for your own.

I don't know how much time there is as I write this. I know, at least, that rejuv is failing. So does Petros Ivanov, who is sworn to secrecy.

How do I face death? With profound anxieties. Anxieties because I know how much there is yet to do.

God, if I could have another lifetime.

But that's yours, sweet. And I'll never know, will I?

Base One has completed its assessment.

You are 17 years old. You are legally adult.

The indices this program uses in Security records indicate a troubled period. Do you think this is an accurate statement?

AE2: Yes.

B/1: Is your life in danger?

AE2: Yes.

B/1: Is the threat internal or external to Reseune?

AE2: I don't know.

B/1: Do you think you can trust the Science Bureau?

AE2: I don't know. I need more information. I want my clearance raised, Base One.

B/1: Working.

Describe the things you want to know.

AE2: Everything. I want this program to do everything it did for Ari senior and I want it to do it without leaving any flags in the system.

B/1: Your request is being processed.

Ari senior has a message.

Stand by.

Ari, this is Ari senior.

You've asked for Base One to assume full operation. The program is assessing your psychological profile, your current test scores, the state of House offices and departments.

Have you considered that the security wall this will create in the House system may be detected by other Bases? Are you knowledgeable enough to create cover?

AE2: Yes.

B/1: I can't foresee your situation when you make this request. I can't advise you in specific. The program, however, is biased to grant this expansion on your request, on a complex weighting of: the length of time you have held your legal majority, the amount and nature of covert activity in other bases, your own test scores and psychological profiles, and a number of other factors you may explore at your leisure.

I had thought about dividing the power of Base One, making it possible for you to acquire information first—without giving you the power to take certain actions through Base One's accesses, this for your protection, and Reseune's.

I decided against that . . . simply because I could not foresee your circumstances. But the program is running as it is because you are asking for a House system rating exceeding that of the present administrators of Reseune.

This may be necessary. It may be a grievous mistake.

Before you proceed, consider that the larger your real power grows, the more it makes you a danger to others. This move of yours, if detected, may increase the number and energy of persons working against you.

Do you still wish to proceed?

AE2: Yes.

B/1: I earnestly advise you, don't use Base One's interactive functions beyond the limits you have used already, until you have a political base to back you: I mean specifically covert actions on a level shutting out Denys Nye, Giraud Nye, Petros Ivanov, Yanni Schwartz, Wendell Peterson, or John Edwards, because they are very likely to catch you at it real-time, in ways that have nothing to do with the House system. You may be brilliant as I was, young Ari, but you are inexperienced at this level. Consider whether a 17-year-old is a match for the experience and political savvy of these people.

It's perfectly safe, however, to use the information-gathering functions of the new level: use that to learn what's going on in the House, by all means, just don't do anything about it until you know damn well you can keep your actions completely covert or until your position is overwhelmingly stronger than any opposition inside Reseune—or the Bureau, or wherever. I am not at all convinced that an inexperienced person can conceal actions within this system.

I am, as you have detected, extremely uneasy about this step. In my day Reseune knew secrets that could mean war or peace.

I did not wield Base One fully until I was 62. I estimate that I had the ability to have handled it when I was 30. But I would have taken it up then with precisely the same caution and by the same degrees I advise you to use at 17. If you cannot survive on wits and knowledge alone, either the situation is worse than mine, or you are not as clever as I was.

Do you wish to proceed, against all these cautions?
AE2: Yes.

B/1: Be aware that this request will begin your assumption of authority over Reseune. Consider the situation inside and outside Reseune, and ask yourself what could result and whether you are ready and able to handle it.

Be aware that others may have anticipated this move and covered their traces. But until you order it to take actions— or until, mark me well, you let slip that you know something you could only have known through a higher Base, you will not create traces. Use that secrecy as long as you can.

Study carefully how others lie to the system, so that when you do it, you will be too good for them to catch.

I have taken only one precaution which will remain in the system until you have control of Administration. Base One will read-only information with no additional prompt, and advise you which information would have been inaccessible to you prior to this expansion.

It will advise you where lies have been planted in the system and show you both sets of information.

I have installed a fail-safe specifically for you, if you should request this power before assuming the administration of Reseune. The system will stop and ask for a special prompt be-fore acting on any level possible as a result of this expansion . . . in plain terms, it will go on acting as it did before, but it will identify and tag certain kinds of information to make you aware what other people think is hidden from you; and it will prevent your accidentally taking actions that would overrun the parameters they believe exist. The key to release the system for action is: Havoc. You may re-set the keyword to suit you. But you should also think about that word—and the conse-quences of ignoring my advice, no matter how hot the fire gets under your feet.

Second thoughts can generally be amended with judicious action; injudicious actions can seldom be recovered with sec-ond thoughts.

Do you understand me, Ari?
AE2: I understand, Base One.

B/1: Your access has been upgraded. This Base is now fully operational. Base One now outranks all other Bases in all Reseune systems.

AE2: Retrieve all previously hidden medical and security records on all individuals under my surveillance.

B/1: Working.

File: Justin Warrick
Emory I
2404: 11/5: 2045

Warrick, Justin.
Estim(ated) Res(ner Index of) 180+ comp(ares) favorab(ly) w(ith) pat [father] (but) lo(w) aggr(e)s(sion level) ref(erence to) presence dom(inant) g(ender)-i(dentical)-p(arent) ergo [I ordered production of] G(rant)ALX [as Justin Warrick's companion]. . . .

File: Justin Warrick
Emory II
2423: 11/10: 2245

Warrick, Justin.
Ref: psychogenesis.

On every evidence I've found in files so far, Justin Warrick was a test case from his conception.

Ari I claims she psyched Jordan into having a PR done. She said things like: "I'm not temperamentally suited to bringing up my own"—I think she meant her own PR. And she said: "Jordan's a loss." Meaning something I don't understand, either that she couldn't work with him, or that she didn't think his slant on his work was what she wanted. I think it was more of the second. But there was ability there, complementary to her own. I think that's what she saw.

She used to work with Jordan. They worked real well at first. But Jordan's upbringing made him a dominant, and she was, and the two of them had a lot of problems which bounced off a sexual encounter they had had when he was 17 and she was 92. That was his only heterosexual relationship, and what went wrong with it had more to do with the fact that he was not hetero to begin with and he had, at 17, begun working with Ari as a student—the whole pattern identical to what happened with Justin.

But in Jordan's case, he had applied to work with Ari, probably because of a genuine admiration for her work. He was young, he was attractive, and Ari's proclivities and his admiration led to a disillusioning experience.

But here's the thing no one's looking at: Jordan Warrick's index increased 60 points during the next ten years. He already had a respectable score. But no one knew what he was until he was working with Ari—because of the publicity and the chance to work *with* her, is the general opinion these days. But the fact is he wasn't Jordan Warrick SP then. He was just damn bright and he was Ari's student.

So I looked back at Jordan's parents. Jordan's mother didn't want him after he was born. She was a researcher. She wanted the bonus you got back then to have a baby in Reseune. But she didn't want a baby. She just picked its father, got pregnant about as clinically timed as you can and still have sex, birthed Jordan and handed him to his father to bring up. His father was an Ed psych specialist who practiced every theory he had on his kid. Pushed him into early learning. And tended to give him things—*lots* of expenditure on things for Jordan. Doted on him.

Anyway, that was Jordan Warrick—not to leave out his companion, Paul, whom he requisitioned a year after his encounter with Ari, and while he was still working with her—but after he had moved out of his father's residence.

After that, his scores came up a lot.

I think Ari intervened with him continually. Ari helped him requisition Paul. Ari claims she talked him into having a PR done when he was about 30, the year after his father died in a seal failure—which was the only family Jordan had except an aunt. So she certainly worked with him. She certainly was dealing with a man who'd just lost someone he loved a great deal, and it's true that the same week they started Justin Warrick, *she* started Grant ALX. Things were pretty good between her and Jordan during that period, and she told Jordan a couple of years later that she had an Alpha test subject she wanted socialized, and would he like to do it and incidentally provide a playmate for his own son.

Jordan agreed. But Ari had picked Grant very carefully, and she had done some very slight corrective work with his set on a couple of things that are easy fixes, nothing beyond that—more than anything, any change in the original Special geneset meant she didn't have to go to Council to get permission and it also meant Grant would be classed as an Experimental, which means Reseune will always hold his contract, no private person can. Ari did Grant's early tape. Ari used Base One to pull up everything she could on Jordan's past and Jordan's father, right around the time she was doing all the search-up for Grant's geneset and all the prep for him. And if Grant was ever part of any other research project, it wasn't in the records or in her notes.

She did have one note that Jordan was a dominating male, but that if he'd been reared by one he'd have curled up and gone under, because that was what he was set to respond to. And something about plants and taller plants getting all the sun. Meaning if Justin was a PR he couldn't turn out *like* his father, because his teacher wasn't Jordan's father, Martin. Martin wasn't a dominant, but he brought up a strong, self-centered dominant who still had his father's tendency to give his son an abundance of affection and material things. *This* was what was going to bring Justin up. And Jordan was much brighter than Martin Warrick, was professionally skilled at manipulation, but with a peculiar emotional blind spot that revolved around his son as an extension of himself—meaning his son was going to *be* himself, and avoid the Bok clone problem that's haunted every PR of a bright parent.

Ari said about Justin, on his school paper: As long as you confuse your father with God you won't pursue this, which would be a shame. I'm requesting you into my wing. It'll do you good, give you a different perspective on things.

I don't know how much of what happened was planned but a lot of it was calculated. She encouraged him in the essay paper. When he did it she approved it, even as much as it duplicated things already tried. She encouraged him;

she snagged him into her wing, into her reach, and she ran an intervention on him.

I've seen the tape (ref. tape 85899) and I know that it was an intervention. She knew she was dying. She had maybe a couple of years. Justin Warrick was the test that would tell her whether or not I would exist—as I do.

She always made such precise procedural steps for people to look at; but when she operated, she always seemed to violate her own rules. That's because she tended to cluster steps and combine operations, because she could pick up on flux-states better than anyone I've ever seen.

The tape of her with Justin bothers me in a lot of senses. But I keep coming back to it because there are a handful of tapes of her doing clinical interventions, scattered through her life, under controlled conditions. But knowing as much as I do about Justin, and about psychogenesis—that tape, terrible as it is, is Ari going without tape, without a clinical situation, without any safeguards; and, here's the eerie part, knowing exactly what the situation was, knowing her reactions from the inside, I can see exactly what she sees, how fast she picks up on flux and how fast she can change an entire program—

Because I've got her notes on what she was going to do, and I can read her body language like no one else.

Justin worked . . . not the way he would have if she'd been able to go on working with him. I know that. I also think I know why my uncles opposed him.

Leaving her work in the hands of a young researcher like Justin Warrick is so in character for Ari, exactly in character with that intervention in the tape. She took chances when she was working that would scare hell out of an ethics board. That—scare me less than they should, maybe, because I can see at least some of what she saw. And I know the reasons she wanted someone to follow her—someone with a special kind of sensitivity and a special kind of vision. It was her macro-system interventions that scared her—that scare me, that make me more and more afraid, and drive me beyond what I can stand, sometimes.

I need him. And I can no more explain to my uncles than Ari could. If I told them in plain language about the macro-system interventions: Listen to me, Denys: Ari put a Worm in the system, it's real, it's working, and I need computer time and I need Justin Warrick's work—I can hear him say: even Ari had her out-there notions, dear, and there's no way you can focus an integration over that range. It just won't happen. And Giraud would say: Whatever it does, we make our money off short-term.

—that's exactly what I'd get.

And Giraud would say to Denys after I was out of the room: We've got to do something about Justin Warrick.

CHAPTER
3

———————————— i ————————————

The landing gear extended as they made their approach at Planys and Grant looked out the window while the blue-grays and browns of native Cyteen passed under the right wing. His heart beat very fast. His hands were sweating and he clenched them as the wheels touched and the plane braked.

He was traveling with Reseune Security: Reseune Security flew with everyone who came and went from Planys, they had told him that. But he was still afraid—afraid of nameless things, because his memory of plane flights involved suspicion, Winfield and Kruger, the crazy people who had tried to re-program him, and an utter nightmare when Reseune Security had pulled him out, drugged and semiconscious, and flown him away to hospital and interrogations.

Twelve hours in the air, and chop and finally monotony over endless ocean in the dark—had calmed him somewhat. He had not wanted to tell Justin—and had not—what an irrational, badly fluxed anxiety he had worked himself into over this trip.

Transference, he told himself clinically, absolutely classic CIT-psych transference. He had gathered up all his anxieties about Justin's safety at home, about his own vulnerability traveling alone into Planys and about knowing no matter what Justin and Jordan insisted, he was not the one of them Jordan wanted most to see—and the plane flight was a convenient focus.

The plane would go down in the ocean. There would be sabotage. There were lunatics who would attempt to shoot it down— The engines would simply fail and they would crash on takeoff.

He had spent a great deal of the flight with his hands clenched on the armrests as if that levitation could hold the plane in the air.

He had been nervous in flight when he had been seventeen, but he had not had cold sweats—which showed that, over the years, he had become more and more CIT.

Now, with the wheels on the ground, he had no more excuses. The anxieties had to attach where they belonged, on meeting Jordan, and the fact that, azi that he was, he did not know what to say to the man he had once called his father; and who had been, whatever else, his Supervisor all during his childhood.

The thought of disappointing Jordan, of *being* that disappointment—was almost enough to make him wish the plane had gone down.

Except there was Justin, who loved him enough to give him the chance to go, who had fought for it and held out for it through all the contrived delays, the breaks in communication—everything, so that when permission came to travel again—*he* could go first. They hoped there would be another chance directly after. But there was no guarantee, there was never a guarantee.

Please, he had said to Jordan, in that last phone call before the flight. I really feel awkward about this. Justin should come first.

Shut up, Justin had said over his shoulder. This time is yours. There'll be others.

I *want* you to come, Jordan had said. Of course I want you.

Which had affected him more than was good for him, he thought. It made a little pain in his chest. It was a CIT kind of feeling, pure flux, which meant that he ought to take tape and go deep and let Justin try to take that ambivalence away before it disturbed his value-sets. But Justin would argue with him. And that curious pain was a feeling he wanted to understand: it seemed a window into CIT mentality, and a valuable thing to understand, in his profession, in the projects he did with Justin. So he let it fester, thinking, when he could be more sensible about it: maybe this is the downside of the deep-set links. Or maybe it's just surface-set flux: but should it make such physiological reactions?

The plane rolled up to the terminal: Justin had said there was no tube-connection, but there was, and there was a good long wait while they got the plane hosed down and the tube-connect sealed down.

Then everyone began to get up and change into D-suits, the way Justin had said they would.

He did as the Security escort asked him. He put on the flimsy protection over his clothes and walked out into the tube and through into Decontamination.

Foam and another hose-down, and a safety-barrier, where he had to strip the suit off and step out, without touching its exterior—

In places he had been, like Krugers', if one had to make a fast transfer, one held one's breath, got to shelter, held an oxy mask tight to one's face with one hand and stripped with the other under a hosing-down that was supposed to take any woolwood fiber down the drain.

Planys was terrifyingly elaborate, a long series of procedures that made him wonder what he had been exposed to, or whether all this was just to make people at this desolate place feel safer.

"This way, ser," one of the Decon agents said, and took him by the elbow and brought him aside into a small alcove.

Body-search. He expected this too, and stripped down when they told him and suffered through the procedure, a little cold, a little anxious, but even Reseune Security people got this treatment going in or out of Planys. So they said.

Not mentioning what they did to the luggage.

"Grant," Jordan said, in person, meeting him in the hall, and:

"Hello, ser," he said, suddenly shy and formal, the surface-sets knowing he should go and embrace Jordan, and the deep-sets knowing him as a Supervisor, and knowing him from his childhood, when all instruction had come from him, and he was God and teacher.

This was the man Justin would have become, if rejuv had not stopped them both a decade earlier.

He did not move. He could not, suddenly, cope with this. Jordan came and embraced him instead.

"My God, you've grown," Jordan said, patting him on the back. "Vid didn't show how tall you'd grown. Look at the shoulders on you! What are you doing, working docks?"

"No, ser." He let Jordan lead him to his office, where Paul waited—Paul, who had doctored his skinned knees and Justin's. Paul embraced him too. Then the reality of where he was began to settle through the flux and he began to believe in being here, in being welcome, in everything being all right.

But there were no guards in the office. That was not the way Justin had warned him it would be.

Jordan smiled at him and said: "They'll send the papers up as soon as they've been over them—Justin did send that report with you, didn't he?"

"Yes, ser. Absolutely."

"Damn, it's good to see you."

"I thought—security would be more than it is." *Are we monitored, ser? What's going on?*

"I told you it's been saner here. That's one of the things. Come on, we're closing up the office. We'll go home, fix dinner—not as fancy as Reseune, but we've got real groceries. We bought a ham for the occasion. Wine from Pell, not the synth stuff."

His spirits lifted. He was still anxious, but Jordan, he thought, was in charge of things; he relaxed a bit into dependency, azi on Supervisor, which he had not done with Justin——had not done since he was in hospital, recovering from Giraud's probes. Had never done, after, because he was always either Justin's caretaker or Justin's partner.

It was like years of pressure falling away from him, to follow Jordan when he said Come, to sink into azi simplicity with someone he could trust—someone, finally, besides Justin, who would not harm him, who knew the place better than he did, and whose wishes were sane and sensible.

It was finally, one brief interlude in all these years, *not* his responsibility.

Only when he thought that, he thought: *No, I can't stop watching things. I can't trust anything. Not even Jordan—that far.*

He felt exhausted then, as if just for a few weeks he would like to go somewhere and do mindless work under someone's direction, and be fed and sleep and have responsibility for nothing.

That was *not* what he could do.

He walked with them to the apartment they had; and inside, and looked around him— *Things are very grim there*, Justin had said. *Very primitive.*

It was certainly not Reseune. The chairs were plastic and metal; the tables were plastic; the whole decor was plastic, except a corner full of real geraniums, under light, and a fish-tank, and a general inefficient pleasantness to the place that had all the stamp of CITs in residence . . . what Justin called a homey feeling, and what he thought of as the CIT compulsion to collect things charged with flux and full of fractals. A potted geranium represented the open fields. The fish were random, living motion. The water was assurance of life-requirements in abundance; and made a fractally repetitive sound which might be soothing to flux-habituated, non-analytical minds. God knew what else. He only knew Justin had let all the plants die after Jordan left, but when things started to go well, Justin began to fuss with a few plants, which always died back and thrived by turns—in time to the rise and fall of Justin's spirits.

Healthy plants, Grant reckoned, were a very good sign among CITs.

Things *felt* safe here, he thought as he gave his jacket up and let Paul hang it in the closet, people were tolerably happy here.

So the improvements in the world, the changes that had made this last couple of years more livable, even happy—had gotten to Planys too, despite the frustrations of the Paxer scare. All the same he wished Jordan knew even a few of the multitudinous signals he and Justin had worked out, the little indicators whether a thing was to be believed.

Maybe Jordan picked up his nervousness, because Jordan looked at him, laughed and said: "Relax. They monitor us from time to time. It's all right. Hello, Jean!" —to the ceiling.

"We know each other," Jordan said then. "Planys is a very small establishment. Sit down. We'll make coffee. God, there's so much to talk about."

<hr />

ii

<hr />

It was very lonely, the apartment without Grant. There was ample justification for worry, and Justin swore he was not going to spend four uninterrupted days at it.

So he read awhile, did tape awhile, an E-dose only, a piece of fluff from library. And read again. Ari had given him an advance copy of Emory's *IN PRINCIPIO*, the first of the three-volume annotated edition of Emory's archived notes, which the Bureau of Science was publishing in cooperation with the Bureau of Information, and which was now selling as fast as presses could turn them out in the Cyteen edition and already on its way on ships which had bid fabulously for it, a packet of information destined for various stations which would in turn pay for the license, sell printout and electronic repros to their own populations and sell more rights to ships bound further on.

Even, possibly, more than possibly, to Earth.

While Reseune accounts piled up an astonishing amount of credit.

Every library wanted copies. Scientists in the field did. But it was selling in the general market with a demand that could only be called hysteria: a volume of extremely heavy going, illustrated, with annotations so extensive there were about three lines of Emory's notes to every page, and the rest was commentary, provided by himself and by Grant, among others: he was the JW and Grant was the GALX; YS was Yanni Schwartz; and WP, Wendell Peterson; and AE2 was Ari, who had gotten the original text out of Archive and provided reference notes on some of the most obscure parts. DN was Denys Nye; GN was Giraud; JE was John Edwards; and PI was Petros Ivanov, besides dozens of techs and assistants who served in editing and collation—each department head and administrator to read and vet the material from his own staff.

Dr. Justin Warrick, it said in the fine print in the table of contributors. Which, secretly, like a little child, he read over and over just to see it confirmed. Grant, they listed as Grant ALX Warrick, E.P., *emeritus psychologiae*, which meant an azi who should have a doctorate in psych, and would have, automatically, if he became CIT. It pleased Grant more than Grant would let on.

CIT silliness, Grant had said. My patients certainly don't care.

But it was there, in print. And meanwhile the general public was buying copies, long waiting lists at booksellers—the Bureau had figured on strong library interest, but *never* anticipated average citizens would buy them, and certainly was bewildered that they were selling at that rate at a pre-publication price of 250 cred per volume—until an embarrassed Bureau of Information cut the price to 120 and then to 75, based on advance orders; and that brought in an absolute flood of orders. There were precious few sales in fiche or tape, except to the libraries: the actual books, printed on permasheet, thank you, were status objects: one could hardly display a microfilm to one-up one's neighbors.

Young Ari avowed herself completely bewildered by the phenomenon.

People know, Justin had said to her, that your predecessor did tremendously important things. They don't know *what* she did. They certainly can't understand the notes. But they feel like they ought to understand. What you ought to do, you know—is write a volume of your own notes: your own perspective on doing the volume. The things you've learned from your predecessor. You *ask* the BI if they'd be interested in the rights to *that*.

Not surprisingly, Information jumped at the chance.

Now Ari was struggling to put her own notes in shape. And coming to him with: Do you think . . . and sometimes just chatter—about the hidden notes, about things as full of revelations as the books he had spent a year helping annotate with the barest explanations of the principles involved.

She had sent a copy of *IN PRINCIPIO* to Jordan.

"Because it has your name in it," Ari had said to him, "and Grant's."

"If it gets through," he had said. "Planys Security may not like it. Not to mention Customs."

"All right," she had said. "So I'll send it with Security. Let them argue with that."

She did thoughtful things like that. In a year and a half in her wing she had come through with every promise she had made, gotten him and Grant a secretary, taken the pressure off—

If something went wrong or something glitched, Florian was on the phone very quickly; and if Florian could not resolve it, it was—Wait, ser, sera will handle it—after which Ari would be on the line, with a technique that ranged rapidly between *This has to be mistaken*— to a flare that department heads learned to avoid. Maybe it was a realization Ari might remember these things in future. Maybe—Justin suspected so—it was because that voice could start so soft, go to a controlled low resonance uncommon at her age—then pick up volume in a punch that made nerves jump: that made his jump, for certain, and evoked memories. But she never raised that voice with him, never pushed him, always said please and thank you—until he found himself actually on the inside of a very safe circle and *liking* where he worked—with a small, niggling fear that he was losing his edge, becoming less worried, less defensive, relying too much on Ari's promises—

Fool, he told himself.

But he grew so tired of fighting, and the thought that he might have reached a situation where he could draw breath awhile, that he might actually have found a kind of safety, even if it meant difficulties to come . . . *later* was all right.

Ari was well aware of what came in and out of her wing, was aggressively defensive of her staff's time—her attention to pennies and minutes was, God, the living echo of Jane Strassen; so that, beyond the annotations which totaled about a hundred twenty pages between himself and Grant, and three months' intensive work, she accepted only design work for her wing, only trouble-shooting after others had done the brute work, and it went, thank God, immediately *back* to junior levels in some other wing when he or Grant had provided the fix, no returns, no would-you-mind's? and no 'but we thought you could do that, we're running behind.'

So he critiqued Ari's work, answered Ari's questions, did the few fixes her wing ran, and had the actual majority of his time to use on his own projects—as Grant did, doing study of his own on the applications of endocrine matrix theory in azi tape, which Grant was going to get a chance to talk over with Jordan—Grant was very much looking forward to it.

They were, overall, happier than he remembered since—a long time; and it was the damnedest thing, waking up in the middle of the night as he did, with nightmares he could not remember.

Or stopping sometimes in the middle of work or walking home or wherever, overwhelmed by a second's panic, of nothing he could name except fear of the ground under his feet, fear that he was being a fool, and fear because he had no choice but be where he was.

Fear, perhaps, that he had not won: that he had in fact lost by the decisions he had made, and it would only take some few years yet to come clear to him.

All of which, he told himself severely, was a neurotic, compulsive state, and he resisted it—tried to weed it out when he found it operative. But take tape for it, he would not; not even have Grant run a little tranquilizing posthyp on him—being afraid of that too.

Fool, he told himself, exasperated at the track his thoughts tended to run, and marked his place and laid the book aside.

Emory for bedtime reading.

Maybe it was the fact he could still hear that voice, the exact inflection she would use on those lines he read.

And the nerves still twitched.

He rattled around an empty apartment in the morning, toasted a biscuit for breakfast, and went to the office—not the cramped, single office he and Grant had used for years, but the triple suite that Ari had leased—physically in the Ed Wing, which was back, in a sense, to where they had begun—simply because that wing had space and no one else did: an office apiece for himself and Grant, and one for Em, the secretary the pool had sent, a plump, earnest lad quite glad to get into a permanent situation where he could, conceivably, come up in rating.

He read the general advisories, the monthly plea from catering to book majo. orders a week in advance; a tirade from Yanni about through-traffic in Wing One, people cutting through the lower hall. Em arrived at 0900, anxious at finding the office already open, and got to work on the filing while he started on the current design.

That went on till lunch and during—a pocket-roll and a cup of coffee in the office; and a concentration that left him stiff-shouldered and blinking when the insistent blip of an Urgent Message started flashing in the upper left corner of the screen.

He keyed to it. It flashed up:

I need to talk to you. I'm working at home today. —AE.

He picked up the phone. "Ari, Base One," he told it.

Florian answered. "Yes, ser, just a second." And immediately, Ari: "Justin. Something's come up. I need to talk to you."

"Sure, I'll meet you at your office." *Is it Grant? God, has something happened?*

"Meet me here. Your card's cleared. Endit."

"Ari, I don't—"

The Base had gone off. Dammit.

He did not meet Ari except with Grant; except in the offices; except sometimes with Catlin and Florian, out to lunch or an early dinner. He kept it that way.

But if something had happened, Ari would not want to argue details over the phone; if something had happened with Grant—

He keyed off the machine, and got up and went, gathering up his jacket, telling Em to shut down and go home, everything was fine.

He headed over to the wing where Ari's apartment was, showed his card to Security at the doors and got a pass-through without question.

Dammit, he thought, his heart pounding, it had better be a good reason, it had better be business—

It had better *not* be because Grant was momentarily not in the picture.

* * *

"Come in," Florian said, at the door. "Sera is waiting for you."

"What does she want?" he asked, not committing himself. "Florian, —is this a good idea?"

"Yes, ser," Florian said without hesitation.

He walked in then, sweating, not only from the trip over. The room, the travertine floors, the couch—was a vivid flash of then and now. "Is it Grant?"

"Your jacket, ser? Sera urgently needs to talk with you."

"About what? —What's happened?"

"Your jacket, ser?"

He pulled the jacket off, jerked a resistant sleeve free, handed it to Florian as Ari arrived in the living room from the right-hand hall.

"What in hell's going on?" he asked.

She gestured toward the sunken living room, the couch; and came down the steps to take a seat there.

He came and sat down at the opposing corner. Not the private living room: thank God. He did not think he could have held together.

"Justin," she said, "thank you for coming. I know—I know how you feel about this place. But it's the only place—the only one I'm absolutely sure there's no monitoring but mine. I want you to tell me the truth, now, the absolute truth: Grant's safety depends on this. Is your father working with the Paxers?"

"My— God. No. No. —How in hell could he?"

"Let me tell you: I've got a report on my desk that says there are leaks out of Planys. That your father—has been talking with a suspect. Security is watching Grant very carefully. They fully expect Jordan to attempt an intervention with him—"

"He wouldn't! Not—not on something like that. He wouldn't do that to Grant."

"Your father could manage something like that without tape, without anything but a keyword, with someone of Grant's ability. I know what Grant's memory is like."

"He *won't* do it. It's a damned set-up."

"It may be," she said quietly. "That's why I wanted to talk

to you, fast, before Security has a chance, because I'll do this: I'll look for all the truth. I'm the one it's against. And I've been aware of this—for a while; from long before Grant got that pass. Grant's gone into the middle of a Security operation that I don't want to agree with. I don't want to think that Grant could work against me, or that you could, but I have to protect myself—which is why I took this chance.''

"I don't understand.'' He felt the old panic—too experienced to give way to it. Keep the opposition calm, keep the voices down, go along with things. He did not think Ari was at the head of whatever was going on, not with what he knew of where authority was in the House. "Ari, tell me what's going on.''

"People who protect me . . . don't want me near you. That's why I waited and let Grant go—because I knew—I know very well that it's a set-up against you, which is why I called you to come here.''

"Why is that? What do you want?''

"Because I have to know. That's first. And I know how you hate this place, but it's the only place, the only place I can trust.'' She reached into her left-hand pocket, and pulled out a little vial. Amber glass. "This is kat. It's a deep dose. You can help me or you can leave now. But this is the chance I have. You go in the tape lab and take this, and let me get you on tape—I promise, I *promise*, Justin, no lousy tricks. Just the truth on tape, for me to use. This is what I need. This is the kind of documentation I can use with the Bureau, if I have to go that far. This is the chance I have to believe you.''

He flashed badly, totally disoriented, unable to think for a few breaths. Then he reached out for the vial and she gave it to him.

Because there was no choice. Not a thing he could do. He only thought—*God, I don't know if I can do this. I don't know if I can stay sane*.

"Where?'' he said.

"Florian,'' she said; and he got up shakily and went after Florian as Florian indicated the hallway to the right.

An open door on the right again was the tape library, with a couch with all the built-ins for deep-study. He walked in and sat down there, set the vial down on the couch beside him and pulled off his sweater, feeling light-headed. "I want Ari here," he said, "I want to talk to her."

"Yes, ser," Florian said. "There's no lead, ser, it's just a patch, let me help you."

"I want to talk to Ari."

"I'm here," she said at the door. "I'm right here."

"Pay attention," he said shortly. And uncapped the vial and took his pill, while the cardiac monitor flashed red with alarms. He looked at the flashes and concentrated, willing himself calmer. "Your patient tends to panic, sera, I hope to hell you remember that."

"I'll remember," Ari said, very quietly.

He worked with the monitor, staring at that, concentrating only on the rate of the flashes. A thought about his father leaked through, about Grant, a single second, and the light flickered rapidly; slow, he thought, that was all, while the numbness started and panic tried to assert itself. He felt a touch on his shoulder, heard Florian urging him: "Lie down, ser, please, just lean back. I've got you."

He blinked, thinking for a moment of the boy-Florian, spinning through the years to Florian grown strong enough to handle his weight, Florian bending over him—

"Be calm, ser," his gentle voice said. "Be calm. Are you comfortable?"

He felt an underlying panic, very diffuse. He felt the numbness growing, and his vision started going out. His heart began to speed, frighteningly, runaway.

"Calm," Ari said, a voice that jolted through his panic, absolute. "Steady down. It's all right. Everything's all right. Hear me?"

iii

"Has your father ever worked with these people?" Ari asked, sitting by the side of the couch, holding Justin's limp hand.

"No," he said. Which meant, of course, to the limit of Justin's knowledge. No, no, and no. She saw the cardiac monitor flash with a very strong rise in heart rate.

"Conspired with anyone against Reseune Administration?"

"No."

"Have you?"

"No."

Not conspiring with anyone. Against Reseune. Against Ariane Emory.

Justin, at least, was not aware of any plot.

"Don't you ever get frustrated with Security?"

"Yes."

"Do you think things will ever change?"

"I—hope."

"What do you hope?"

"Keep quiet. Live quiet. People believe me. Then things change."

"Are you afraid?"

"Always."

"Of what?"

"Mistakes. Enemies."

He hoped if he could work with her—it would prove something about himself and his father, in a calmer world—

He was afraid for Grant more than Jordan. Jordan had his Special's status to protect him. Grant—if they interrogated him—would be subject to things they might try to impose on him, ideas and attitudes they might try to shape—Grant would resist it. Grant would throw himself into null and stay there: he had before. But if they kept working at him—

If *he* were arrested, here, in Reseune, if Reseune Administration was determined to make a case, then they could do that. He thought that could be the case—that politics always mattered more than truth. And more than a Warrick life—always.

"Jordan's not a killer," Justin said. "He's not like that. Whatever happened was an accident. He made his mistake in trying to cover it, that's what I know happened."

"How do you know it?"

"I know my father."

"Even after twenty years?"

"Yes."

He was close to the upturn, when the drug would fade. And she was all but hoarse from questions and from strain.

She thought: *I almost know enough to take on what Ari did. Almost. But he's not the boy she worked with.*

I could Work him to make him want me. So easily. So easily.

She remembered the tape, remembered it with sexual flashes that troubled her.

And thought, thinking of the possible intersections with so many, many knot-ups in his sets: *Damn, no.* Damn, *damn,* Ari, not so fast, not so reckless.

I could make him happy. I could take all of that away—

Politics is real and everything else takes second place, he knows that—*There's that on top of everything that's wrong in him.*

I could make him worry less. I can make him trust me more.

Is even that—fair? Or safe—in the world the way it is, or inside Reseune?

She got up, cut the recorder off and sat down on the edge of the couch beside him. She touched his face very gently, saw the monitor blips increase. "Hush, it's all right, it's all right—" she said, until she could get the monitor blips down again.

"Justin," she said when it was running even, "I believe you. You'd never hurt me. You'd never let me be hurt. I know all those things. I don't think they're going to make a move on Grant—not now that I've got you on record. I can tell my uncle what I have, and at the same time I'll tell him Grant's in my wing, and he'd better not move against him. That's what I'm prepared to do, because I believe you. Do you understand me?"

"Yes." A little flutter from the monitor.

"Don't be anxious about this place. This is my home. My predecessor isn't here anymore. That's all gone. That's all gone. You're safe here. I want you to remember these things. I can't get what I'd like out of hospital, without them knowing I'm doing this—but I want you to do the deep-fix for me, the way Grant could do it. Can you do that? Bear down hard, feel good, and remember this."

"Yes. . . ."

"I want you to think: I'm going to believe this forever. I promise you, if you trust me, if you come to me and if Grant comes to me when you need help, I'll do the best I can. You can rest now. You'll wake up feeling fine, and you'll be all right. Do you hear me?"

"Yes."

No flutter now, just a strong, steady beat. She got up, signaled Florian and Catlin to be very quiet, patted Justin gently on the shoulder. You stay with him, she signaled Florian.

And to Catlin, in the hall, she said: "What's the news?"

"Nothing more than we had," Catlin said.

"Stand by in case Florian needs you." She went to her own office and phoned Denys directly.

"Seely," she said, "I need Denys, right now." And when Denys came on: "Uncle Denys, how are you?"

"I'm quite well, Ari, how are you?"

"I wanted to tell you something. I've gotten very nervous about the situation, you know, with Grant being out and all, and Grant *is* vulnerable, so I asked Justin to talk with me about it—"

"Ari, this involves exterior Security. I strongly suggest you let this alone."

"I've done it already. I want an order, uncle Denys, for Grant to be immune to Security, I don't care if something should go on at Planys with Jordan, I have an agreement with Justin—"

"I'm sorry, Ari, this isn't at all wise. You don't *tie down your Security people. You have no business making promises to Justin, especially to Justin. I've talked to you about this."*

"This is the agreement, uncle Denys. Justin's agreed to take a probe with *my* security."

"Ari, you're interfering in a matter you have no expertise in whatsoever, that involves your safety. I won't have that."

"Uncle Denys, I've been thinking a lot. It runs like this: I'm getting a lot more grown-up. People couldn't ever make a campaign out of killing a cute kid. Paxers and all these groups haven't come out into the open all at once just by coincidence. They see me getting older, they know that I'm real, they know I'm going to be a lot of trouble to them someday, and they're going to throw everything they've got at me in the next few years. But you know what occurs to me, uncle Denys? That could be true on this staff too, inside Reseune. And I'm not going to have my staff tampered with by anybody except me."

"Ari, that's halfway prudent, but you're meddling with a kind of situation you're not equipped to deal with."

"I perfectly well am, uncle Denys. I'm not going to be reasonable on this. I want Grant back without any problems. Florian's going to meet the plane and bring him up here, and I'm going to talk to him, myself, *with* trank. If I find out anyone else has, I'm going to be real upset. I don't care if it's Jordan, or if it's Reseune Security, either one, I'm going to be real upset."

"*Ari, —*"

"I'm just telling you, uncle Denys. I know you don't like it. And I *don't* want to fight with you. Look at it from my point of view. You're getting up there in years, you could have a stroke or something—where would that leave me, if I don't have control of my own wing? I'd *have* to trust a lot of people all of a sudden, without knowing what's going on. And I don't ever want to be in that situation, uncle Denys."

"*We've got to talk about this.*"

"We can. Only I want your promise that you're not going to let Security touch Grant even if you think Jordan did something to him: I'll tell you how Justin feels about it—if Jordan did something like that, Justin would be real mad. And that would mean Justin would be on my side about it. But if *you* did, then Justin would be mad at me. There's an old proverb about muddying up the water, do you know it? I'm getting old enough I don't want other people's notions of what's good for me muddying up the waters I have to swim in for the rest of my life, uncle Denys. That's exactly what it comes down to."

"*I appreciate your feelings, Ari, but you'd better gather your data before you interfere with an operation, not after.*"

"We can talk about this as much as you like and you give me advice I know is going to be worth listening to. But then's then. Now is, I'm not going to have them messed with by anybody. They're in my wing and I've made promises I'm going to keep. If you do anything else, you cut me down with my own staff, and I'm not going to have that, uncle Denys. That's a promise."

There was a long silence on the other end. "*Have you discussed with Justin the chance that Grant might have been tampered with?*"

"*He's* afraid of it. He's the one brought it up with me. He's willing to trust *me* in this, uncle Denys, not Reseune Security,

strange as that may seem—but then, by what he tells me
Reseune Security isn't very polite. I've *got* his deposition that
Grant went out of here clean, uncle Denys. I've got it under
deep probe, and I'm quite sure of it. So we'll find out when
Grant gets back, won't we? I'll be happy to lend you a tran-
script of the interview.''

Another long silence. *"That's very kind of you. Dammit,
Ari, Justin's got medical cautions, he's got major problems, I
don't care if he thought this would be better, you're a
seventeen-year-old kid—"*

"Eighteen in two months, which is going on twenty in the
way Base One reckons. And damned good, uncle, *damned*
good . . . or what's all your work good for, you want to answer me that one, uncle Denys? I've been running interventions on Florian and Catlin for more than five years, so I'm not
really likely to slip up, am I?''

*"I'm telling you, Ari, dammit, you've seen the tape Ari
made, you know you're dealing with a man with a damn tenu-
ous hold on sanity where you're concerned, and you want to
go running interventions on him? We're talking about a thirty-
six-year-old man who's lived half his life with a problem, and
you want to meddle with it, alone, without any protection for
yourself or him if he has a heart attack or slides over the mental edge. You want to know what you're meddling with, young
sera, you could be working in your office, minding your own
business someday, and have that young man come through the
door with a knife, that's what you're playing with. We're dealing with a grown man a long time and a whole lot of business
past that incident when he was your age—he's changed, what
Ari planted in him has had time to mutate unwatched, he won't
go in for therapy, and like a fool, because I agreed with him,
he had to become self-guiding, I let him decline therapy. Now
it's turned out to be a major mistake. I had no idea my niece
was going to let her glands interfere with her common sense,
my dear, I certainly had no idea she was going to take this
unstable young man to her bosom and make an adolescent fool
of herself, no indeed, I didn't. And, my God! the kind of pressure you can put on this young man with your well-intentioned
meddling— Don't you understand, child, Reseune has never
intended any harm to Justin Warrick? We know his value,*

we've worked with him, we've done the best we could to secure his future and to prevent him from precisely the kind of blow-up you're courting with your meddling. And whose fault will it be then?''

"All that's very fine, uncle Denys, but I know what I'm doing, and my reasons stand."

A long silence.

"We'll talk about this," Denys said then.

"Yes. We will. But in the meantime you call Planys and call Security there and tell them be damned careful they don't lay a hand on Grant."

"All right, Ari. You get your way on this. We'll talk about it. But I don't just get that transcript. I get the tape of the session. You know what a transcript is worth. If you want my support in this let's try a little cooperation, shall we?''

"That's all I want, uncle Denys. You're still a dear."

"Ari, dammit, we're not talking about a little thing here."

"My birthday's coming up, uncle Denys. You know I'd like a party this year. I really would."

"I don't think this is the time to discuss it."

"Lunch, the 18th?"

Back, then, to Base One to be sure that call went the way uncle Denys said.

Be careful, Ari senior had said, using the information in the expanded base, because it was so easy to slip up and reveal what one should not have known—like exactly what Security was doing half a world away.

So one lied. One tried to get very good at it.

She went back to the library, because Catlin reported that Justin was coming out of it, quietly, still a little fuzzed—which was not a bad time to explain something.

So she sat down on the couch where Justin lay drowsing with the lights dimmed, with a light blanket over him and Florian keeping watch near him.

"How are you?" she asked.

"Not uncomfortable," he said, and a little line appeared between his brows as he tried to move. He gave that up. "I'm a bit gone yet. Let me rest. Don't talk to me."

On the defensive. Not the time with him, then. She laid her

hand on his shoulder. "You can try to wake up a bit," she said. That was an intervention too, but a benign one. "Everything's fine. I knew you were all right. And I've talked to uncle Denys and told him keep hands off Grant, so Grant's going to be safe, but I do need to talk to you. Meanwhile you're going to stay in the guest room tonight. I don't think you ought to go back to your apartment till you're really awake."

"I can leave," he said.

"Of course you can, when you're able to argue, but not tonight. If you like, I'll have Florian guard your door all night, so it'll be very proper. It's completely in the other wing from my room. All right? As soon as you can walk all right, Florian will put you to bed."

"Home," he said.

"Sorry," she said. "I need to talk to you in the morning. You shouldn't leave before then. Go to sleep now."

That was, in his state, a very strong suggestion. His eyelids drifted lower, jerked, lowered completely.

"Guest bedroom," she told Florian. "Soon as he can. I do want you to stay with him, just to be sure he's safe."

---

iv

It was a strange bed, a moment of panic. Justin turned his head and saw Florian lying on his stomach on the second bed, fully dressed, boyish face innocent in the glow from the single wall-light. Eyes open.

He thought that he remembered walking to this room, that it was down a hallway he could remember, but he was still disoriented and he still felt a touch of panic at the remembrance of the drugs. He thought that he ought to be distraught to be where he was, flat-tranked as he was. He lay half-asleep, thinking that as the numbness let up he would suffer reactions. He was still dressed, except his sweater and his shoes. Someone had put a blanket over him, put a pillow under his head. It was, thank God, not Ari's bedroom.

"You're awake, ser?"

"Yes," he said, and Florian gathered himself up to sit on the edge of the other bed.

"Minder," Florian said aloud, "wake Ari. Tell her Justin is awake."

Justin shoved himself up on his hands, caught his balance, rubbed at his stubbled face.

"What time—?"

"Time?" Florian asked the Minder.

"0436," it said.

"We should start breakfast," Florian said. "It's near enough to the time sera usually gets up. There's a guest kit in the bath, ser. A robe if you like, but sera will probably dress. Will you be all right while I check on my partner?"

"Sera is almost ready," Catlin said, and poured him coffee, Catlin—whose blonde hair was for once unbraided, a pale rippled sheet past black-uniformed shoulders. "Cream, ser?"

"No," he said, "thank you."

Kids, he thought. The whole situation should be funny as hell, himself—at his age—virtually kidnapped, tripped, and finally solicitously fed breakfast by a pack of damned kids . . .

Not feeling too badly, he thought. Not as rough as one of Giraud's trips, in any sense. But he was wrung out, his lungs felt too open, and his limbs felt watery and altogether undependable.

Which they would, considering what a physiological shock that much cataphoric was; which was the reason for the mineral and vitamin pill Catlin put on a dish and gave to him, and which he took with his coffee without arguing.

It was a cure for the post-kat shakes, at least.

Ari arrived, in a simple blue sweater and blue pants, her black hair loose as she almost never wore it nowadays. Like Ari-the-child. Ari pulled back the chair at his right and sat down. "Good morning. —Thanks, Catlin." As Catlin poured coffee and added cream. And to him: "How are you feeling? Are you all right?"

"You said you had something important to say," Justin said.

"About Grant," Ari said, straightway. Then: "—We can make anything you want for breakfast."

"No. Thanks. Dammit, Ari, let's not do games, shall we?"

"I'm not. I just want to make sure you get something to eat. Have some toast at least. There's real honey."

He reached for it, smothering temper, patiently buttered it and put on a bit of the honey. An entire apiary set-up over in Moreyville, along with several other burgeoning commercializations. Fish. Exotics. Frogs. Moreyville was talking about expanding upriver, blasting out space on the Volga and creating new flats for agricultural use.

"This is the thing," Ari said, "I talked to uncle Denys last night and Denys pulled Security away from Grant. We had a bit of a fight about it. But I told him I couldn't trust having people in my wing gone over by people I don't know. It came down to that. So this is the deal we made. I run my own Security checks, and if I'm satisfied, that's all that gets done. What you have to do is agree that if there is a question, —I do an interview and get it settled."

He stared at the piece of toast in his hand, without appetite. "Meaning you run another probe."

"Justin, I hope there won't be any more questions. But this Pax thing is really dangerous. It's going to get worse—because they're seeing I'm serious. There aren't very many people anywhere I can trust. There aren't very many people anywhere you can trust either, because when politics gets thick as it's going to get—you know better than I do how innocent people get hurt. You remember you asked me to do something for your father. Well, I have: I probably stopped him from being arrested last night, at least on suspicion, and I know I stopped Grant from getting probed by Security. Probably your father won't even know how close it was, and if you'll take my advice, please don't tell him. Grant's going to get home all right. Your father's safe. And you're not any worse off this morning than yesterday, are you?"

"I don't know." *Shaken up, dammit, which I wasn't, yesterday. I don't know, I don't know, I don't know, and, God, where's a choice?*

"You don't want to deal with Security," Ari said. "Giraud doesn't like you, Justin, he really doesn't like you. I don't need professional psych to pick that up. I want you to stay; and that means everybody in the universe will know you could be a pressure point against me—they could put pressure on you, or

Grant, or Jordan. Giraud certainly is going to put the pressure on and try to prove something against you or your father—if we don't have contrary evidence that you're working with me. That's what I need. I need it from you and I need it from Grant, and if you do that, then you'll be my friend and you'll have Security working to protect you. If you don't—I've got to put you and Grant out—outside, where you *can't* be trusted, because every enemy I've got will think of you and Grant and Jordan just as levers to be used. That's the way it is. And I think you know that. That's why you told me last night you hoped if you stayed close to me—you could make things better. You said that. Do you remember?"

"I don't remember. But I would have said that."

"I want you to be in my wing, I want you to work with me—but being on the inside of my Security means if I have the least idea something could be wrong, —I have to ask questions. That's the way it is."

"Not much choice, is there?" He took a bite of the toast, swallowed, found the honey friendlier to his stomach than he had thought it would be. "You expect me to order Grant to take a probe from a seventeen-year-old kid?"

"I don't want him to be upset. I wish you'd at least explain to him."

"Dammit, I —"

"He's safe, isn't he? When you see him off the plane, you'll know I kept my promise; and you can tell him why I'm doing it. Then you'll both be safe from anybody else. You won't have to worry about people making mistakes anymore, or blaming you for things. And I'm not a kid, Justin. I'm not. I know what I'm doing. I just don't have much real power yet. That's why I can't reach out of my wing to protect my friends, that's why I'm doing such a damn stupid thing as bringing you on the inside under *my* Security wall—you and a few others of my friends."

"Us. Grant and me. *Sure*, Ari. Sure, you are. Let's have the truth for a minute. Are you working some maneuver around your uncles—or did Giraud suggest this?"

"No. I trust you."

"Then you're damn stupid. Which I don't think you are."

"You figure it. You and Grant are the only adult help I can

get that, first, I have to have, because I need you; second, that I can constantly check on, because there's nobody but you who needs something I can do, that only I'm willing to do. Sure I can hire help. So can my opposition.''

"So can your opposition—threaten my father.''

"Not—past my net. You're part of it. You'll tell me if you think he's threatened. And you figure it: are you safer on your own? Is Grant? Not at all. Besides which—if your safety is linked to mine—it's not really likely your father would make a real move against Reseune, is it?''

He stared at her, shocked; and finally shrugged and took another bite of toast and washed it down.

"You know, I tried this same move with your predecessor when I was seventeen,'' he said. "Blackmail. You know what it did for me.''

"Not blackmail. I'm just saying what is. I'm saying if you go out that door and I put you out of my wing—''

"I get it from Giraud faster than I can turn around, I get it and Grant gets it, every time he finds an excuse. That's real clear. Thanks.''

"Justin—Giraud might *make up* a case. I hate to say that. There's a lot good about Giraud. But he's capable of things like that. And he's dying. Don't tell that. I'm not supposed to know. But it's changed a lot of his motives. He and Jordan never got along—not personally, not professionally, not at all: they had a terrible fight when Jordan was working with Ari— really, terribly bitter. He disagrees with what he sees as a whole Warrick attitude—an influence toward a whole slant of procedure, a kind of interventionist way of proceeding that in his mind permeated Education and got out into the tapes through what he called 'Warrick's influence.' Which isn't so. Ari knew what she was doing. She knew absolutely what she was doing, and what Giraud hates so much was really Ari's— but you can't make him understand that. In Giraud's mind Jordan was the source of that whole movement—in fact, I think in Jordan's own mind Jordan was the source of the whole movement—which was never true. But Giraud won't believe it. He *wants* to settle the Centrists before he dies, because Denys is getting on in years too, and Giraud foresees a time when his generation will be gone and I'll still be vulnerable.

He sees your father as a pawn the Centrists could use. He sees you as a reservoir of Warrick influence in Reseune, me as a kid thinking with her glands, and he's desperate to get you away from me. So I've not only got to convince myself you're clean-clearance, I've got to convince uncle Denys *and* Giraud I'm absolutely sure what I'm doing. I can handle them, however crazy I make it sound . . . because *I'm* going to tell them I've got Ari's notes on your case.''

He swallowed hard.

''Have you?''

''That's what I'm going to tell them.''

''I heard what you're going to tell them! I also know you just evaded me. You do have them, don't you?''

''You also know that whatever I say occasionally about what I'd *like* to be the truth, I do lie sometimes. Yanni says there are professional lies and they're all right. They're what you do for good reasons.''

''Dammit—''

''I'm lying to protect you.''

''To whom? You have *her* kinds of twists, young sera. I hope to hell it doesn't extend deeper.''

''I'm your friend. I wish I were more than that. But I'm not. Trust me in this. If you can't—the way you say—who can you? I've kept you out of Detention. And I'll give you the session tape, I always will. With Grant too. I don't ever want you to doubt each other.''

''Dammit, Ari.''

''Let's be honest. That's an issue, and I'm disposing of it. Let's try another. You think I'll intervene with you—the way I'm going to tell Denys. You know—let's be plain about it—you're safer with me running unsupervised than with Giraud with all the safeguards there are. You're worried about trusting yourself and Grant to a kid. But I'm Ari's student. Directly. And Yanni's. I'm not certified . . . not just because I've never bothered to be. There are a lot of things I can do that I don't want on Bureau records yet. I confess to some very immature thoughts. Some very selfish thoughts. But I didn't do it. You woke up down the hall, didn't you?''

He felt his face go red. And expected a flash, in this place, under strained circumstances, but it was faint and almost without charge, just the older face, Ari getting ready for work, matter-of-factly, leaving him there with the kind of damage he had taken. . . .

He felt resentment, that was all . . . resentment much more than shame.

"You *did* something," he said to the seventeen-year-old. *His* seventeen-year-old.

"I told you calm down about this place," she said. "I figured it would bother you. I didn't think that was unethical."

"Ethics had nothing to do with it, sera. No more than with her."

She looked a little shocked, a little hurt. And he wished to hell he had kept *that* behind his teeth.

"Sorry," he said. "I didn't mean that. But, dammit to hell, Ari! If you've got to take these trips, stay off the peripheries with me!"

"It's embarrassing for you," she said, "because I'm so young, —isn't it?"

He thought about that. Tried to calm down. Temper. Not fright. And what she had said. "Yes, it's embarrassing."

"For me, too. Because you're so much older. I feel like you're going to critique everything I do, all the time. It makes me nervous, isn't that funny?"

"That's not the word I'd pick for it."

"I *will* listen to you."

"Come on, Ari, let's not do games, didn't I say? Don't play little-girl with me. You've stopped listening to everyone."

"I still listen to my friends. I'm not my predecessor. You'll remember me saying that too, —don't you?"

Another jolt at nerves. "I think that's only a question of semantics."

She reacted with a little flicker of the eyes, and a laugh. "Point. But there, you're pretty quick this morning. Aren't you?"

It was true. That self-analysis was what kept him from total panic. "You have a lighter touch than Giraud," he said. "I give you that, young sera." *Young sera* annoyed her. He knew it did. He saw the little reaction on that too. A man didn't go to bed with *young sera*. And she was being honest. He saw the little frown he expected, that, by all that was accurate about flux, said that she was probably being straightforward this morning—or the reactions would have showed. "But I want the tape of what you did. And I want to talk to Grant."

——————————————— V ———————————————

It was riding with Amy that afternoon—herself on the Filly, Amy on the horse they called Bayard—Amy had found that in a story, so the third filly had a name, unlike goats and pigs who were usually just numbers, except a few who were exceptional.

Filly's just the Filly, Ari had said. And the Mare's Daughter they called the Daughter, or Filly Two, and Filly Two was Florian's even if he couldn't own her: no CIT was ever to ride her. But the third was Bayard, and that was Amy Carnath's horse; and the fourth and fifth and sixth belonged to Maddy and Sam and 'Stasi, what time they were not doing little runs into the fields, doing work, delivering items out where trucks would crush the plants and a human walking was too slow.

There was going to be a stable and an arena just for the horses someday, Ari had decided. Space in the safe zones was always at a premium and uncle Denys called it extravagant and refused to allow it.

But *she* had notions of exporting to Novgorod, animals just to look at and watch for a few years, but someday to sell use of, the way the skill tapes of riding and of handling animals sold as fast as they could turn them out—to people who wanted to know what pigs and goats and horses were like and how they moved, and what riding a horse felt like. Spacers bought those skill tapes, marketed as entertainment Sensatape. Stationers did. People from one end of space to the other knew how to ride, who had never laid eye or hand on a horse.

That more than paid for the stable and the arena, she had argued; *and* the earth-moving and the widening of Reseune's flat-space: the horses did not need the depth of soil that agriculture did, and the manure meant good ground.

They eat their weight in gold, Denys had objected, with no, no, and no.

Grain is a renewable resource, she had said, nastily. It likes manure.

No, said Denys. We're not undertaking any expansions; we're not making any headlines with any extravagance in this political atmosphere; it's not *prudent*, Ari.

Someday, she had said, defeated.

Meanwhile the horses were theirs, unique, and did their small amount of work.

While out in the riding pen was the best place in Reseune besides her apartment to go to have a talk without worrying about security; and it had its own benefits, when it came to being casual and getting Amy Carnath to relax and talk about really sensitive things.

Because Amy was not happy lately. Sam had taken up with Maria Cortez-Campbell, who was a nice girl; Stef was back with Yvgenia; and Amy—rode a lot and spent a lot of time studying and tending the export business, which had sort of drawn her into a full sub-manager rating in the whole huge Reseune Exports division and a provisional project supervisor's rating in the Genetics Research division.

Amy was always the brightest. Amy was getting a figure, finally, at seventeen, at least something of a figure. She was getting pretty in a kind of long-boned way, not because she *was* pretty, but because she was just interesting-looking, and might get more so.

And Amy was too damned smart to be happy, because there just happened to be a shortage of equally smart boys in her generation. Tommy was the only one who came close, and Tommy was Amy's cousin, not interested in the same field, and mostly interested in Maddy Strassen anyway. *That* pair was getting halfway serious, on both sides.

"How are things?" she asked Amy when they were out and away from everyone, under a tranquil sky. And prepared herself for a long story.

"All right," Amy said, and sighed. That was all.

Not like Amy at all. Usually it was *damn Stef Dietrich*, and a long list of grievances.

She didn't know this Amy. Ari looked at her across the moving gap between the horses, and said: "It doesn't sound all right."

"Just the same old stuff," Amy said. "Stef. Mama. That's the condensed report."

"You'll be legal this month. You can do anything you damn please. And you've got a slot in my wing, I always told you that."

"I can't *do* any damn thing," Amy said. "Justin—he's *real*. I've got a pack of stuff in Exports. Merchandising stuff is all I do. That's all I use my psych for. That's not your kind of business. I don't know what you'd want me for."

"You've got a clean Security clearance, cleanest of all my friends. You're good at business. You'd be a good Super, you'd be good at most anything you wanted to take on, that's your trouble. You get small-focused into doing it instead of learning it; and I want you learning for a while. Remember when I snagged you into the tunnels and we started off the whole gang? That's why I asked you out here before I talked to anybody. You were always first."

"What are you talking about?" Amy suddenly looked scared. "First at what?"

"That this time it's for real. That this time I'm not talking about kid pranks, this time I'm talking about getting a position in the House. Things are shifting, they're shifting real fast. So I'm starting with you, the same way I did back then. Will you work for me, Amy?"

"Doing what?"

"Genetics. Whatever project you want to come up with for a cover. A real one. A put-together till you can make up your mind. I don't care. You go on salary, you get your share of your own profits—all that."

Amy's eyes were very large.

"I want you and Maddy in two different divisions," Ari said, "because I'm not going to put you two one over the other. That'd never work. But between you and me, you're smarter than she is, you're steadier, and you're the one I'd trust with the bad stuff. And there could be. Giraud is on the end of his rejuv. That's secret. A very few people know, but probably more and more will guess. *When* he dies, that's an election in Science. That's also about the time the Paxers and the rest of the people who want me dead—for real, Amy."

"I know it's real."

"You know why they made me and how they taught me, and you know what I am. And you know my predecessor had enemies who wanted her dead, and one who killed her. The closer I get to what she was, the more scared people get— because I'm kind of spooky, Amy, I'm real spooky to a lot of people who weren't half as afraid of my predecessor— Are you scared of me? Tell me the truth, Amy."

"Not—*scared* of you. Not really. *Spooky* is a good word for it. Because you're not—not the age you are; and you *are*, with us. Maddy and I have talked about it, sometimes. How we— sometimes just want to do something stupid, just for relief sometimes. Like sometimes—" Amy rode in silence a moment, patting Bayard's shoulder. "My mama gets so mad at me because I do spooky things, like she thinks I'm a kid and she worries about me, and she treats me like a kid. One time she yelled at me: Amy, I don't care what Ari Emory does or what Ari Emory says, you're my daughter—don't you look at me like that and don't you tell me how to bring you up. And she slapped me in the face. And I just stood there. I—didn't know what to do. I couldn't hit her. I couldn't run away crying or throw things. I just—stood there. So she cried. And then I cried, but not because she hit me, —just because I knew I wasn't what she wanted me to be." Amy looked up at the sky. There was a glitter of tears in the sunlight. "So, well, mama's got the notion I'm going to leave when I can, and she's sorry. We had a talk about it, finally. She's the one who's scared of you. She doesn't understand me and she thinks you're all to blame for me not having a childhood. That's what she says. You never got a chance to be a child. I don't know, I thought I had a childhood. We had a hell of a good time. Stuff mama doesn't know. But I don't like it anymore. I'm tired of *little* games, Ari, you know what I mean. I'm tired of Stef Dietrich, I'm tired of fighting with mama, I'm tired of going to classes and playing guessing-games with Windy Peterson on his damn trick questions and eetee rules and catch-you's. I think Maddy's about the same."

"Can you work with Sam?"

"Hell, he's got that airbrain of his—that's not nice to say, is it? I can't see what he sees in her."

"*Don't* mess him up, Amy."

"I won't. I'm through with all of it. You know what I want? I want exactly what you've got with Florian. No fuss. No petty spats. No jealousy. Moment I can afford it—"

"You want to take me up on the offer, I'll reckon you'd be a lot more efficient with an assistant. *My* feeling is you'd be frustrated as hell with anything but an Alpha and there's probably only a handful of those still unContracted. I'll give you a printout of all the numbers there are. Green Barracks is the most likely source. Which means somebody more like Catlin, but still, —you could fix that."

Amy just stared. And blushed a little.

"Someday," Ari said, "you'll be a wing Super yourself. That's what I intend. Someday I'll run Reseune, and we're not playing just-suppose now, we're dealing with long-term. I want you to have the kind of support you're going to need; I want you to have somebody capable of protecting you *and* of handling jobs you're too busy to do, and in your case, male and smart are two real necessities. Another female—you'd kill. Do I psych you right?"

Amy laughed suddenly, and colored a little. "I don't know. —I need time to think about this."

"Sure. You've got five minutes."

"No fair, Ari."

"Same thing as under the stairs. Same thing as then. I need my friends now, I need you first. And there's a real danger—if I'm a target, you could be too."

Amy bit her lip. "I don't mind that. I really don't. I mind the row it's going to make with mama. You know what I think? She wants to hang onto me. She sees you as more of an influence than she is, and she always planned me to go into Ed psych, never mind I'm better at other things."

"Hell, look at me. You think a PR doesn't have to figure out who's who?"

"I know that. But your—predecessor—isn't around to give you looks across the breakfast table."

"Whose life are you going to live? Yours or hers?"

Amy nodded finally. "Or mine or yours? I'm *mine*, Ari. I don't want you supporting me. If it's a real job, if it's *my money*, I'm fine."

"Deal."

"Deal," Amy said.

"So now we go get Maddy. And then we go for Sam. And Tommy."

" 'Stasi's all right," Amy said. "*I* don't mind her. But Stef Dietrich can go walk, for what I think."

"Stef's not in my crew," Ari said. "No hard feelings, but he's a troublemaker, and I don't need him." She stretched in the stirrups and settled again and said: "We get Maddy. Sam and Tommy. 'Stasi, I've got no objection to. But everybody comes in in just the same order they always did. Seniority. Something like that. I'll tell you: I've got one major problem, one major vulnerability, and one major help—and they're all Justin Warrick. He'll help us. But there's a lot coming at him. And he and Grant are the only ones *with* us who aren't *us*, you know what I mean."

"He's smart enough to be trouble," Amy said.

"I've thought about that. My uncles don't want him near me. The Warrick influence, they call it. They say he's poison. I know other things. I can tell you stuff, Amy, if you're in with me."

"I am."

"Denys is interested in Ari's notes—Ari's *notes* and the psychogenesis project—but I've held back on him. I put all the stuff in three blocs: one, I don't talk about. And the general notes—that's the published stuff, and the stuff that's going to be published. The Rubin project stuff: that's mostly secret, but that whole security wall is a farce—I'm public, and anybody who understands endocrine theory can figure a lot of what happened to me— You know one of the things they really want to keep secret? *Justin Warrick.* Because he's not Jordan, but he's sure not a Bok clone either, and he could become a voice inside Reseune—if they ever let him have a forum; because he's smart, he understands what I am, and he's a Special in everything but title, one of Ari's students—that's something they don't publicize either—another Special, PR of a Special, a lot more important than Rubin, no matter what they've sold the Defense department. Ari worked him like everything—but they don't tell Defense that either, because they're scared as hell of him and his influence. I think Denys is sure Ari worked with him. Denys is the one who's kept him from getting treatment—for things that really bother him, things Ari did with him—and her murder really messed him up, terribly, not just that his father did it, but that he needed her—so much.''

''What did she do?''

''A real major intervention. Right before she was murdered. Something she never finished, something that pretty well set the pattern of Justin's life. Beyond that—it's personal to him, and I won't say. But it was rough.''

''Like the stuff they did to you?''

She thought about that a moment. ''A lot, yes. A lot. With some differences. *Jordan* wanted him to be like Jordan. He wouldn't have been. Ari knew what she wanted out of that geneset and she got it. That's the real story. She manipulated CIT deep-sets . . . with real accuracy.''

Amy gave her a look.

''Psychogenesis can go two ways,'' Ari said, ''just like any other kind of cloning. Either an identical—or a designer job. I'm as close an identical as you're likely to get. I told Justin I wasn't my predecessor and he said that was only a game of semantics. And I think he's right about that. There were real differences: my maman; Ollie; Denys—he wasn't Geoffrey Carnath, not by half, thank God. A lot of different things happened. But I had Florian and Catlin; I had no doubt the theories I was handed—worked. I could feel it work. I know what put me ahead of Ari. I had to work. I was scared. I couldn't just sink into out-there and survive on people taking care of me. I learned to focus-down and to work real-time, and to think out-there too. That's the real lesson. Bok's clone never came in out of the dark, never owned anything, never *was* anything. You know what *I'd* have answered to the kind of questions that poor woman got? Go to hell! And if piano-playing was what I did, damn, I'd do it! And maybe I'd spit in the eye of math teachers who didn't teach me the kind of things Bok must have learned—like *being* in space, dammit! Like living like a spacer! Like knowing math is life and death! —Bok's clone got dry theory. She was creative, and they gave her dry dust. They cushioned her from everything. And *they* couldn't understand her music. She was a lousy pianist. She couldn't transcribe worth shit. But I wonder what kind of music she heard in her head, and why she spent more and more time there? I'm not sure she *did* fail. Maybe the damn geniuses couldn't talk to her. Maybe their notation didn't work for her. I wonder what the whole symphony was, and whether she was playing accompaniment. —Huh.'' She shook herself. ''That's spooky, too, isn't it?''

''They ran her stuff through computer analysis. It came up neg.''

''With Bok's theories. Yes. But she never knew her genemother.''

''With her teachers' stuff?''

''Might be. Or something completely off in the beyond.''

''I'd like to pull those files. Just to see what they tried.''

''Do it. Do any damn thing you want. We're research, aren't we? You pull all your projects out of the other wings, you put them into our budget, and our credit balance will hold just fine for that kind of thing. The guppies and the bettas can buy a lot of computer time.''

---

vi

The airport lobby was mostly deserted, RESEUNEAIR'S regular flights all departed, the passengers that came and went in this small public area of Reseune all on their way to Novgorod or Svetlansk or Gagaringrad. There was the usual presence of airport security, and a handful of black-uniformed Reseune Security down from the House, waiting to meet their comrades in from Planys. The same as he was there for Grant, Justin thought; nothing more.

But Florian had gone off into the deplaning area he had no admittance to, had assured him: ''Sera Amy Carnath is just across the room, ser, and so is Sam Whitely, both friends of sera's: I've asked them keep their distance, so if you do get in trouble here, they have a pocket com and they can advise me, but I'm on the regular Security band—'' This with a touch near the small button Florian wore next to his keycard. ''I'll be monitoring Security. If anything should happen, go along with it and trust we can unravel it.''

The two watchers kept to their side of the lounge, a big-boned, square-faced youth who was already huge, hard muscle and a way of sitting that said he was no accountant—Whitely was a Reseune name, but from the Town, not the House; Justin remembered seeing him in Ari's crowd. And Julia Carnath's girl Amy, Ari's frequent shadow, thin and bookish, and sharp, very sharp, by her reputation among the staff. Denys Nye's niece and a boy who looked like he could bend pipe bare-handed—a combination that would give Security pause, at least, Security tending to abhor noisy incidents.

He felt safer with the kids there.

Damn, he had lived this long to be protected by children. To be co-opted by a child who was the same age as himself when he had fallen victim to her predecessor—that was the peculiarly distressing thing. Not that he had a chance, taking on Ari in the prime of her abilities, but that her successor reached out so easily, and just—swept him in and put him in this situation, with Grant on the other side of those doors likely wondering what Ari's personal bodyguard was doing involving himself in the baggage check and in the body search Florian was bound to insist on— Grant would start with a little worry in his look, an initial realization that something was amiss, and quietly go more and more inward, terrified, going through the motions because in that situation there was nothing to gain, nothing to do except hope to get through to his partner and hope that his partner was not already in Detention.

Florian had refused to take so much as a note: I'm sorry, ser; I have to follow regulations here. I'll get him through as quickly as I can.

Not knowing what was toward, not knowing what could have happened to his partner, and that partner waiting to tell him—

God, to tell him he was going up to Ari's floor. That he was going to have to take a probe. That it was all right—because his partner said so, of course, having just had one himself.

He thought it remarkable that he could sit through this night-mare, sit watching the guards in their small group, the two kids talking, listening to the ordinary sounds from the baggage de-partment that meant they were active back there, probably lin-ing up the luggage on the tables where Reseune Security would go through it and check everything item by item, nothing cur-sory on this one, he figured. Examination right down to the integrity of seams on one's shaving kit or the contents of opaque bottles.

He was used to packing for Security checks. No linings, everything in transparent bottles, transparent bags, as little clothing as possible, all documents in the briefcase only, and those all loose-leaf, so they could feed through the scanners.

Take sweaters. Shirts rumpled untidily in searches, and Security always questioned doubled stitching and double-thick collars.

He stretched his feet out in front of him, leaned back and tried to relax, feeling the old panic while the minutes went by like hours.

Sure, it's all right, Grant. I'm sure I wasn't tampered with. Like hell.

But what have we got, else? Where can we go, except hope Ari's reincarnation isn't going down Ari's path?

If she's got those notes, dammit, she knows what her predecessor meant to do with me. She can change it—or she can finish it the way the first Ari would have, make me into what the first Ari planned. Whatever that is. I thought once that might have been the best thing—if Ari had lived. If there ever was a design. Now it's too imminent. Now it's not what Ari could have given me. I'm the adult. I've got my own work, I've got my own agenda—

And Grant, my God, Grant—what have I dragged him into? What can I do?

The doors opened, and Grant came out, carrying his own briefcase, Florian behind him with the luggage.

"Bus, ser," Florian said, waving a hand toward the doors as Justin stood up and started toward Grant.

Their paths in that direction intersected.

"I'm certainly glad to see you," Grant said. He had that slightly dazed look that went with a transoceanic flight and a complete turnabout of hours. Justin threw an arm about him, patted him on the back as they walked.

"How was the trip?"

"Oh, the ground part was fine, Jordan and Paul—everything's all right with them, I really enjoyed the time; just talk, really—a lot of talk—" Doors opened behind them, and

Grant's attention shifted instantly, a glance back, a loss of his thought. "I—"

The doors ahead opened automatically, one set and the others, onto the portico where the bus waited.

"Are we all right?" Grant asked.

"Ari's being sure we are," Justin said, keeping a hand on Grant's back, cautioning him against stopping. Florian put the luggage right up onto the bus deck and got up after, giving a sharp instruction to the driver to start up as Grant stepped up onto the deck and Justin followed him on the steps.

"We've ten more passengers," the driver objected.

"I've a priority," Florian said. "—Get aboard, ser."

Justin crowded a step higher as Grant edged his way past, as Florian shut the door himself.

The driver started the motor and threw them into motion.

"You can come back down after the others," Florian said, standing by the driver as Grant sat down on the first bench and Justin sat down beside him.

"What are we doing?" Grant asked quietly, reasonably.

"We're quite all right," Justin said, and took Grant's wrist and pressed it, twice, with his fingers where the pulse was. Confirmation. He felt Grant relax a little then.

Florian came back and sat down across from them. "Catlin will hold the elevator for us," Florian said. "House Security at the doors will be just a little confused when the bus comes without the rest of the passengers. There's nothing really wrong. They'll probably move to ask the driver what's going on, and we just walk right on through—absolutely nothing wrong with what we're doing, ser, only we just don't need a jurisdictional dispute or an argument over seniority. If we're stopped, absolutely there's no problem, don't worry, don't be nervous, we can move very smoothly through it if you'll just let me do the talking and be ready to take my cues. Ideally we'll walk straight to the doors, through, down to the elevator—Catlin and I have double-teamed senior Security many a time."

"That'll take us up to Wing One residencies," Grant said quietly.

"That's where we're going," Justin said. "There's a little

boundary dispute going on. Ari's coordinating this through the House systems so we *don't* end up with Giraud."

"Fervently to be wished," Grant said with a shaky little sigh, and Justin patted him on the knee.

"Terrible homecoming. I'm awfully sorry."

"It's all right," Grant murmured, as undone as Justin had seen him in many a year. Justin took hold of his hand and squeezed it tight and Grant just slumped back against the seat with a sigh, while the bus started the upward pitch of the hill.

Florian was listening to something through the remote in his left ear. He frowned a little, then his brows lifted. "Ah." A sudden twinkle in the eyes, a grin. "Security was complaining about the bus leaving. House Security just reported it's a request from sera; ser Denys just came on the system to confirm sera's authority to take Grant into custody. We're going to go through quite easily."

"We *are* in some trouble," Grant said. "Aren't we?"

"Moderately," Justin said. "Did you have trouble at Planys?"

"None," Grant said. "Absolutely none."

"Good," he said, and, considering they were within earshot of the azi driver, did not try to answer the look Grant gave him.

The lift doors let them out in the large, barren expanse of Ari's outside hall, baggage and all—which Catlin and Florian had appropriated, and Florian spoke quietly to empty air, advising Ari they were on the floor.

The apartment door opened for them, down the hall.

And Justin slipped his hand to Grant's arm as they walked. "We got into a bit of trouble," Justin said in the safety of Ari's private hall. "We have Giraud on our backs. They were going to plant something on you, almost certain. We've got a deal going with Ari."

"What—deal?"

He tightened his fingers, once, twice. "Take a probe. Just a handful of questions. It's all right, I swear to you."

"Same deal for you?" Grant asked. Worried. Terribly worried. Not: *do you promise this is all right?* But: *Are you all right?*

Justin turned Grant around and flung his arms about him, a

brief, hard embrace. "It's all right, Grant. She's *our kid*, all right? No games, no trouble, she's just taking our side, that's what's going on."

Grant looked at him then, and nodded. "I haven't any secrets," Grant said. His voice was thin, a little hoarse. "Do you get to stay there?"

"No," he said. "Ari says—says I make her nervous. But I'll be in the room outside. I'll be there all the while."

Justin flipped pages in the hardprint Florian had been thoughtful enough to provide him—the latest *Science Bureau Reports*, which he managed to lose himself in from time to time, but the physics was hard going and the genetics was Reseune's own Franz Kennart reporting on the design of zooplankton, and he had heard Franz on that before. While a biologist at Svetlansk had an article on the increasing die-off of native Cyteen ecosystems and the creation of dead-zones in which certain anaerobic bacteria were producing huge methane pockets in valleys near Svetlansk.

It was not, finally, enough to hold his attention. Even the pictures failed, and he merely read captions and isolated paragraphs in a complete hodgepodge of data-intake and stomach-wrenching anxiety, old, old condition in his life—reading reports while waiting for arrest, doing real-time life-and-death design-work while awaiting the latest whim of Administration on whether he could, in a given month, get word of his father's health.

He flipped pages, backward and forward, he absorbed himself a moment in the diagrams of Svetlansk geology and looked at the photos of dead platytheres. There seemed something sad in that—no matter that it made room for fields and green plants and pigs and goats and humans. The photo of a suited human providing scale, dwarfed by the decaying hulk of a giant that must have lived centuries—seemed as unfeeling as the photos from old Earth, the smiling hunters posing with piles of carcasses, of tiger skulls, and ivory.

For some reason tears rolled down his face, startling him, and his throat hurt. For a damn dead platythere. Because he was that strung, and he could not cry for Grant, Grant would look at him curiously and say: *Flux does strange things, doesn't it?*

He wiped his eyes, turned the page and turned the page again until he was calm; and finally, when he had found nothing powerful enough to engage his attention, thought: *O God, how long can a few questions take?*

The first Ari did Grant's designs. She's got access to those. She's got the whole manual. The same as Giraud.

Giraud left him a z-case.

Has he gone out on her?

They'd call me. Surely they'd call me.

He laid the magazine on the table in front of him and leaned his elbows on his knees, ground the heels of his hands into his eyes and clasped his hands on the back of his neck, pulling against a growing ache.

Suppose that Jordan did plant something deep in him— Grant could do that, could take it in, partition it—

Jordan wouldn't do that. God, surely, no.

The door opened, in the hall; he looked up, hearing Ari's voice, hearing her light footsteps.

She came out into the front room, not distressed-looking. Tired.

"He's sleeping," she said. "No trouble." She walked over to the couch where he was sitting and said: "He's absolutely clean. Nothing happened. He's asleep. He was upset—of course he had reason. He was worried about you. I won't stop you from waking him. But I've told him he's safe, that he's comfortable. I'll give the tape to Giraud; I have to. Giraud's got a real kink in his mindsets on what he calls your influence. And you know what he'd think if I didn't."

"Whether you do or not, he's still going to think it. If that tape proved us innocent beyond a doubt—he'd find one."

She shook her head. "Remember I told Denys I've got Ari's working notes? I just tell him I'm quite well in control of the situation, that when I'm through it won't make any difference what Jordan did or didn't do, that if he's worried about the Warrick influence he can stop worrying, I'm working both of you."

It was credible, he thought; and of course it sounded enough like the truth under the truth to feed into his own gnawing worries and remind him of Emory at full stretch—layers upon layers upon layers of truth hidden in subterfuge and a damnable sense of humor. He rubbed the back of his neck and tried to think, but thoughts started scattering in panic—except the one that said: No choice, the kid's the only force in the House that ultimately matters, no choice, no choice, no choice.

. . . *Besides which*— he heard her saying over the breakfast table —*if your safety is linked to mine*—*it's not really likely your father would make a real move against Reseune, is it?*

"Let me tell you about Giraud," she said. "Sometimes I hate him. Sometimes I almost love him. He's absolutely without feelings for people he's against. He's fascinated by little models and microcosms and scientific gadgets. He views himself as a martyr. He's resigned to doing dirty jobs and being hated. He's had very few soft spots—except his feud with your father, a lot of personal anger in that; except me—except me, because I'm the only thing he's ever worked for that can put arms around him and give him something back. That's Giraud. We're on opposite sides of him. I don't say that to make you feel sorry for him. I just want you to know what he's like."

"I know what he's like, thanks."

"When people do bad things to you—it makes this little ego-net problem, doesn't it, isn't that what I learned in psych? There's this little ego-net crisis that says maybe it's your fault, or maybe everybody thinks you're in the wrong, —isn't that what goes on? And ego's got to restructure and flux the doubt down and go mono-value on the enemy so there's no doubt left he's wrong and you're right. Isn't that the way it works? You know all that. If you think about that mono-value it restarts all the flux and it hurts like hell. But what if you need to know the whole picture about Giraud, to know what you ought to do?"

"Maybe nobody ever gets that objective," he said, "when it's his ass in the fire."

"Giraud fluxed you. Fluxed you real good. Are you going to let him get away with it or are you going to listen to me?"

"You do this under kat, sera?"

"No. You'd feel the echo if I had, —wouldn't you? You're so fluxed on me you can't think straight. You're fluxed on me, on Giraud, on Jordan. On yourself. On everybody but Grant.

That's who you'll protect. That's the deal, and I'm the only one who can offer it in the long run. Giraud's dying.''

He stood there, adrenaline coursing through him, but the body got duller with overload. The brain did. And flux just straightened out, even when he knew she was Operating, even when he knew step by step what she was doing: even when he realized there had been deep-level tweaks that had prepared for this, even when he felt amazement that she did it from around a blind corner and improvising as she went.

The knot unkinked. He was wide-open as drugs could send him, for one dizzy instant.

"All right," he said. "That's got one little flaw: Grant's not safe when you can meddle with him."

"Grant would never do anything against you. That's as controlled as I need. I'd be a fool to meddle with the one stable point you've got—when what I want is to be sure where *you* are. You're the one I'd intervene with—if I was going to do it. But if Grant's safety is assured, you're going to remember— anytime you think about doing anything against me—that much as your father might want to, *he* hasn't got the power to protect himself, much less you; and I have. I'll never hurt Jordan. I'll never hurt Grant. I can't promise that with you. And right now you know exactly why—because you're my leverage on a problem that threatens a whole lot more than just me."

It was strange that he felt no panic. Deep-set work again. He felt that through a kind of fog, in which intellect took over again and said: *And you're my leverage. Aren't you?*

But aloud, he said: "Can I see Grant?"

She nodded. "I said so. But you will stay here—at least for a few days. At least till I get it straightened out with my uncles."

"It's probably a good idea," he said, quite calm, even relieved, past the automatic little flutter of alarm. Flux kicked back in. Defenses came up all the way. He thought about the chance that Giraud would arrest them even over Denys' objections.

Or arrange their assassination. Giraud was not a man who worried about his own reputation. A professional—in his own nefarious way—who served a Cause, Ari was right about that.

Giraud would sacrifice even Ari's regard for him—to be sure in his own mind, that Ari was safe.

Giraud would do it dirty, too. It was Ari's regard for them he had to terminate. It was his ideas Giraud had to discredit.

There *had* been a plot to incriminate him through Grant. He was sure of that. Every trip to Planys was a risk. They were cut off again. *No* more visits. No chance to see Jordan. They were lucky to get Grant back unscathed. And if Giraud could work on Jordan, indirectly—

Jordan knowing his son and his foster-son had joined Ari's successor—

There was no end to the what-ifs, no way to untangle truth and lies. Anyone could be lying. Everyone had reason. Every move Jordan made in Planys—was a risk. Failing to get to them, Giraud might well move on Jordan to get leverage on them in Reseune, to create doubts in Ari's mind—

And Ari said—*I'm working both of you*—

God.

He went to the hall and to the open library door; and into the dim room where Grant lay on the couch, asleep and very tranked. Florian was there, shadow in the corner, just sitting guard. Catlin was not. Catlin was somewhere else in the apartment, in the case he had violated instructions to stay to the front rooms, he thought.

He laid his hand on Grant's shoulder and said: "Grant, it's Justin. I'm here, the way I said."

Grant frowned, and drew a deep breath and moved a little; and opened his eyes a slit.

"I'm here," Justin said. "Everything's all right. She said you're all right."

A larger breath. Eyes showing white and pupil by turns as Grant struggled up out of the trank and reached after him. He took Grant's hand. "Hear me?" Double press on the inside of the wrist. "It's all right. You want Florian and me to carry you? You want to go to bed?"

"Just lie here," Grant murmured. "Just lie here. I'm so tired. I'm so tired—"

His eyes closed again.

"I'm doing quite well," Ari said, over a bite of salad; lunch, at *Changes*, the 18th December. "They're back in their own residency. Everyone's happy. There's no problem with Jordan, no lingering messiness. I just wasn't about to let them out where Giraud could get at them. You shouldn't worry. I can take care of myself. Is that enough said?"

"You know what I think about it," Denys said.

"I appreciate your concern. But," she said with a small quirk of her brow, a deliberate smile, "you probably worried about Ari senior this way too."

"Ari was murdered," Denys said.

Point.

And feeler? Denys was upset. Giraud was upset. Giraud *hated* disorder and his own impending death was creating maximum disorder: there were beginning to be rumors in the House—no leak: Giraud's own appearance, increasingly frail despite his large bones—was its own indicator of a man in failing health.

"One thinks she was murdered," Ari said. "Who knows? Maybe the pipe just blew. I've tried that door. A breath of air would disturb it, at certain points. A blown cryo line is just that. Isn't it? The line blows, she gets caught in the spray, falls, hits her head. The door closes quite naturally. Maybe murder was a useful story. *Murder* let you take fairly extreme measures."

"Is that what Justin says?"

"No. Dr. Edwards."

"When did John say a fool thing like that?"

"Not specifically. He just taught me scientific procedure. I never rule anything out. I just think some hypotheses are more likely than others."

"Confession makes it more likely, doesn't it?"

"I suppose it ought to. All things equal." She cut up a cucumber slice. "You know the kitchen's getting a little lazy. Look at this." She impaled a large lettuce rib. "Is that a way to serve?"

"Let's stay to business, dear, like why in hell you're being a fool about this man. Which has much more to do with glands than you want to admit. If you don't realize your vulnerability, I can assure you it's going to dawn on him, just as soon as the waves stop.''

"Except one thing, uncle Denys: Justin's not Jordan. And he can't kill. He absolutely can't, for the same reason he can't work real-time. He'd freeze. He can't even hate Giraud. He feels other people's pain. Ari exacerbated that tendency in him. She leaned on it, hard. You see I *do* have those notes. I know something else, too: Jordan was hers. She just couldn't use his slant on things, so she conned Jordan into a replicate, and she took him, she absolutely took him. If she hadn't died, Justin would have slid closer and closer to her over the years—either healed the breach with Jordan or broken with him—because there's something very sad about his relationship to Jordan, and he would have learned it.''

"What's that, mmmn?''

"That Jordan would have smothered him. Ari was never afraid of competition. Jordan was; and that relationship—Justin and his father—would have become more and more strained under Ari's influence. That's exactly what I project. Jordan is an arrogant, opinionated man who had intentions for his replicate, but they weren't going to work, because his son, with a good infusion of independence from Ari's side, was going to go head to head against him and make his life miserable; and I don't think Jordan's ego would ever let him see that.''

"You don't even know Jordan Warrick.''

"Ari did. It's my predecessor talking now. She set his whole life up. She provided Grant as an ameliorating influence on Justin, a partner of equal potential—Grant's predecessor was a Special, remember?—but deep-setted to be profoundly supportive of his Contract, which is exactly what a boy being pressured by his father to succeed—would rely on, wouldn't he, for the unqualified emotional support he'd need? Grant was always the leverage Ari would have to get Justin away from Jordan when the time was right; and now I have him. I'm going on Ari's instructions on this. She valued Jordan's abilities, she just wanted them to support her work—which, by what everyone tells me, is exactly the point where she and Jordan clashed: Jordan accused her of taking his ideas and claiming them. Justin's voiced similar reservations, of course. And he's confessed to resentments. But I've got that covered.''

"How, pray tell?"

"I'm a little smarter than my predecessor. I've kept him out of my bed and dealt strictly with his *professional* qualifications.''

"I'm relieved.''

"I thought you would be. I know Giraud will be ecstatic. I *know* what he thinks went on while Justin was in my apartment. You can tell him not. I may have scared Justin out of good sense, but I've never scared him too much. I've behaved myself, I did a few psych-tweaks on Ari's intervention with him while he was under, and he's really glad I let him alone. Pretty soon, he'll be all the way over to grateful.''

"You know, young sera, you're getting entirely too confident for your age.''

"I'm a lot of things too much for my age, uncle Denys. Most people find that completely uncomfortable. I really appreciate it that I can be myself with you. And with Giraud. I really do. I appreciate it too that you can be sensible with me. You're not dealing with little Ari anymore. I'm much, much more like my predecessor. More than I've let on in public, which is exactly, of course, what she'd do in my position. My enemies think they've got more time than they do, which is one way of dealing with the problem. And positioning myself. —Which is why I've really, urgently got to talk to you about Giraud, uncle Denys.''

"What about Giraud?"

"You're really very fond of him, aren't you? He's very much your right hand. And what are you going to do when he dies?''

Denys drew in his breath and rested his hand beside his plate. *Score one.* Denys looked as taken off guard as she had ever seen him. There was an angry frown, then a clearer expression. "What do you suppose I'll do?"

"I don't know. I wonder if you're thinking about it.''

"I'm thinking about it. We're both thinking about it.'' Still the anger. "Your actions aren't helping. You know how volatile the situation in Council is going to be.''

"I know Giraud's worried. I know how worried he is about

me. 'The Warrick influence.' God, I've heard that till I'm deaf. . . . Let me tell you: Justin's *not* plotting against me.'' She saw the unfocusing of Denys's eyes, and rapped the table sharply with her knuckles. *"Listen* to me now, uncle Denys.'' The focus came back. "Stop thinking I'm a fool, all right? I need him for very specific, very *professional* reasons. He's working in an area I need, or *will* need, in future.''

"Nothing you couldn't do, young sera.''

"Maybe. But why should I, when I can have someone else do it, on his level, and save myself the time?''

"He'll like that.''

"Oh, he'll get credit. I've told him. And unlike Jordan, Justin grew up number two in everything. He's got a good deal more flexibility than Jordan.''

"What are you going to do with Jordan in your administration, pray tell? Let him loose? That would be abysmally stupid, Ari. And that's exactly what your young man is going to ask of you—what he already *has* asked of you, why not be honest? I'm sure he has, just the same as he connived his way into your sympathy.''

"He's asked. And I asked him if he thought Jordan himself would be safe—or whether Jordan could defend himself against people who'd want to use him. Like the Paxers.''

"Young woman, you *are* meddling.''

"It doesn't take *my* abilities, uncle Denys, to guess what kind of stuff Giraud would like to have planted on Grant and Jordan—about the time you break the news the Centrists are in contact with him. I'm sorry to mess Giraud up. I know he's furious with me. I'm sorry about that. But Giraud's messing up a much more important operation—mine. And I won't stand for it.'' She poured more wine. They had chased the waiter away and asked for him to respond only to the call-button. "You just don't give me enough credit, uncle Denys. Remember what I said about muddying the waters. I don't like that. I don't like it at all. Giraud's not thinking straight and I wish you'd straighten him out; he's tired, he's ill, and in this, I just don't know how to talk to him.''

"I thought you knew everything.''

"Well, say that I know enough to know he's not well, he's trying to hide that from the world, he doesn't want to admit it to me, and it's a guaranteed explosion if I try to reason with him. Excluding trank, which I'm not about to do to my uncle. You're the only one he'll listen to in this, you're the only one who can get him calmed down, because he knows you're objective and he won't believe that about me. And there's something else I want you to tell him. I want you to tell him . . . the Warrick influence isn't the only thing going in Reseune. He should believe . . . he should definitely believe . . . the Nye influence is terribly important to me. Indispensable to me . . . and to Reseune.''

"That's gratifying.''

"I haven't gotten to my point yet. This is terribly delicate, uncle Denys. I don't want you to take this wrong. And it's so hard to discuss with Giraud—but . . . Giraud's so hardheaded practical, and he's been such an influence—on me; on Reseune— What do you think he'd feel—about having a replicate done—like me?''

Denys sat still, a long, long moment. "I think he'd be amazed,'' Denys said. "He'd also point out that he's not documented to the extent you are.''

"It's possible it'll work. It's even probable. All I'd need is the ordinary House stuff. Damn, this is so awkward! I don't know how to approach asking him. I don't know how he feels about dying. He's—never brought it up with me. I gather he doesn't want me to know. But I know a lot more about psychogenesis than you knew when you started; I know a lot I haven't written up—I know it from the inside, I know what matters and what doesn't and where you came close to a real bad mistake. And I really think I could run it with Giraud. If he'd let me.''

"Dear, when one's dead, there's not a precious lot one can do to stop you from any damn thing, now, is there?''

"It matters what you want. And what Giraud wants, I mean, his opinion is the most important, because that has to do with his psychsets, and whether his successor would be comfortable with what he is. That's critical. And there's who would be the surrogates. You're not young yourself, to take on another kid. I thought about Yanni, Yanni's got the ability, and the toughness. Maybe Gustav Morley. But you'd be best, because you know things no one else *can* remember about your upbringing, and you can be objective, at least you could with me. But you weren't related to me. That's a difference to think about. That could be a lot of stress, and I'm not sure you want to cope with that now, with Giraud.''

Denys had laid the fork down altogether. ''I'd have to think about that.''

''At least talk to him. Please make him understand—I *don't* want to fight with him. I need him, I'll need him in things I can't foresee yet. That's why I want to do this. Tell him—tell him I love him and I know why he's doing these things to stop me, but tell him I know something too and he should let me alone and let me operate. Tell him—tell him I understand all his lessons. I've learned from him well enough to protect myself. —And tell him if he wants to know what it's like to *be* a successor—I can tell him.''

''I'd find that a point of curiosity too,'' Denys said after a moment, ''what degree of integration there is. *Is* there identity?''

Gentle smile. ''Profiles? Say they're real close. What it feels like, uncle Denys, what it feels like—is, you think,—*I'd never do that.* But eventually you would. You almost remember—*remember* things. Because they're part of the whole chain of events that lead to the point you go on from. Because you *are* a continuance, and what your predecessor did was important and the people she knew are still there, the enemies and the friends are still there for reasons of what she was and what she did—more, you *understand* what she felt about things and how it all fitted, from the gut, in your glands, in your bloodstream, and, oh, it makes more and more sense. You see yourself on an Archive tape and you feel this incredible—identity—with that person. You see a little slump; you straighten your own shoulders—*Stand straight, Ari, don't slouch.* You see a little upset—you feel personally threatened. You see anger. Your pulse picks up a bit. I *will* write a paper someday, when the subject's much more commonplace. But I don't think it's a thing I want to have in the *Bureau Reports* right now. I think it's one of those processes Reseune can bastardize for the other agencies that want to do it with easy types. But they'll always send the Specials to us, because they're going to be the real problem cases: Alphas always are. Even CITs. And that means more and more of the best talent—begins at Reseune.''

Denys gazed at her a long time without speaking.

"I *am* very much the woman you knew," she said. "Never mind the kid's face. Or the fact my voice hasn't settled yet. There is a kind of fusion. Only I'm already working on Ari's final notes, not her starting hypotheses. Psychogenesis is a given with me. I'll do much more, much more than she did. Isn't that what you wanted?"

"Much—more than we expected."

She laughed. "Which way do I take that?"

"That we're very proud of you. I—personally—am very proud of you."

"I'm glad. I'm very glad. I'm very grateful to you, uncle Denys. And to Giraud. I always will be. You see: Ari was such a cold bastard. She learned to be, for very good reasons. But that part didn't have to be exact. I can love my uncles, and I can still be a cold bastard when I have to be, just because I'm very self-protective—because no matter what the advantages I've had, I'm a target and I know it. I won't be threatened. I'll be there first. That's the way I am. I want you to know that."

"You're very impressive, young sera."

"Thank you. So are my uncles. And you're both dears and I love you. I want you to think about what I want to do—about Giraud; and talk to Giraud, and tell me how he feels about it."

Denys cleared his throat. "I don't think—I don't think he'll turn you down."

Is there identity?

She knew damn well that Denys was asking for himself.

What's it like?

Will—I—remember? That was the really eetee one, which a sane man knew better than to wonder. So she flirted it right past him now; and made him sweat.

"I'll tell you where an interesting study might be, uncle Denys. Getting me and Giraud together someday and letting us compare notes. *I* have the illusion of memory. I wonder if he will."

Denys had not taken a bite in a half a minute. He sat there a helpless lump.

Shame on you, she thought to herself. *That's awful, Ari.*

But something in her was quite, quite satisfied.

What in hell's the matter with me?

I'm madder than hell, that's what. Mad that I'm young, mad that I'm dependent, mad that I'm trapped here and Denys is being Denys, and mad that Giraud's timing is so damn lousy, leaving me no way to get that seat. Dammit, I'm not ready for him to die!

Denys' fork rattled, another bite. He was visibly upset.

How can I enjoy doing that? My God. He's an old man. What's gotten into me?

Her own appetite curdled. She poked at the salad, extracting a bit of tomato.

She thought about it that night, listlessly dividing attention between a light sandwich Florian had made her, the evening news, and doing a routine entry on the keyboard—which she preferred to the Scriber when she was listening to something: the fingers were output-only, and what they were out-putting was in a mental buffer somewhere. Pause. Tick-tick-tick. Pause. While the visual memory played out lunch and uncle Denys and the logical function worked on the politics of it. *Is* there identity? —An eetee kind of question in the first place, never mind that she had eetee feelings about it—she knew how to explain them, in perfectly solid and respectable terms: she was used to deep-study, she could lower her threshold further by wanting to than most people could on E-dose kat, the tapes involved a person identical to her in the identical environment, and the wonder would be if the constant interplay of tape-flash and day-to-day experience of the same halls, the same people, the same situations—did not muddle together in a flux-habituated brain.

Denys understood that, surely, on the logical level.

People surely understood that.

Damn, *she* was not dealing well with that aspect of it. She dealt with massive movements in the populace. Microfocus failed her.

The average, harried, too-busy-for-deepthink Novgorod worker.

Listen and learn, Ari, sweet: ordinary people will teach you the truest, the most sane things in the world. Thank God for them.

And beware anyone who can turn them all in one direction. That one is not ordinary.

People were aware . . . of Reseune's power, of the power her predecessor had wielded.

IN PRINCIPIO was a phenomenon, Ariane Emory's basic theories and methodologies and the early character of Reseune, set almost within the most educated laymen's grasp, so that there was, in the public mind, at least the glimmering of what no demagogue could have made clear before that book aroused such strange, such universal interest in the popular market.

It had spawned eetee-fringe thinkers of its own, a whole new and troublesome breed who took Emory for their bible and practiced experimental so-called Integrations on each other, in the idea it would expand their consciousness, whatever that was. There were already three cases down in the Wards, Novgorod CITs who had all drug-tripped their way to out-there on massive overdoses, run profound interventions on each other and now outraged staid old Gustav Morley by critiquing his methodology. A handful of admirers had outraged Reseune Security, too, by trying to leave the lounge down at the RESEUNEAIR terminal and hike up toward the House, proclaiming that they had come to see Ariane Emory—with the result that Reseune was urgently considering building a new terminal for commercial flights, *far* down from the old one where, in the old days, Family and ordinary through travelers using RESEUNEAIR had once mingled with casual indifference. A handful of would-be disciples had turned up over in Moreyville looking for a boat, until wary locals, thank God, had figured out what they were up to and called the police.

My God, what do I do if I meet one of these lunatics? What are they after?

It's a phase. A fad. It'll go. If it weren't this they'd be getting eetee transmissions on their home vids.

Why didn't we see this?

But of course we saw it. Justin saw it. There's always the fringe. Always the cheap answer, the secret Way—to whatever. Novgorod's in chaos, Paxers threatening people, wages aren't rising to meet spot shortages—

Danger signs. People yearning after answers. Seeking shortcuts.

Seeking them in the work of a murdered Special—

In the person of her replicate, as the Nyes fade, as the unsta-

ble period after that assassination births more instabilities, elections upon elections, bombings, shortages, and the Child—the Child verges on womanhood and competency in her own right, announcing herself with the recovery of Ari senior's legendary lost notes—

Damn well what I expected Science to understand—

But Novgorod's understanding it at a completely different level . . .

The children of azi's children—the constituency of Reseune: Ari's own creation, no theory in a Sociology computer. It's there. It's ready.

And Giraud, damn him, can't hold on to that seat long enough for me.

''Vid off,'' she said, and leaned back and shut her eyes, feeling that general pricklishness that meant her cycle was right on schedule.

Tomorrow I should work in, stay away from people.

I hurt Denys today. I Had him, I didn't need to take that twist. Why in hell did I do that?

What am I mad about?

Adrenaline high, that's what's going on. Not mentioning the rest of the monthly endocrine cocktail.

Damn, that was an underhanded shot I took. Denys didn't deserve that.

I know what Ari came to. Her temper, her damnable temper—the anger she was always afraid to let out—

Frustration with the irrational—with a universe moving too slow for her mind—

God, what's going on with me?

She tasted blood, realized she had bitten her lip, and unfocused.

She pressed her hands against her forehead, leaning back in the chair, shut her eyes . . . thinking about that tape, Justin's tape, thinking—

God, no. Not when she was fluxing this bad. Not when she could think of it as surrogate. Leave the damn thing in the cabinet, locked up, safe. Let it be.

It was—oh, God! not for entertainment—

Dammit, Ari, get off it!

Watch the damn fish. Watch the fish procreate and breed

*and spawn and live their very short lives, back and forth, back
and forth in the tank beside the desk.*

*Sex and death. Breeding and devouring their own young if
god did not take precautions and intervene with the net. How
long can an ecosystem survive, inputting both the biomass of
its own dead and its own births, and the artificial sunlight?*

*If you put them with big fish there won't be any blue fish at
all. . . .*

Do you know whether a fish sees colors? . . .

Breathing grew more even. Time reached a slower pace.
Eventually she could sigh, bring the emotional temperature
down, and postpone thinking. She got up and logged off and
went to her bedroom, quietly, not to draw Florian and Catlin's
notice.

She just wanted bed, that was all. But she sat staring at the
dresser-top corner, where Poo-thing rested, well-worn and dis-
reputable. No condemnation there.

She thought about putting him in the drawer. What if she
had brought Justin to her room while he was here; and there
was poor Poo-thing to laugh at?

That was the whole trouble—that there were no more
games, there was no more give-and-take with friends, no more
throwing a dart to see if it got one back, and having uncle
Denys come back at her, hard-edged wit, a little sting to put
her in her place. She tried to get a rise out of him and there was
no bounce-back, no humor, nothing but the wary fencing of an
old man who was no longer the power—just the threatened.

Floating-in-black-space.

*Welcome to the real world. Poo-thing's worn out. Denys is
a scared old man. And you're what he's scared of. People
won't argue with you: who wants to lose all the time?*

*I could do any damn thing I want in Reseune. Like take any-
body, anything, teach them what I could do—in one day, I
could scare hell out of this place, make them understand I'm
holding in—*

Everybody'd love me then, wouldn't they?

Poo-thing stared, with wide black eyes.

*I ought to take you to work, set you on the desk. You're the
best conversationalist in Reseune.*

Dammit, someone pull a prank on me, someone make me laugh, someone for God's sake answer me.

I can see all the star-stations, all the azi-sets, the whole thing in slow flux, so damned slow, and so dangerous—

Where's the advice, Poo-thing?

Amy, and Maddy and Tommy and Sam. Florian and Catlin. Justin and Grant. Yanni. And Andy down in AG.

It's talking, fool. The whole universe is talking. Listen and be amazed.

Nelly. Maman and Ollie. Denys. Giraud-present and Giraud-soon-to-be.

The static of the suns.

". . . Sera?"

She drew a long breath.

Short-focused again, black-clad figure in the doorway, tall and blond. Worried.

"I'm fine," she said; and discovered her legs asleep. Foolish predicament, gratefully foolish. She rubbed her aching thighs and levered herself up with absolute gracelessness, leaning on the headboard.

When she could stand she went over to the dresser, picked up Poo-thing and put him in the drawer.

Catlin looked at her strangely for that too. But she doubted Catlin had ever understood Poo-thing in the first place.

viii

Punch and sugary cookies. Ari nipped one off the table herself, ignoring the kitchen's more elaborate confections, savored the plain flavor, and took a drink of the green punch which she preferred, thank you, from the non-alcoholic bowl.

A little girl slipped up through the crowd of Olders and snatched a handful; and a second. Fast escape. That was Ingrid Kennart, aged six. Ari chuckled to herself, on a fleeting memory. And frankly could not recall for a second whether it was a flash off some Archive tape or out of her own past.

New Year's, God, of course it had been a New Year's. The music changed, live this year—a handful of the techs had a band, not bad, either. But the glitter was the same. And maman and Ollie—

She caught a flash of silver jewelry out of the corner of her eye and for a second saw a ghost—but it was only Connie Morley, who was tall and thin and wore her dark hair upswept and elegant—

She had a second of triste, no reason, just looked away across the floor where Olders were sitting—Denys: Giraud was in Novgorod this season. Petros Ivanov. Dr. Edwards. He could, she swore, never be *John* to her, no matter how old she got. And old Windy Peterson and his daughter, out dancing, Peterson *trying* to learn the new step.

Maddy Strassen was beautiful, really beautiful in silver-blue satin—no shortage of partners for her or 'Stasi, her faithful shadow. And Amy Carnath—Amy was out on the floor with a very correct, very confused-looking young azi who was, however, doing quite well with the step—blond, crewcut, and terribly handsome: Security, stiff as they came when Amy had gotten her hands on him, but loosening up a bit, to the amusement of all of them and the evident disquiet of Amy's mother. The lad was Alpha, and social as far as Green Barracks went— yes, sera! with a real snap in the voice. Quentin, his name was: Quentin AQ-8, who just *might* have ended up being Contracted to House Security or RESEUNESPACE, or outside, if any of a small handful of qualified agencies had wanted to pay the million and a quarter for his Contract, for an azi who had to be Supered directly from Reseune, and whose reflexes were dangerously fast. Quentin AQ would have found himself in someone's employment in another year.

Quentin was, Florian and Catlin reported, a very happy, if very over-anxious young man. And Amy was—

—in love, probably described it. At least it was a very healthy dose of infatuation, which made Amy Carnath insist Quentin was her partner, Quentin was going out onto the floor, fashions and customs changed, and people were forgetting *why* the old rules existed with the earliest azi: it had gotten to have completely different reasons, and it was going to stop. The youngers did it at their parties; the Olders could just accept it, so there: thus Amy Carnath.

Florian, Ari had said then, so Amy and Quentin were not out there alone. And after a while there were a few others.

But mostly Florian and Catlin shadowed her very closely, and Florian refused 'Stasi with an earnest: *I'm terribly sorry. I'm on duty.*

That was the way the world changed. In the House, Florian and Catlin were shadowing her with the attention they had used in Novgorod.

No relaxing. No let-down.

The Novgorod authorities were scared out of their minds about the New Year's crowds and the chance of an incident.

Hell of a thing. The Paxers were *not* Ari's design, she was more and more convinced. A cultural inheritance, an ugly little side-trip in the independence-prioritied mindsets that had founded Union. The grandsons and granddaughters of rebel scientists and engineers—blew up kids in subway stations, and wanted to run the government.

They talked about potential Worms in *Justin's* designs twenty, thirty generations down. Union had a few after three generations, real serious ones, and she was scared going into a controlled situation like New Year's with Family and staff, with Florian and Catlin to watch with a trained eye for anything Unusual. To have a Novgorod citizen's choice—kilometers of walking in ped-tunnels or twice daily percentaging the headlines and the mood of politics to decide whether to risk a ten-minute subway ride—not mentioning the chance of some ordinary z-case putting the push on you for your keycard—*hell* of a way to live. But Novgorod citizens hated the idea of a master-system for keycards: a danger to their freedom, they argued.

They had, she thought, a higher anxiety threshold than she did; but they were holding their own, that was the good part, hell with the Paxers, people held on; and she, Ari Emory, she followed the situation and wondered if there was perhaps merit in the idea of a major program to buy-off thousands of military azi still rejuvable, bring them back to Reseune for re-training, exactly the way they had done before she was born—

No question then of the bad precedent of having armed troops keeping order in Novgorod, but a loan of a civilian agency from Reseune Administrative Territory to the municipality of Novgorod. If these were the times they lived in, as well have a response for it, if it meant enforcement standing line-of-sight in every ped-tunnel and subway in Novgorod.

Manpower was the original reason Reseune existed; and she was working out the proposal to land on Denys' desk. And expected Denys to say no. Reseune was making profit again and Denys was determined to hold the line against what he called her out-there ideas.

She sighed, watching uncle Denys from across the room, and seeing a tired lump of a man who had some very strange turns: who had, she had discovered it in Denys' Base in the House system—a huge volume of unpublished work that she ached to talk with him about, work on inter-station economics that was bound to cause a ripple when it did come to light . . . *she* did not understand it, but it was very massive and very full of statistics; a huge work on the interaction of economics with the Expansionist theory of government that was absolutely fascinating; a massive study of the development of consumer society in azi-descended population segments, including specific tracing of psychsetted values in several generations of testing; a study of replicate psychology; a history of Reseune from its inception; and work on military systems, of a kind that looked very much like Giraud's work—until she put her finger on the telltale phrases and turns of speech and realized to her shock that Giraud did not write the things published under Giraud's name. They were Denys' writings. And this secret store of them, this absolute treasure-house of ideas, —kept in Archive? Never brought forward, just meddled with from time to time, adjusted—an enormous work-in-progress, from a man so obsessively retiring that he maneuvered his brother into a Special's status so that Giraud could have the reputation and do the public things, while Denys stayed in the background, appearing to devote himself exclusively to administrative work and the day-to-day decisions and approvals for R&D and implementations.

Besides bringing up a kid for a few years—letting *her* into that intense privacy, hosting birthday parties and putting up with Nelly and two junior Security trainees—while writing these things that never appeared, only grew and grew.

Strange man, she thought, objective about Denys for the

first time in her life. Willing to take on Giraud's replicate—oh, yes. Beyond any doubt. And facing Giraud's death with—not quite grief: a sense of impending catastrophe.

No difficult question at all why Denys had been so willing to take her in, why he had thrown all Reseune into turmoil to re-cover Ariane Emory's abilities for Reseune: Denys was bril-liant, Denys had the old problem with Alphas—that lack of checks, lack of boundaries, that floating-in-black-space prob-lem, that meant no minds to bounce off, no walls to return the echo. Denys was brilliant, and quite eetee and self-defensive: and incapable, perhaps, of believing his work was finished—hence the perpetual adjustments. A mind working on a macro-system that only kept widening . . . a perfectionist, with the need to be definitive.

No need of people at all. Just a student of them.

And facing death—Giraud's and his own—with incredulity. Denys was the center of his own universe, Giraud his willing satellite, and of course Denys was interested in psychogenesis, Denys was so damned interested he had almost lost his balance with her, Denys wanted immortality, even without personal continuance—and she had only to hold out the promise: if Giraud was essential to the universe—who more than Denys?

She turned, set the cup on the edge of the table, and started, expecting the person behind her to be Florian, about to take the cup; but it was Justin; and she was chagrined in that half-second, at being that on-edge, and at being caught being fool-ish.

He took her hand, said: "I think I remember how," and of-fered the other hand.

She stared at him, thinking: *How much has he had?* and lifted her hand to his, fingers locked in fingers, the two of them moving out onto the floor to an older, slower number. He *had* been drinking, probably no few drinks, but he moved with some grace, surely as aware as she was of the fact other dan-cers broke step to gawk at them, that the music wobbled and recovered.

He smiled at her. "Ari never danced. But her dinners were always good for a week of office gossip."

"What in hell are you trying to do?"

"What I'm doing. What you did—with Florian—and young

Amy. Good for you. Good for you, Ari Emory. Damned right. —I thought—a little social rehab—twice in a night—figuring you have a sense of humor—''

Other dancers were in motion, recovering their graces. And Justin's smile was thin, deliberately held.

"You're not in some kind of trouble, are you?"

"No. Just thinking—I've lost a big piece of my life— staying inconspicuous. What the hell. Why not?"

She caught a glimpse of Denys' chair, near the door. Vacant.

And thought: *God. Where are the edges of this thing?*

The music finished. People applauded. She stared a second at Justin, a second that felt all too long and public.

I've made a serious mistake.

Cover it, for God's sake, it's like the Amy/Quentin thing, people will take it that way with cue enough—

She walked with Justin hand-in-hand from the floor, straight for Catlin. "Here's the one to teach you the new steps. She's really amazing. —Catlin, *show* Justin, will you?"

As the band started up again, and Catlin smiled, took Justin by the hand and took him back to the floor.

Grant—was over by the wall, watching, with worry evident.

"Florian," she said, "go ask Grant what the hell Justin's up to."

"Yes, sera," Florian said, and went.

Denys was gone from the room. So was Seely.

Justin's linked himself with me—publicly. Not that everyone didn't know. But that I let it go—that, they'll gossip about.

She looked to the floor, where Justin made a brave and even marginally successful attempt to take up on Catlin. And to the corner of the room, where Florian and Grant were in urgent converse.

Denys—walked out.

Florian came back before the end of the dance. "Grant says: it's CIT craziness. I had no notion of this. Grant asked your help but he says if he intervenes it may be public and tense. He says Justin's been on an emotional bent ever since he and Grant went back to their own residency—Grant says he's willing to speak to you about it, but then he said: Sera intervened: ask sera if this is the result of it.''

Ari frowned. "Dammit."

"Maddy," Florian said.

Which was a better idea than she had, fluxed as she was. "Maddy," she said. "Go." *Dammit, dammit! He's pushing, damned if this is innocent. Denys was here, the whole Family watching—*

She took a deep breath. *No more easy course. He's no kid. Denys isn't. Now they're not dealing with me as a kid either, are they? Grant thinks this is an emotional trip—or that's what Justin's told Grant to say.*

Damn, I should haul him in for a question-and-answer on this little trick, damn, I should.

And he'd never trust me, never be the same Justin, would he?

Catlin and Justin were leaving the floor. Maddy Strassen moved in with Maddy's own peculiar grace, said something to Catlin and appropriated Justin's arm, walking him over to the refreshments while the band took a break; and 'Stasi Ramirez was moving in from the other side.

Thank God.

She drew quieter breaths, sure that Denys had his spies in the room, people who would report to him exactly the way things went.

Like Petros Ivanov.

Which could only help, at this point.

Grant—stayed as unobtrusive as Grant's red-haired elegance could ever be, over in a corner of the room, having a bit of cake and a cup of punch. And talking to young Melly Kennart, who was twelve. Completely innocent.

Maddy partnered Justin through two dances. Ari took the second one with Tommy Carnath, who was looking a little grim. "Patience," Ari said, "for God's sake, we've got a problem."

"He's the problem," Tommy said. "Ari, he's moving on you. Your uncle's mad."

If Tommy saw it, so did a lot of other people.

And nothing could cover it. All she could do was signal she was not responding to the overture.

Embarrass him and send him off? He was vulnerable as hell to that. Laying himself wide open to it. Betting his entire career and maybe his life on that move, and *not* stupid, no, no way that a man who had run the narrow course he had run all his life suddenly made a thorough break with pattern on a flight of emotion. No matter if he was drunk. No matter what. Justin *had* thought about what he was doing.

And put her on the spot. Support me in front of the whole Family or rebuff me. Now.

I'll kill him.

I'll kill him for this.

---

ix

"Ser Justin's here," Florian said, via the Minder, and Ari said, without looking up from her desk:

"Damn well about time. Bring him to the den. *Him*, not Grant."

"Grant's not with him," Florian said.

Florian had not let him in yet: the Minder always beeped in her general area to let her know when an outside access opened. It did then; and she waited to finish her note to the system before she stirred from her chair, told Base One log-off, and walked down the hall to the bar and the den.

Justin was there, in the room that held so many bad memories—walking the narrow margin behind the immense brass-trimmed couch, looking at the paintings. While Florian waited unobtrusively by the bar—unconscious echo on Florian's part: he and Catlin had never seen the tape.

She chose this place.

Favor for favor.

"I want to know," she said, to his back, across the wide expanse of the wood-floored pit, "what in *hell* you hoped to accomplish last night."

He turned to face her. Indicated the painting he had been looking at. "That's my favorite. The view of Barnard's. It's so simple. But it affects you, doesn't it?"

She took in her breath. *Affects you, indeed. He's Working me, that's what he's after.*

"*Grant* asked me for help," she said. "You've got *him* scared. I hope you know that. What are you trying to do? Unravel everything? It's damned ungrateful. I kept Giraud off your tail. I kept you out of Detention. I've taken chances for you—What do you expect I should do, shout across the room? I do you a favor. I do every damn thing I can to help you. What do you do for me? Push me in public. Put me in a situation. I *don't* think I'm that much smarter than you are, Justin Warrick, so don't tell me you were just going from the gut. I'll tell you you wanted me in a corner. Back you or not, on your damn timetable; and if Tommy Carnath saw it and Florian saw it and 'Stasi Ramirez saw it, you tell me whether Yanni Schwartz or Petros Ivanov or my uncle missed it.''

He walked around the edge of the pit, to the front of the bar.

"I apologize.''

"*Apologize* won't handle it. I want to know—simply and clearly—what you want.''

"You can always ask that. Isn't that the agreement?''

"Don't push me. *Don't* push me. I'm still trying to save your butt, hear me?''

"I understand you.'' He leaned against the bar and looked at Florian. "Florian.''

"Ser?''

"Scotch and water. Do you mind?''

"Sera?''

"My usual. His. It's all right, Florian.'' She walked down the steps and sat down on the couch, and Justin came down and sat. Put his elbow on the couch-back in the same way as all those years ago, unconscious habit or scene-following as deliberate as hers . . . she did not know. "All right,'' she said, "I'm listening.''

"Not much to say. Except I trusted you.''

"*Trusted* me! —For what, a damned fool?''

"It was just—there. That's all. What would I do? Work in your wing, be your partner another twenty years till Denys dies? Keep my head down and my mouth shut and attend all those damn parties, twenty lousy years of going through every social function, all the department functions, everything—with every CIT in the House feeling like he has to explain himself to Security or your uncle if he's spotted talking to me? Hell of a life, Ari.''

"I'm sorry,'' she said shortly. Which was true: she had had

a dose of it too, in growing up; and she had seen it happen to him and felt it in her gut. "But that still doesn't say why you did it. Why you had to wait for a damned sensitive time—I just got things smoothed over with Denys, I *just* got things settled, and you throw me a move like that."

"Sorry," he said bitterly.

"Sorry?"

"Times are always sensitive— Always. It's always something. I'm cut off from my father again, dammit, because of Giraud. I've got your word he's safe. That's all I've got."

His voice wobbled. Florian set the whiskey down by his hand, on the shelf behind the couch, and ghosted her direction, putting the vodka-and-orange by hers.

"Which," he continued, after a drink, "I don't doubt. But that's why. Others do doubt my father's safety. Giraud is one. So damned easy to have an incident—a confusion on the part of some poor sod of an azi guard—isn't it? Terrible loss—a Special. But as you say, —Giraud's dying. What can he care? You underestimate him—if you think he's not going to try to be rid of my father—except—except if he finds things *aren't* settled at Reseune, and I'm a threat he can't get at. Next to you. *Then* he'll doubt. And Giraud, scheming bastard that he is, —never makes precipitate, reckless moves. *I* want his attention. I want it on me until he's dead. It's that simple."

It made sense, it made a tangled, out-of-another-mindset sense, if you were Justin Warrick, if you knew Giraud, if you had no power and nothing to bluff with except Ari Emory and a potential for trouble.

"So," he said, "I just—saw a chance. I didn't thoroughly plan it. I just saw what you did with the Carnath girl—Amy—and thought—if you blew up, well, maybe I could patch it. If you covered me—it'd get to Giraud. Maybe it'd look like more than it was and worry hell out of him. I'm sorry if it's fouled *you* up; but I doubt it has; fouled up your plans to keep me pure in Security's sight, maybe; worried Denys, I'm sure; —but messed up anything for you, personally, —I very much doubt it."

"Nothing like the mess you've made for yourself."

"Good. On both counts."

"You're a damned fool! You could *tell* me, you know, you could trust I can keep an eye to Jordan—"

"No, I can't trust that. I can't trust that, when you're *not* in contact with the military, when you're *not* in Giraud's position and you're not in Denys' chair either. I can't depend on your knowing what they're up to, I'm sorry."

He *didn't* know Base One's extent. Had no idea. And there was no telling him. Not on any account. She sipped her vodka-and-orange, set it down and shook her head.

"You could at least have consulted me."

"And put you on your guard? No. Now done's done. I'm being honest, since you've asked. I'm asking you one more thing: run a probe if you like, but *don't* give the tape to Denys."

"Who said I did?"

"I don't know. I just have my suppositions what would appease Denys. Don't give this one out. It can only harm my father. It sure won't make me look any better to either one of the Nyes."

"Except if I don't they'll be sure I'm going along with what you did."

"So you are turning the tapes over."

"The ones I admit to running. I've never let them have Ari's notes on you. I've never shown them what I did to settle some of the damage Ari left. The unresolved stuff. I've never shown them the little intervention that lets you be here, this close to me, without sweating."

"Without worse than that. Without much worse than that. I'm still getting tape-flash now and again. But most of the charge is gone. I only remember—at much more distance than I've ever had—or I never could have done what I did at the party; never could have come here; never could have contemplated—my real plan for irritating Giraud."

"That being?"

"Going to bed with you."

That jolted, hard. It was so matter-of-fact she was half embarrassed, only dimly offended at first blink.

"Not," he said, "that I thought of doing anything you hadn't flatly asked me—once and twice, and recently. Make you happy—make Giraud quite, quite unhappy. And not in a way that could hurt you . . . I never wanted that. To be honest, I wasn't sure I could. So I just—took a different course when it offered itself, that's all. I hope I don't offend you. And I wouldn't mention it, except I'd rather explain it with my wits about me, thank you, where I can at least string things together in my own defense. So there you are. That's why.''

It was a deliberate move that made it psychologically harder for her to insist on a probe . . . quieten things down: defuse the situation. And tell enough of the truth to make everything reasonable.

Come in here without Grant, too. *That*, when he knew he was potentially in trouble.

Damn, possibilities multiplied ad infinitum when it involved motives and an unacknowledged Special whose stresses came from everywhere and everyone—not least the fact that she had Worked him under kat, grabbed hold of things which were profoundly important to him and tried, at least, to tie up the old threads—far as one could in a mind that had changed so much since Ari's notes; and considering the psychological difference of their reversed ages.

Very tangled. Very, very tangled.

"You've messed up work of mine," she said. "You've made me problems. I've got reason to be mad. And I supported you out there, dammit."

"Yes," he said. "Which I hoped you'd do."

"It's a damn mess." She swallowed down any assurances she could give of Jordan's safety. Or how she knew. Frustrating as it was to look like a fool, better that than be one. "Dammit, you've put me at odds with Giraud. I don't see why I should have to handle problems you've made me because you could betray my interests and trust I'd forgive you. That's a hell of a thing."

"I didn't have a choice."

"You damn well did! You could have told me."

He shook his head, slowly.

"You're really pushing me, Justin. You're damn well pushing me."

"I didn't have a choice."

"And now I've got to cooperate and keep Giraud's hands off you or he'll blow your whole little scheme, is that it?"

"Something like. What else can I say? I hope you will. I *hope* you will; and I don't hope for too much in my life."

"Thanks."

He nodded, once, ironically.

"So you get off cheap," she said. "You get everything you want and you don't even have to go to bed with me."

"Ari, I didn't mean that."

"I know. Not fair."

There was a deep-link in his sets—to Ari. And she knew that. Knew that it was active, in this place, at this time.

That it was double-hooked. He hoped to snare her into it—to irritate Giraud. He was still maneuvering: she knew where it was going.

But there were deeper hooks than he knew.

"You want me to?" he asked.

"I don't know," she said. Then: "No. Not like it was pay for something. There's a security wall down the hall. There's a guest accommodation on the other side. You go there. Florian will get you through. I'll call Grant to come up. Florian and Catlin will supervise Housekeeping, shutting down your apartment, packing up what you'll need. If they leave anything out, you can go back with them to get it."

He looked shocked.

"You want my help," she said, "it does cost. It costs you the apartment you have. It costs you your independence. It costs you convenience the way it costs me. But you're not going to go into Security and you're damn sure not going to spill what you know about me to Giraud either. Which is the other part of your threat, isn't it?"

"I don't know what I know—"

"I'm sure you could figure it. You come and go through that security door; your cards will admit you. You'll move into Wing One facilities, and I don't know who I'm going to have to bump to make room for you, but you're going inside Wing One security, and inside my security; and I don't want any argument about it."

"None," he said quietly.

————————————— X —————————————

"Grant is here," the Minder said, and Justin leapt up off the couch, was at the door almost before Grant could open it, as Grant came alone into the apartment.

"Are you all right?" Grant asked, first-off.

"Fine," Justin said, and embraced him. "Thank God. No trouble?"

Grant shook his head, and drew a breath. "I got the call, I told Em hold the office down—I walked out into the hall and Catlin picked me up. Walked me all the way to the lift. She said she'd go to the apartment and bring essentials and anything we call down for."

No questions, nothing. Habit of half a lifetime. "We can talk," Justin said, realizing that fact—that there was nothing, now, that could be secret if Ari wanted it, nothing that anyone *but* Ari was going to reach, here, in this place. It was a moment of vertigo, old cautions tumbling away into dark on either side. The thought shook him, left him lonely for reasons he could not understand. "God, it's not home, is it?"

Grant held on to him. He felt himself shivering, suddenly, he had no notion why, or what he feared, specifically, only that nothing seemed certain any longer . . . not even their habits of self-defense.

Not home. Not the place he had always lived, not the obscurity they had tried to maintain. They were closer and closer to the center of Reseune.

"No probe," he said. "Ari asked why—reasonable question. I told her. This is her notion of increased security. I've got to show you around this place. You won't believe it."

He got control of his nerves, turned Grant around and gave him the full perspective of the living room and dining room.

It was a huge apartment by any standards: a front hall mostly stone, roofed in plasticized woolwood; a sitting-room with a gray sectional, black glass tables; and beyond that a dining hall with white tile, white walls, black and white furnishings— *My God*, Justin's first thought had been, an emotional impact of stark coldness, an irrational: *one red pillow, anything, to save your sanity in this damn place—*

"It's—quite large," Grant said, —diplomatically, he thought: "isn't it?"

"Come on," he said, and took Grant the tour.

It was better in the halls, pastel blues and greens leading off to a frost-green kitchen and a white hall to a suite of rooms in grays and blues—a lot of gray stone, occasional brown. A sybaritic bath in black and silver, mirrored. Another one, white and frost-green glass.

"My God," Grant said, when he opened another door on the master bedroom, black and black glass and white, huge bed. "Five people could sleep in that."

"They probably have," Justin said. And suffered a moment of flashback, a bad one. "They promise us sheets and supplies. There's some sort of scanning system they run things through, even our clothes. It puts some kind of marker on it. If we pass the door with anything that hasn't gone through scan—"

"Alarm sounds. Catlin explained that. Right down to the socks and underwear." Grant shook his head and looked at him. "Was she angry?"

He did not mean Catlin. Justin nodded. "Somewhat. God knows she's got a right to be, considering. But she's willing to listen. At least—that."

Grant said nothing. But the silence itself was eloquent as the little muscle twitch in the eyes toward the overhead. *Do we worry about monitoring?*

Because Grant knew—Grant knew everything that he had confessed to Ari and then some, as far as their intention to divert Giraud. But there were things between himself and Ari he could not say where monitoring might exist, things she might go after under probe, but he could not bring them out, coldly, and have her know that Grant knew: the feeling he had had in that room in Ari's apartment, the shifting between then and now—

The gut-deep feeling—passing at every other blink between then and now; to look into Ari's eyes gone by turns young and old—knowing, for the first time since he was younger than she was now—that the sexual feelings that haunted every touch of other human beings, every dealing he had with humanity—had a focus, had always had a specific, drug-set focus—

He might have gone to bed with her. He could have gone to

bed with her—in one part of his imagining. More, he had *wanted* to, for about two heartbeats—until he had flashed, badly, waiting on her answer, and known that he would panic; and was caught somewhere between a fevered hope of her and a sweating terror. As if she was the key.

Or the destruct.

God, what has she done to me?

What keys has she got?

"Justin?" Grant said, and caught his arm. "Justin, —"

He held to Grant's shoulder and shuddered. "O God, Grant. . . ."

"What's wrong?" Grant's fingers gripped the back of his neck, pressed hard. "Justin?"

His heart raced. He lost vision for a moment, broken out in sweat, feeling himself nowhere at all, if Grant were not holding to him.

That's what Ari wanted—all those years ago. Wanted me—fixed on her—

I've lost everything, dragged Grant and Jordan with me—

This is all there'll ever be, sweet—

Worm. Psychmaster. She was the best there ever was—

Pleasure and pain. *Deep-set links—*

His heart made a few deep, painful beats. But he could adjust to that, the way he adjusted to everything, always. Life *was*, that was all. One lived.

Even knowing that the worst thing that had been done to him all those years ago was not sexual. Sex was only the leverage.

Endocrine-learning and flux, applied full-force, the kind of wrench that could take a vulnerable, frightened kid and twist him sideways into another research, another path for his entire existence.

She saw to my birth.

One could live. Even with the ground dropping out from under one's feet. Even with black space all around.

"What did she do?" Grant asked him, a sane, worried voice out of that mental dark, a hard pressure around him, at the back of his neck. "Justin?"

"She gave me the keys a long time ago," he murmured. "I knew, dammit, I knew—I should have seen. . . ."

Things began to focus then. Vision came back, the edge of

Grant's shoulder, the stark black and white room that was not home, the knowledge that, foreseeably, they would not go back to the friendly, familiar apartment with the brown stone and the little breakfast nook that had always seemed safe, no matter what they knew about Security monitoring. . . .

"She knew she was dying, Grant. She was the best damned analyst going— She could read a subject like no one I ever saw. D'you think she never knew Giraud?"

"Ari senior?" Grant asked.

"Ari. She knew Giraud was no genius. She knew who would follow her. Do you think she didn't know them better than we do? Ari said—I was the only one who could teach her. The *only one*. That she needs my work. And she's working off Ari's notes, doing what Ari told her to do . . . all down the line."

Grant pushed him back. He stared up into Grant's worried face, seeing it as a stranger would, in an objective way he had never looked at Grant, the unlikely perfection—Ari's handiwork too, from his genesets to his psychset.

Everything was, everything. No good, any longer, in fighting the design. Even Grant was part of it. He was snared, he had always been.

She wanted Jordan. Jordan failed her. She saw to my creation. Designed Grant.

Fixed me on her—in one damnable stroke—

Everything's connected to everything—

Field too large, field too large—

"Justin?"

God, is the kid that good, does she know what she's doing to me?

Whose hand was on the switch in there? Which Ari?

Does it even matter—that one could set a path that sure— that the other could operate, just take it up and go—

Grant seized his face between his hands, popped a light slap against his cheek. "Justin!"

"I'm all right," he said.

I'm scaring hell out of him. But I'm not scared. Just— Cold as hell now. Calm.

Helps, when you know the truth, doesn't it?

"—I'm all right. Just—went a little sideways for a moment.'' He patted Grant's shoulder, distanced himself a few steps and looked down the hall, the strange, not-home hallway. ''Like—I'd waked up. Like—for a moment—I could just shake it all off. Think right past it.'' He felt Grant's hand on his shoulder, and he acknowledged it with a pressure of his own—scared again, because he was alone where he was standing, and Grant wanted to be with him, but he was not sure Grant could be—that anyone could be. And Ari was out so far ahead of him, in territory that was hers and her predecessor's, in places that he could not reach.

Places Jordan had never been.

Ultimate isolation.

''Our poor kid,'' he murmured, ''*is* Ari. Damn, she is. No one ever caught up to her. She's going out into that place no one else can get to and no one can really speak to. That's what's going to happen to her. Happening to me . . . sometimes.'' He blinked and tried to come back. To see the lights again. The damned stark decor. Black and white dining room down the hall. ''God, Housekeeping's got to have a red vase or something, doesn't it? Pillows. Pictures. Something.''

''What are you talking about?'' Grant asked.

The Super's training tried to assert itself. *Get yourself together. You're scaring him.* ''Flux. Not a damn thing human in this apartment. Until we get a few things up from ours. Things with color. Things that are *us*. God, this place is like a bath in ice water.''

''Is that what's the matter?''

''Something like.'' He blinked rapidly, trying to clear his eyes of the fog and focus short-range. ''Maybe just—thinking this was where we would have ended up, if Ari had lived a little longer. This would have been ours.''

''Justin, what in hell are you talking about?''

''Common sense. Ari didn't want to ruin Jordan. She needed his abilities. She was dying. She knew the Nyes for pragmatic sons of bitches. Conservative as hell. She wasn't. And *they* were going to have her successor. Don't you think she worried about that? And if she'd had two more years, even six more months, I think—I damn well know—I wouldn't have been what she took in. I might have been able to fight Giraud. Might have had some input into Ari's upbringing.

Might be in Administration, might be high in the Bureau, by now, maybe sitting in Peterson's chair, who knows?''

Now—I'm not that person.

But Ari's following her predecessor's program. Following her notes.

It's a dangerous course for her. If Ari hasn't the perspective to figure that out, to figure me out—it's very dangerous.

Not because I wish her harm.

Because I can't help it. I have ties—I can't shed.

"I don't want to hurt her, Grant."

"Is there a question of it?"

It was too much to say. Ari had sworn there was no monitoring, but that was only the truth she wished were so: her capabilities were another story. Ari would lie by telling what she wished instead of what she would do: Ari had confessed that to him—manipulative in that admission as in anything else she did. *Never take me for simple . . . in any sense.*

"No," he answered Grant. "Not by anything *I* want."

Are you listening, Ari?

Do you hear what I'm saying?

—————————————— xi ——————————————

"Message," the Minder said, waking Ari out of sleep, and waking Florian.

"Coded private, Base Three."

Giraud.

Giraud was in Novgorod. Or had been when she went to sleep.

"Damn," she said; and rolled out of bed and searched for her slippers and her robe.

"Shall I get up, sera?"

"Go back to sleep," she said. "It's just Giraud going through the overhead. What else did I expect? Probably one from Denys too. . . ."

She found one slipper and the other as she put her arms into the sleeves, found the sashes and lapped them. "A little light," she said, "dammit, Minder. Eight seconds. On in the hall."

The room light came up a little, enough to see her way to the door, while—a backward glance—Florian pulled the covers over his head and burrowed into the dark. Eight seconds. She opened the door to the outside, blinking in brighter light, rubbing her eyes, as the light faded behind her.

She shut the door, and saw Catlin in the hall, in her nightrobe, her hair loose. "Back to bed," she told Catlin. "Just Giraud."

Catlin vanished.

She wanted a cup of something warm. But she was not about to rouse either of them: they had worked themselves to exhaustion getting Justin packed and upstairs before the rest of House Security could get at Justin's belongings or Justin's notes, and getting enough essentials through the Residency scanners to give them a choice of clothing and the basics for breakfast and to put their working notes into their hands again—after which, she reckoned, Justin might be a good deal happier.

Giraud certainly would not be.

She went into her office, tucked up in the chair and said, "Minder, message. I'm alone."

"Message, Base Three to Base One. Ari, this is Giraud."

All right, all right. Who else?

"Abban's flying down with this tape and flying back again tonight. He'll probably be on his way back to the airport by the time the system's alerted you. I can't afford this time. He can't. But I expect you know what's got me upset."

Three guesses, uncle Giraud? Is this about the dance?

Or have you heard your niece's latest?

"I'm terribly worried, Ari. I've made multiple tries at recording this message. The first one wasn't polite. But I think I can understand at least the reasons behind your reasons.

"I'm not going to yell at you. Isn't that what you always used to say: if you're going to yell at me, uncle Giraud, I'm not going to listen.

"We're both too old for that, and this is much too important for temper to get into it. So please, listen to this all the way through. It's ephemeral in the system unless you capture and copy—which you may do. If you do, I leave it to your discretion whether to send it to Archive, but I advise otherwise for reasons which may occur to you. This message is cued only to

Base One. Unless I am dangerously mistaken, that will assure you are the only recipient.

"There's been another bombing. You may have heard."

Damn. No.

"*Major restaurant. Five dead, nineteen injured. New Year's Day crowds. That's what we're dealing with. Lunatics, Ari. People who don't care about their targets.*

"*Let me go through this point by point, as logically as I can, why what you've done regarding young Warrick isn't advisable.*

"*I advised you in the first place against coming to Novgorod. I foresaw a press furor that could well lead to more bombings, and the public is damn tense—putting up with it, surviving, but ready to find a focus for their problems, and I don't want that blood on you, understand. Certainly we don't need to make you a center of controversy.*

"*Your suggestion to lend enforcement and surveillance help under Reseune's aegis is a damned fine one. I'm ashamed not to have thought of the means: Novgorod city government's touchy and suspicious of anything that massive with Reseune's stamp on it, but they're desperate, and that gives them an alternative to the several other routes they don't want to go— they don't want the precedent of calling on the regular military; they don't have the funds to Contract more personnel. Reseune Security in the subways is bound to be a target, but no sitting target, either—and we can muster enough to handle it: borrow the transport and the weapons from the military, at a level where Novgorod doesn't have to be acutely aware of that connection; shore up Jacques, too: the armed forces are chafing at what they call a do-nothing policy across the board. Success at something, success at anything, would make the whole administration of Union look a damned sight better.*

"*Which brings up another point, Ari. One I'm no happier talking about than you can imagine—but you and I both know that I'm on the downward slide.*"

Pity, uncle Giraud?

Shame on you.

"*Just de-charge the situation and listen to me. I want you to start thinking clearly about what in hell you're going to do when I die, because I can assure you your enemies are planning for it.*

"Khalid is beyond the two year rule. He could challenge Jacques again now. He could, but he hasn't filed. The Centrists are nominally backing Jacques. They're scared of Khalid: he's not someone they can control and Corain in particular sees Khalid as a clear danger to himself, someone who'd like to take the helm from him—and Corain's no young man any longer. Khalid calls Corain a tired old grandfather . . . behind closed doors, but that kind of thing gets passed along, in private circles.

"Me, he calls a dead man. Not particularly pleasant, but I'm getting used to the idea. He doesn't know yet how right he is."

My God, uncle Giraud. What a view of things!

"Look at Council, Ari. Catherine Lao's almost my age. That's your most valuable ally besides Harad and myself. I'm going. Jacques is a very weak figure and Gorodin's grooming a replacement in the senior end of the admiralty board, in a man named Spurlin, able, but very middle-of-the-spectrum, very strictly the interests of his own Bureau, blow anyone else. Are you following this?"

Too well. I'm ahead of you.

"I made a terrible mistake, Ari, when I moved against Warrick without consulting you. We crossed one another, and to your damage. I made a further mistake when I didn't level with you then. Now I have reason to suspect you've passed at least my Base . . ."

Oh. Dear.

". . . and possibly Denys' as well—either that or you have an uncanny timing.

"I confess that threw me. I didn't know then what to do. I'm old and I'm sick and I'm scared, Ari. But I'm not going to get maudlin. Just in that very bright mind of yours, you should realize that your uncles have human weaknesses. I should have taken immediate measures I failed to take. When I was younger I might have done better, but I'm not sure I would have. Doubts like that, you understand, are the bane of any reasoning mind. Do I not act because I see too much and the choices are too wide—or because I just can't make a choice?

"I'm making one now. A desperate one. I'm laying out the truth for you. Jordan Warrick is in direct contact with a man named McCabe, in air systems maintenance, who has direct links to Mikhail Corain's office. I'm appending the entire report into Base One . . ."

You're supposed to have put all the security reports into House systems, uncle Giraud. And this is totally new. How much else have you held out?

". . . along with all our current files on Planys security. It's quite a mass of information. Suffice it to say, quite honestly, Warrick is repeating an old pattern. You'll find in there a transcript from a meeting of Warrick with Secretary of Defense Lu, back in Gorodin's administration, a very secret transcript, that never came out at the hearings. Warrick was dealing, right before your predecessor's death, for his transfer out to Fargone, and all that goes with it. Warrick was discovered in his scheme. It collapsed. Everything went up in smoke. Ari caught him dealing with Corain and I imagine Ari told him the truth of what was going on with his son.

"Jordan Warrick saw that tape. I can attest to that. Exactly what his professional skills are capable of making out of it, with his own knowledge of his son, I don't know—but I know, you know, young Warrick knows, and I'm damned sure Jordan Warrick knows—that it was more than sexual gymnastics and more than a blackmail trip. He knew at that point that, A, Denys and I wouldn't let him get his son back in his hands to work with; and B, Ari had been working on him for a number of sessions he couldn't estimate. In Jordan Warrick's place, what would you conclude?"

My God, Giraud.

"Jordan Warrick is very well aware of his son's association with you. We've monitored very closely—to know what he does know. And what he can see is his son increasingly involved with you, with more and more to lose in any accident to you. That part of what you've done is instinctively correct, Ari. I tried to prevent it in the first place, afraid you were being an adolescent about the matter, but somewhere in the flux, your instincts are still quite true. And now I remember, as old men will, that Ari was very much the same. So I rely on that; and I warn you: Jordan has never trusted his son. Justin has never

understood his father. Justin—is an idealist and an honest man, and as such, he is very useful as an instrument. But he is vulnerable to his father; and his father is your implacable enemy, your enemy on principle, your enemy in his opposition to Reseune and all it stands for. I worry less about your having sex with this man than about your public defense of him—your stripping away the political isolation we've placed him in. We've kept him powerless to harm you. That you might sleep with him is, at this point, an inconsequence. If it would cure the sexual infatuation I would be delighted.

"But bringing this man into prominence in Reseune—is deadly.

"Let me go afield a moment. I know you're able to compass this interconnection of facts.

"Gorodin's medical reports look worse than mine. I don't know about Lao's. I figure that I have, granted nothing goes catastrophically wrong, maybe this year in tolerable health. After that, Lynch is going to have to take more and more of the operations and leave me the decision-making. Which I plan to make you privy to, along with Denys.

"What will happen when I die . . . if I can prevail on my brother to leave Reseune, I'll appoint him proxy and he can stand for election. If. Denys is not taking my death well.

"I haven't thanked you properly for your—vote of confidence in me. Frankly, I'm not sure what the proper response is to finding out I'll be replicated—a little flattered, I suppose, not exactly personally involved, except as it consoles Denys. I'm sure I won't know personally. I'm not even sure that it's true, or that I'm that important, although Denys is, and in the context of my value to him—I can well see there might be a point to it. But if it is true, for God's sake don't make it public. The public can accept the entity you call the cute kid. But I was always a sullen brat, your predecessor would have told you that; and I'm sure you can think what kind of furor it could stir up if my enemies could look forward to another round with Giraud Nye. I suppose Justin does know what you intend. He's altogether too close to your affairs; and I hope to hell he hasn't gotten that word to Jordan; because if he has, it's in Corain's office by now, and I can about swear that will be exactly the route.

"I don't want Denys to take guardianship of my replicate. Give that job to Yanni. He's at least as hardheaded as our father was; and I really want Denys in Novgorod, in office, and on the job, if any force can move him. You're not able to take Reseune Administration: you'll be at most twenty, and it needs a much more experienced hand. The logical candidate to administer Reseune is Yanni Schwartz. But you must above all else start taking a more public role and establishing a more professional image. You have to stand for that seat in your own right, at the right time.

"But don't count on your enemies standing still for that day. Khalid, I'm sure, has never forgotten what you and I did to him. I'm virtually certain, but I can't prove, that there is some very vague linkage among the Paxers, the Rocher party, the Abolitionists, and some allegedly respectable elements in the Centrist party, some of which links go perhaps very high indeed. I don't say that Khalid is bombing subways. I do think that he's prepared to use the whole issue of your existence and the Paxer movement against you—the fear of Reseune's power—all of that—

"The moment I'm dead, I figure there'll not only be the election in Science, but Khalid will challenge Jacques. We're caught in a situation in this. We're not enthusiastic about Gorodin's man Spurlin. Gorodin's health won't let him run again. Lu is disaffected, a bitter man. We're pressing Jacques to resign now and appoint Spurlin as proxy. He sees this as an Expansionist plot—correctly. But he doesn't admit that he can't beat Khalid again; and he won't look at his own polls that show him slipping badly. A case either of a man being pressured by Corain to hold on in hopes of a change in the polls; or a man being a fool. Corain tells me privately that he's urged Jacques to step down. He says Jacques refuses, that Jacques privately resents the label as a seat-warmer and a mouthpiece for Gorodin, Jacques is determined to hold the office in his own right, after Gorodin dies—a case of one man's vanity impinging on Union's future.

"What I'm afraid is going to happen is the following: two elections going, and no knowing how Gorodin's health will be. And in the wake of media interest in my death, and Denys' succession to the seat—that's precisely when I'm afraid Jordan

Warrick is going to break his silence and come up with charges of his own, one of which is very likely going to be a claim of his own innocence and the claim that I blackmailed him into accepting blame for Ari's death. I think you can see the mess you're about to create in rehabilitating his son. I hope you can see it. Your predecessor wouldn't fail me in this."

God. Dear God.

Is he innocent?

"There's no way in hell Jordan Warrick can testify or be questioned, without a major change in the law. He can make charges with the same immunity that he has in keeping silent. He can say anything. And this is a man who's waited two decades for this chance . . . who will have his chance, now, because we gave up our chance to have linked him to the Paxers. We still can, if you're willing to use your head. I'm afraid it wouldn't win you young Warrick's gratitude. But then again, you're much cleverer than I am, young sera. And maybe you can navigate those rocks.

"You have your predecessor's notes in Justin Warrick's case. You have run an intervention on him, I very much suspect, of what sort I will not speculate: I only know that the gesture he made at the party last night would once have been impossible for him. Having had him under probe a number of times, I know him and I know the nature of his problems, only some of which stem from that session with your predecessor—"

Damn you. *Damn* you, Giraud!

"Not to stand in the way of young love, Ari, sweet, but Justin's father put a damned heavy load on him. If you've got Ari's notes you know that. You count yourself expert enough to take on a case Petros and Gustav won't touch, I'll trust you can add up the stresses on Justin Warrick and figure out what's going on with him. And you can add up the stresses that will result if he hears his father claim he was framed and unjustly treated.

"I'm at the point where I have to surrender a good many things to young hands. I thought that, frankly, I could rid you of a very unpleasant decision. You've appropriated it to yourself by your maneuvers to forestall me and to prevent me from discrediting Jordan Warrick. I neither beg nor plead with you

at this point. I'm accustomed to being the villain in the Family. I have no objection to bowing out in that role. If you would care to turn your back in the affair of Jordan Warrick, I could foresee that you could turn proof of his activities to your considerable personal advantage in dealing with Justin Warrick. I'm sure you understand me. If you decide on that course you have only to call on me.

"You assuredly know now why I have taken extreme precautions to prevent this tape from seeing Archives. It's potentially deadly. Never mind my reputation. Your own safety is in question, and if you use that famous wit of yours, you will look to that to the exclusion of all else.

"Above all, keep power out of the hands of people you would want to protect. Out of a hundred thirty-three years of living, love, that's the highest wisdom I can come to.

"I'll keep you posted. Abban may make many of these flights. I don't trust regular communications. Don't you.

"Above all, take this for a storm-warning. I'm taking excellent care of myself. I've given up my few vices for your sake, to buy you time. Remember my offer. Position yourself carefully, and don't be careless with your associates. Justice, guilt and innocence are irrelevant. Motivation and opportunity are the things you have to watch. Nothing else has any validity."

"Endit."

She sat still a long while.

"Log-off," she said finally.

And got up and went back to the bedroom.

Florian waked when she came in. Or had never been asleep. She got in beneath the covers. And stared into the dark.

"Is there trouble, sera?"

"Just Giraud," she said, and rolled over and put her arm around him, burrowed down against his shoulder, smothering the anger, fighting it with all she had. "God. Florian. Do something, will you?"

2424: 2/3: 2223

B/1: Ari senior has a message.
Stand by.
Ari, this is Ari senior.
You've asked about power.
That's a magic word, sweet. Are you alone?
AE2: Yes.
B/1: You are 18 years old. You are legally adult. You have authority of: Wing Supervisor; Alpha Supervisor.

You have flagged for systems surveillance: Denys Nye; Giraud Nye; Petros Ivanov; Yanni Schwartz; Wendell Peterson; John Edwards; Justin Warrick; Jordan Warrick; Gustav Morley; Julia Carnath; Amy Carnath; Maddy Strassen; Victoria Strassen; Sam Whitely; Stef Dietrich; Yvgenia Wojkowski; Anastasia Ramirez; Eva Whitely; Julia Strassen; Gloria Strassen; Oliver AOX Strassen; and all their associations.

Additionally you have flagged for exterior surveillance and news-service monitoring: priority one: Mikhail Corain; Vladislaw Khalid; Simon Jacques; Giraud Nye; Leonid Gorodin; James Lynch; Thomas Spurlin; Ludmilla deFranco; Catherine Lao; Nasir Harad; Andrew McCabe; and all their households.

Do you wish to add or subtract?

AE2: Continue.

B/1: Ari, this is Ari senior.

You are monitoring inside and outside Reseune. You hold economic and administrative power inside Reseune with a rating of: excellent performance.

I advise against any move against Administration on the grounds of: chronological age.

NewsScan profile indicates No security anomaly within Reseune's internal surveillance. Do you disagree?

AE2: No.

B/1: You've asked about power. There are three parts to that. Taking it. Holding it. Using it. Taking it and holding it are very closely related: if you pay less attention to the second than to the first you are in trouble, because the same dynamics that put you in power will operate as well for someone else against you.

Let me tell you: physical force will only work on lower levels. Don't discount it. But the most effective way to power is through persuasion. This means psych, personally applied, and massively applied. If you have followed my work this far, you understand when I say that the press is one of the most valuable tools you will have to work with.

There are at least three possible situations with the press. A, Completely free; B, Free in some areas, controlled in others; C, Completely controlled. In the first instance, the press is vulnerable to direct manipulation; in the second, vulnerable to direct manipulation in some areas, but vulnerable to tactics which increase public distrust of official information; in the third state, rumor is potentially more powerful than the press, and with an efficient organization you can equally well turn that situation to your advantage. Which of the three do you estimate is the case?

AE2: The second.

B/1: Analysis indicates a period of unrest.

Intersection of data indicates reason for concern.

Your NewsScan profile is: low activity; predominantly favorable. Consider carefully the effects of a change in this profile at this time.

Always respect the power of public opinion. Need I say that to a Reseune-trained operator?

Remember that change in social macrosystems operates rarely like earthquake, more frequently like subsoil ice, deforming the terrain in general ways, by gravity and topological constraints. The potential for cataclysmic events is comparatively easy to figure: figuring the precise moment or trigger of fracture is not; while the temporal component in slow change is relatively easy to figure, the total direction of change is complex, involving more individual action. Politicians frequently ride the earthquakes; while Reseune has always operated best in the subsoil, slowly, with frequent small adjustments.

I distrust such models. But I trust I am giving them to an adult who understands me.

I urge you consider the changes in Novgorod and in Cyteen in your own lifetime, and in mine, and in Olga's. I predict they will be extreme, and I urge you watch several areas.

a) An early problem will be the pressure of CIT population increase, particularly in Novgorod, particularly on stations such as Esperance and Pan-Paris, which do not lie on the routes of proposed expansion: eventually CITs will find that jobs are not as easy to come by, and that will lead to increased power for the Abolitionists who call for the cessation of azi production.

b) Interstellar government having its capital resident in a world-based city is increasingly fraught with problems, however much the situation has been advantageous to Reseune. It may in your lifetime produce difficulties and threaten Union: placing the capital specifically at Novgorod instead of Cyteen Station exposed Union politics to Cyteen influence and to Cyteen economics in ways which I do not think healthy. Be alert for that sentiment. It will come, though perhaps not in your lifetime.

It is possible in the future that for reasons presently unforeseen, Novgorod may diminish in power and influence within

Cyteen and consequently pose less problem, but I doubt it: geography favors it and the presence of Union government fattens it. I foresee it clinging to the government by every means possible, including dirty politics and gerrymandering which could threaten Union. Particularly beware the intersection of a) and b) or b) and c).

c) The discovery that Reseune has tampered with social dynamics at Gehenna and elsewhere could create widespread panic and distrust of Reseune's influence.

d) The mere potential for Earth's further intervention in Alliance affairs or outside human space, acts as a destabilizing force in Alliance-Union relations; an actual or perceived threat from that quarter could worsen relations.

e) The opportunity for major gains by political opposition during the interregnum of your guardians, and the death and defeat of various of my own allies in the interim, will likely effect the rise of major new political forces, some of whom may well be radically Abolitionist. I predict that within a decade or so of my death Mikhail Corain will be viewed as too moderate to control his own allies, and it is foreseeable that a more radical figure will unseat him, possibly changing the Centrists considerably. Particularly look to the effects of your own emergence into public life. I had enemies. You will face opposition which may have superstitious roots, in fear of the unknown, in fear of you as a political force, and in fear of what the science which brought you into being could mean—to a society only recently adapting to rejuv. Uncertainty of any sort creates demagogues.

f) A major new discovery of non-human intelligence might destabilize the situation I left, and might come at any time. I urge you press for expansion in safe areas and for necessary precaution against hostile contact. We do not know our time limits and we are scarcely stable enough in my time to deal with that eventuality.

g) There may be major divergences from my policies inside Reseune, and there exists the chance that you have either made personal enemies on-staff or that you are perceived as standing for policies others oppose.

h) A major breakdown could occur within a designed azi population, or there may be major difficulties in CIT-azi inte-

*grations within a given population. I hope this does not come
to pass, but my best estimate of a problem area would be Pan-
Paris, where economic constraints and military retirees may
pose hardships: next most likely: Novgorod, in the third generation . . . where the old rebel ethos of the founders of Union
may well find difficulty mixing with the Constitution-venerating
descendants of the wartime worker-azi, and where population
pressures and Cyteen's ability to terraform new habitat on that
site may run a narrow race indeed.*

I hope time has proven me wrong in some of these things.

*But I urge you to study these situations and to prepare re-
sponses to them, before you make any move on your own.*

*Avoid precipitate action: by this I mean, don't be too quick
to take what you're not ready for; don't be so late that you
have to move hastily and without adequate groundwork.*

*Power of any kind lays heavy responsibility on you; and it
changes your friends as it changes the way your friends regard
you. Do not be naive in this regard. Do not assume. Do not
overburden your friends with too much trust.*

*Above all remember what I said in the beginning: respect
the power of public opinion.*

NewsScan shows mention of you: 3 articles in last 3 months.

Mention of Giraud Nye: 189 articles in last 3 months.

Mention of Mikhail Corain: 276 articles in last 3 months.

Mention of Reseune: 597 articles in last 3 months.

Mention of Paxers: 1058 articles in last 3 months.

Continue?

**AE2: Base One, give me the nature, location, and time of
Ari senior's last entry into the House system.**

B/1: Working.

Entry by TransSlate; 1004A, 2404: 10/22: 1808.

**AE2: Give me the location and time of Ari senior's
death.**

B/1: Working.

1004A.

Autopsy ruling: 2404: 10/22: 1800 to 1830 approximate.

**AE2: 1004A is the cold lab in Wing One basement. Cor-
rect?**

B/1: Correct.

AE2: Who else has accessed this information?

B/1: No prior access.

AE2: Replay entry.

B/1: Working.

Order: Security 10: Com interrupt: Jordan Warrick, all outgoing calls. Claim malfunction. Order good until canceled.

AE2: Base One, is that the last entry from Ari from any source?

B/1: Working.

Affirmative.

AE2: Base One, at what time did Jordan Warrick enter Wing One basement security door on 10/22, 2404?

B/1: Working.

Wing One basement security door coded 14. Jordan Warrick's key accessed D14 at 1743 hours, that date.

AE2: Departure, same visit?

B/1: 1808 hours, that date: duration of visit: 25 minutes. . . .

AE2: Record current session to Personal Archive. Give me the full transcript, Autopsy, Ariane Emory; all records, Jordan Warrick, keyword: Emory, keyword: trial; keyword: murder; keyword: hearings; keyword: Council; keyword: investigation.

CHAPTER 4

"The first bill on the agenda is number 6789, for the Bureau of Trade," Nasir Harad said, "Ludmilla deFranco, Simon Jacques co-sponsors, proposing restructuring of the Pan-Paris credit system. Call for debate."

"Citizens," Mikhail Corain said, lifting his hand. "For the bill."

"Finance," Chavez said. "For the bill."

"Move to forgo debate," Harogo said, "in the absence of opposition."

Corain cast a look down the table, toward Nye, who had reached for his water glass.

It was a bargain, the time-saving sort. The acquiescence of the Expansionists in the move designed to take pressure off the ailing Pan-Paris central bank, the promise of military contracts, the private assurance that Reseune would grant more time on the considerable sum Pan-Paris owed—of course it would: Pan-Paris was Lao's central constituency and the bill was the first step in a long-proposed settlement on the Wyatt's Paradise–Pan-Paris loop that called for a fusion-powered station at Maronne Point, where there was only dark mass, but enough to pull a ship in.

There were four bills lined up, Expansionists falling all over themselves after decades of opposition, finally diverting funds from the slow construction of Hope to the more immediate difficulties of home space and a trade loop that had gotten, since the War, damnably short of exportable commodities.

Major construction, finally, beyond the rebuilding of stations damaged in Azov's desperate push in the last stages of the War; beyond the endless restructurings of debt and adjustments necessary when the merchanters associated into Alliance and left Union banks holding enormous debt.

Seventy years later, a policy shift to save that trade loop became possible only because the special interests that had blocked it suddenly discovered there was nothing left to do.

"Move to suspend debate," Harad said in his usual mutter. "Second?"

"Second," Corain said.

"Call for the vote."

A clatter from down the table. Nye had knocked the water glass over his papers, and sat there—sat there, with the water running across his notes, in a frozen pose that at first seemed incongruous, as if he were listening for something.

Then Corain's heart ticked over a beat, a moment of alarm as he saw the imminent collapse, as Lao, next to Nye, rose in an attempt to hold him, as of a sudden everyone was moving, including the aides.

But Giraud Nye was slumping down onto the papers, sliding from his chair, completely limp as the azi Abban shoved Lao aside and caught Nye in his fall between the seats.

The Council, the aides, everyone broke into tumult, and Corain's heart was hammering. "Get Medical," he ordered Dellarosa, ordered whoever would go, while Abban had Nye on the floor, his collar open, applying CPR with methodical precision.

It was quiet then, except the aides slipping from the chamber—strange that no one moved, everyone seemed in a state of shock, except a junior aide offering to spell the azi.

Medical arrived, running steps, a clattering and banging of hand-carried equipment, Councillors and aides clearing back in haste to let the professionals through, then waiting while more medics got a portable gurney through and the working team and Abban, clustered about Nye, lifted him and lifted the gurney up.

Alive, Corain thought, shaken: he could not understand his own reaction, or why he was trembling when Nasir Harad, still standing, brought the gavel down on Chairman's discretion for an emergency recess.

No one moved to leave for a moment. Centrists and Expansionists looked at each other in a kind of vague, human shock, for about a half a hundred heartbeats.

Then Simon Jacques gathered up his papers, and others did, and Corain signaled to his own remaining aides.

After that it was a withdrawal, increasingly precipitate, to reassess, to find out in decent discretion how serious it was, whether Nye was expected to recover from this one.

Or not.

In which case—in which case nothing was the same.

_____ ii _____

"*. . . collapsed in the Council chamber,*" the public address said, throughout Reseune, and people stopped where they were, at their desks, in the halls, waiting; and Justin stood, with his arms full of printout from the latest run on Sociology, with that vague cold feeling about his heart that said that, whatever Giraud was to him personally—

—there was far worse.

"*He stabilized in the emergency care unit in the Hall of State and is presently in transit via air ambulance to the intensive care unit in Mary Stamford Hospital in Novgorod. There was early consideration of transfer to Reseune's medical facilities, but the available aircraft did not have necessary equipment.*

"*His companion Abban was with him at the time of the collapse, and remains with him in transit.*

"*Secretary Lynch has been informed and has taken the oath as interim proxy, for emergency business.*

"*Administrator Nye requests that expressions of concern*

and inquiries regarding his brother's condition be directed to
the desk at Reseune hospital, which is in current contact with
Stamford in Novgorod, and that no inquiries be made directly
to Novgorod.

"Reseune staff is urged to continue with ordinary schedules.
Bulletins will be issued as information becomes available."

"Damn," someone said, on the other side of the room,
"here it goes, doesn't it?"

Justin took his printout and left, out into the hall beyond the
glass partitions, where people lingered to talk in small groups.

He felt stares at his back, felt himself the object of attention
he did not want.

Felt—as if the ground had shifted underfoot, even if they
had known this was coming.

"It's the slow preparation," a tech said in his hearing. "He
may already be dead. They won't admit it—till the Bureau has
the proxy settled. They can't admit anything till then."

It was a dreadful thing—to go to Denys now. But a call on
the Minder was too cold and too remote; and Ari faced the
apartment door and identified herself to the Minder, with
Florian and Catlin at her back, and nothing—nothing to protect
her from the insecurity in front of her—an old man's impending bereavement, an old man facing a solitude he had never—
Giraud himself had said it—never been able to come to grips
with.

If Denys cried, she thought, if Denys broke down in front of
her he would be terribly ashamed; and angry with her; but she
was all the close family he had left, who did not want to be
here, who did not want, today, to be adult and responsible, in
the face of the mistake this visit could turn out to be.

But she had, she thought, to try.

"Uncle Denys," she said, "it's Ari. Do you want company?"

A small delay. The door opened suddenly, and she was facing Seely.

"Sera," Seely murmured, "come in."

The apartment was so small, so simple next her own. Denys
could always have had a larger one, could have had, in his long
tenure, any luxury he wanted. But it felt like home, in a nostal-

gic wrench that saw her suddenly a too-old stranger, and Florian and Catlin entering with her . . . grown-up and strange to the scale of this place: the little living room, the dining area, the suite off to the right that had been hers and theirs and Nelly's; the hall to the left that held Denys' office and bedroom, and Seely's spartan quarters.

She looked that direction as Denys came out of his office, pale and drawn, looking bewildered as he saw her.

"Uncle Denys," she said gently.

"You got the news," Denys said.

She nodded. And felt her way through it—herself, whom Union credited for genius in dealing with emotional contexts, in setting up and tearing down and reshaping human reactions—but it was so damned different, when the emotional context went all the way to one's own roots. Redirect, that was the only thing she could logic her way to. Redirect and refocus: *grief is a self-focused function and the flux holds so damn much guilt about taking care of ourselves.* . . . "Are *you* all right, uncle Denys?"

Denys drew a breath, and several others, and looked desperate for a moment. Then he firmed up his chin and said: "He's dying, Ari."

She came and put her arms around Denys, self-conscious— God, guilty: of calculation, of too much expertise; of being cold inside when she patted him on the shoulder and freed herself from him and said: "Seely, has uncle Denys still got that brandy?"

"Yes," Seely said.

"I have work to do," Denys said.

"The brandy won't hurt," she said. "Seely."

Seely went; and she hooked her arm in Denys' and took him as far as the dining table where he usually did his work.

"There's nothing you can do by worrying," she said. "There's nothing anyone can do by worrying. Giraud knew this was coming. Listen, you know what he's done, you know the way he's arranged things. What he'll want you to do—"

"I damned well *can't* do!" Denys snapped, and slammed his hand down on the table. "I don't intend to discuss it. Lynch will sit proxy. Giraud may recover from this. Let's not hold the funeral yet, do you mind?"

"Certainly I hope not." *He's not facing this. He's not accepting it.*

Seely, thank God, arrived with the brandy, while Florian and Catlin hovered near the door, gone invisible as they could.

She took her own glass, drank a little, and Denys drank, more than a little; and gave a long shudder.

"I can't go to Novgorod," Denys said. There was a marked fragility about the set of his mouth, a sweating pallor about his skin despite the cool air in the room. "You know that."

"You can do what you put your mind to, uncle Denys. But it's not time to talk about that kind of thing."

"I *can't*," Denys said, cradling the glass in his hands. "I've told Giraud that. He knows it. Take tape, he says. He knows damned well I'm not suited to holding office."

"It's not a question of that right now."

"He's *dying*, dammit. You know it and I know it. And his notions about my going to Novgorod—dammit, he knows better."

"You'd be very good."

"Don't be ridiculous. A public speaker? An orator? Someone to handle press conferences? There's no one less suited than I am to holding public office. Behind the scenes, yes, I'm quite good. But I'm much too old to make major changes. I'm not a public man, Ari. I'm not going to be. There's no tape fix for age, there's no damned tape fix to make me a speechmaker . . ."

"Giraud isn't exactly skilled at it, but he's a fine Councillor."

"Do you know," Denys said, "when I came down to the AG unit that time—that was the first time since I was nine, that I'd ever left these walls?"

"My God, uncle Denys."

"Didn't add that up? Shame on you. I came down to see my foster-niece risk her lovely neck, the way I watched from the airport remotes when your predecessor would come screaming in, in that damned jet. I hate disasters. I've always expected them. It's my one act of courage, you understand. *Don't* ask me to handle press conferences." Denys shook his head and leaned on his elbows on the table. "Young people. They risk their lives so damned lightly, and they know so little what they're worth."

He wept then, a little convulsion of shoulders and face, and Ari picked up the decanter and poured him more, that being the only effective kindness she could think of.

She said nothing for perhaps a quarter, perhaps half an hour, only sat there while Denys emptied another glass.

Then the Minder said: *"Message, Abban AA to Base Two, special communications."*

Denys did not answer at once. Then he said: "Report."

"Ser Denys," Abban's voice said, cold with distance and the Minder's reproduction, *"Giraud has just died. I'll see to his transport home, by his orders. He requested you merge his Base."*

Denys lowered his head onto his hand.

"Abban," Seely said, "this is Seely SA. Ser thanks you. Direct details to me; I'll assist."

Ari sat there a very long time, waiting, until Denys wiped his eyes and drew a shaken breath.

"Lynch," Denys said. "Someone has to notify Lynch. Tell Abban see to that. He's to stand proxy. He's to file for election. Immediately."

---

iii

The Family filed into the East Garden, by twos and threes, wearing coats and cloaks in the sharpness of an autumn noon.

With conspicuous absences, absences which made Ari doubly conscious of her position in the forefront of the Family— eighteen, immaculate in mourning, and correct as she knew how to be—wearing the topaz pin on her collar, the pin Giraud had given her . . . *something that's only yours*. . . .

The funeral was another of those duties she ᵊould have avoided if she could have found a way.

Because Denys had made a damnable mess of things. Denys had fallen to pieces, refused the appointment as proxy Councillor of Science, and refused to attend the funeral. *Denys* was over at the old Wing One lab, supervising the retrieval and implantation of CIT geneset 684-044-5567 . . . precisely at this hour—at which Ari, even with compassion for his reasons, felt a vague shudder of disgust.

It left her, foster-niece, as nearest kin—not even directly related to Giraud, but ranking as immediate family, over Emil Carnath-Nye, and Julia Carnath-Nye, and Amy. She felt uncomfortable in that role, even knowing Julia's attachment to Giraud was more ambition than accident of blood. Hell with Julia: there was prestige involved, and she hated to move Amy out of her proper place, that was the uncomfortable part. The Carnath-Nyes stood, an ill-assorted little association of blood-ties far from cordial these days—Amy bringing Quentin as she had brought Florian and Catlin, for personal security in troubled times, not to flaunt him in front of the Family and her mother's disapproval; but that was certainly not the way Julia Carnath took it.

Julia and her father Emil resented having Abban standing beside them; and took petty exception to the man—*man*, dammit, who had been closer to Giraud in many ways than any next-of-kin, even Denys; who had held Giraud's hand while he died and taken care of notifications with quiet efficiency when no Family were there to do anything.

That attitude was damned well going to go: she had served notice of it and scandalized the old hands before now. Let them know what she would do when she held power in the House: hell with their offended feelings.

Amy was there; Maddy Strassen was in the front row, with aunt Victoria—maman's sister, and at a hundred fifty-four one of the oldest people alive anywhere who was not a spacer. Rejuv did not seem near failing Victoria Strassen: she was wearing away instead like ice in sunlight, just thinner and more fragile with every passing year, until she began to seem more force than flesh. Using a cane now: the sight afflicted Ari to the heart. *Maman would be that old now. Maman would be that frail.* She avoided Victoria, not alone because Victoria hated her and blamed her for Julia Strassen's exile to Fargone.

The Whitely clan was there: Sam and his mother; and the Ivanovs, the Edwardses; Yanni Schwartz and Suli; and the Dietrichs.

Justin and Grant were not. Justin had sent, all things considered, a very gracious refusal, and let her off one very difficult position. It was the only mercy she had gotten from Family or outsiders. Reporters clustered down at the airport press area, a half hour down there this morning, an appointment for an interview this afternoon, a half a hundred frustrated requests for an interview with Denys—

I'm sorry, she had said, privately and on camera. *Even those of us who work lifelong with psych, seri, do feel personal grief.* Coldly, precisely, letting her own distress far enough to the surface to put what Giraud would call the human face on Reseune. *My uncle Denys was extremely close to his brother, and he's not young himself. He's resigning the proxy to Secretary Lynch out of health considerations— No. Absolutely not. Reseune has never considered it has a monopoly on the Science seat. As the oldest scientific institution on Cyteen we have contributions to make, and I'm sure there will be other candidates from Reseune, but no one in Reseune, so far as I know, intends to run. After all—Dr. Nye wasn't bound to appoint Secretary Lynch: he might have appointed anyone in Science. Secretary Lynch is a very respected, very qualified head of the Bureau in his own right.*

And to a series of insistent questions: *Seri, Dr. Yanni Schwartz, the head of Wing One in Reseune, will be answering any specific questions about that. . . .*

. . . No, sera, that would be in the future. Of course my predecessor held the seat. Presently I'm a wing supervisor in Research, I do have a staff, I have projects under my administration—

Every reporter in the room had focused in on that, sharp and hard—scenting a story that was far off their present, urgent assignment: she had thrown out the deliberate lure and they burned to go for it despite the fact they were going out live-feed, with solemn and specific lead-ins and funeral music. She handed them the hint of a story they could not, with propriety, go for; and kept any hint of deliberate signal off her face when she did it.

But they had gone for it the moment they were off live-feed: to what extent was she actually in Administration, what were the projects, how were the decisions being made inside Reseune and was she in fact involved in that level?

Dangerous questions. Exceedingly dangerous. She had

flashed then on bleeding bodies, on subway wreckage, on news-service stills of a child's toy in the debris.

Seri, she had said then, direct, not demure: with Ari senior's straight stare and deliberate pause in answering: *any wing administrator is in the process.*

Read me, seri: I'm not a fool. I won't declare myself over my uncle's ashes.

But don't discount me in future.

I came here, she had reminded them in that context, *as a delegated spokesman for the family. That's my immediate concern. I have to go, seri. I have to be up the hill for the services in thirty minutes. Please excuse me. . . .*

It was the first funeral she had attended where there was actually burial, a small canister of ash to place in the ground, and two strong gardeners to raise the basalt cenotaph up from the ground and settle it with a final thump over the grave.

She flinched at that sound, inside. So damned little a canister, for tall uncle Giraud.

And burial in earth instead of being shot for the sun. She knew which she would pick for herself—same as her predecessor, same as maman. But it was right for Giraud, maybe.

Emil Carnath called for speeches from associates and colleagues.

"I have a word," Victoria Strassen said right off.

O God, Ari thought.

And braced herself.

"Giraud threw me out of my sister's funeral," Victoria began in a voice sharper and stronger than one ever looked for from that thin body. "I never forgave him for it."

Maddy cast Ari an anguished look across the front of the gathering. *Sorry for this.*

Not your fault, Ari thought.

"What about you, Ariane Emory PR? Are you going to have me thrown out for saying what the truth is?"

"I'll speak after you, aunt Victoria. Maman taught me manners."

That hit. Victoria's lips made a thin line and she took a double-handed grip on her black cane.

"My sister was *not* your maman," Victoria said. "That's the trouble in the House. Dead is dead, that's all. The way it works best. The way it's worked in all of human society. Old growth makes way for new. It doesn't batten off the damn corpse. I've no quarrel with you, young sera, no quarrel with you. You didn't choose to be born. Where's Denys? Eh?'' She looked around her, with a sweeping gesture of the cane. ''Where's Denys?'' There was an uncomfortable shifting in the crowd. ''Sera,'' Florian whispered at Ari's shoulder, seeking instruction.

''I'll *tell* you where Denys is,'' Victoria snapped. ''*Denys* is in the lab making another brother, the way he made another Ariane. *Denys* has taken the greatest scientific and economic power in human history and damned near run it into bankruptcy in his administration, —never mind poor Giraud, who took the orders, we all know that—damned near bankrupted us all for his eetee notion of personal immortality. You tell me, young sera, do you remember what Ariane remembered? Do you remember her life at all?''

God. It was certainly not something she wanted asked, here, now, in an argumentative challenge, in any metaphysical context. ''We'll talk about that someday,'' she said back, loudly enough to carry. ''Over a drink, aunt Victoria. I take it that's a *scientific* question, and you're not asking me about reincarnation.''

''I wonder what Denys calls it,'' Victoria said. ''Call your security if you like. I've been through enough craziness in my life, people blowing up stations in the War, people blowing up kids in subways, people who aren't content to let nature throw the dice anymore, people who don't want kids, they want little personal faxes they can live their fantasies through, never mind what the poor kid wants. Now do we give up on funerals altogether? Is that what everyone in the damn house is thinking, I don't have to die, I can impose my own ideas on a poor sod of a replicate who's got no say in it so I can have my ideas walking around in the world after I'm dead?''

''You're here to talk about Giraud,'' Yanni Schwartz yelled. ''Do it and shut up, Vickie.''

''I've done it. Goodbye to a human being. Welcome back, Gerry PR. God help the human race.''

The rest of the speeches, thank God, were decorous—a few

lines, a: *We differed, but he had principles*, from Petros Ivanov; a: *He kept Reseune going*, from Wendell Peterson.

It ascended to personal family then, always last to speak. To refute the rest, Ari decided, for good or ill.

"I'll tell you," she said in her own turn, in what was conspicuously her turn, last, as next-of-kin, Denys being exactly where Victoria had said he was, doing what Victoria had said, "—there was a time I hated my uncle. I think he knew that. But in the last few years I learned a lot about him. He collected holograms and miniatures; he loved microcosms and tame, quiet things, I think because in his real work there never was any sense of conclusion, just an ongoing flux and decisions nobody else wanted to make. It's not true that he only took orders. He consulted with Denys on policy; he implemented Bureau decisions; but he knew the difference between a good idea and a bad one and he never hesitated to support his own ideas. He was quiet about it, that's all. He got the gist of a problem and he went for solutions that would work.

"He served Union in the war effort. He did major work on human personality and on memory which is still the standard reference work in his field. He took over the Council seat in the middle of a national crisis, and he represented the interests of the Bureau for two very critical decades—into my generation, the first generation of Union that's not directly in touch with either the Founding or the War.

"He talked to me a lot in this last year: Abban made a lot of trips back and forth—" She looked to catch Abban's eye, but Abban was staring straight forward, in that nowhere way of an azi in pain. "—couriering messages between us. He knew quite well he was dying, of course; and as far as having a replicate, he didn't really care that much. We did talk about it, the way we talked about a lot of things, some personal, some public. He was very calm about it all. He was concerned about his brother. The thing that impressed me most, was how he laid everything out, how he made clear arrangements for everything—"

Never mind the mess Denys made of those arrangements.

"He operated during the last half year with a slate so clearly in order that those of us he was briefing could have walked into his office, picked up that agenda and known exactly where all the files were and exactly what had to be priority. He confessed he was afraid of dying. He certainly would have been glad to stay around another fifty years. He never expressed remorse for anything he'd done; he never asked my forgiveness; he only handed me the keys and the files and seemed touched that I did forgive him. That was the Giraud I knew.''

She left it at that.

I have the files. That was deliberate, too. The way she had done with the press.

Not to undermine Lynch, damned sure. Denys refused the seat and someone had to hold it; Reseune was in profound shock. Certain people were urging Yanni to declare for the seat, challenge Lynch.

No, Denys had said, focused enough to foresee that possibility. No challenge to Lynch from anyone. He's harmless. Leave him.

What Yanni thought about it she was not sure. She did not think Yanni wanted that honor.

But Denys' refusal had jerked a chance at Reseune Administration out of Yanni's reach. And *that*, she thought, however much any of them in Reseune had suspected Denys would refuse the seat, that had to be a disappointment.

She made a point of going over to Yanni after the services, catching his arm, thanking him for his support and making sure the whole Family saw that.

Making sure that the whole Family knew Yanni was not out of the running in future, in her time. ''I know what you're doing,'' she said fervently, careless of just who could hear, knowing some would. ''Yanni, I won't forget. Hear?''

She squeezed his hand. Yanni gave her a look—as if he had not believed for a second it was more than a salve to his pride and then caught on that it was altogether more than that, in that subtle way such indicators passed in the Family.

Not a word said directly. But there were witnesses enough. And Yanni was profoundly affected.

Hers, she reckoned, when it came down to the line, in the same way Amy and Maddy and the younger generation were.

And others in the House would see the indicators plain, that she had declared herself on several fronts, and started making acquisitions, not on a spoils system for the young and upcoming, but for a passed-over senior administrator who enjoyed more respect in the House than he himself imagined.

Signal clearly that Yanni was hers and let Yanni collect his own following: Yanni took no nonsense and let himself be taken in by no one. *Yanni* had stripped his own daughter of authority when she had abused it, and favored no one except on merit: that was his reputation—when Yanni thought of himself as a simple hardnosed bastard.

Yanni had some reassessing to do. Figure on that.

Yanni was not going to be taken in by the bootlickers and the Stef Dietrichs in the House or elsewhere.

He had been one of maman's friends. She thought with some personal satisfaction, that maman would approve.

<hr>

iv

<hr>

She took the outside walk back to the House, around the garden wall, toward the distant doors: it was, thank God, quiet, after the pressure of the interviews. *Damn Victoria*, she thought, and reckoned that Maddy had wanted to sink out of sight.

"Do you wonder why we do such things?" she murmured to Florian and Catlin. "So do I."

They looked at her, one and the other. Catlin said, in Florian's silence: "It's strange when someone dies. You think they ought to be there. It was that way in Green Barracks."

Ari put her hand on Catlin's shoulder as they walked. Memories. Catlin was the one who had seen people die. "Not slowing down, are you?"

"No, sera," Catlin said. "*I* don't intend to be talked about."

She laughed softly. *Count on Catlin*.

Florian said nothing at all. Florian was the one who would have taken in every signal in the crowd; and work over it and work over it to make it make sense. Florian was the one who would worry about the living.

"He's gone," Ari said finally, at the doors. "Damn, that *is* strange." And looked at Florian, whose face had just gone quite tense, that listening-mode that said he was getting something attention-getting over the Security monitor. One or the other of them was always on-line.

"Novgorod," Florian said. "Jordan Warrick—has declared his innocence— He says—he was coerced. Reseune Security is issuing orders to place him in detention—"

Ari's heart jolted. But everything came clear then. "Florian," she said while they were going through the doors, "code J Red, go. We're on A; go for Q and we're Con2."

Make sure of Justin and Grant: Catlin and I are going for Denys; get home base secure and stay there; force permitted, but not as first resort.

That, before they were through the doors, while a Security guard whose com would not be set on that command-priority gave them a slightly puzzled look at their on-business split-and-go.

"They're not saying much," Catlin said as they went.

"Out to the news-services?"

"That, first," Catlin said. "Com 14 is loaded with incomings."

Reporters at the airport, at the edge of a major news event and hemmed in by an anxious, noncommunicative Security.

"Damn, is Denys on it? What in hell is he doing?"

Catlin tapped the unit in her ear. "Denys is still in the lab; Base One, relay Base Two transmission? —Affirmative, sera. He's sent word to defer all questions; he's saying the charges are a political maneuver, quote, ill-timed and lacking in human feeling. He says, quote, the Family is returning from the funeral and people are out of their offices: Reseune will have a further statement in half an hour."

"Thank God," she said fervently.

Denys was awake. Denys was returning fire.

Damned well about time.

-----------------v-----------------

It was a good day to stay home, Justin reckoned—given the situation in the House, given a general unsettled state in Security now that its chief was dead: *I don't want to be alarmist,* Ari had said in a message left on the Minder, *but I'd be a lot easier in my mind if you and Grant didn't go anywhere you don't have to for the next few days—work at home if you can. I'm going to be busy; I can't watch everything; and Security is confused as hell—a little power struggle going on there. Do you mind? Feel free to attend the services. But stay where people are.*

I'll take your advice, he had messaged back. *Thank you. I know you have a lot to take care of right now. I don't think our presence at the services would be appropriate, or welcome to his friends; but if there should be anything Grant or I can do in the wing to take care of details, we're certainly willing to help.*

She had not asked anything of them—had more or less forgotten them, Justin reckoned, small wonder with the pressure she was under. The news was full of speculations about Denys' health, about the political consequences of Reseune yielding up the seat Reseune had held on Council since the Founding—about whether the Centrists could field a viable candidate inside Science, or whether Secretary and now Proxy Councillor Lynch had the personal qualifications to hold the party leadership which Giraud had held.

"There's nothing wrong with Denys' health," Grant objected, the two of them watching the news in the living room.

"I don't know what he's about," Justin said. And trusting then to the freedom Ari swore they had from monitoring: "But losing Giraud is a heavy blow to him. I think it's the only time I've ever felt sorry for Denys."

"They're doing that PR," Grant said; then: "Denys had to get Ari's backing, isn't that ironic as hell?"

"He's what—a hundred twenty-odd?—and that weight he carries doesn't favor him. He'd be lucky to see ten, fifteen more years. So he *has* to have Ari's agreement, doesn't he?"

"It's not going to work," Grant said.

Justin looked at Grant, who sat—they *had* found a scattering of red and blue pillows—in a nest at the corner of the couch, his red hair at odds with half of it.

"Denys *has* to set the pattern," Grant said, "has to give him that foundation or there's no hope for Giraud. I firmly think so. Yanni may have known their father in his old age, but Yanni's much too young to do for Giraud what Jane Strassen did—not mentioning how they've treated him—"

"He owes them damned little, that's sure enough."

"And there's always the question what's in and not in those notes Ari-younger got from her predecessor," Grant said. "I think Ari knows a lot she's not putting in those notes. I think *our* Ari is being very careful what she tells her guardians."

"Ari says sometimes—not everything was necessary."

"But whatever *is* necessary—is necessary," Grant said. "And Denys can't know—isn't in a position to know, that's what I think; and she's keeping it that way."

"The Rubin boy's going into chemistry, isn't he?"

"Fine student—test scores not spectacular, though."

"Yet."

Grant made a deprecating gesture. "No Stella Rubin. No one to tell him when to breathe. Hell is necessary for CITs, do we make that a given? You warned them not to let up on him too much—but the project is still using him for a control. Put the whole load on Ari; go easy on Ben Rubin; see what was necessary. . . . I'll bet you anything you like that Denys Nye had more to do with that decision than Yanni Schwartz did. *Yanni* never went easy on anyone."

"Except—Yanni's got a family attachment in the way. Rubin's suicide really got him, and Jenna Schwartz, remember, had some little thing to do with that. It could well be Yanni's going easy."

"But Rubin's still a control," Grant said. "And what he's proving—"

"What he's proving is, A, you can't do it with all genesets; B, some genesets respond well to stress and some don't—"

"Given, given, but in the two instances we have, —"

"And, C, there's bad match-ups between surrogate and subject. Don't discount the damage Jenna Schwartz did and the damage the contrast between Jenna Schwartz and Ollie Strassen did to the boy."

"Not to mention," Grant said, holding up a finger, "the fact Oliver AOX is male, and Alpha; and Stella Rubin is female and not that bright. I'd *like* to do a study on young Rubin. No edge to him, not near the flux swings. The instability goes with the suicide, goes with the brilliance—Among us, you know, they call it a flawed set."

"And do a fix for it."

"And lose the edge, just as often. —Which brings us back to young Ari, who's maybe given the committee all she knows—which I don't believe, if she's as much Ari as she seems, and our Ari—doesn't take chances with her security. I very much think access to those programs is a leverage of sorts—and do you know, I think Denys would have begun to guess that?"

Justin considered that thought, with a small, involuntary twitch of his shoulders. "The committee swears no one can retrieve from Ari's programs without Ari's ID. And possibly it's always been true."

"Possibly—more than that. Possibly that Base, once activated—can't be outmaneuvered in other senses. Possibly it's capable of masking itself."

"Lying about file sizes?"

"And invading other Bases—eventually. Built-in tests, parameters, —I've been thinking how I'd write a program like that . . . if she were azi. The first Ariane designed me. Maybe—" Grant made a little quirk of his mouth. "Maybe I have a—you'd say innate, but that's a mistake—in-*built* resonance with Ari's programs. I remember my earliest integrations. I remember—there was a—even for a child—*sensual* pleasure in the way things fit, the way the pieces of my understanding came together with such a precision. She was so very good. Do you think she didn't prepare for them to replicate her? Or that she'd be less careful with a child of her own sets, than with an azi of her design?"

Justin thought about it. Thought about the look on Grant's face, the tone of his voice—a man speaking about his father . . . or his mother. "Flux-thinking," he said. "I've wondered— Do you love her, Grant?"

Grant laughed, fleeting surprise. *"Love* her."

"I don't think it's impossible. I don't think it's at all unlikely."

"Reseune is my Contract and I can never get away from it?"

"Reseune is my Contract: I shall not want? —I'm talking about CIT-style flux. The kind that makes for ambivalences. Do you love her?"

A frown then. "I'm scared of the fact this Ari ran a probe.

I'm scared because Ari's got the first Ari's notes—which include my manual, I'm quite sure. And what if—what if—This is my nightmare, Justin: what if—in my most fluxed imaginings, Ari planned for her successor; what if she planted something in me that would respond to her with the right trigger? —But then I flux back again and think that's complete nonsense. I'll tell you another nightmare: I'm scared of my own program tape."

Justin suffered a little sympathetic chill. "Because Ari wrote it."

Grant nodded. "I *don't* want to review it under trank nowadays. I know I could take enough kat to put me flat enough I could take it—but then I think—I can handle things without it. I can manage. I don't need it, God, CITs put up with the flux and they learn from it. And I do—learn from it, that is."

"I wish to hell you'd told me that."

"You'd worry. And there's no reason to worry. I'm fine—except when you ask me questions like that: *do I love Ari?* God, that's skewed. That's the first time I ever wondered about it in CIT terms. And you're right, there's a multi-level flux around her I don't like at all."

"Guilt?"

"Don't do that to me."

"Sorry. I just wondered."

Grant shifted position in the nest of pillows, against the arm. "Have you ever scanned my tape for problems?"

"Yes," Justin said after a little hesitation, a time-stretch of hesitation, that felt much too long and much too significant. "I didn't want to make it evident—I didn't want to worry you about it."

"I worry. I can't help but worry. It's too basic to me."

"You—worry about it."

Grant gave a small, melancholy lift of the brows, and seemed to ponder for a moment, raking a hand through his hair. "I think she asked something that jolted me—deep. I think I know where. I think she asked about my tape—which, admittedly, I have a small guilt about: I don't use it the way I'm supposed to; I think she asked about contact with subversives; and I dream about Winfield, lately. The whole scene out at Big Blue. The plane, and the bus with those men, and that room. . . .''

"Why didn't you tell me that?"

"Are dreams abnormal?"

"Don't give me that. Why didn't you tell me?"

"Because it's not significant. Because I know—when I'm not fluxed—that I'm all right. You want me to take the tape, I'll take it. You want to run a probe of your own—do it. I've certainly no apprehensions about that. Maybe you should. It's been a long time. Maybe I'd even feel safer if you did. —If,'' Grant added with a little tilt of the head, a sidelong glance, a laugh without humor. "If I didn't then wonder if *you* weren't off. You see? It's a mental trap."

"Because you got a chance to see Jordan. Because the damn place is crazy!'' Of a sudden he felt a rush of frustration, an irrational concern so intense he got up and paced the length of the living room, looked back at Grant in a sudden feeling of walls closing in, of life hemmed around and impeded at every turn.

Not true, he thought. Things were better. Never mind that it was another year of separation from his father, another year gone, things no different than they had ever been—things were better in prospect, Ari was closer than she had ever been to taking power in her own right, and her regime, he sincerely believed it—promised change, when it would come.

They're burying Giraud today.

Why in hell does that make me afraid?

"I wish," Grant said, "you'd listened to me. I wish you'd gone to Planys instead."

"What difference? We'd have still been separate. We'd still worry—"

"What then? What's bothering you?"

"I don't know." He rubbed the back of his neck. "Being pent up in here, I think. This place. This—'' He thought of a living room in beige and blue; and realized with a little internal shift-and-slide that it was not Jordan's apartment that had come back with that warm little memory. "God. You know where I wish we could go back to? *Our* place. The place—'' Face in a mirror, not the one he had now. The boy's face. Seventeen and innocent, across the usual clutter of bottles on the bathroom counter, getting ready for an evening—

Tape-flash, ominous and chaotic. The taste of oranges.

"—before all this happened. That's useless, isn't it? I don't even want to be that boy. I only wish I was there knowing what I know now."

"It was good there," Grant said.

"I was such a damned fool."

"I don't think so."

Justin shook his head.

"I know differently," Grant said. "Put yourself in Ari's place. Wonder—what you would have been—on her timetable, with her advantages, with the things they did to her— You'd have been—"

"Different. Harder. Older."

"—someone else. Someone else entirely. CITs are such a dice-throw. You're so unintentionally cruel to each other."

"Do you think it's necessary? Can't we learn without putting our hand in the fire?"

"You're asking an azi, remember?"

"I'm *asking* an azi. Is there a way to get an Ariane Emory out of that geneset—or me—out of mine—"

"Without the stress?" Grant asked. "Can flux-states be achieved intellectually—when they have endocrine bases? Can tape-fed stress—short of the actual chance of breaking one's neck—be less real, leave less pain—than the real experience? What if that tape Ari made—were only tape? What if it had never happened—but you thought it had? Would there be a difference? What if Ari's maman had never died, but she thought she had? Would she be sane? Could she trust reality? I don't know. I truly don't know. I would hate to discover that everything until now—was tape; and I was straight from the Town, having dreamed all this."

"God, Grant!"

Grant turned his left wrist to the light, where there was always, since the episode with Winfield and the Abolitionists, a crosswise scar. "This is real. Unless, of course, it's only something my makers installed with the tape."

"That's not good for you."

Grant smiled. "That's the first time in years you've called me down. Got you, have I?"

"Don't joke like that."

"I have no trouble with reality. I *know* tape when I feel it. And remember I'm built right side up, with my logic sets where they belong, thank you, my makers. But flux is too much like dreams. Tape-fed flux—would have no logical structure. Tape-fed flux is too much like what Giraud did in the War, which I don't even like to contemplate—building minds and unbuilding them; mindwiping and reconstruction . . . always, always, mind you, with things the subject can't go back to check; and a lot left to the imagination. I honestly don't know, Justin. If there's a key to taping those experiences— *Giraud* could have had some insight into it, isn't that irony?"

It made some vague, bizarre sense, enough to send another twitch down his back, and a feeling of cold into his bones.

"Talking theory with Giraud—" But Giraud was dead. And yet-to-be. "It wasn't something we ever got around to."

"The question is, essentially, whether you can substitute tape for reality. I'm very capable, Justin; but I sweated blood on that flight to Planys, I was so damned helpless during the whole trip. *That's* what you give up: survivability in the real world."

Justin snorted. "You think I don't worry."

"But you could learn *much* more rapidly. Back to the old difference: you flux-learn; I logic my way through. And no aggregate of CITs is logical. Got you again."

Justin thought about it; and smiled finally, in the damnable gray apartment, in the elegant prison Ari appointed them. For a moment it felt like home. For a moment he remembered that it was safer than anywhere they had been since that fondly-remembered first apartment.

Then the apprehension came back again, the great stillness over Reseune, deserted halls, everything in flux.

There was sudden break-up on the vid, the news commentary thrown off in mid-word.

The Infinite Man appeared on screen. Music played. One never worried about such things. Someone kicked a cable, and Reseune's whole vid-system glitched.

Except it was also something Reseune Security did, for selected apartments, selected viewers.

My God, he thought, a sudden rush of worry, lifelong habit.
*Were they monitoring? Have they gotten through her security?
What could they have heard?*

---

vi

"Uncle Denys," Ari had relayed on the way, via Base One
and Catlin's com unit, "I need to talk to you right away."

"Lab office," Seely had relayed back.

Shocked looks followed them through the labs from the time
they had entered, techs who knew that things were already Odd
with Denys, azi who were reading the techs if not the situation,
and worried as hell; and now an unexplained break-in of conspicuous Family coming straight from the funeral, in mourning, and headed for lab offices at high speed—small wonder
the whole lab stopped and stared, Ari thought; and at least she
could freely admit to knowing as much as she knew, excepting
what Planys was doing.

Past the tanks, the techs, the very place where she had been
born, where likely by now half a dozen Giraud's were in
progress—up the little stairs with the metal rail, to the small
administrative office Denys had commandeered: Seely was evidently keeping a look-out through the one-way glass of the lab
offices, because Seely opened the door to let them in before
she had made the final turn of the steps.

Denys was behind the desk, on the phone—with Security,
by what it sounded. Ari collected herself with a breath.
"That's fine," she said, when Catlin whisked a chair to her
back; she took off her gloves and her jacket, gave them to
Catlin and sat down as Denys hung up the phone.

"Well, sera," Denys said, "we have the result of your
baulking Security at Planys."

"Where is Jordan?"

"Under arrest at Planys. He and his companion. Damn
him!"

"Mmmn, *Justin* is accounted for."

"Are you certain?"

"Quite. *Justin* is the one I want to talk to you about."

"Ser," Florian said when they had let him in, Florian in House uniform and without his coat, so Florian and therefore probably Ari had had time, Justin reckoned, to come in next door first.

But it made him anxious that it was not a call over the Minder, or a summons to Ari's apartment or her offices, just a Minder-call at the door, Florian asking entry.

And the vid still showed nothing on the news channel except that single logo.

"There's been an incident," Florian said, preface, and in the half-second of Florian's next breath: *O God*, Justin thought, *something's happened to Ari*; and was bewildered in the same half-second, that the fear included her, her welfare, which was linked with their own. "Your father," Florian said, and fears jolted altogether into another track, "—has gotten a message to the Centrists, claiming innocence."

"Of *what?*" Justin asked, still tracking on *incident*, not making sense of it.

"Of killing Dr. Emory, ser."

He stood there, he did not know how long, in a state of shock, wanting to think so, wanting to think—

—*but, my God, during Giraud's funeral—what's he doing? What's going on?*

"We don't know all the details yet," Florian said. "Sera doesn't want to admit to ser Denys just how far her surveillance extends, please understand that, ser, but she does know that your father is safe at the moment. She's asking you, please, ser, understand that there's extreme danger—to you, to her, to your father, no matter whether this is true or false: the announcement has political consequences that may be very dangerous, I don't know if I need explain them. . . ."

"God." *Ari's safety. Everything*— He raked a hand through his hair, felt Grant's hand on his shoulder. Florian—seemed older, somehow, his face utterly without the humor that was so characteristic of him, like a mask dropped, finally, time sent reeling. . . . *Could it be true?*

"She wants you to pack a small bag, ser. Sera's interim staff is on the way up to this floor, and sera asks Grant to stay here and put himself under their orders. . . .''

"Pack for *where?*"

Separate us? God, no.

"Sera wants you to go with her to Novgorod—to defuse this matter. To speak to the press. She wants to take the politics out of the question—for your father's sake, as much as her own. Do you understand, ser? There'll be a small question-and-answer at Reseune airport; that's safest. She's asking a meeting with Councillor Corain and Secretary Lynch. She earnestly hopes you won't fail her in this—''

"My God. God, Grant—'' *What do I do?*

But Grant had no answers. *CITs are all crazy*, Grant would say.

Ari's out of her mind. Take me to Novgorod? They don't dare.

They need me. That's the game. My father under arrest. They want me to call him a liar.

Reseune Security doesn't need to kill him. They can use drugs. It takes time. Time I can buy them to operate on him—

Would Ari—do this to us?

Would Florian be here without her orders?

In front of those cameras—if I get that far— How can they stop me from any charges I can make?

Grant.

Grant—being here, in Ari's keeping. That's what they're offering me—Grant's sanity—or my father's.

He looked up into Grant's face—far calmer, he thought, than his own, Grant's un-fluxed logic probably understanding there was no choice in his own situation.

I have faith in my makers.

"Grant comes with me," he said to Florian.

"No, ser," Florian said. "I have definite instructions. Please, pack just the essentials. Everything will be inspected. Grant will be safe here, with sera Amy. There will be Security: Quentin AQ is very competent, and sera Amy will have her friends for help here. No way will any general Security come onto this floor or interfere with the systems. No way will sera Amy do anything to harm Grant."

A gifted eighteen-year-old, with a thin, earnest face and a

tendency to go at problems head-on: an eighteen-year-old who, he had always thought, liked him and Grant. Honest. And sensible as an eighteen-year-old had any likelihood of being.

God, they *all* were. "It's a damn Children's Crusade," he said, and caught Grant's arm. "Do what they say. It'll be all right."

"No," he said in front of the cameras, in the lounge at Reseune airport. "No, I haven't been in contact with my father. I hope to get a call through—when we get to Novgorod. It's the middle of their night. They—" He tried, desperately, not to look nervous: *Don't look guilty*, Ari had said, before they left the bus. *Don't look like you're hiding anything. You can be very frank with them, but for God's sake think about the political ramifications when you do it. Be very careful about making charges of your own, they can only muddy things up, and we have to rely on uncle Denys—we can't offend him, hear me?*

"My father—is in Detention at the moment," he said, finding the pace of things too much, the dark areas too extensive. The truth seemed easier to sort out than lies were, if one kept it to a minimum. "All I can tell you—" No. *Can* meant dangerous things. "All I know how to tell you—is that there's an inquiry. My father told me—at the time it happened—exactly what he told the Council. But there were things going on at the time—that might have been a reason. That's why I'm going to Novgorod. I don't know—Ari herself doesn't know—who's telling the truth now. I want to find out. Reseune Administration wants to find out."

"I can assure you," Ari said, beside him, "I have a very strong motive for wanting to know the truth in this case."

"Question for Dr. Warrick. Are you presently under any coercion?"

"No," Justin said firmly.

"You are a PR. Are you—in any way—more than that?" He shook his head. "Standard PR. Nothing extraordinary."

"Have you ever been subject to intervention?"

He had not expected that question. He froze on it, then said: "Psychprobe is an intervention. I was part of the investigation. There were a lot of them." They would question his sanity for that reason; and his reliability. He knew that. It would cast doubt on his license for clinical practice and cast a shadow on his research. He knew that too. The whole thing took on a nightmarish quality, the lights, the half-ring of reporters. He became quite placid, quite cold. "There was an illicit intervention when I was a minor. I've been treated for that. I'm not presently under drugs; I'm not operating under anyone's intervention. I'm concerned about my father and I'm anxious to get to Novgorod and answer whatever questions Council may have: I'm most concerned about my father's welfare—"

"Is he threatened in any way?"

"Ser, I don't know as much as you do. I'm anxious to talk with him. For one thing, I want to be sure what he did say—"

"You're casting doubt on his statement through Councillor Corain, as valid, or as coming from him."

"I want to be sure that he did send that message. I want to hear it from him. There are a lot of unanswered questions. I can't tell you what you want to know. I don't know."

"Sera Emory. Do you know?"

"I have ideas," Ari said, "but I'm being very careful of them. They involve people's reputations—"

"Living people?"

"Living and dead. Please understand: we're in the middle of a funeral. We've had charges launched and questions asked that depend on records deep in Archive, about things that are personal to me and personal to Justin—" She reached and laid her hand on his, clenched it. "We had come to our own peace with what happened. Justin's my friend and my teacher, and now we wonder what did happen all those years ago, and why Justin's father wouldn't have told *him* the truth, if there was more to it. We don't understand, either one of us. That's why we're going outside Reseune. We're going to handle this at the Bureau level—at Council level, since they're the ones who did the first investigation, if we have to go that far. But it's not appropriate for us to investigate this on a strictly internal level. Dr. Warrick has made charges; they need to be heard in the Bureau. That's where we're going—and I think we ought to get underway, seri, thank you. Please. We'll have more statements later."

"Dr. Warrick," a journalist shouted. "Do you have any statement?"

Justin looked at the man, blank for a fraction of a second until he realized that Dr. Warrick was the way the world knew him. "Not at the moment. I've told you everything I know."

Florian touched him as he got up, showed him a route through to the boarding area, for the plane that waited for them. *RESEUNE ONE*.

A solid phalanx of regular Security made a passage for them, an abundance of Security that clearly said: This is official; Administration is involved.

It answered to Ari. Giraud was a wisp of ash and a group of cells trying to achieve humanity; and meanwhile Ariane Emory was in charge, with all the panoply of Reseune's authority around her.

He went quickly through the doors, and down the corridor into the safeway and into the plane, where he stopped in confusion, until Florian took him by the arm and guided him to one of a group of leather seats, and settled him in.

"Would you like a drink, ser?"

"Soft drink," he said, while Ari was settling in opposite him, while the plane was starting engines and more Security was boarding.

"Vodka-and-orange," Ari said. "Thank you, Florian." And looking straight at him: "Thank *you*," she said. "You handled that very well."

He gazed back at her in a virtual state of shock, thoughts darting in panic to the Security around him, the fear that one of them could simply pull a gun and spray the cabin; fear for Grant back in the apartment, that, no matter what Florian said about general Security not having admittance to that level, an eighteen-year-old girl was in charge, along with a Security guard no older than she was, and anything could happen; fear that something might be happening with Jordan; or that Paxer lunatics might somehow have rigged a missile that could take the plane out of the sky—

There was not a damned thing he could do, except say what he was supposed to say, trust . . . God, that was the hard part. Let go all the defenses, do whatever Ari told him, and hope that another eighteen-year-old knew better than he did how to handle the situation.

"I was seventeen," he said to Ari, quietly, while the engines were warming up, "when I thought I knew what I was doing well enough to send Grant to Krugers. You *know* what that came to."

Ari snapped her seat buckle across, and reached up to take the drink Catlin handed her. "Warning taken. I know. But sometimes there aren't any choices, are there?"

vii

RESEUNE ONE made cruising altitude, and Ari took a sip of her drink and checked the small unit she had clipped to her chair arm, remote for the more complex electronics in the briefcase in its safety rack beside her seat, the first time she had ever carried it. She pushed the check button. It flashed a reassuring positive and beeped at her.

System up, link functioning.

Across from her, in his seat beside Justin, Florian nodded to her smile and nod at him. Florian had done the updating into the code system—of course it worked; and worked, so long as she made no queries, as a very thorough observer in Reseune's state-of-the-art net, simply picking up on all her flagged items and routing them to her as they came up in the flow.

Not even Defense had cracked that code-upon-code jargonesque flow Reseune Security used: one hoped.

Ari picked up her drink again and leaned back. "Everything's all right," she said to Justin. "No troubles we don't know about, and we're picking up our Bureau escort in about five minutes."

Justin looked from the window at his right toward her, truly looked at her, eye to eye across the low table that divided the seats. He had darted glances toward every movement in the plane, tense as Florian or Catlin when they were On; he was tracking even on the working of the plane's hydraulics, and the light from the window touched taut muscle in his jaw, mature lines of worry set into his brow and around his mouth: the years had touched him, no matter the rejuv. *He worries so* much, she thought. He's too smart to trust anyone. Certainly not Reseune. Now, not even his father. He'll doubt Grant himself if he's gone too long.

That's what he's trying to figure out—trying to estimate where I am in this, and whether Grant is safe, and how much I'm a young fool and how much I've got him fluxed and how much he can believe now of anything I say or do.

I'm not the kid he knew. He's begun to figure that; and he's started to wonder when it happened, and how far it's gone, and who was working on him while he was under kat. He's scared—and embarrassed about being scared of me; but he knows he has every right to be afraid now.

The brain has to rule the flux, Ari-elder; I think I've finally understood what you mean. Whether he slept with me or not, I'd have come round to this, I do think I would: you didn't bring up a fool, Ari-elder. Neither did maman and my uncles.

Ollie doesn't write because he values his neck, that's the truth. This universe is dangerous, and Ollie's just as upset as Grant is back there, alone, with strangers. He's trusted nothing since maman died. He works for Reseune Administration.

"We can talk now," she said, with a slide of her eyes toward the rear of the plane where the regular Security people sat. The engine noise was as good as any Silencer, given that Security did not have any unreported electronics back there; but the carry-bag at Florian's feet had its own array of devices, which one had to trust was up to what Florian vowed it was— and Florian's Base One clearance was quite adequate for him to find out whether it was up to date.

"An explanation would do," Justin said. "What are you doing?"

"I'd be ever so happy if I knew. I'm not choosing the timing on this. I'm afraid Councillor Corain is and it's not like him. I'm afraid the information has gotten to someone else, like Khalid, and he had to jump fast to be first—which is why it came out in the middle of the funeral, not tonight."

Justin looked taken off his balance. "You know about things like that. I'm sure I don't."

"You *know*, Justin, you know damn well, you just haven't had uncle Giraud's briefings; and it *still* caught us. Giraud knew there was a leak. He knew what your father would say;

he warned me what your father would say if he got a chance. The question isn't even whether it's true. Let's assume it is." He was going to slip her, she saw it coming, and she maintained his attention with an uplifted finger, exactly, *exactly* Ari senior's mannerism: she knew it. "*What* does it do for your father?"

"It gets him the hell out of Planys. It gets him clean, dammit, it gets him his standing with the Bureau—"

"All of which I'm not averse to—in my own time. My own time isn't now. It can't be now. *Think* about it, Justin; you can handle Sociology equations. Try this one, try this one near-term, like the next few years—tell me what's going to happen and what's going to result from it. *That's* first. That's the thing that matters. What does it do to him, what's going to happen? Second question: where does he stand, where does he think he stands, what side has he just taken—and don't tell me your father's naive, *no* one in Reseune is naive, just under-briefed."

He said nothing. But he was thinking, deep and seriously, *on* what she had said, and around the peripheries: who am I dealing with, what is she up to, has Denys choreographed this business? He was much too smart to take anything at one level.

"Did you leak it to Corain?" he asked.

Oh. That *was* a good one. It jolted a thought loose. "*I* didn't. But, God, Denys might have, mightn't he?"

"Or Giraud," Justin said.

She drew a long breath and leaned back. "Interesting thought. Very interesting thought."

"Maybe it's the truth. Maybe whoever leaked it is in a position to know it's the truth."

Florian was interested: Florian was watching Justin with utmost attention. She reckoned that Catlin was. God, Ari thought, and found herself smiling. He's not down, is he? I *see* how he's survived.

"Easier to answer that," she said, "if I had an idea what happened that night, but there's no evidence. I thought there might have been a Scriber record. There was just the TranSlate. There's nothing there. The sniffers were useless; there'd been too many people in and out before they thought about it. Psychprobe would have been the only way. And that didn't happen. And won't. It doesn't matter. Giraud talked about 'the

Warrick influence.' Giraud made an enemy. Now what do we do about that enemy?''

A slower man, an emotional man, would have blurted out: *Let him go.* She sat watching Justin think, relatively sure of some of the tracks—the fact that Jordan's name was in Paxer graffiti; that Jordan's ideas had opposed her predecessor; that there was one election shaping up in Science and another virtually certain in Defense, both critical, both of which, if the Centrists won—could destroy Reseune, shift the course of history, jeopardize all Reseune's projects, and all her purposes. . . .

Perhaps three, four, minutes he sat there, deep-focused and calm as kat could have sent him. Then, in with careful control:

"Have *you* run the projections of Jordan's input?''

She drew breath, as if one of a dozen knots about her chest had loosed. *There* is *an echo*, she thought, imagining that dark place, that floating-in-null place. She took her own time answering. "Field too large," she said finally. "*I* don't aim at him. I want him safe. The problem is—he's quite intelligent, quite determined, and even if he didn't leak that message— what's he going to do if he gets in front of the news cameras? What's he going to do to every plan for solving this that I could have come up with?''

"I can solve it. Give me fifteen minutes on the phone with him.''

"There's still a problem. He won't believe a word of it. Giraud said it: that tape was an intervention. Your father saw it—''

He reacted to that as if it had hit in the gut.

"You haven't,'' she said, "have you? Ever. You don't know what Ari did. You should have asked to see it. You should have gone over that damned thing as often as it took. It fluxed me too, fluxed me so I wasn't thinking straight: it took Giraud to point out the obvious. If *I* could see what Ari did, so could your father. Your father didn't see it as a seventeen-year-old kid, your father saw it as a psychsurgeon who had to wonder exactly how often and how deep Ari's interventions had been. He had to wonder how far they'd gone. You and Grant worry about each other when you've been separate three days. I know. You know they can't run an intervention on Jordan—

but don't you think he has to wonder—after twenty years—just whose you are?"

Justin leaned forward and picked up his drink from the table, breathing harder: she marked the flare of his nostrils, the intakes and the quick outflow. *And the little body moves that said he wanted out of that round.* "Florian," he said, "would you mind terribly—I think I'd like something stronger."

She could read Florian too, instant suspicion: Florian distrusted such little distracting tactics, with thoughts engendered of lifelong training. He was not about to turn his back on an Enemy.

"Florian," she said, "his usual."

Florian met her eyes, nodded deferentially then and got up, not even looking at Catlin, who sat beside her: there was no question that Catlin was on, and hair-triggered.

"You can talk to your father," she said to Justin, "but I doubt he's believed you entirely for years. Not—entirely. He *knows* you were psychprobed, over and over again; and he doesn't believe in Reseune's virtue. If you try to reason with him—I'm afraid what he's going to think, do you see? And I'm not just saying that to get at you, Justin, I'm *afraid* what he's going to think, and I don't think you can do anything to stop him, not with reason."

"You forget one thing," he said, leaning back against his seat.

"What's that?"

"The same thing that keeps Grant and me alive. That past a certain point you don't care. Past a certain point—" He shook his head, and looked up as Florian brought the drink back. "Thank you."

"No problem, ser." Florian sat down.

"If he gets into public," Ari took up the thread of thought, "he can do himself harm, he can do me harm, of course—which I don't want. It's possible that your father has been psychologically—very isolate, for a very long time: insular and insulated from all the problems going on in the world. If he was protecting you against the release of that tape—which may be a real motive for him lying until now—he evidently believes you're capable of handling it or he's been told something by someone that makes him desperate enough to risk you as well as himself—*if* that message actually came from him, which is a question . . . but it doesn't really matter. What he'll do—that matters. And we have an image problem in all this mess, you understand me?''

Justin *was* understanding her, she thought so by the little motions of his eyes, the tensions in his face. ''What is there to do?'' he said. ''You've left Grant back there; I don't know what they're doing to my father at Planys—''

''Nothing. They're not going to do anything to him.''

''Can you guarantee that?''

She hesitated awhile over that answer. ''That depends,'' she said. ''That very much depends. That's why you're with me. *Someone* has to do something. I'd wanted to be inconspicuous for a while more, but I'm the only one who face the media knows and I'm the only one who has enough credit with them to patch this mess up—but I need you, I need your help. Possibly you'll double on me. I don't know. But whether it's true or false what they're saying, it's going to be terribly hard for your father to handle this or to back away from the cameras if he gets the chance. You're my hope of stopping that.''

Another small silence. Then: ''How did you get Denys's permission for this move?''

''The same way I've gotten you into my residency. I told Denys you're mine, that I ran a major intervention, that Grant is far more of a hold on you than your father is; that you'd choose him over your father if it came to a choice, because your father can take care of himself; while Grant—'' She shrugged. ''That kind of thing. Denys believes it.''

That got through to him, just about enough threat to make sure he understood. Justin sat there staring at her, mad, very mad. And very worried. ''You're quite an operator, young sera.''

The compliment made her smile, though sadly. ''Giraud died too soon. The Paxers aren't going to sit still in all this commotion. The elections are going to be chaos, there may be more bombings, more people dead—the whole thing is going to blow wide if we don't head it off. You know all of that. Your work is exactly in my field. That's one thing at stake. So you can put your father in a position where he has to do something desperate and put himself out front of something he can't control and I don't think he has any idea exists; or you can help me defuse this, calm him down and let me run a little game with Denys—put your father wise to it if you can, I don't mind; encourage your father to wait until I *do* run Reseune. We can double-team Denys, or you can blow everything to hell with the newsservices—by asking to get your father in front of the cameras; by doing things that make you look like you're under duress—"

"The truth, you mean."

"—or by doing things that give you a bad image. You can't look like a traitor to your own father. You're very good with bright people and design-systems; but you don't know where the traps are, you're not current with the outside world, you're not used to the press and you're not used to picking up on your own public image. For God's sake take advice and be careful. If you get stubborn about this you can lose every leverage you've got."

He stared at her a long time, and sipped his whiskey. "Tell me," he said finally, "exactly what sort of thing I should watch out for."

Grant watched, entranced by the precision, as the cards crackled into a precise shuffle in the girl's fingers. "That's amazing," he said.

"This?" Sera Amy looked pleased and did it again. "My mother taught me, God, I guess from the time my fingers were big enough." She shot a series of cards to her and to him. Quentin AQ was the silent presence in the room, a tall, well-built young man in Security uniform, who sat and watched—a young man altogether capable of breaking a neck in a score of different ways: Grant had no illusions about his chances if he made a move crosswise of Amy Carnath. He had looked to spend the time confined to his room at best and under trank or under restraint at worst; but young sera had instead made every attempt to reassure him: *It won't take long, they'll meet with the Bureau, I don't doubt they'll have everything straightened out in a couple of days*: and she had finally, after a mid-afternoon lunch, declared that she would teach him to play cards.

He was touched and amused. Young Amy was taking her

recently-acquired Alpha license very seriously, and doing outstandingly well: the game did keep his mind off what, if he were half-tranked and locked in solitude, would have been absolute hell—a situation which was still hell, what time he let himself worry whether the plane had landed yet, whether Justin was safe, what was going on with Jordan in Planys.

He wished he were on that plane; but he figured he was actually doing more good for Justin as a hostage, being civil and cool-headed and not pouring fuel on the fires of juvenile excitement—or Administration paranoia.

Poker was also an interesting game, in which Amy said an azi had two considerable advantages, first, profound concentration, and second, the ability to conceal one's reactions. Sera was right. He very much wanted to try it with Justin.

When Justin got home.

It was the little thoughts like that, that sent panic rushing through him, with the thought that something could happen, that somehow an order could come through that sera Amy could not resist or that authorities elsewhere could take Justin into custody; and, Reseune holding his Contract, they might not meet again. Ever.

Then he might not sit placidly waiting for re-training. Then he might do something incredibly unlikely for an azi designer, and get his hands on a weapon: in a very fluxed way it seemed what a CIT might do and what was the best thing to do. At other moments—he was fluxing that wildly—he knew that his own personal CIT might fight to be free, but he would never turn a weapon on sera Amy, nor on Quentin AQ, and that Justin could never—he had told the truth to ser Denys—never harm any of the people who had harmed him. His CIT might threaten with a weapon, but pull the trigger—Justin could not, not even if it was Giraud, who was dead anyway.

No, when it came to it, Grant thought, studying the hand young sera had dealt him—he could not see himself surrendering to the hospital; but he could not see himself shooting to kill, either.

Young Amy told him that the secret of the game she was teaching him was to keep one's intentions and one's predicaments off one's face. Young Amy was very intelligent, and quite good at it herself, for a CIT. Possibly she was playing more than one game and trying to read more than what cards he held, the same way he was trying to read her for more information than she was willing to give.

So meanwhile he gambled for small markers, because one was supposed to play for money, but he owned none that was not Justin's; and he would not risk that, even at the minuscule levels young Amy proposed. He risked nothing that was Justin's, was very glad to have enough liberty in the apartment to know that Justin's papers were safe, and generally to catch what bits of information he could . . . dumb-annie was a role he still knew how to play. *I'll be all right*, Justin had said to him. And after all was said and done, he had to rely on that, like any azi—while he kept fluxing on Winfield and the Abolitionists and the fact that at thirty-seven he was legally a minor; and Amy Carnath at eighteen was legally an adult. *Dammit*, he wanted to shout at her, *take advice. Tell me what's going on and listen to someone with more experience than you have.*

But that was not likely to happen. Amy Carnath took Ari Emory's orders; and whether it was Denys Nye or Ari Emory managing things now—he could not at all figure.

———————————— **viii** ————————————

The airport stirred boyhood memories, himself in the terminal gift shop, begging a few cred-chits from Jordan for trinkets and gifts for home: Justin thought of that as they walked the safeway from the plane to the Novgorod terminal, with armed Security going ahead of them and crowding close behind.

No passage through the public terminal: Ari had explained that; no transfer to a car in the open. Things were too dangerous nowadays. They took a side door, hurried downstairs to a garage where cars waited with shielded windows.

There Security laid hands on him and took him apart from Ari and Catlin and Florian. Ari had warned him it would happen and asked him to do exactly what Security told him, but they were damned rough, and their haste and their force getting him into the car was more than it need have been.

He kept his mouth shut about it, sandwiched in between two guards in the back seat, and with a heavy hand on his shoulder as the doors locked. Then the man let go of him and he settled back, watching as the first few cars left the garage. Their own driver joined the tight convoy, whisking out past *RESEUNE ONE*'s wing, along the edge of the field and out a guarded gate where they picked up more escort.

It was the sort of official protection, he thought, that must have attended Giraud Nye in these troubled years. He sat between the hard-muscled bodies of two of Reseune's senior House Security, with another, armed, in the front- seat passenger side, and one driving. He watched the road unfold to the river, the bridge and the drive—he remembered it—which led up to the government center, green crops growing in the interstices, a handful of trees which had prospered in the years since he had ridden this road at Jordan's side, taking the tour—

The Hall of State loomed up around a turn, suddenly filling the windshield; and he felt a chill and a sense of panic. "Aren't we going to the Bureau?" he asked his guards quietly, calmly. "I thought we were going to the Science Bureau."

"We follow the car in front of us," the one on the left said.

He figured that much. Damn, he thought, and sat and watched, wishing he had Grant's ability to go Out awhile. He wanted this day done with. He wanted—

God, he wanted to go home.

He wanted a phone, and a chance to talk to Jordan, and to find out the truth, but the truth, Ari had said it, was the least important thing.

He was numb, in overload, total flux. He tried to find answers and there was no information to give them to him, except the ones Ari herself led him through, bringing order where none existed—or finding the only way through, he did not know any longer. He had found himself agreeing to lie to the press, agreeing to deny his father's innocence—to which he himself could not swear—

He found himself doubting Jordan, doubting Jordan's motives, Jordan's love for him, everything in the world but Grant. Doubting his own sanity, finally, and the integrity of his own mind.

Not even Giraud did this to me. Not even Giraud.

Flux of images, the older Ari, the younger; flux of remembered panic, interview in Ari's office:

. . . You make my life tranquil, sweet, and stand between me and Jordan, and I won't have his friends arrested, and I won't do a mindwipe on Grant, I'll even stop giving you hell in the office. You know what the cost is, for all those transfers you want. . . .

. . . I told Denys you're mine, that I ran a major intervention, that Grant is far more of a hold on you than your father is; that you'd choose him over your father if it came to a choice. . . .

The convoy drew up under the portico at the side of the Hall of State. He moved when his guards flung the door open and hastened him out and through the doors—not so roughly this time: this time there were news cameras.

Ari stopped and took his arm. The thought flashed through his mind that he could shove her away, refuse to go farther, tell the cameras everything that had happened to him, shout out the fact that Reseune was holding Grant hostage, that they had worked on him to divide him from his father, that Jordan might well have spent twenty years in confinement for a lie—

He hesitated, Ari tugging at his arm, someone nudging him from behind.

"We're going to meet with Secretary Lynch," Ari said, "upstairs. Come on. We'll talk to the press later."

"Is your father innocent?" someone shouted at him out of the echoing chaos.

He looked at that reporter. He tried to think, in the time-stretch of nightmare, whether he even knew the answer or not, and then just ignored the question, going where Ari wanted him to go, to say whatever he had to say.

"You do this one alone," Ari told him when they reached the upstairs, turning him over to Bureau Enforcement. "I'll be getting the hearing on monitor, but nobody from Reseune will be there. The Bureau wants you not to feel pressured. All right?"

So he walked with blue-uniformed strangers still of Reseune's making, taught by Reseune's tapes—who brought him into a large conference room, and brought him to a table facing a triple half-ring of tables on a dais, where other strangers took their seats in a blurred murmur of conversation—

Strangers except Secretary-now-Proxy for Science Lynch: Lynch he knew from newscasts. He settled into his chair, grateful to find at least one known quantity in the room, at the head of the committee, he supposed. There was a pitcher of water in front of him, and he filled a glass and drank, trying to soothe his stomach. Ari's staff had offered him food on the plane, but he had not been able to eat more than the chips and a bite of the sandwich; and he had had another soft drink after the whiskey. Now he felt light-headed and sick. *Damn fool*, he told himself in the dizzying buzz of people talking in a large room, *quit sleepwalking. Wake up and focus, for God's sake, they'll think you're drugged.*

But the flux kept on, every thought, every nuance of everything Jordan had last said to him; everything Ari had said that might be a clue to what was going on or whether the threat was threat or only show for Denys and Security.

Secretary Lynch came up to the table where he was sitting, and offered his hand. Justin stood up and took it, felt the kindness in the gesture, saw a face that had been only an image on vid take on a human concern for him; and that small encouragement hit him in the gut, he did not know why.

"Are you all right?" the Secretary-Proxy asked.

"A little nervous," he said; and felt Lynch's fingers close harder on his. A little pat on his arm. Giraud's career-long associate, he suddenly remembered that with a jolt close to nausea, and felt the whole room go distant, sounds echoing in his skull in time with the beating of his heart. *Where does Ari stand with him? Is this choreographed?*

"You're inside Bureau jurisdiction now," Lynch said. "No Reseune staff is here. Three Councillors are in the city: they've asked to audit the proceedings: Chairman Harad, Councillor Corain; Councillor Jacques. Is there any other witness you want? Or do you have any objection to anyone here? You understand you have a right to object to members of the inquiry."

"No, ser."

"Are you all right?" It was the second time Lynch had asked. Justin drew in a breath and disengaged his hand.

"Just a little—" *Light-headed. No. God, don't say that.* He thought his face must be white. He felt the air-conditioning on sweat at his temples. "I was too nervous to eat. I don't sup-

pose I could get a soft drink before we start. Maybe crackers or
something.''

Lynch looked a little nonplussed; and then patted his shoulder and called an aide.

Like a damned kid, he thought. Fifteen minutes, a pastry
and a cup of coffee, that little time to catch his breath in an
adjoining conference room, and he was better collected—was
able to walk back into the hearing room and have Secretary
Lynch walk him over to Mikhail Corain and to Simon Jacques
and Nasir Harad one after the other, faces he recognized in
what still passed in a haze of overload, but a less shaky one:
God, he was fluxed. He had had nightmares about publicity,
lifelong, felt himself still on the verge of panic—still kept
flashing on Security—the cell—the Council hearings. . . .

Giraud's voice, saying things he could not remember, but
which put a profound dread in him.

Wake *up*, dammit! No more time for thinking. Do!

''Dr. Warrick,'' Corain said, taking his hand. ''A pleasure
to meet you, finally.''

''Thank you, ser.''

When did that message actually come from my father? That
was what he wanted to ask.

But he did not, not being a fool. *Audit,* Lynch had said: then
the Councillors were not here to engage in questions.

''If you need anything,'' Corain said, ''if you feel you need
protection—you understand you can ask for it.''

''No, ser. —But I appreciate your concern.'' *This is a man
who wants to use Jordan. And me. What am I worth to him?
Where would his protection leave me?*

Out of Reseune. And Grant inside.

Corain patted him on the arm. Simon Jacques offered his
hand, introducing himself, a dark-haired, neutral kind of man
with a firm grip and a tendency not to meet his eyes. ''Councillor. . . . Chairman Harad.'' —as he shook Harad's thin hand,
meeting a gray stare appallingly cold and hostile. *One of
Reseune's friends.*

''Dr. Warrick,'' Harad said. ''I hope you can clear up some
of the confusion in this. Thank you for agreeing to appear.''

''Yes, ser,'' he said. *Agreeing to appear. Who asked me?*

Who agreed in my name? How many things have gone out, in my name, and Jordan's?

"Dr. Warrick," Lynch said, taking his arm. "If we can get this underway—"

He took his seat at the table; he answered questions: No, I have no way of knowing anything beyond my father's statements. He never discussed the matter with me, beyond the time—just before the hearing. When he was leaving. No, I'm not under drugs; I'm not under coercion. I'm confused and I'm worried. I think that's a normal reaction under the circumstances. . . . His hand shook when he picked up the water glass. He sipped water and waited while committee members consulted together, talking just under his hearing.

"Why do you believe," a Dr. Wells asked him then, "—or did you ever believe—your father's confession?"

"I believed it. He said so. And because—" *Bring out some of the sexual angle*, Ari had said on the plane. *It plays well in the press. Scandal always gets the attention, and you can work people en masse a lot easier if you've got their minds on sex: everybody's got an opinion on that. Just don't mention the tape and I won't mention the drugs, all right?* "Because there was a motive I could believe in—that everyone in Reseune believed in. Me. Ariane Emory blackmailed me into a relationship with her. My father found out."

The reaction lacked surprise. The interrogator nodded slowly.

"Blackmailed you—how?"

He slid a glance toward Mikhail Corain, though it was a committee member who asked the question. He said, watching Corain's reactions in his peripheral vision: "There was a secret deal for Jordan's transfer to RESEUNESPACE. Ari found out Jordan had pulled strings to get past her, and she made a deal with me—not to stop my father's transfer." Corain did not like that line of questioning. *So*, he thought, and looked back at the questioner. "She told me—that she intended me to stay in Reseune; that she meant to teach me; that she saw potential in my work she wanted developed, and that she wanted a guarantee Jordan wouldn't mess up the psychogenesis project. It looked like it would be a few years. Then she said she'd approve my transfer to go with him. Probably she would have. She usually kept her promises.''

Slowly, slowly, there began to be consultation. *They knew,* he thought to himself. *They knew—the whole damn committee—even Corain— All these years; my God, the whole damn Council and the Bureau—there was no secrecy about me and Ari. But something I said—they didn't know.*

God! What am I into? What deals did Giraud make, what am I treading on?

''You wanted to keep the sexual relationship secret,'' Wells said. ''How long did that continue?''

''A few times.''

''Where?''

''Her office. Her apartment.''

''Who initiated it?''

''She did.'' He felt the heat in his face, and leaned his arms on the table for steadiness. ''Can I say something, ser? I honestly think, ser, the sex was only a means to an end—to make me guilty enough to drive a wedge between me and my father. It wasn't just the encounter itself. It was the relationship between her and my father. I'm a PR, ser. And she was not my father's friend. I thought I could handle the guilt. I thought it wouldn't bother me. From the other side of the event it looked a lot different; and she was a master clinician—she was completely in control of what was going on and I was a student way out of his limits. My father would have understood that part of it, when I couldn't, at the time. I didn't plan for him to find out. But he did.''

A thought flashed up with gut-deep certainty out of the flux: *He didn't do it. He couldn't kill anyone. He'd have been concerned for me. He'd have wanted to work the situation, get me clear before he did anything—and I can't tell them that. . . .*
—to change an instant later into: *Anyone can do anything under the right stress. If that was the right stress for him—the unbearable point—*

Lynch asked: ''Did your father confront you with the discovery?''

''No. He went straight to her. I had a meeting with Ari for later that evening. I didn't know she was dead until they told me, after I was arrested.''

Then—then the thing that had been trying to click into place snapped into lock, clear and plain, exactly where the way out was: *Disavow what Jordan's said—be the outraged son, defending his father: put myself in a position to be courted by both sides. That's the answer.*

Out of everything that Ari had said on the plane, exactly where she was trying to lead him. Her pieces, handed him bit by bit—*damn, she's an operator.* But there was a way to position all of it so he could step to either shore, play the emotional angle, the outrage—oppose Jordan and be won over; or win Jordan over—whichever worked, hell with Corain, hell with all the would-be users in this mess: he could maneuver if he could just get a position and focus everyone's efforts on him, to persuade *him.* It collected information, it collected a small amount of control, and he thought, he *thought* it possibly exceeded the perimeters where Ari had intended he should go— but only enough to worry her and keep her working on him and his position, *not* so long as he could tread a very narrow line between opposition and cooperation.

Under fire. When he always did his best thinking. He picked up the glass and took a second drink, and his hand was suddenly steady, his heart still pounding: *Damn, Giraud did a piece on me, didn't he? Shot my nerves to hell. But the mind works.*

"Were you aware of any other person who might have had a motive for murder?"

"I'm not aware of any," he said, frowning, and plunged ahead unasked. "I'll tell you, ser, I have a major concern about what's going on here."

"What concern?"

"That my father's being used. That if he did recant his confession—that can't be checked any more than the confession can be. No one knows. No one can know. He's a research scientist. He's been twenty years out of touch with current politics. He could make a statement. He could say anything. God knows what he's been told or what's going on, but I don't trust this, ser. I don't know if he's been told something that made him come out with this, I don't know if he's been promised something, but I'm extremely worried, ser, and I resent his name being caught up in politics he doesn't know anything about—he's being *used*, ser, maybe led into something, maybe just that people are taking this up that had absolutely nothing to say to help him twenty years ago and all of a sudden everyone's interested, *not* because they know whether he's guilty or innocent, but because it's a political lever in things my father's not in touch with, for reasons that don't have anything to do with my father's welfare. I'll fight that, ser."

There was silence for about two breaths, then a murmur broke out in the room.

Now the knives were going to come out, he thought. Now he had found his position and now he had built Jordan a defense no matter what he had said.

His hand was shaking nearly enough to spill the water when he took his next drink, but it was the after-a-fight shakes. Inside, he had more hope for himself and Jordan and Grant than he had had since he had known where they were taking him.

Corain bit his lip as young Emory courteously shook his hand during the mid-session recess, as she said earnestly, in the insulation of her personal Security and his: "It's politics, of course: Reseune understands that; but it's very personal with Justin. He's not political. He sees what happened to his father in the first place as political and now he sees it all starting up again now that Giraud's dead and there are elections on. I've advised him to tone it down; but he's terribly upset."

"You should advise him," Corain said coldly, "if that's his primary concern, he should stay away from the media, young sera. If he raises charges, they'll go before Council."

"I'll pass him that word, ser." With a little lift of the chin. Not Ari senior's smile, not that maddening, superior smile; just a direct look. "Possibly my predecessor slipped and fell. *I* have no idea. I'm interested in the truth, but I *really* don't think it's going to come out in this hearing."

If Ari senior had said that, it would surely have meaning under meaning. He looked this incarnation in the eye and was absolutely sure it did. Reseune was pulling strings in Science, damned right it was.

"I hate it," Ari Emory said, assuming a confidential friendliness, "that this has blown up now. Politics change, positions change—and develop common interests. I'll administer

Reseune before too many years; there's a lot I can do then, and there are changes I want to make. I want you to understand, ser Corain, that I'm not welded to the past."

"You have a few years yet," Corain said. And thought: *Thank God.*

"A few years yet. But I've been in politics a long, long time. If my predecessor were alive right now, she'd look at the general situation and say something has to be done to calm it down. It's not good for either party. All it does is help Khalid."

Corain looked at the young face a long, long moment. "We've always maintained a moderate position."

"We absolutely overlap, where it comes to solving Novgorod's problems. And the Pan-Paris loop. All of that. I think you're entirely right about those bills—the way I know I'm right about Dr. Warrick."

"You don't have any power, young sera."

"I do," she said. "At least within Reseune. That's not small. Right now I'm here because I know people, and Justin doesn't; and because Justin's my friend and quite honestly, I don't think his father is any danger to me personally and neither does Reseune Administration. So it's psychology of a sort: I want people to know that I support Justin. He sees his father in danger of getting swept up in causes he knows his father wouldn't support; and that's where Reseune is going to insist on its sovereignty to protect its citizens, both him and his father. It can end up in court; and it can get messy. And that just helps the Paxers, doesn't it, that I don't think you like either. So is there a way out of this? You've got the experience in Council. You tell *me*."

"First off," Corain said, with a bitter taste in his mouth, "young Warrick has to back off the charges he's making."

She nodded. "I think that's a good idea."

"If I gave the committee the idea that I blame Councillor Corain," Justin said carefully, quietly, "I certainly want to apologize for that impression, that came to my attention at recess. I'm sure he has my father's welfare at heart. But I *am* afraid of violent influences that could have involved themselves in this—"

ix

It was after midnight before they made the hotel, via the underground entrance, the security lift straight to the upper floors that Reseune Security had made their own: Ari sighed with relief as the lift stopped on the eighteenth floor—a sprawling, single interconnected suite on this VIP level of the Riverside, and one that Giraud still had reserved for the month, in a hotel that Reseune Security knew down to its foundations and conduits.

Abban met her at the lift, and Ari blinked, surprised at first, then ineffably relieved to see Abban's competence handling what Florian and Catlin had had no opportunity to oversee, quietly on the job, no matter that they had buried Giraud that morning, no matter that Abban had been through hell this week. He had to have flown up from Reseune this afternoon, after the rest of the staff arrived.

"Young sera," Abban said. "Florian, Catlin, I've already made the checks: sera will want the master bedroom, I'm sure; ser Justin to the white room or the blue—as sera pleases."

The blue bedroom was far off across the suite, down a hall and past the tape studio; the white was next to the master suite, connected by a side door, if it was unlocked: white had lately been her room, when she had been in Novgorod with uncle Giraud. *I'd rather my old room,* was her thought; but that was too emotional a thing to say, Abban was not terribly social, even after all those years, and it was the pressure of the day and her exhaustion that made her wish she was a child again, with Giraud next door to handle all the problems. "He can take white," she said, and looked at Justin, who was altogether exhausted. "Go with Kelly, Justin, he'll see you settled—is there anything to eat, Abban? Justin's starved."

"We thought meals might be short. Staff has a cold supper ready on call for any room; white wine, cheese and ham; or if sera prefers—"

"You're a dear, Abban." She patted his arm and walked wearily through the main doors of the VIP suite, Abban walking at her right, Florian at her left, and Catlin a little behind as they passed the guards into the long main hall of Volga sandstone. "I really appreciate your doing this. You didn't have to."

"Giraud asked me to close down his office and collect his personal papers. And ser Denys has asked me to oversee House Security, in somewhat Giraud's capacity, I hope on a tolerably permanent basis. It's only part of my job."

"I'm glad someone's looking after you. Are you all right, Abban?"

Abban was well above a hundred himself, having had one Supervisor for most of his life. He was very lost now, she thought, with Denys focused now on Giraud-to-come. Somebody had to take him—or give him Final tape and a CIT-number, which Abbban was ill suited for. All Abban had gotten since Giraud had died seemed to be snubs from the Family and responsibility for all the details, precious little grace for what he was suffering, and it made her mad.

"Perfectly well, thank you, sera. Ser Denys has offered me a place in his household."

"Good." She was surprised and relieved. "Good for Denys. I worry about you."

"You're very kind, young sera."

"I do. I know everything's in order; the staff's got it going. Go get some rest yourself."

"I'm perfectly fine, young sera, thank you: I prefer to stay busy." They stopped at the door of the master bedroom, a small suite within the suite, and Abban opened the door on manual. "I'll handle the staff and order your suppers—Florian and Catlin are staying right in your bedroom, aren't they? I'd advise that."

"Yes. Don't worry. It's all right." Abban would, she thought, have preferred Justin in the blue room, at the other end of the floor; and likely Giraud and therefore Abban had never believed there was no bed-sharing going on. "I assure you, *just* Florian and Catlin. Everything's fine. Get us our suppers and we'll all be in for the night."

"Remember even the main Minder is a limited system: you're on manual for the door. Please don't forget to lock it."

"Yes," she said. That would nettle Florian and Catlin—Abban's damned punctilious superiority, as if they were still youngers. She smiled, glad at least Abban had that intact.

"Go," she said. "It's all right." And Abban nodded, gave her a courteous "sera" and left her to Florian and Catlin.

"He's doing fine," Florian said, with precisely that degree of annoyance she had figured. "*Abban* for head of Security. . . ."

Abban's nit-picking outraged Florian; Catlin found his reminders merely a waste of her time and treated them with cool disdain. That was the difference in them. Ari smiled, shook her head and walked on into the living area of the master suite, gratefully turned the briefcase over to Catlin and fell into a formfit chair with a groan, while Florian went straight to the Minder to read out the entries since Abban would have set it sometime today.

"God," she sighed, leaned back in the soft chair and let it mold around her, feet up. "How are we, clean enough?"

"Nothing's clean enough in this place," Catlin said. She set the briefcase on the entry table, opened it, pushed a button and checked the interior electronics. "Everything's real nervous," Catlin said. "I'll be glad to get out of here."

Florian nodded. "Minder was set up at 1747, only staff admitted since then."

"It was supposed to be set by 1500," Catlin said, cool disapproval.

"Abban did the set." Snipe. "Probably re-set it when he came in." Double snipe. "I'll ask him. —Sera, just sit here awhile. Let us go over everything."

"God," Ari moaned, and reached down and pulled off her shoes. "If there's a bomb I don't care. I want my shower, I want my supper, I want my bed, I don't care who's in it."

Florian laughed. "Quick as we can," he said, and left the Minder and went and looked at Catlin's readouts, then unpacked his own kit, laying out his equipment.

Carelessness was the one direct order they would never obey. No one checked out her residences except them and that was the Rule. Catlin had made it, years ago, and they all still respected it. No matter the inconvenience.

So she tucked her knees up sideways in the chair and shut her eyes, still seeing the cylinder going into the ground, the cenotaph slamming down; Abban's pale face; Justin's, across from her on the plane, so pale and so upset—

Damned long day. Damnable day. Corain was willing to deal but Corain was being careful, Corain was playing as hard and as nasty as he could. Corain had gotten to Wells, on the Bureau committee, and after the recess the questions had gotten brutal and detailed.

What is your present position in Reseune? Who approved it?

When was the last time you spoke to your father? What was his state of mind?

Have you ever had treatment for psychological problems? Who administered it?

You have an azi companion, Grant ALX-972. Did he come with you? Why not?

Have you ever been subject to a psych procedure you haven't previously mentioned to this committee?

Justin had held his ground—occasionally outright lying to the committee, or lying by indirection, a flat challenge to the opposition inside the Bureau to see if they had the votes to mandate another psychprobe: they don't have, she had assured him in the recess; but let's don't put that to the test, for God's sake.

He had held up, absolutely no fractures, till his voice began to give out: the temper built, the nerves steadied—he always did that, nervous as hell because politics gave him flashes, because that mind of his saw so many possibilities in everything, and sorted and collated over so wide a range he had trouble thinking of where he was and what was going on around him, but he had stalled off, found his equilibrium—she had recognized that little intake of breath, that set of the shoulders the instant she saw it on camera in the adjoining room, known that all of a sudden the committee was dealing with a Justin Warrick who was *in* that room, and starting onto the offensive.

Good, she had thought then, *good. They think they can push him. He hasn't even been here till now. Now he is. He's too smart to go over to Corain. He'll never follow anyone's lead who's making mistakes: he's got far too much impatience with foul-ups and he said it while he was under kat: No one helped my father then. Not one of his damn friends. He has a lot of hostility about that.*

They'll find out they're dealing with a Special, after he's made off with their keys and their cred-slips—damn, he's good when he cuts loose; everything they say his father has, including the temper—once you get it going, once you get him to stop analyzing and move. He's still learning these people and he hates real-time work with a passion. Field-too-large. He's never learned to average and extemp the way I have: Justin wants exactitudes, and you don't get that in real-time and you don't get it in politics. The same precision that makes him so valuable in design, that's why his designs are so clean—that's why he's so damn slow, and why he keeps putting embellishments on them—patches, for intersects he can see and the other designers, even Yanni, damned well can't—

Someday, when we get back, out of this, we've got to talk about that. . . .

There's got to be a search-pattern he's using that isn't in program, even if he's got total recall on those sets—

If he could explain it—

I can almost see it. There's something in the signature of the designers themselves—a way of proceeding—he's comprehending on a conceptual level. But he's carrying it into CIT work—

"They're sending a tray up," a strange voice said, and Justin, lying on the bed and almost gone, felt a jolt of panic: it should be Grant's voice; and it was not.

Kelly, the man's name was. Security. He passed a hand over his eyes, raked fingers through his hair and murmured an answer.

He was all right, he kept telling himself; he was safe. Kelly was on his side, there only to protect him.

He levered himself up off the bed, dizzy from fatigue, the down-side of the adrenaline high he had been on hour after hour. "I don't think I can eat."

"I have orders you should, ser," Kelly said, in a tone that said he would, bite by bite.

"Damn." A thought got to him. "I have a hospital appointment tomorrow. Rejuv. God." He thought of making the request through Kelly, but by his experience, nothing got done through lower levels. "Is Florian or Catlin still in the net?"

"Yes, ser."

"Tell them give me a call. Tell them I'm without my medication." He went into the bath and splashed water into his face and onto the back of his neck, worried now about Grant. He had no liking for taking medication from any random stock in Novgorod; he thought about Ari's elaborate security precautions around Grant and worried about the breach it could create, or whether there was any motive for anyone at Reseune to substitute drugs.

"Ser Justin?" Florian hailed him, from the wall-speaker. "This is Florian. Do you mean your prescription? We have that."

"Thanks. Have they made arrangements for Grant? He's on the same schedule."

"We thought of that. It's taken care of, ser. Do you need it tonight?"

"Thank you," he said, relieved. Trust Florian. *No* detail dropped. "No, I'm going to rest tonight, it sends me hyper— God knows I don't need it before bed." It also hurt like hell; and he was not looking forward to it. Could *not* go through tomorrow's hearings on pain-killer.

"Yes, ser. It's all right then. Have a good sleep."

"Endit," he said to the Minder. And heard the suite door open. His heart jumped.

Kelly, he told himself. Dinner was a little early. He toweled his face dry, hung the towel on the hook and walked out into the bedroom.

No Kelly.

Not *like* Security. "Minder," he said. "Minder, get Florian AF. Next door."

No sound.

"Minder, give me an answer."

Dead.

O my God.

"It's Abban, sera," the Minder said; and Ari levered herself out of the chair to manual the door herself, Florian and Catlin still being occupied about their checks in the bedroom.

"Sera!" Florian said sharply from behind her, and she stopped as he hurried to get the door himself. The Rule again. "I'll set supper out," he said quietly then, and with a little smile: "The shower's safe."

"I'm so glad." She started on her way, looked back as the door opened and Abban showed up with the catering staff.

As suddenly there was a pounding on the adjoining door from Justin's side. "Florian!" she heard him shout.

Then the whole wall blew outward, a sheet of bright fire, a percussion like a fist slamming against her; and she fell over a chair arm, complete tumble onto her knees and into the narrow wedge against the wall as flames shot up, as of a sudden a volley of gunshots exploded from her right, shells exploded to her left, and she stared in a split-second's horror, flinging up her arms as a flying body came at her, bore her over and cracked her head against the floor.

Second explosion, jolting the bones. "Sera!" Florian gasped into her ear, and she tried to move, cooperating by instinct as he tried to haul her along the floor behind the chair, with fire lighting the smoke and heat already painful. One more shot went off and exploded, and Florian fell on top of her, covering her with his body, protecting her head with his arms.

In a moment more there was a dreadful quiet, except the crackle of the fire that lit the lowering pall of smoke—then a sudden scrape of the chair pulled away and flung tumbling. Florian moved. She saw Catlin's stark, grim face upside down above her in the orange light, felt Florian's knee bruise her leg and his hand press her shoulder as he tried to get up and they tried to get themselves sorted out: he hauled himself up and got an arm around her with Catlin on the other side, Florian stumbling and catching himself on the wall.

A solid wall of fire enveloped the open door, a tumult of voices outside—*Theirs or ours?* Ari wondered desperately— The fire enveloped bodies on the floor, half-exploded, unrecognizable except the black Security uniforms—where Abban had been standing—and the heat burned her hands and her face—

Who's the Enemy? What's waiting out there? What's first? Can you run through fire that thick? Is it burning in the hall?

She felt the hesitation in Florian and Catlin, only a second; then Florian breathed, to someone not present: "Florian to Security Two—somebody's turned off the fire-systems. Re-engage, system two. That's an incendiary. Acknowledge."

"They're answering," Catlin said.

"Who's *they*?" Ari said, and choked on the smoke. The fire blinded, burned them with the heat, worse by the moment. "Dammit to hell, where's the hand extinguishers?"

As suddenly the fire-systems cut on with a wail of sirens.

There was fire: Justin was aware of that first, of blistering heat that drove him to move before he was fully conscious, of smoke that stung his nose and his throat and his lungs—deadly as the fire and harder to evade. He clawed his way up over debris of shattered structural panels and hot metal, felt one cut his leg as he went over, lost his balance and wormed through underneath the massive bureau that had come down onto the end of the bed—away from the fire, that was all he could think of at the moment, until his vision cleared and he could see the hallward door through the smoke, beyond the ruin of ceiling and wall-panels piled on the furniture.

There was a blank then. He came to on his knees, clinging to the door handle, trying to get to his feet again, finding fire on his left, the lights only clusters of suns in a universe gone to murk, to fire and shouts coming from somewhere. He pulled the manual latch, got the door unlocked, and pulled it open against the obstruction of debris around him.

Another blank. He was in the hall, dark figures rushed at him and one hit him, flinging him against the irregular stone of the wall. But that one stopped then, and hauled him up and yelled at him: "Get to the exit! That way—"

He felt the stiff material of a firesuit; felt a mask pressed to his face; felt himself dragged along while he inhaled cleaner air. Then he saw the emergency exit for himself, and tried to go under his own power—through the doors into clean air. The man yelled something at him, shoved him through—

Blank. Someone caught hold of him. There were people around him, in the stairwell.

"How far up is it?" someone shouted at him. "Where did you come from?"

He could not answer. He coughed and almost fell; but they helped him, and he walked.

———————————————— X ————————————————

"Kelly EK is dead," Catlin reported calmly, between listening to the net.

The rescue copters were still coming in at the pad outside Mary Stamford Hospital, and Ari angrily fended away the medtech who was trying to see if the lump on her head needed scan: "For God's sake, let me *alone*! Catlin, *where*, in the room?"

"In the hallway," Catlin said. "Alone. They identified him by his tags. —They're searching out on the far side of the building now, where the exit stairs let out: a lot of the guests went that way."

"God." Ari wiped a hand over her face—reflex: there was Neoskin on her hand and sweat stung.

The fire teams had it under control, the report ran. Explosions had gone off at several points on the floor, in the blue room and the white. *The explosives were rigged in White,* Florian had said, vastly chagrined. *A periphery scan wouldn't pick them up, but we'd have found them if we'd run the check from the top. But Abban psyched us. He had the trigger: I saw the flash from the briefcase on the table; and that rig was state-of-the-art.*

It had gone so fast, Justin's urgent shout through the connecting door, the split-second warning that had triggered Florian's something's-wrong reflexes and brought Catlin, armed, out that bedroom doorway the instant after the initial explosion, in a chain of thought that went something like: explosions-can't-happen-with-adequate-checks; there's-Abban-who-ran-the-checks; *fire!*—about a nanosecond before Abban's fire came back at her a hair off. A good shot with a regular pistol and a better one with explosive rounds, that was what it had come down to, while Abban had hesitated one fatal synapse-jump between target A and target B.

Giraud's orders, Ari thought. Giraud ordered me killed. . . .

Rescue teams had gotten into Justin's charred room. They were searching through the wreckage; but from the time they had said that the heavy display cabinet had crashed down beside the connecting door and shielded that area from the force of the blast, and that they had found the hall door open, then she had believed Justin had to have gotten out. There were two dead of smoke inhalation that they had found; Kelly burned, evidently, beyond recognition, *not* with Justin, where he should have been; several severely burned trying to get to her—God help them; but Security from the floor below had gotten up there with emergency equipment and a unit captain with good sense had gotten Florian's advisement the fire systems were not operating and gotten to the control system to turn them on again—Abban had seen to that little detail too—while another had ordered all personnel who could not reach fire control equipment to get out, immediately . . . a damned good thing, because the majority were azi, who might well have tried to help her without fire-gear and died trying.

"Damn!" Astringent stung the wound on her head. They had already pulled a finger-wide fragment of plastic out of her shoulder. Florian was in worse shape, having caught several, and having bled profusely, in no condition to be running check-in, but Florian was at one door and a reliable guard was at the other, making sure badges got checked and that Reseune personnel were accounted for.

Abban and the two with him were dead. *I don't know if they were his*, Catlin had said. *There wasn't time to ask.*

An arriving ambulance jumped a curb, and Justin reeled back, stumbled and recovered himself in the dark, in the chaos of lights and firefighting equipment, announcements over loud-hailers, guests in night-robes and pajamas huddled together in the street outside and onto the gravel garden area. Firelight spread through smoke, smoke hazed the emergency lights and the floods around the entrance and down the drive.

He was on the street then. He did not know how he had gotten there, or where the hotel was. He was wobbling on his feet and he found a bench to sit on, in the dark. He dropped his head into his hands and felt clammy sweat despite the night chill.

He was blank for a time more. He was walking again, confronted with a dead end in the space between two buildings, and a stairway down. *Pedway*, the sign said.

Find a phone, he thought. *Get help. I'm lost.*

And then he thought: *I'm not thinking clearly. God, what if—*

It was someone on staff. Security had checked it.

Abban—had checked it.

Was it aimed at me? Was I the only one?

Ari—

He stumbled on the steps, caught himself on the rail, and made it to the bottom, to security doors that gave way to his approach, to a lighted tunnel that stretched on in eerie vacancy.

"Uncle Denys," Ari said; and of a sudden the load seemed too much—*Uncle Denys*, the way she had said in the hospital when she had broken her arm, when they had handed her the phone and she had had to tell Denys she had been a fool. Not a fool this time, she told herself that; lucky to be alive. But the report was nothing to be proud of either. "Uncle Denys, I'm all right. So are Florian and Catlin."

"Thank God for that. They're saying you were killed, you understand that?"

"I'm pretty much alive. A few scratches and some burns. But Abban's dead. Five others. In the fire." There was a limit to what they could say on the net, via the remotes Florian had set up with the mobile system. "I'm taking command of Security here myself. I'm issuing orders through the net. Security is compromised as hell, understand me. Someone got inside." Her hand started to shake. She bit her lip and drew in a large breath. "There've been two other bombings tonight—Paxers blew up some track in center city, they're claiming the attack on the hotel, and they're threatening worse; I'm in contact with the Novgorod police and all our systems—"

"Understood," Denys said, before she had to say more than she wanted. *"I'm relieved. We've got that on the net. God, Ari, what a mess!"*

"Don't be surprised by much of anything. It's all right, understand. Bureau Enforcement is moving on the hotel situation. Watch the net."

"Understood. Absolutely. We'd better cut this off. I'll up your priorities, effective immediately. Thank God you're safe."

"I plan to stay that way," she said. "Take care of yourself. All right?"

"You take care," Denys said. *"Please."*

She broke the contact, passed the handset back to Florian.

"We have confirmation," he said. "The plane has left the ground at Planys. They expect touchdown about 1450 tomorrow."

"Good," she said. "Good." From the fragile amount of control she had.

"Councillor Harad is waiting on-line; so is Councillor Corain. They've asked about your safety."

Strange bedfellows, she thought. But of course they would—Harad because he was an ally; Corain because, whatever he feared from her, he had more to fear from the Paxers, the radicals in his own spectrum; and the radicals in Defense.

"I'll talk to them. Have we got reporters down there?"

"Plenty."

"I'll talk to them."

"Sera, you're in shock."

"That's several of us, isn't it? Damn, get me a mirror and some makeup. We're in a war, hear me?"

The mirror in the ped-tunnel restroom showed a soot-streaked face that for a heartbeat Justin hardly knew for his own. His hands and arms were enough to raise question, the smell of smoke about his clothing, he had thought; and now he turned on the water full, took a handful of soap and started washing, wincing at bruises and burns.

The dark blue sweater and pants showed soot, but water and rubbing at least got the worst off and ground the rest in. He went through an entire stock of soap packets and dried his hair and his shoulders under the blowers, looked up again and saw a face shockingly pale. He was starting to need a shave. His sweater was burned and snagged, he had a tear above the knee and a gash where the tear was. Anyone who saw him, he thought, would report him to the police.

And that would catch him up in Cyteen law.

He leaned against the sink and wiped cold water across his face, clamping his jaws against a sick feeling that had been with him since he had come to. Thoughts started trying to insinuate themselves up to a conscious, emotional level: *It was Ari's wall; whoever did this was staff—whoever did this—*

Abban. Giraud's orders. But I'm only the incidental target. If she's dead—

The thought was incredible to him. Shattering. Ariane Emory had years to live. Ariane Emory had a century yet, was part of the world, part of his thinking, was—like air and gravity—there.

—someone else is in charge, someone else—wanting—someone to blame.

Paxers. Jordan.

Amy Carnath waiting in the apartment, with Grant, with Security—if Ari's dead—what can anyone do—

They've got Jordan, got Grant—I'm the only one still free—the only one who can make them trouble—

Something was wrong. Grant heard the Minder-call in the other bedroom—they had given him Justin's, which was his own as well, out of courtesy, he thought, as the larger room, or perhaps because they had known. Florian had re-set the Minder to respond to Amy Carnath, so nothing of what it was saying got to him, but he reckoned that it was not minor if it wakened young sera in the small hours of the night. After that he heard both Amy and Quentin stirring about and talking together in voices he could not quite hear with his ear to the door.

He slammed the door with his open palm. "Young sera, is something wrong?"

No answer. "Young sera? Please?"

Damn.

He went back to the large and unaccustomedly empty bed, lay staring at the ceiling with the lights on and tried to tell himself it was nothing.

But finally sera Amy came on the Minder to say: "Grant, are you awake?"

"Yes, sera."

"There's been an incident in Novgorod. Someone bombed the hotel. Ari's all right. She's coming on vid. Do you want to come to the living room?"

"Yes, sera." He did not panic. He got up, got his robe, and

went to the door, which Quentin opened for him. "Thank you," he said, and walked ahead of Quentin as far as his own living room, where Amy was sitting on the couch.

He took the other side of the U, Quentin took the middle, between him and Amy; and he sat with his arms folded against too much chill, watching the images of emergency vehicles, smoke billowing from breached seals on the hotel's top two floors.

"Were people killed?" he asked quietly, refusing to panic. Sera Amy was not cruel. She would not bring him out here to psych him: he believed that, but it was a thin thread.

"Five of Security," Amy said. "They say the Paxers got a bomb in. They aren't saying how. I don't know any more than that. We're not supposed to do things on the phones that give away where people are or what's going on or when they're going to be places. That's the Rule."

Grant looked at her past Quentin. Not panicking, not yet; but the adrenaline flood was there, threatening shivers, pure fight-flight conflict.

"I had a call from Dr. Nye warning me not to let you loose," Amy said. "He says he'd really like me to send you downstairs to Security, but I told him no. I lied to him. I said you were locked up."

"Thank you," Grant said, because something seemed called for.

And watched the vid.

Makeup covered the minor burns, but she left the visible bruise and the burn on her cheek; she put two pins in her hair, but she let it fly loose about her face. She had a clean sweater in her luggage that Security had rescued from the suite, but she chose to meet the cameras in what she was wearing, the tailored, gray satin blouse, with the blood and the burns and the soot, and the watermark the firefighting foam had made.

She was also sure, having stalled off twice, that the clips would hit the morning news with full exposure in Novgorod.

"They tried," she said grimly, in answer to the first question, which asked her reaction to what had happened; and she confronted the cameras with a rapid-fire series of answers that got around the fine question of who had done it and gave her the launching point that she wanted—

"We are very well, thank you. And I have a personal statement, which I'll give you first. Then questions.

"I don't know yet why this happened. I know part of it; and it was an attempt not quite to silence me, because I have no voice in politics—but to kill me before I do come of age enough to acquire one.

"It was a power move of some kind, because whoever did it wanted power without process. It cost the lives of brave people who tried despite fire and the dangers of more explosions, to rescue me and others; more, it was a clear attempt to destroy the political process, no matter who instigated it, no matter who perpetrated it. I don't think that the Paxers had anything to do with this. That they're anxious to claim they had is typical of the breed: and they hope to benefit from it—*benefit* from it, because that's exactly what's going on: that a handful of individuals too few to make a party and incapable of winning votes in debate thinks it can wear down the majority by terror—creates an atmosphere in which every fool with a half-conceived program can try the same thing and add to the confusion they hope to use. Let me tell you: whether this was the Paxers or one individual with a personal opinion he thinks outweighs the law, it's the peace under assault, it's our freedoms under assault, and every one of these attacks, no matter how motivated, makes the lawful rest of us that much more certain we don't want killers in charge of our lives and we damned well don't want their advice on how to conduct our affairs.

"Let me tell you also that within an hour of the disaster, Chairman Harad and members of the Council, Simon Jacques and Mikhail Corain, called me to express their profound outrage. *Everyone*, no matter what political party, understands what's threatened by actions like this. I don't need to say that to the people of Novgorod, who've held out against the tactics of the extremists and who've equally well held out against offers of help from the central government. I take my example from Novgorod. People can persuade me with ideas but there's no way in hell they're going to move me with violence or the possibility of violence.

"This isn't the first time in history someone's tried this; and by everything I've ever learned, the answer that works with them is exactly the kind of contempt Novgorod turns on them and their ideas—contempt, but no patience, *no* patience. Every time the Council sits to debate honest differences, *everybody* wins, precisely because civilization is working and the majority and the minority are trying to work out a fair compromise that protects the people they represent. That's why these types who want their own way above all have to destroy that; and that's precisely why the best answer is a consensus of all the elected bodies that ideas are valuable, peaceful voices deserve serious consideration, human needs have to be dealt with in a wise distribution of resources, and the principle of life itself has to be high on our list of values, just under our regard for the quality of life and the freedom to speak our opinions. Whoever did this, from whatever misguided notion of right above the law, he hasn't scared me into retreat, he's made me know how important law is; and I will run for office, someday; I'll run, and I'll respect the vote in my electorate, whatever the outcome, because an honest contest is one thing, but creating chaos to undermine the people's chosen representative isn't dissent, it's sabotage of the process, the same as the bombers are trying, and I'll have no part of that either."

Hear that, Vladislaw Khalid.

"If my electorate does think I should sit on Council I'll remember the cost it takes to *have* Council at all; and I'll remember that we have to have it, no matter the types who think they're above the law and so right they can take lives with impunity.

"That's the end of my personal statement. I've been very happy until now being as private as I could be; and I can't be now, because somebody decided to kill people to keep me from ever speaking out. So now I will speak up, loud and clear and often as there's something to say, because that's the best way I know to fight the ones who want me silenced.

"I'll take questions."

It was all right, she thought. She got off with a: "I'm sorry, my voice is going"; and a tremor in the hand she used to wipe a stray strand of hair—no need to pretend the latter: she had hid it until then, and got away from the cameras and had to sit down quickly, but she had gotten through it and said exactly what she had wanted to say.

"Is there any word?" she asked Catlin, who had been monitoring the net.

"No, sera," Catlin said.

She let go her breath and took the water Florian handed her. "Damn." Tears threatened, pain and exhaustion and the frustration of the situation. It was dawn. She had not slept since the morning of Giraud's funeral. Yesterday. God. "I'm going to make a phone call to Amy," she said in a controlled, quiet voice. "Ask Lynch to set up a very brief meeting with the Councillors and proxies at hand; and with the Bureau; I want to be at the airport by 0900."

"Sera, you haven't slept. Allow for that."

She sat a moment and thought about that. The blast kept replaying in her memory. The burned bodies. The smoke-filled halls, the lights shining out of haze.

She had no desire to shut her eyes at the moment, or to put food into her stomach, or to disturb her wounds by wrestling herself into the sweater she had brought: such little pains unnerved her, when there was so much worse to think about.

So one did not think about what-if and might-have-been. One handled things at the present, and trusted one's long-prepared decisions.

One Worked the whole of Union if that was what it took. One promised order where order did not exist; one held out the promise of moderation and rapprochement to shore up Corain, who was the opposition she preferred to Khalid.

One moved close to center for a while, to move the opposition closer to one's position—granted, of course, that they were trying to do the same: and granted at that point the clever and the quick would make the next jump out, leaving the opposition sitting bewildered at the new center.

Working the macrosystem, Ari senior would say.

While everything else went to hell and nothing that one wanted—stayed for long.

Except Florian and Catlin. Except the one flawless loyalty—the one thing that Ari's murderer had not dared to face.

* * *

Justin waked, winced at stiffened joints and the cramped position the thinly-padded bench in the restroom afforded; waked and tried to move in a hurry at the sound of the outer doors, to rake his hair into some kind of order and get to his feet before the intrusion passed the second doors; but he was only halfway up and off his balance before he faced two men in work-clothes, who stared at him half a heartbeat in surprise. He just turned to the sink, natural as breathing, turned on the water, wet his hands and ran them through his hair.

Except the two men showed up in the mirror, close behind him.

One moment he panicked. The next he thought: *Hell, they're not Reseune Security*, and turned around with a right elbow and all the strength he had—shocked as it connected, but still moving in the tape-taught sequence, full spin and a punch to the breastbone.

He stared a split-second at the result, one man flung backward against the corner, the other down—*God*, he thought, and then seeing the first man bracing to go for him, darted for the door and knocked it banging, went through the second the same way, and came out into a tunnel already beginning to fill with morning traffic.

What if I was wrong? That man could die. I may have killed someone.

Then: *No. I read it right.*

And: *I haven't studied that tape since I was a kid. I didn't know I could do that.*

He slowed to a fast walk, shaking in the knees and hurting in his shoulders and his back and knowing he was attracting attention with his unshaven face and his agitated manner: he tried to match the pace of the general traffic, put his hands in his pockets and tried to look more casual, all the while thinking that the men could be after him now with more than robbery in mind.

Damn, I'd have given them the keycard and wished them luck using it, let *them lead the police on a chase—*

God. No. Novgorod doesn't have a check-system. There's no tracking system, they refused to put it in.

He turned on one foot—his neck and shoulders were too

stiff—caught his balance, looked back and moved on. He was not sure he could even recognize the men among the crowds—

More strangers than I've ever seen at once in my whole life—too many faces, too many people in clothes too much alike. . . .

People jostled him and cursed him: *Damn z-case*, a man said. He rubbed an unshaven chin and, since shutters were opening and shops were lighting up in this section of the tunnels, he found a pharmacy and bought a shaving kit; and a breakfast counter and bought a roll-up and a glass of synth orange. But the boy took an extra look at the keycard and made him nervous.

Justin Patrick Warrick, it said, *CIT 976-088-2355PR*, which was damning enough; but in faint outline behind that was the Infinite Man emblem of Reseune Administrative Territory.

"Reseune," the boy said, looking up, checking the picture, he thought—in case it was stolen. "Never seen one of those. You *from* there?"

"I—" He had not tried talking. His voice was hoarse and cracked. "I work in the city offices."

"Huh." The boy slid it into the register slot and handed it back with the cup and the roll on the lid. "You return the cup and lid we refund half." The number *3* was on both.

"Thanks." He went over to the counter, unlidded the drink, and took down the roll with huge gulps of the sugary, iced drink, no matter the rawness of his throat—uneasy on his stomach in the first few moments and then altogether equal to anything *Changes* could offer at twenty times the price. He leaned there a moment with his eyes watering, just breathing and letting his stomach get used to food.

Where in hell am I going? What am I going to do?

He wiped his blurring eyes, went back to the counter with the cup and the lid, among other customers, delayed a moment until they were served. "Where can you get the news?"

"They got a board down to the subway."

"Where?"

"Straight on, to your Wilfred tunnel, go right. —You been up to that fire at the Riverside?"

"Up all night with it," he said. "You hear anything—who did it, why?"

The boy shook his head, and served another patron. Justin waited.

"Emory was on vid this morning," the boy said; and Justin's heart skipped. "Madder'n hell."

"Emory's all right?"

"*She* was, yey." The boy broke off to take a card and pour a drink. "You *from* Reseune?"

Justin nodded. "Can I use a phone? *Please.*"

"I can't do that." Another customer. The boy yelled, pointing past the woman: "Down to the corner, public phone."

"Thanks!"

He went, walking fast, with the traffic, in the direction the boy had said, passing some casual walkers. *Call the Bureau. Ask for protection. They* can't *think I'm responsible. They can't blame anyone but Reseune Security—*

Abban, the head of it—

He saw the sign that said *Phone*, and kept his keycard in his hand. He knew the Bureau number: he had had it memorized for years—but he had never used a phone outside Reseune, and he picked up the receiver, reading instructions: *Lift receiver, insert card, key in or touch 0 and voice in. . . .*

"Ser."

He turned and saw a gray uniform, a tall, heavy-set body. Novgorod police.

He dropped the receiver and hit the officer a glancing blow getting past him; and ran, desperately, through the crowds.

But his keycard, he realized to his horror, dodging past a group of workers and down a side tunnel—his keycard was still in the phone-slot.

----------------- **xi** -----------------

". . . My own Security was remiss at best," Ari said, in what of a voice she had left, sitting at the table in the conference room where Justin had sat. "Reseune will be conducting an internal investigation. I will tell you this, seri, —" Her voice cracked, and she took a drink of water. She had gotten her clothes changed, her hair pinned up—Catlin and Florian had helped; and she had the shakes—even if they had gotten her a cup of coffee and a liquid breakfast, which was all she could stand on her smoke-irritated throat. "I'm sorry. The voice isn't much. —I was about to say: I'm functioning as temporary head of Reseune Security; I'm ordering transfers; I'm posting and making assignments. I'm prepared to continue in that post at least administratively if Family council confirms it, though I'm quite aware my age and experience in Security are at issue: my view of my position is as someone qualified to assess the individuals in charge of operations and to make sure communications go through. I feel—to put this delicately—that my uncle's death has left some disarray in the department; the death of the acting head in the fire—is extremely unfortunate."

"Do you feel," Lynch asked, "that there is a chance the attempt was entirely internal?"

She drew a breath and took another drink of water. "Yes. I don't discount that possibility. Reseune is in transition. Dr. Nye—my surviving uncle—is very much affected by his brother's death. There are questions about his own health. But there are certainly experienced administrators who can deal with the problems if Reseune's own council should give them that mandate."

"In short, you feel Reseune can handle the problems."

"I have no doubt."

"Internally," Dr. Wells said, Corain's voice in Science. "But there is, pardon me, sera Emory, some question in my mind, regarding Dr. Warrick's disappearance. You say he was lodged in the room next to yours—but you know he cleared that area."

"Yes."

"Do you consider there's a chance he ran?"

"I don't think that likely, no."

"Why? Because his father is detained by Reseune?"

"Because," she shot back, "of his testimony before this committee. The Paxers were damned—excuse me: were extremely quick to take advantage of the hotel bombing; I'm scared mindless that there may well have been Paxer agents hovering around the hotel because we were there, and that whether or not they were the ones who planted the bomb—they may have been in a position to recognize Dr. Warrick among the evacuees and to kidnap him.''

"Certain people might suggest other agencies.''

"We certainly have no motive to. We brought him here.''

"His father remains in detention.''

"Under protective guard, in view of a security breach that put him in contact with unauthorized personnel. We don't know *what* else could have gotten to him. The attempt on my life makes that more than a remote possibility. In the meanwhile I'm extremely worried about Justin Warrick's whereabouts and about his physical condition.''

"While Dr. Jordan Warrick remains under arrest.''

"You can call it what you like, ser; the facts are as I gave them.''

"Under your direction of Security.''

"Under my direction.''

"From whom are you taking your orders?''

"I operate within the directives of Reseune Administration. I'm reviewing Jordan Warrick's security and I will be in communication with him; and with Reseune Administration; I'm not empowered to make changes without consultation.''

"Is he aware of his son's disappearance?''

"No, ser. We hope to have better news for him. Justin's well aware of his personal danger—he may well have hidden somewhere until he can be sure of the situation. That's my best hope.''

"Is there any likelihood,'' Lynch asked, "that one of the blasts was aimed at him?''

"The blast was incendiary and directional; they put it in his room because my security could have found it immediately if it had been inside. It was elaborately shielded, it was mounted, more than likely, my security tells me, behind the very large bureau—a floor-to-ceiling cabinet—against that wall.'' Her voice cracked. She took another drink. "Excuse me. Justin was at a connecting door at the time, right against that wall—he was trying to warn me or my staff of something: we don't know what. The wall blew; the bureau spun half about and fell against the bed between him and the blast; and the plastic fragments hit that and the far wall. He was protected. That's how we know he survived the blast and we know he made it out of that room. Possibly he had seen something *in* the room that shouldn't have been there. I want to ask him. I want to know why his personal guard was found dead down the hall, *not* in the room. There are a lot of unanswered questions revolving around Dr. Warrick.''

"For the record, you don't consider any possibility that Dr. Justin Warrick was part of a conspiracy."

"Absolutely not. For the record, I'm worried about a problem inside our own staff, within the area of personnel attached to my late uncle—and I'm very hesitant to be more specific than that even with this distinguished committee and guests. I'm continuing to answer questions, but I'm *exceedingly* anxious to get to the airport and get home, to carry reports to members of the Reseune staff who may decide to take action. The attack proves well enough that lives may be in danger."

"From what source?" Wells asked.

"Again, ser, I don't feel I should make charges: the next step is internal investigation, after which appropriate authorities from my Territory will be in contact with the Bureau."

"You're extremely young to lecture this committee on judicial matters."

"I believe, ser, that I'm factually right; and I hold an administrative post within Reseune which requires legal expertise—I refer to my post as wing supervisor, ser. It is correct for me to bring my information before Reseune authorities: I can appeal to the Bureau only in a personal matter, and it would be irresponsible to treat this as a personal incident: its implications are far more extensive."

"Specifically?"

"The possibility that Reseune law is being violated. That security is compromised to the extent I can't be sure of my Administrator's security. Either his involvement—or his safety from persons who may be. I have to say that much, to make you understand it could cost lives if we delay in this committee, or if a message goes out of here to Reseune." *God. Let's not have a debate on this. We can't leak it that Jordan Warrick is on a plane, it's too damn vulnerable till it's on the ground; and* after *it is—*

It lands at 1500. God knows into what.

"Then perhaps Reseune should ask for Bureau Enforcement."

"Perhaps Reseune will. At the moment I ask you to realize that Reseune's internal stability is threatened. Its sovereignty is at issue. I hope to find I'm wrong. I'd *like* for this to have come entirely from outside. I don't see a reasonable possibility that it did."

"You talk about personnel attached to your late uncle, the Councillor. I have questions about that."

How many of the Bureau have ties to Giraud?

Lynch himself?

God, have I made a mistake?

"In consideration of sera Emory's health," Lynch said, "and request for consultation with her staff—"

"Mr. Chairman, —" Wells objected.

"—we'll take a recess at this time." The gavel came down. "Committee will re-convene at 1930 hours, sera Emory's health permitting."

She let go the breath she had been holding, and shoved back the chair from the table. "Thank you, ser Secretary," she said in what voice she had left; and looked to the side as Florian came up to her and cut the microphone off.

"Sera," he said in a low voice. "He's in the tunnels. Novgorod police almost had him. He left his keycard. They're sure it's him."

She almost had to sit down. She leaned on the table. "He's run?"

But they could not discuss it; Lynch was moving up on her other side. She turned and took his hand. "Thank you."

Lynch nodded. "Take care, sera."

Harad wished her much the same.

"Sera," Jacques said stiffly, non-committal.

And Corain: Corain gave her a long and wary look as he shook her hand.

_____ **xii** _____

"Another, ser?" the guard asked, appearing by Jordan's seat.

"I could stand it," Jordan said. "Paul?"

"Yes," Paul said. And after the guard had walked down the aisle toward the bar: "You can't complain about the service."

"Sun off the right," Jordan observed. They were reaching cruising altitude again, after refueling at, he supposed, Pytho. In the dark. But the dawn-glow was visible ahead of the plane; and ever so slightly to the right.

From Pytho the plane could have gone to Novgorod or to Reseune. If it held course as they bore, it was Reseune—which was not, he was sure, any sort of good news.

Paul took his meaning. Paul was steady as ever, his support through the years; and now.

He wanted to see Reseune: it was strange that he could feel that way. But it was part of his life; it was civilization; and he was in some part glad to be going home. He hoped to see Justin.

He feared—much worse things.

"We've picked up a tailwind," one of the guards had said, in his better-than-average hearing. "We're going to beat our schedule."

The tunnels afforded few hiding places, only nooks, the dim recess of the news-shop; that took money to enter but the crowded doorway offered Justin a brief refuge and a vantage to scan the tunnel up and down. Then another public restroom, and a quick shave: he had kept the shaving kit and left the damned keycard; but he was afraid to stay there long—

The crowd in a restaurant, the general drift toward another corridor—another appeal to a shopkeeper: "Can I use your phone? I was robbed: I need to call my office—"

"Better call the police," the shop-owner said.

"No," Justin said; and seeing the look of suspicion on the man's face: "Please."

"Police," the man said into the receiver.

Justin turned and left, moving quickly into the crowds, dodging away, heart pounding. The strength the breakfast had lent him was gone. He felt the stiffness and the sprains, and his skull ached. He found himself farther down the corridor than he had thought, found another gap in his memory; and looked behind him in panic.

There were police at the intersection. He saw them look his way.

He turned back again and dived down a stairs: *Subway*, it said. He jostled past other walkers, came out at the bottom.

"Hey," someone yelled behind him.

He ran, out onto the concrete rim, evaded a headon collision and dodged around a support column.

People dived away from him, scrambled out of the way in panic: the whole strip was vacant. "Stop right there!" a voice thundered behind him, and screams warned him of a weapon drawn.

He dodged wildly aside and something slammed like a fist into his back; but he saw safety ahead—saw the black of Reseune Security, a man yelling: *"Don't shoot!"* and a gun in that man's hand too, aimed toward him.

But a numbness was spreading from his shoulder across his back, and balance went. He fell on the concrete, conscious, but losing feeling in his limbs.

"I'm Justin Warrick," he said to the black-uniformed officer who knelt down to help him. "Call Ari Emory."

And: "No," he heard the officer say, not, he thought, to him: "This man is a Reseune citizen. He's under our authority. File your complaints with my captain."

They wanted to take him to hospital. They wanted to take him to the Novgorod police station. They told him that it had not been a bullet but a high-velocity trank dart that had penetrated his shoulder: "I'm very glad to know that," he said, or tried to say, past the numbness of his mouth. And was equally relieved when the agent told him they had reached Ari, and that *RESEUNE ONE*, already on the runway, had turned back to hold for him.

------------------------------ **xiii** ------------------------------

"I'll walk," he said, and did, facing the climb up the passenger ramp; but Florian had come halfway down to help him and Ari was waiting at the top, in the doorway, with the frown he expected.

Ari put her arm around him when he made it through the doorway; so did Catlin, fending away other Security personnel; and steered him for the nearest seat. But he stopped, resisting their help for a moment, scanning the group of Security staff for Abban or for strangers. "Who's back there?" he asked. "Ari, who oversaw the plane, do you know?"

"The pilot and co-pilot," Ari said, in a voice only a little less hoarse than his. "And staff we're sure of."

"Abban—"

"Dead," Catlin said, and patted his shoulder. "We're onto it, ser. Come on."

He let go the seat then, eased himself into it, leaned back and stared at Ari in a dull, all-over malaise as she sat down opposite him. "Thanks for holding the plane," he said between breaths.

"Where in hell were you?"

"Went shopping," he said, as the door thumped to and sealed. For a moment he was disoriented. "Sorry." He knew her suspicions—and Florian's and Catlin's. He felt a dull surprise that they let him this close to her. "I wasn't anywhere. I got disoriented. Wandered off." The plane began to move, pale landscape swinging past the windows in the edge of his vision. "I just walked until I knew I was in the tunnels; and I found Security and I told them find you."

"That's not half of what I hear. Novgorod is real nervous about people acting odd around the subways."

He shut his eyes, just gone for the moment, exhausted, and the seat was soft, comfortable as a pillow all around him, while he was trying to organize his thoughts. The engines began to drown out sound, a universal white-out. Someone leaned near him and drew the belt over him. He looked up at Catlin as the catch snapped. The plane was gathering speed. Ari was belting in. Catlin and Florian dropped into the seats by him.

The takeoff had a peculiarly perilous feel. Maybe it was the drug that dizzied him; maybe it was the steep bank the pilot pulled, an abrupt maneuver unlike anything he had ever felt. He gripped the arms of the seat, remembering the chance of sabotage, remembering the fire—

"Wes, back there, is a class one medic," Ari said to him, raising her voice over the engine-sound. "He's got the equipment. When we level off we can get you an almost-real bed. How are you doing?''

''Fuzzed. They shot me with numb-out.'' He tried to focus on here and now, the list of things he wanted to ask her. ''Giraud—Jordan—could be in danger.''

''I'm head of Security at the moment,'' Ari said. ''I'll tell you—I'm quite aware of our problems. I went to the Bureau, I laid the problems out, and when we land we're going to call Family council—that's why I desperately want you there. For one thing, you've a vote. For another, you can probably tell things I can't, about what's gone on all these years.''

''You're challenging Denys?''

Ari nodded. ''I'm bringing your father in. He's already left Pytho. *That* was for his protection, to get him home where there are witnesses. I could divert the plane. But that would tell too much. Say that I can hide certain orders from Denys. Not a whole plane. It's due in at 1500. We're projecting arrival about 1400. We're running that close. I can stall its landing, divert it to Svetlansk or somewhere, *after* we've landed. I hope to have Denys thinking I'm coming back for safety reasons. But he probably won't accept that.''

He had thought he had had all he could take, already. He sat there with adrenaline pouring into his exhausted system and wondered why he was relatively calm. *We're going to die*, he thought. *Somewhere along this—they're going to get us. Somewhere in the networks of Security orders, the airport, the military—the Bureau—House Administration—*

''The first thing he'll move on,'' he said, ''is my father and your friends. And they haven't got a way of finding it out.''

''I sent Amy a very simple message this morning. It contained a codeword. There's a good chance she's been able to warn the others: she's on Base One right now, and that's a lot of defense in itself. Don't worry.''

''God.'' He took several slow breaths. ''Why are you trusting me?''

Ari gave a one-sided smile—her predecessor's expression, so like her it affected his pulse rate. ''I could say, because you know how safe your father and Grant are with Denys right now. Or because you made your choice when you told them to call me. —But the real reason is, I always could read you—

better than anyone in the House. You're my friend. I never forget that.''

''You choose a damned peculiar way to show it.''

The smile hardened. ''I choose what works. I don't get my friends killed letting them run into a situation I can see and they don't. I don't argue about some things. I'm self-protective as hell. But you're special with me. You always have been. I hope we never come to odds.''

He felt a profound unease at that. And reckoned she meant him to.

''I want to help your father,'' she said. ''But you have to keep him from bringing this to Council. You have to get me the time. Give him time to know *me*, not the Ari he remembers.''

''He'll do that for me.''

''He won't trust you.''

That hurt. It was also true. ''But he'll give me the time. He won't betray his friends, but if I ask him I can get that from him. He *is* reasonable, Ari. And he does care what happens to me.''

''That's clear too.'' She leaned her head back, turned her face toward Florian, beside her. ''Tell Wes come help him. I'm going to trank out about half an hour. I've got to have it.''

Justin thought the same. He unbuckled, levered himself out of his seat, and let the Security medic take his arm and steady him on his way aft.

xiv

Grant rested his head on his hands and wiped them back through his hair. ''Here,'' Quentin said, and offered him a soft drink from their own kitchen.

''Thank you.'' He took it and sipped at it, sitting on the couch, while Amy Carnath pored over the output that they had linked up to the living room monitor.

Justin was all right; the plane was up. They were on their way back; the worst of their fears had not come true; but they were not home yet.

Ari had stalled the press conference till dawn, putting out

bulletin after bulletin, each more appalling than the last, until she had come on herself and fueled a whole new set of speculations—*not* laying it indubitably to the Paxers, but by implication taking into Khalid, perhaps even intimating the existence of high-level complicity, virtually declaring for office—

Then, after the news conference, a message came through Base One to sera Amy, and Base One started pouring out instructions. . . .

Amy, this is Ari, via Base One. This is all pre-recorded, so you can't talk back and forth, just listen and do this.

Something's happened. I can't know what in advance, but if you're getting this, something drastic will have happened, and I'm either in hospital, dead, or somewhere outside Reseune and in trouble.

First thing, protect yourself.

Second, the warning flasher we talked is out over the House system now, so everybody knows to take precautions.

Help them if you can. Base One is now available for you to use on Florian's and Catlin's level, and that means you can get information and perform operations without leaving a flag, even for Denys or Giraud. The Help function is under Tutor if you need it.

I don't think they'll go at you. They know Base One uses lethal force. I don't advise your taking other people up onto the floor, but use your discretion in extreme need.

Don't use Base One to request information outside Reseune. I can, but for various reasons I haven't incorporated that routine under this access—mostly that it's hard not to give yourself away. I've encoded every single contingency I can think of and if I've activated this, I've probably fired you off a list of pertinent items via a code transmission in the net to Base One.

As follows:

Assassination attempt; from inside Reseune; Jordan Warrick; not involved; Jordan Warrick moved; to Reseune; trust Grant; but; Justin Warrick; whereabouts uncertain; in Novgorod; watch out for; Denys.

Grant drank his soft drink and stared bleakly at the computer flow, codes, mostly, which he could not read, which, very likely, Amy could not read, but the advanced system which

had annexed their home unit very probably did read, and Base
One answered Amy's questions.

"Damn," Amy said.

Grant did not like that. He waited for illumination, and
finally got up, but Quentin's instant, wary attention dissuaded
him from taking a step in any direction.

"What's wrong?" he asked quietly. "Sera?"

"Oh, damn!" She spun her chair around. "Security's just
gone off-line. The whole net is down."

"Denys is aware," Grant said with a cold feeling; and then
saw the black screen come to life again.

*This is the House System emergency function. Someone has
attempted interrupt. The Bureau has been notified and the interrupt documented.*

*The System is now re-integrating. Source of the interrupt:
Security main offices.*

Control of the System has now passed to Ariane Emory.

*All Security personnel, stand by further orders through nor-
mal channels: Security main offices are downgraded to: Unreliable; House Administrative offices downgraded to:
Unreliable; control re-routed to: RESEUNE ONE.*

"God," Grant breathed, and sat down.

"Well, Denys has done it," Ari said, and leaned back in her
seat, watching the system-flow transit the briefcase flat-screen,
Florian and Catlin reading over her shoulder.

"That sounds like my predecessor's work," Florian said.

"It might well be. And mine. —I'm surprised at Seely
letting Denys try that."

"Seely is likely following orders," Catlin said. "Seely
would have advised against it."

"Might not be there?"

"Might not," Catlin said, "but mostly, I think, they're pre-
paring to defend the Administrative wing."

"Makes sense," Florian said. "The system may have
downgraded his Base, sera, but I'm sure he's already gone to
manual on those locks."

"Negotiation's what he's aiming for. He has absolutely
nothing else to gain. *Denys* wants to be immortal. *Giraud* is

down there in that tank, and Denys can't keep his hand on everything.''

"Security won't like to be used against the House," Catlin said. "Abban I can understand. Seely I can. Some of the others—"

"Yakob?" Florian suggested.

"Could be odd tape. Could be odd tape on that whole senior wing. They've had twenty years to do it. I don't trust any of them."

"Don't count the Administrative systems as gone, sera," Florian said. "There could be a way—check and see if there's any order for Q system equipment credited to Administrative."

"Security 10: acquisitions: Administrative: computer equipment: search. —Why? You think that could have been the tamper in Security?"

Florian leaned on her seat-back, nodded vigorously as she looked up over her shoulder. "Acquisitions might not turn it up either," he said. "You can rig modules you could port in a suitcase, right down to the memory. Giraud could do it, easy. Right past Decon and everybody."

"Security 10: widen search, last item: computer equipment: twenty-year range: search. —You're right. Denys isn't stupid—even about the House systems. It makes damn good sense: divert Base Two to an alternate system, outflow without respecting any command-level inflow—like a one-way filter, to shut out the House system and still run it?"

"It's more complicated than that, but that's generally the idea. Your predecessor was full of tricks. He'd know there were protections—"

"He *does* know. What about airport defenses? Can we get in there?"

"As long as we have affirmative control while we're going in, and it's talking to us," Florian said, then shrugged. "Unless that system can do something I can't figure. It's always possible. Jeffrey BJ's supposed to be in charge at the airport, and I don't know there's anything wrong with him; but I'd say the best thing to do is check the flight schedules, make sure nothing's inbound, and then use the override to reorient and then lock down: that way if Denys' Base is going to touch anything off it won't hit anything."

"I can name you a handful," Catlin said, "who can make sure that power stays down."

"*You* two take it."

He came around and sat down carefully in the chair next to her, and took the microphone. Catlin perched on the leather arm of his chair; and for a few moments it was all their peculiar jargon and names she did not know, but Catlin and Florian did.

Meanwhile she watched the dataflow. Search negative. She was only moderately interested. It made thorough sense, what Florian suggested; and Giraud could well have gotten the equipment in years ago. They had had all her childhood to set it up, and make sure it functioned.

Kill the airport defenses first, get the plane on the ground; and then figure something could go wrong with the precip towers: envelope rupture would make things uncomfortable for anyone trying to get to the House; figure that Denys might simply have ordered the buses uphill and parked them.

Search: she keyed, *airport: bus, ser # ?; graph.*

The schematic of Reseune turned up both buses, at the front of the Administrative wing.

She keyed orders to the main boards at the precip towers. They were an hour away from the field.

Then she got up and went, herself, back where her Security staff sat talking together: they had heard the net go down and re-establish itself, each and every one of them who had been listening to the net, and that was all of them, she figured.

"We're doing all right," she said. "Stay seated: listen. Florian's taking the defenses down. Wes, Marco, you stay with me and Dr. Warrick, on the plane: we're going to be busy as hell and someone's got to coordinate whatever they can set for our protection. Dr. Warrick's a friendly, but he doesn't know the Rules: if so happen we have to move, you see he does what you tell him. The advance team is going to have to get into Administrative, and Florian and Catlin are going to be leaders going in. Tyler, you're First after either one of them."

"Yes, sera," Tyler said, a smallish, wiry man, white-haired and crew-cut. Tyler had served as one of Ari senior's staff. Two of the others were retired marines, Wes was a Green Barracks instructor, and the rest ranged from diplomatic security to Marco, who was a systems programmer.

"We'll have a number of other Security on call-up," she said. "Take that advisement from Catlin: she's doing the organization, Florian's doing the special work, Catlin will brief you: we've kept this operation in ready-state for the last two years, not quite like we're improvising, all right? We just didn't know our target. Now we do. And we know right where the keys are. All right?"

"Yes, sera."

She patted Tyler's shoulder, walked back down the narrow aisle past the galley and the staff restrooms; and opened the door of the bedroom. Justin was asleep, completely out.

Burns and bruises, Wes had said. Memory gaps were the serious part; but, as Wes put it, you have one go off next to you, you drop a few things. Nothing unusual.

"Wake up," she said. "Justin. I need you up front."

XV

"They're in," Amy said. "That's the Tower. They're on the ground."

Grant, leaning on the back of the couch, breathed again.

Amy had confused hell out of Security, changing the whereabouts of everyone on her list for protection, lying with one output while she monitored the whereabouts of every Security unit in the buildings they could access, called Security personnel on the Approved list to Wing One, and secured the doors.

While Sam Whitely down at the motor pool arranged transport for Green Barracks personnel and Maddy Strassen and 'Stasi Ramirez and Tommy Carnath had simply gone missing to unlikely places as lies in the net persuaded any inquirers they had taken refuge in B lab and down in the Ag lab.

Call to Family council, the advisement flashed out on the net: *Ariane Emory, calling emergency session via House System, to consider the question: nomination of Dr. Yanni Schwartz to replace Denys Nye as Administrator of Reseune, meeting to be held at 1700 or as soon as practical.*

Grant stood back and folded his arms. *He* had no vote. He

was following the scroll of activity on the monitor, that had accelerated markedly ever since *RESEUNE ONE* had entered approach. That last advisement came as a vast relief to more than himself, he thought: a calculated bit of psych, a tag of grim humor: Emory in full flower.

There were Security orders all over the system of a sudden, outpouring from Base One.

Ari did not look up from the screen; and Justin did not speak, following the flow on an auxiliary Florian had used. Occasionally she gave a voice input or pushed a key; and changes happened. Queries were incoming: *RESEUNE ONE*'s crew, forward, kept their posts, keeping the plane ready to move away and, if the airport seemed threatened, to take to the air again.

He had much rather stay on the ground; and he wished to hell he had some knowledge of the codes that might have told him where things stood.

"We're all right," Ari said. "Sam's got the trucks up from Green; they're going up the hill—no challenge yet. He's holding inside Administration, probably inside Security itself."

She made more changes.

She could, she said, open any doors that were not disabled or under an outlaw Base's control.

Makes it easier, Florian had said, stuffing the pockets of his jacket with various small components out of his own kit— probes and wire, mostly, with some sort of system evident. And Florian had taken a small bag from a locker, and another from a second locker; and handled those very carefully, while Catlin had arranged things with the Security agents aft.

They must be halfway up the hill now, Justin thought.

"*Sera*," the intercom said suddenly, communication from *RESEUNE ONE*'s crew. "*We've got a phone relay from Administration. Dr. Nye, asking to speak with you personally, sera.*"

"Don't divert your attention," Justin muttered.

"Damn right. —Put it over the intercom; we're all intimate here. —Justin, punch that yellow button on your arm-rest and pass me the mike, will you? This one's engaged."

"Ari," Denys' voice said over the intercom. *"I really think you're being a little excitable."*

Ari laughed, never taking her eyes from the screen in front of her. She held out her left hand and Justin laid the mike-wand into it. "Are you hearing me, uncle Denys?"

"I'm hearing you fine, dear. I wish you'd make clear exactly what's going on here, and call off your troops before they do serious damage to the wing."

"You want to unlock those doors, uncle Denys? We can talk about this. I promise you'll be safe. I'll even continue Giraud."

"I don't know what happened in Novgorod: I'm sure it's more than you've told me. Can we talk about this?"

"I don't mind."

"I'm willing to resign. I want protection for myself and my people. I think that's reasonable."

"Perfectly reasonable, uncle Denys. How do we make that official?"

"You stop your people. You guarantee me custody of Giraud's replicate. I'm perfectly willing to accept retirement. I have the means to make taking this place extremely expensive; but there's no need. I have the feeling you must blame me for the events in Novgorod—"

Ari laughed again, with less humor, Justin thought. "I really don't know, uncle Denys. I don't entirely care. I've rather well overrun the course you set for me; and it's *my* time. The changing of the seasons. Perfectly natural. You can have a wing, you can have your comforts— I know that matters to you, uncle Denys. You can work on your books, — I do know about that. They're wonderful. You have so much valuable yet to do. . . ."

"You're very flattering, young sera. I want Seely."

Ari was silent a moment. "Under some restrictions. I can agree to that."

"You don't touch him!"

"I wouldn't hurt Seely, uncle Denys. We can work something out. I promise you. I won't file charges. Your life will be exactly the same. You don't travel anyway; and you'll have Giraud to occupy you and Seely, won't you? You were a damned good parent, you know; and very kind, really you

were. You could have done a lot of things to me Geoffrey did
to Ari senior; and you took a chance with the program and
didn't. I really have quite a warm feeling for you about that,
uncle Denys; and for Seely; and for Giraud. Giraud and I got to
be really close at the last; and I really don't think he did it, I
think it was a worm in Abban's tapes. I think it was something
you put there. Maybe not. I may have an over-active imagination. —They're going to take those doors down, uncle Denys;
and practically speaking, —you're running out of time.''

''*Stop them.*''

''Are you going to come outside, uncle Denys? With
Seely?''

''*All right. When you get up here. I want a guarantee of
safety.*''

''You have it in my word, uncle Denys.''

''*I want you here to control your people. Then I'll open the
doors.*''

Justin shook his head. Ari looked at him and said: ''All
right, uncle Denys. I'll be up there.'' She pointed at the button
on Justin's seat. Justin pushed it, breaking contact.

''*Ari?*''

Ari pushed a button on her chair arm. ''We're finished.
Break contact.''

''Ari,'' Justin said, ''he wants you in range.''

Ari watched the screen and said: ''That might be, but he's in
an awfully bad position.'' She picked up her own microphone.
''We've got contact with Denys. He says hold off, he's just
resigned. Confirm; pick it up. —Justin: *you* stay here.''

''Dammit, Ari, —''

''*I* wouldn't be going up there, except I hope we can do this
without a shot. I'm enough for Security to worry about; they
don't need another one. If something goes badly wrong, this
plane is going back to Novgorod, and you can tell the Bureau
the whole damn mess, then do what you like. But I'd prefer
you back in Reseune, running another of my sets. I'll even let
you pick the surrogates.''

He stared at her.

''I have a lot of unfinished business,'' Ari said, standing by
the seat. ''If I don't make it out of this—getting me back is a

real priority. Gehenna is only *one* of the problems. And you need me the same as I need you.''

She gathered up Marco, and Wes unsealed the door, and sealed it again after her.

It was true, he thought as that door closed. Everything else considered, —it was true.

Then he thought of what she had said: *only* one *of the problems*; and: *the same as I need you.* . . .

<hr>

xvi

''I don't like this,'' Florian said, crouched close to Catlin, where the bus and the hill made a little cover a curve away from the glass main doors. His hands were cold, exposed to the air: he protected the left one under his arm and watched the data-flow on the hand-held monitor in his right.

''It's a case of What's he got,'' Catlin said, tucked down tight, chest against arms against knees.

''Seely isn't sera's kind of problem,'' Florian said.

Catlin looked at him, quick and hard. ''Sniper or something bigger up there. You want those doors?''

''Grenade will handle that. They're doing final prep in there now, I'm sure of it, now sera's left the airport. This whole thing is a set.''

''Go, then,'' Catlin said. ''You time it. There's got to be a trigger in that hall.''

Florian took a breath, flexed a stiffened hand and an injured shoulder. ''Photocell, likely. Floor and body-height, with an interrupt, electric detonator, best guess—I'm first in on this one.''

The shockwave shook the bus; and Ari was already ducking when Marco grabbed her and pulled them both down, but she fought to get a look as the bus made the turn.

Smoke billowed up from the area of the Administration Wing front doors. She could see the other bus parked on the slope. The black-uniformed group there was in sudden motion, running uphill.

Her driver stopped.

Marco pulled her flat and threw himself over her.

As the air shook and clods peppered the windows.

Florian picked himself up, wiped his eyes and staggered to his feet as someone helped him, he was not sure who, but it was from behind and it was friendly if it got him up again.

He saw Catlin ahead of him in the dim hall, saw her arm a grenade and wait, the thing live in her hand—because somebody like Seely could give it back to you.

She threw it, but a black blur came out that door.

Florian snapped his pistol up and fired; and the grenade blew the whole doorway to ruin. Catlin had fired too. She took another shot, point-blank, to be sure.

Florian leaned against the wall and caught his breath. The net was saying that the teams from Green Barracks had gotten into Security—up the lift shafts from the tunnel system: easy job, till they got to the traps and the defenses.

The whole hall was filled with bluish smoke. The fire alarms had gone off long since.

Catlin walked back to him, swinging her rifle to cover the hall beyond, while he kept a watch over her blind-side. "One more," she said.

He nodded.

He was not glad of this one. Denys had been kind to them. He remembered the dining room, remembered Denys laughing.

But it was sera's safety in question, and he had only a second's compunction.

Catlin had less.

The front doors were in ruins, the smoke still pouring out when Ari climbed off the bus; and Florian and Catlin both came out under the portico to meet her.

"Denys is dead," Florian told her first off. "I'm sorry, sera. It was a set-up."

"What about Seely?"

"Dead," Catlin said.

Ari walked up onto the porch and looked into the hall. Bodies lay scattered in the dim emergency lights, under a lowering canopy of smoke. She had known that place since childhood. It did not look real to her.

Denys gone. . . .

She looked back at Florian and Catlin. Catlin's expression was clear-eyed and cool. It was Florian who looked worried. Florian, who had a gash running blood down his temple and another on his cheek, not mentioning what he had had from Novgorod.

She did not ask. Not anywhere near witnesses.

―――――――――― xvii ――――――――――

The Reseune corporate jet touched smoothly, braked, and swung into a brisk roll toward the terminal and Decon—always a special treatment of plane and passengers, when a flight came in from overseas.

"It's going to take a while," Justin said, hand on Grant's shoulder; and they might have gone to sit down, then, in the comfort of the VIP and press room. But he watched it roll up to the safeway; watched the windows after it had come to rest. He could make out shadows moving inside, nothing more.

But one of them was Jordan and another was Paul.

Everything's all right, he had said, when *RESEUNE ONE* had let him speak to the incoming plane, when Grant was on the way down from the hill and Reseune was stirring to heal its wounds. *Don't worry. Yanni Schwartz is the new Reseune Administrator. Welcome home.*

He worried. He watched out the window mostly, while Decon did its work, hosing down the plane in foam. He and Grant exchanged stories in distracted bits and pieces, what they had known, and when, and what they had been in a position to pick up.

He worried until the doors opened and gave up two tired travelers.

After which they had the lounge to themselves, Ari had said, for as long as they wanted; and the sole surviving bus waiting out under the portico, to get them back up the hill.